Irish author **Abby Green** ended a very glamorous career in film and TV—which really consisted of a lot of standing in the rain outside actors' trailers—to pursue her love of romance. After she'd bombarded Mills & Boon with manuscripts, they kindly accepted one, and an author was born. She lives in Dublin, Ireland, and loves any excuse for distraction. Visit her at abby-green.com or email abbygreenauthor@gmail.com.

After spending three years as a die-hard New Yorker, **Kate Hewitt** now lives in a small village in the English Lake District with her husband, their five children and a golden retriever. In addition to writing intensely emotional stories, she loves reading, baking and playing chess with her son—she has yet to win against him, but she continues to try. Learn more about Kate at katehewittbooks.com.

Also by Abby Green

Rush to the Altar
Billion-Dollar Baby Shock
Bride of Betrayal

Also by Kate Hewitt

Back to Claim His Italian Heir
Pregnancy Clause in Their Paper Marriage
Spaniard's Waitress Wife

Passionately Ever After… collection

A Scandal Made at Midnight

Discover more at millsandboon.co.uk.

INESCAPABLE DESIRE

ABBY GREEN

KATE HEWITT

MILLS & BOON

All rights reserved including the right of reproduction in whole or in part in any form. This edition is published by arrangement with Harlequin Enterprises ULC.

This is a work of fiction. Names, characters, places, locations and incidents are purely fictional and bear no relationship to any real life individuals, living or dead, or to any actual places, business establishments, locations, events or incidents. Any resemblance is entirely coincidental.

Without limiting the exclusive rights of any author, contributor or the publisher of this publication, any unauthorised use of this publication to train generative artificial intelligence (AI) technologies is expressly prohibited. HarperCollins also exercise their rights under Article 4(3) of the Digital Single Market Directive 2019/790 and expressly reserve this publication from the text and data mining exception.

® and TM are trademarks owned and used by the trademark owner and/or its licensee. Trademarks marked with ® are registered with the United Kingdom Patent Office and/or the Office for Harmonisation in the Internal Market and in other countries.

First published in Great Britain 2026
by Mills & Boon, an imprint of HarperCollins*Publishers* Ltd,
1 London Bridge Street, London, SE1 9GF

www.harpercollins.co.uk

HarperCollins*Publishers*, Macken House, 39/40 Mayor Street Upper, Dublin 1, D01 C9W8, Ireland

Inescapable Desire © 2026 Harlequin Enterprises ULC

Bodyguard's Royal Temptation © 2026 Abby Green

Keeping His Enemy Close © 2026 Kate Hewitt

ISBN: 978-0-263-41822-4

03/26

Printed and Bound in the UK using 100% Renewable Electricity at CPI Group (UK) Ltd, Croydon, CR0 4YY

BODYGUARD'S ROYAL TEMPTATION

ABBY GREEN

MILLS & BOON

This is for Paddy Kerr. Thanks for the invaluable
sailing and boats advice. And this is also for
the rest of the Brookfield Walkies group, Jo and
Anita. Not to mention the dogs: Gunner, Poppy, Juno,
Orwell and Peggy. Thanks for the many steps and
things put to rights on our little treks around IMMA.
The perfect recipe for staying sane(ish). x

CHAPTER ONE

THE VOICE DRONED ON... 'Given our location between North Africa and Southern Europe, and the fact that we are steeped in history dating back thousands of years, with influences from the Moors to the Greeks, Spanish and French, we are uniquely positioned to—'

'To promote our rich diverse culture and stunning natural beauty by encouraging investment in industry and especially tourism. Having French as our official language and with most citizens speaking English and at least two or three more, we're accessible to many, in terms not only of tourism but also industry. We need to encourage our young, well-educated and multilingual population to stay, and not emigrate as so many have in the past, but to do that we need to prove we can provide investment opportunities.'

Her Royal Highness, Crown Princess Cassandra Theodora Sophia Beatriz Clotilde Mansur de Roche—to give her her full name and title—finished off the end of her chief advisor's lecture without even thinking about it. Anything to stay awake. His voice was so unfortunately monotonous. Her older brother, the recently abdicated king, had warned her about this.

She was also standing in front of open French doors

that led out to a terrace, in a bid to remain alert with the help of the sea breeze. The view of aforementioned stunning scenery beyond the palace offices was helping. The blue ocean glittered and foamed under the sparkling sun, she could see a pod of dolphins frolicking and wished she were out there too, in her little kayak, exploring the nooks and crannies of the coast. The dolphins would regularly keep her company.

But that had been when she'd been the mere spare to the heir. Just a plain princess. Before the world had blown up a couple of months ago when it had transpired that her older brother was *not* the biological heir of the late king. He was in fact the product of an affair their late mother, the queen, had had with a lover. Probably one of her bodyguards.

Cassie had always wondered if the whispered rumours were true because the only physical trait she and her brother shared was their distinctive blue eyes. Where she was blonde, and fair, he was dark. Well, now she knew. Now everyone knew.

Everything had changed and suddenly Cassie had been pushed to the top of the heir queue. The coveted spot. A part of her was still in denial, although these daily lectures covering everything from history to geography, economics and politics were helping to drum it home.

In a few short weeks, she would be crowned Queen of Sadat Sur Mer. At that reminder there came a familiar tightening in her chest and her breathing became shallower. She'd worked hard to overcome the anxiety that had dogged her childhood dominated by two parents who'd hated each other and who had expressed that frequently and volubly within the palace walls. She'd battled it by focusing on being as sunny and amenable as possible, in a bid to distract one or other of her parents from hating on each other at any given time.

She'd been so successful at projecting a happy-go-lucky front that she'd managed to almost fool herself into believing it was her default disposition. And it had worked most of the time—her bright beaming smile would often help divert attention from her parents' rigid tension and barely concealed contempt for one another.

So the return of the old anxiety was not welcome. Nor was the fact that her brother was no longer here to guide her or to help her with this transition. Not his fault—but the backlash against him for not being of the king's line had been fierce. The people had loved Caius and had felt personally betrayed by something that had been entirely out of his control.

It had been decided that he would serve Cassie better by leaving Sadat Sur Mer until her coronation day, to let things calm down and give the people time to adjust to her taking on the role of monarch.

Cassie knew Caius would be with her if he could but she couldn't help but also feel a little irrationally betrayed by the fact that now she was all on her own to deal with this massive change in their situation. She'd always been able to count on his solid and comforting presence, even if he'd been on the other side of the world, making headlines for his playboy antics before he'd been crowned king. He'd barely had enough time to settle into the role before the scandal of his birth had hit them.

It wasn't that she didn't want to be queen, she'd just never expected to be in this position. He'd been brought up prepared to be ruler. She hadn't. And now everyone was looking to her to be their supreme leader. Daunting, to say the least.

A pang of old grief struck her to think of her twin sister, Christabel, who had died at birth. If she had lived, who was to say that Cassie would have even become queen? Maybe her sister would have relished the role and been more suited? But she wasn't here, and Cassie was, and that was a humbling reminder that she had to accept this new reality for her sister's sake as much as hers.

'Your Highness?'

Cassie reluctantly turned from the view to see folders open on the desk. 'Yes, Pierre.'

'One more item to discuss before we finish.'

She could make out the A4-size photo of a blandly handsome face from where she stood. Clearly they'd moved on from her chief advisor's favourite subject to his next favourite subject—a prospective mate. The king to her queen. The sire to her heirs, who would carry her name to ensure the line didn't disappear. The band around her chest got tighter and she countered it by forcing a bright smile as she walked over to the desk and sat down behind it.

'You've prepared some candidates, I see.'

'Yes, Your Highness. The men in this folder are all from eminently suitable royal lineages. As you might appreciate considering recent events, it's absolutely crucial that we restore faith in our people by choosing someone with impeccable pedigree.'

With superb comic timing, Cassie's beloved cockapoo, whose pedigree was murky to say the least, ambled over from her bed to where Cassie sat, and Cassie scooped her into her lap, ignoring Pierre's pinched expression of disapproval. She didn't appreciate the reference to her brother being somehow *less* just because his royal blood was a little diluted.

She sent Pierre a tight smile. 'Thank you, I can look through these on my own.'

Her advisor all but clicked his heels together and bowed. 'Very well, Your Highness, we can make arrangements to meet your preferred candidates.'

Cassie hid a sigh and said, 'Pierre, you really don't have to bow to me. I would prefer to keep things a little less formal than they have been.' Especially as they'd been in her father's time. A father who had shown scant interest in Cassie, or only when she'd diverted his attention by being sweet and pretty and happy.

Pierre looked as scandalised as if she'd started to strip off her clothes.

'Your Highness, there is a long tradition of protocol to follow. It is my duty to ensure this is preserved, now more than ever given our recent tribulations.'

Cassie swallowed her frustration. It would take time to shake things up a bit. She knew that. 'Pierre, as always I appreciate all your counsel and hard work.'

Looking slightly mollified, the older man left and when he had Cassie slumped back into the chair, snuggling Zoe close. Caius, her brother, had warned her that the old guard would be hard to encourage into modern times.

She sat up again and looked at the open folder. The first candidate was someone she was distantly related to. *Euw.* No. She flicked to the next candidate. A prince known for his love of illegal substances. A hard no. The next one had gambled away his family's fortune and was known to be on the lookout for a new monarchy to feather his nest. No. The last one in the folder was gay—an open secret. *No.*

Cassie shut the folder and tried not to feel disheartened. If she truly felt one of them might be a possibility as her life partner then she would do her best to give them a chance. She didn't want to be obstructive.

Even Caius, who'd partied as hard as the rest of them while he was crown prince, before ascending to the throne, had agreed to discuss forming an engagement with a crown princess from one of Europe's most illustrious bloodlines and monarchies. That arrangement had dissolved once the scandal had hit.

But before that had happened, when Cassie had asked her brother how he could endure the thought of a marriage of convenience he'd shrugged and said, 'This is our world, Cass. We don't have the luxury of choosing our own partner. And in any case, it's better like this, we both know there's no such thing as love or happy ever afters.'

Cassie hadn't responded to that because her dirty little secret was that she did want to believe in love and happy ever after. Especially after enduring a childhood watching two people slowly and torturously annihilate each other, spreading toxicity and infecting everything around them with cynicism.

A cynicism that her brother had embraced, telling Cassie all he needed out of a marriage was an heir and maybe a spare and no drama or histrionics.

She wasn't even sure when this burning desire had rooted itself within her. Maybe it had its genesis in knowing she had got to live and her sister hadn't, so she wanted a more authentic experience.

But once it had become apparent that she would become queen, she knew she couldn't embark on that life of service with someone by her side that she only tolerated. And none of the men in that folder came even close to being tolerated, never mind a potential *real* partner.

She wasn't naive enough to expect actual *love*, but was it too much to hope for respect? Companionship, kindness. Even passion? Although that was still an abstract concept. No one had ever stirred her desires like that. She was still a virgin. Not from lack of opportunity—she'd gone to the local university and had friends of both sexes but, as a princess, it wasn't exactly easy to indulge in a relationship when every public move you made was studied and scrutinised. When you had your own security detail.

Her brother had cautioned her before he'd left Sadat Sur Mer, saying, 'Cass, I know you've got a soft heart but you need to be strategic about who you choose. If you can find someone who will let you rule and be by your side and give you heirs, that's all you need. You can find passion and excitement elsewhere if you're discreet about it. This is a job.'

'Is that what you'd planned to do?' Cassie had asked her brother, feeling almost doubly betrayed by his blatant cynicism.

He'd shrugged. 'Sure, and I wouldn't have judged my queen for doing the same, as long as we were both discreet.'

But that hadn't worked for their parents. Their respective infidelities hadn't eased matters, they'd caused bitter tension. Cassie had always secretly suspected that her father had been in love with their beautiful mother, and he hadn't been able to tolerate her affairs, or the fact that she didn't love him.

Cassie sighed out loud in the massive and ornate palace private office. All the more reason for her *not* to pursue finding a real relationship. Maybe her brother was right.

But then something rebellious sparked to life within her as she realised that perhaps embarking on a life of duty would be a lot more palatable if she felt she'd *lived* a little first.

Maybe that was why Caius had been so sanguine about a life of service with someone he would never love. Because he'd had his fun as one of the world's most notorious playboys and he'd felt ready to settle down to a more sedate and discreet life. Cassie stood up abruptly and put the dog down.

She started to pace back and forth as a plan formed in her head. An audacious plan. She'd never rebelled in her life, too busy trying to make sure everyone around her was happy. She'd never joined the club of Euro royalty who indulged in an endless merry-go-round of exclusive parties, shopping and sybaritic opulent experiences.

She stopped pacing as it struck her that the reason she hadn't ever indulged like that was because it didn't really appeal. She was more introverted. She liked reading. She loved clothes and fashion but for her own pleasure, not to show off in public. She'd never been able to indulge in the side of her that veered towards bright colours and floaty ethereal dresses more suited to a free spirit than a princess.

She'd always wondered if maybe her sister would have been the more extroverted one.

But maybe she could find out what that freedom would be like. Just for a brief moment, before the world as she knew it turned into something else. A life of duty and service. Surely if she felt as if she'd taken something for herself, this desire for a more fulfilling personal life wouldn't have such an appeal.

She just needed to live a little. To take a leaf out of her brother's book and enjoy her freedom before it was gone for good. *Maybe even lose her virginity.* Her skin felt hot at that audacious idea, but it also took root. She had no desire to offer herself up to her prospective king as some kind of sacrificial virgin.

The days of expecting such archaic things were long gone and she knew well that not one of those prospective kings in the folder was a virgin. So why should she be?

But if she wanted to indulge in a last bid for freedom,

she needed time, privacy and a chance to be anonymous. She knew she'd go unrecognised among throngs of people who didn't expect to see a princess in their midst. She wouldn't stand out in a crowd, if she didn't want to.

Where would she find throngs of people? In a busy tourist location.

She went back to the desk and picked up the phone, summoning Pierre back into the room.

He arrived within seconds, a hopeful look on his face, no doubt because he expected her to have chosen a suitable potential king candidate. She was going to disappoint him.

Determined not to be swayed from her course of action, she said, 'Pierre, I'm taking personal leave for the next ten days. A holiday.'

His eyes popped and his face flushed. His mouth opened but Cassie put up her hand, stopping him from saying a word. She said firmly, 'It's not up for discussion. Please rearrange my schedule.'

CHAPTER TWO

ARES DRAKOS REALLY resented having to make a last-minute dash across the globe from Manhattan to Greece. The island of Crete, specifically. He also resented, but with less force, the fact that he'd had to cancel a date with his current lover. Although if he was being totally honest with himself, he had planned on it being the last time he'd see her. She hadn't turned out to be all that interesting, in or out of bed, and he found his capacity to indulge in the games of modern dating becoming less and less appealing.

There were very few people who could call in a favour like this, because he was very selective in who he chose to protect, but Caius Mansur de Roche, recently disgraced abdicated king, was one of them. Thanks to an alcohol-infused bonding session they'd had way back in some bar in… New Orleans? Or maybe it had been Costa Rica.

Ares had been there on a job, Caius had been there raising hell. Ares—who usually loathed the rich and entitled, and royalty were the worst of that lot—had found himself actually liking the crown prince. So much so that, when he'd realised there was a paparazzo lurking, he'd tipped the crown prince off and he'd managed not to land himself on the front pages yet again.

They'd somehow always endeavoured to meet up if they were in the same place at the same time. But when Caius had abdicated and asked Ares to take over his sister's—the new crown princess's—security, Ares had refused, point-blank. He didn't do cosseted royals. He'd had a short, sharp experience with European royalty and they needed babysitters, not security. He'd vowed never again. He didn't need the money or the headache.

He used to work as a one-man security operation, highly sought after because of his legendary skills, but he now ran an exclusive security company with a very select band of employees that he trusted implicitly. They had become *the* go-to security agency in a very short space of time, not just because of their discretion and skill but because Ares had also invested in new cutting-edge decryption software, making him millions overnight but also giving him and his company an edge over everyone else. An edge he did not take advantage of, which had only garnered him even more respect.

But then Caius had contacted him again the day before and told him that his sister, Crown Princess Cassandra, had taken an unscheduled holiday break, leaving Sadat Sur Mer, the small island monarchy for Greece.

By the time she'd made it to the other side of security at the private airport in Athens, she'd somehow given her bodyguards the slip.

Ares had said, 'She's due to be crowned queen soon,

right? So she's probably just making the most of her time clubbing and shopping and lounging about on yachts. I know I would.'

His friend had sounded uncharacteristically tense. 'No, Ares, she's not like that. She's quiet. She doesn't go clubbing. So, even if she is on some kind of a mission to have an…experience, she's not street smart, not like us. She's innocent, and I can't be certain about this but I do mean *literally*.'

Ares had made a face. 'That is too much information, my friend, even for you.'

But his friend had pleaded, 'Look, Ares, you know I don't scare easily. But she's only sending me texts to let me know she's OK, no more details. No information about where she is. She's out there on her own, without any protection. Our security team has let her down. Left her vulnerable. She's my baby sister. Even though it's not my fault, it *is* down to me that she's now the crown princess. I need to know she's OK and I know your team will locate her within hours if you put them on it. You know money isn't an issue.'

Ares's insides had clenched at that. He'd once had baby sisters and he could remember the way it had been totally instinctive to want to protect them. Until his family had left him for dead. He'd walked away from them as soon as he could and neither they nor his older brother had come looking for him, showing him that they hadn't ever needed him. The distance between them now seemed more vast than ever.

He'd felt himself weakening and said gruffly,

'And you know money shouldn't be discussed among friends.'

He'd taken a breath and then, 'Look, I have some meetings in Europe I've been putting off scheduling. I'll do it.' He'd felt the strangest sensation as he'd committed to that, as if he'd just committed to something momentous.

Caius had sighed volubly with relief. 'Thanks, man, I really owe you.'

Except now Ares was bitterly regretting that his friend had somehow managed to worm his way into Ares's very smallest soft spot to butter him up. Because from where he was sitting, at an incredibly tacky Cretan bar with the absolute worst affront to music pounding so loud around him that he could feel it in his bones, Crown Princess Cassandra Mansur de Roche, with a heap of middle names he couldn't care less about, was having the time of her life and looked to be in no need of rescuing or protecting at all.

He knew it was her even though her naturally blonde hair had streaks of pink, red and purple running through the long wavy locks. And even though her eyes were heavily made up and there were tiny diamanté stickers artfully placed across her cheeks. And... he couldn't be sure but from where he was sitting her eyes looked darker so maybe she was using coloured contacts, because one of her most distinctive physical traits was her incredibly blue eyes.

It irritated Ares that he could recall her picture in his mind with absolute precision. That honey-blonde hair, kissed by the sun. Wide, almond-shaped blue eyes under dark arching brows. Not too thin, not too thick. Just perfect. Like her nose, with the slightest patrician bump.

A perfectly oval-shaped face with high cheekbones. Delicate jaw, but defined. But it was her mouth that had sent little sparks of heat into his veins. Plump and full. Generous. Wide. Far too sensual a mouth for a woman who had to appear at all times to be mindful and demure.

Ares had taken one look at that mouth and had scoffed at her brother's quaint notion that she might still be an innocent. No way no how. Not with a mouth that sent all sorts of dark desires into a man's head. *Or just yours, maybe?*

He scowled at that and took another slug of beer, hoping that might douse the very unwelcome buzz of awareness in his body. He was only human and she was a beautiful woman, but blonde princesses with electric-blue eyes who looked as though they'd just stepped off a Disney movie set were not his type. The awareness was an aberration.

He assured himself again that she was not in need of specialist protection. She was dancing with total abandon in the middle of the dance floor, arms in the air, inviting the eye to move over her perfect, lissome body. Long legs encased in snug denim that cupped her perfectly shaped bottom, which Ares could see all too well as she turned away from him.

Her graceful back was bare, as she was wearing a sparkly butterfly-shaped top that seemed to be held together by two mere strings, at her neck and mid-back.

Her waist was slim and her hips...surprisingly womanly. Sending another flash of heat into Ares's blood.

Dammit. He was not going to sit here and ogle a spoiled entitled princess, crown or otherwise, who clearly needed no help. He fished for his phone in the pocket of his jeans, fully intending to take a photo of Caius's precious baby sister in action to send to him before letting him know her location so her own useless bodyguard/babysitters could take over again. And then he could get on with protecting people who *really* needed to be protected, but just as he lifted the phone up, he saw something and cursed volubly. He couldn't leave her now.

Cassie knew that she must look as if she were having the time of her life and, boy, was she really trying her hardest, but the truth was that she knew she'd made a mistake coming to Crete in a bid to stay anonymous among the crowds.

It was *too* busy. And, she'd realised, she wasn't used to being in crowds without a cordon of space around her—not a bad thing, but more jarring than she had expected.

So far, her attempt at making the most of her freedom was looking a little pathetic. But the truth was that she'd really liked the idea of going to a regular holiday destination, rather than some rarefied resort. She'd wanted to feel as though she was experiencing the real world for once.

Her close friends were people in Sadat Sur Mer who were still at university or who had jobs and families.

They also weren't available to spontaneously flit away for a few days of hedonism, demonstrating the gulf between her and them that she'd always tried her best to pretend wasn't there.

Hedonism, Cassie berated herself. More like Cassie-no-matesism. Just when she was beginning to feel like a total fool for going to all the trouble to disguise herself—after realising most people here were too wasted to know who they were, never mind her—two guys about her age approached her on the dance floor, crowding her a little so she had to move back.

She was slightly assured because they looked less out of it than everyone else.

'Hey, you look lonely, want some company?' One of them leant towards Cassie and shouted in her ear over the pounding music.

He held out a glass with a bright pink liquid in it and a little umbrella cocktail stick poking out from the top. 'Try it, it's nice.'

Of course she wasn't going to accept a drink from a complete stranger. At that moment Cassie realised that, somehow, these two amenable-looking guys had manoeuvred her so that they were in a corner of the club and they were blocking her view of the dance floor. She was alone. No one knew where she was and actually this whole idea had been really stupid.

She forced a bright smile. 'Thanks, guys, but I'm actually on my way out to meet a friend in another bar, and I'm late.'

'But you looked like you were having fun. Stay for one drink, come on.' This was said by the other guy, who had a cute friendly face. Cheeky chappie. But Cassie felt uneasy.

'I'd really like to but—'

'Then do.' The other guy, more forceful now, holding the drink towards her. Cassie's skin went cold. She felt herself tensing her muscles ready to use a couple of moves to extricate herself when a large shape loomed over them all and a hand reached into where Cassie stood and grabbed her arm.

'*There* you are. I've been waiting an hour. Come on.'

Cassie was so stunned at first that she let herself be tugged towards the stranger, barely aware of the two guys falling back. She registered things—tall, broad, powerful, dark messy hair and short beard, intense eyes, dark brows, and…the fact that the stranger was hands down the most gorgeous specimen of a man she'd ever seen in her life.

His face was hard and stern but it was also *beautiful*. His mouth in particular was captivating. Firmly sculpted. She had a strange urge to reach up and trace its shape with a finger. Cassie felt a little dazed.

Taking advantage of her surprise, his hand moved down her arm, and he took her hand to lead her out of the bar before her brain had time to catch up with her body. Simultaneously she was registering an electrical charge flowing through her blood out to her skin, making it prickle. *Awareness*.

They were outside on the busy street and Cassie's ears were still ringing from the loud music when she realised what had just happened. She pulled her hand free of the man's and looked up at him. 'What the hell do you think you're doing?'

He stood back and looked her up and down. Cassie realised he was even taller than she'd first thought. At least six feet four. Wearing a shirt with rolled-up sleeves and jeans. Jeans that sat low on narrow hips and hugged powerful thighs and long legs like a second skin.

Mortified to realise she'd just blatantly ogled him, she looked back up and folded her arms across her chest. His dark gaze dropped and Cassie looked down to see her stance was pushing her breasts together and up. The top precluded a bra and she'd been conscious that she didn't have the small tidy breasts a top like this merited but it had been too late to change earlier, before she'd lost her nerve completely and left her four-star hotel.

She refused to be conscious of him *ogling* her even though it made the awareness coalesce into a feeling of tightness deep in her core. She automatically pressed her thighs together to stem the sensation.

'Do you want to explain why you just manhandled me out of that bar?' she said, sounding unbearably prim.

He looked so stern, Cassie had a totally unexpected and disturbing image of this man putting her over his knee and lifting his hand—she blurted out in a panic, 'I was having fun.'

He arched a brow and finally deigned to speak. 'Really? It didn't look much like fun dancing on your own.' His voice matched the rest of him, deep and masculine. The slightest hint of an accent. And censure.

He was echoing her own thoughts and the fact that her decision to take this trip had been so spontaneous and last minute that she really hadn't thought it through much at all. He was also unwittingly pressing on the wound of the fact that she was alone because her brother had had to more or less abandon her.

She felt exposed and lashed back. 'Watching me, were you? Just waiting for a moment to step in and make it look like you're some sort of saviour? Well, those guys weren't bothering me at all. In fact, if you don't mind, I'm going to go back in.'

Cassie went to walk around the man mountain, because that's what he was. Powerful. With well-honed, defined muscles. Thick corded muscles. Under dark olive skin.

But before she could take another step he said, 'Wait, stop.'

Cassie wasn't sure why she did. But something about him was just too…intriguing, while also being seriously annoying. *Disturbing*.

She didn't turn around. Waiting. He moved to stand in front of her again. She looked at him and raised a brow this time. A look of definite irritation crossed with something else she couldn't decipher crossed his face. Then he gritted out as if almost loathe to give her the information, 'They had spiked that drink. Most likely with a roofie. They weren't drunk, did you notice that? They're probably on a mission to spike girls' drinks all night until they get lucky. You were pretty obviously alone so you were an easy target.'

'Can you stop saying that, please? And I'm not an

easy target. I could have defended myself. I had no intention of taking that drink.' But she might have if they hadn't creeped her out. Cassie had to acknowledge that.

Mr Tall Dark and Stern pointed out, 'You wouldn't have had a hope of defending yourself if you'd taken a sip of that drink.'

Cassie shivered a little. No. She wouldn't have, and she might have let her guard down. And she had ditched her bodyguards. And the royal house of Mansur de Roche did not need adverse headlines before her coronation.

She forced herself to stand tall and say, 'OK, well, look, I appreciate you had my best interests in mind and were only trying to help.'

She held out her hand and he looked at it dumbly. She said, 'I'm offering my hand in thanks for your concern.'

As if she'd shocked him with her gesture he took it, wrapping her much smaller hand in his. She noticed his palms felt a little rough and that sent another electric jolt right to a spot between her legs. She pulled her hand back. 'OK, thanks, bye now.'

She turned to go in the opposite direction but then the man said, 'Wait. Where are you going?'

Cassie stopped and turned around again. She had to admit helplessly, 'I don't actually know. I'd like to have a drink and a dance but that place was just...*awful*.'

'There's not much better here but I know a spot if you'd like to have a drink with me.'

Cassie hovered uncertainly. Had this man been telling the truth? If she accepted his invitation was she in fact being incredibly stupid and naive and jumping from the frying pan into the fire?

She imagined if her sister were here and braver than Cassie, more spontaneous. Before she could think about it too much she acted on instinct. 'OK, yes.' She smiled and his eyes widened. He was looking at her mouth.

Then those dark eyes moved back up and with almost a scowl on his face he said, 'Come on.'

Cassie was totally bemused. This man had clearly not been born with the charm gene and yet perversely it was what made her feel safe to go with him.

He led her over to where a motorbike rested at an angle. A proper motorbike. Not a scooter as most people used here. Cassie loved motorbikes. Caius had secretly taught her how to ride them when she was much younger. The royal staff would have had collective heart attacks if they'd known. Their parents probably would have been too busy arguing to notice.

The man took a helmet out of a back compartment and handed it to her. She put it on. Then he put on his own helmet. He got onto the bike, the movement stretching the denim material over his thighs. Cassie's legs suddenly felt a little rubbery. She realised—as if someone had just punched her—this was *it*. She was experiencing desire. Lust. Attraction. She'd spent years wondering what it must feel like and now she knew. Like a fever.

He was sitting on the bike looking at her, holding out a hand. 'Use me for balance, put your foot—'

'I know,' she said, stepping forward to put the ball of her foot on the footpeg. She ignored his hand, putting hers on his shoulder and stepping up, lifting her other leg over the body of the machine, sitting down.

She slid right down in the hollow between them until her body was flush against his, breasts pressed against his broad back. His very broad and strong back. It felt so much more formidable when she was pressed up against him like this.

He turned his face towards her. 'Wrap your arms around me and hold on.'

Cassie didn't need any encouragement. These last few seconds had been the most exciting of her life to date. She wrapped her arms around his lean torso and with a roar of the throttle that scattered people around them, they were off.

What the hell are you doing, man? The voice in Ares's head wasn't his, it was Caius's, and he scowled inside the helmet. His logic had been: Get the princess out of that situation and then...when she'd been about to walk away it had been: Keep her with you so you know where she is. Keep her safe.

But as he roared along a coastal road now, with her arms around his waist, hands linked together, all too close to a part of his anatomy that was *very* reactive to her proximity, Ares had to admit that his motives had been much more instinctive and less altruistic. Completely unprofessional.

He had sent off a text to Caius though, just before he'd gone over to disrupt the nefarious plans of those idiots, telling his friend that he had located her. And... she was technically under his protection for now.

So yeah, taking her off to a quieter part of the island to have a drink and a dance was totally acceptable. Ares leaned into a turn in the road and her hands tightened around him, making his erection twitch. He gritted his jaw and resisted the urge to take one of her hands and put it between his legs where he throbbed for her. He couldn't remember the last time a woman had turned him on this easily. She was no mere woman. She was a queen in waiting. A totally out-of-bounds woman. And yet, apparently, blonde Disney princesses *were* his type.

Doubts assailed him again. This had been a really stupid idea. He should have just told her who he was and that she was under his protection until her team were back in place. As soon as they stopped, that was what he would do and then he would take her back to her hotel.

The bike stopped and Cassie took the helmet off, shaking out her hair. They were on the edge of a gorgeous little marina/harbour with houses and buildings jostling along the edge, all different colours. Bustling bars and cafes, restaurants. People sitting outside eating and drinking. A very faint sound of disco music coming from the other end of the stretch.

Night had fallen properly now and a crescent moon hung in the sky like a bauble. Stars twinkling.

It was a world away from the over-touristy place she'd been. Using her hand, she balanced on him and got off the bike. Her legs felt wobbly as the adrenalin left her system. She avoided looking at the man as he got off the bike and took off his helmet. She suddenly felt shy. It had been so intimate, wedged up against him, her hands wrapped together just over his—

'Where is this place?' she asked, hoping he wouldn't see how it had affected her.

'It's Rethymno, a little quieter than where we were.'

'It's lovely. Quaint. And yes, quieter, thank you.' She cast a glance at him and felt heat climb into her cheeks. She could remember how flat and hard-muscled his torso had felt under her arms. How she'd wanted to undo her hands and slip one under the material of his shirt.

He said, 'Look, I need to tell you—'

For some reason Cassie didn't want him to finish his sentence. She stuck out a hand and said, 'I'm Cloe.' She mentally crossed her fingers at the white lie, assuring herself that one of her names *was* actually Clotilde, so it wasn't a total untruth.

He looked at her for a long moment and then he took her hand, saying, 'I'm Ares.'

Reluctantly she took her hand out of his, liking it far too much. 'You're Greek?'

He nodded.

She smiled. 'Well, that makes sense. We're in Greece.' She cringed inwardly. She was being an idiot.

Cassie glanced around quickly and said, 'Look, I owe you a drink for potentially saving me from a pretty horrific situation. How about that bar over there?'

He looked to where she was pointing and Cassie held her breath. She could hear some kind of jazzy funky music beat. A world away from the disco inferno they'd just left behind.

After what felt like an eternity, Ares said, 'Sure, after you.'

Relief swept through Cassie. Because this man had single-handedly woken her desire. Like Sleeping Beauty. Cassie suppressed a slightly hysterical giggle. She blinked her eyes a few times. The dark contacts she'd put in were scratching a little but she couldn't drop her guard now. She knew she was being reckless by evading her bodyguards and it was the most rebellious thing she'd ever done, but, that tacky bar earlier aside, this was turning into one of the most thrilling evenings of her life.

Pathetic. She ignored the little voice and stepped into the bar, very aware of the tall solid presence behind her.

Cassie was still a little unused to not being automatically recognised so when the greeter came over and skipped over her to look up at Ares, it was a little jolting but not entirely unwelcome. Ares stood beside her, and as they were led to a table in a corner booth, he lightly touched her back. *Her bare back.*

Electricity sparked up and down her spine and between her legs felt sensitive and hot. She slid into the booth, and he followed her, accepting the menu from the server, who couldn't seem to take her eyes off him. Cassie couldn't blame her.

Sitting beside him now, she could really take him in. The hard planes of his face, that mouth. Deep-set eyes. Softened by the beard that hugged his jaw. Messy hair. He should look thoroughly disreputable but there was something about him that Cassie recognised. *Class.* He couldn't hide that. Intriguing.

He looked at her and she swallowed. She was not used to this at all. 'So, um, do you come from this island?'

He shook his head. 'No, the mainland.'

He hadn't cracked a smile once since they'd met. Cassie smiled for both of them. Being sunny came easily. She'd been doing it all her life. 'Care to narrow it down a bit?'

His gaze was fixed on her mouth and then it moved up over her face. She'd never felt so self-conscious. She was very aware of the heavy make-up, contacts and glitter. He looked as if he was holding back a scowl. Definitely not Mr Charming.

'Athens.'

Then he said, 'What about you?'

Cassie tensed but kept the smile in place, because it seemed to unnerve him. 'Oh, I'm just here for a few days on holiday.'

'From where?' he all but bit out.

Cassie waved a hand. 'A little place you'll never have heard of, near the South of France.'

Luckily the server came back and took orders for drinks before he asked her to elaborate. Cassie ordered a sparkling wine and Ares ordered something non-alcoholic. When the server left, he put an arm across the back of the seat. Cassie was very aware that his fingers rested within touching distance of the top of her back.

Feeling a little out of her depth but trying to ignore it, she asked, 'So are you here on holiday too?'

He shook his head. 'No, work.'

Cassie made her smile brighter. 'You're not fond of long sentences, are you?'

There was the faintest glimmer in his eyes to show that her remark had made its mark. So maybe there was some humour after all. And why on earth was he so appealing when he wasn't even going out of his way to charm her? Was she hard-wired to be drawn to people who she felt she had to humour? That cut a little too close to the bone and Cassie felt her smile slipping just as the drinks were delivered.

She took a quick sip to hide the sudden onset of introspection. Ares took a sip too of his drink and Cassie couldn't avoid looking at the way his throat moved… leading down to the top of his chest, revealed by a couple of open shirt buttons. She could see dark hair, curling. He was so *male*. She'd never thought she'd find someone so unashamedly masculine attractive.

She put down her drink. 'So, what is your work, then?'

He put down his glass but kept his hand around it. Cassie couldn't help but notice his long fingers, blunt nails. She could just look at him all day. He was mesmerising.

'I dabble in a couple of things…investment, and logistics.'

'Sounds…vague,' Cassie said. He obviously wasn't going to elaborate.

'What about you?'

Cassie fiddled with her glass, avoided his eye. She could be vague too. 'I, um, just graduated university not long ago.' That was true. She'd graduated from the main university on Sadat Sur Mer.

'What did you study?'

'Economics and international relations. And languages.' Except she'd been speaking at least four languages fluently since she was a child.

'You're not working yet?' he asked.

She'd been working her whole life as a princess, but he couldn't know that. Cassie crossed her fingers on her lap, under the table. 'I'm actually starting a new job within the next few weeks, hence this holiday.'

Ares arched a brow. 'I guess that's as good a time as any for a holiday.'

Relieved he wasn't asking for more information on her *job*, and worried where the conversation might stray next, Cassie blurted out, 'Would you like to dance?'

He looked at her and drew back slightly. Cassie's insides dropped. Had that been a really gauche thing to do? She was so inexperienced at this. She'd always been so protected and cosseted, and, even if she'd liked a guy, they were usually so intimidated by who she was that they wouldn't come near her. In a way she could understand now why Caius had socialised with the people he had, because it simply would have been too awkward not to.

But suddenly Ares said, 'Yes, OK.' And he was sliding out of the booth and holding out his hand.

CHAPTER THREE

WHAT THE HELL are you doing, man? You were meant to tell her who you were as soon as you arrived. This is such a bad idea, tell her now—but at the feel of Cassie's small hand sliding into his, all of Ares's thoughts stopped dead.

This had to be better than sitting next to her and breathing in her evocative scent, musky and flowery and earthy all at once. It had taken all of his control not to let his fingers touch her hair, test if it felt as silky as it looked. Even with those lurid colours through it, nothing could dim the golden blonde strands.

He led her to the small space where other couples had moved together as the music changed and became more sultry. He turned and faced her. She was taller than he'd expected her to be. Even without the heels she'd be above average height.

He tugged her towards him and she came with a tiny stumble that brought her flush with his body. She was all slim, lithe curves and her breasts pressed against his chest. He already knew they were bigger than he might have first thought because he'd seen her cleavage, unwittingly presented when she'd folded her arms in front of him. And then, on the bike, pressed against him. She wore no bra. The thought of those perfect orbs of flesh, loose and unbound—Ares gritted his jaw to try and maintain some semblance of control as he spread his hand across her back.

She felt incredibly delicate and yet there was a latent strength. He had a sense not to underestimate her. After all, she'd managed to ditch her bodyguards and avoid her brother.

He looked down at her and she lifted her face. She smiled. It made something inside Ares ache. Why was she so smiley? So perky? She was a princess way out of her depth. She could have been unconscious somewhere now if it hadn't been for him. But again he had that sense that perhaps she would have surprised him by managing to get out of that predicament. She was using a false name to avoid detection.

Then his gaze went to her mouth. It opened slightly and he had a glimpse of pink tongue. White teeth. A fire started raging in his blood. He'd never been more tempted by a woman. By a woman who was so far out of his bounds that—

Before Ares could formulate another word, she'd reached up and pressed her mouth to his, a chaste and surprisingly sweet gesture. But any thought of *sweet* fast dissolved as the kiss morphed into burning hot heat and intense need. Ares couldn't resist. Didn't want to resist. So he didn't.

Cassie's heart was thumping so hard she felt sure the entire island must be able to hear it. One minute she'd been looking up into that gorgeous face, at that provocatively sexy mouth, and the next she'd done the most audacious thing. She'd kissed him, reaching up on tippy-toe. Winding her arms around his neck.

His mouth had felt hard and unyielding under hers. Warm but unmoving. *She'd made a bad mistake. This guy wasn't remotely into her at all.* She'd been about to pull back, her insides curdling with humiliation, and she'd taken a breath against his lips and then everything had changed.

He'd reciprocated. No. He'd taken over. Masterfully. Pulling her even closer with his arms, welding her to him so tight that she swore she could feel every ridge of his hard musculature. His arms were like steel. And she *loved it*.

His mouth moved over hers now, coaxing a response that Cassie gave instinctively. She had been kissed before but she'd always had to make the move because guys were so intimidated and then nothing much had happened. They'd been like deer in the headlights. Those experiences had only reinforced her impression that perhaps she wasn't destined for a life of passion. But now...she was being given a crash course.

Ares's tongue touched hers and an electric shock went straight to between her legs. She pressed her thighs together as if that could contain the sense of burgeoning tension and excitement.

The kiss deepened and became explicit. Testing, tasting. Luxuriating. It was as if they had all the time in the world for this exquisite pleasure. Bodies pressed together, tongues duelling.

Slowly, Cassie realised that her back was against a

wall. Ares had manoeuvred them off the main floor to a corner near the booth.

He broke the kiss and lifted his head. Cassie felt drunk. It took an age for her to be able to open her eyes. And he was blurry at first and then came back into focus. Her mouth was tingling, and between her legs felt swollen and hot and damp.

As if reading her mind, he inserted a thigh between her legs and Cassie almost whimpered as the movement caused a friction that made her bite her lip. She wanted to rub against him, to alleviate the building tension.

He put his hands on her waist and his hands and the wall were the only things holding her up. He shook his head. 'You are...a temptress.'

Cassie felt like giggling. But then she didn't as one of his hands moved up over her waist, tracing the curve, moving closer and closer to the underside of her breast. And then she sucked in a breath, all thoughts of giggling gone as his hand cupped the weight of her breast. And then his thumb moved back and forth across one tight and tingling nipple.

Cassie's thighs tightened around Ares's and she felt a flutter of sensation at her core. She was holding onto his arms and she couldn't reach all the way around they were so thickly muscled.

She felt primitive. Him man, her woman. She wanted to climb him and wrap her legs around him. She said, without even really thinking, 'Please, Ares, touch me, show me...how it can be.'

He cupped her breast more firmly and bent his head and captured her mouth in another searing hot kiss.

Deep and explicit straight away, no leading into it. Cassie welcomed it, wrapping her arms around him again, opening herself up to his hands, inviting him to touch her, moving against him in a way that had her starting to gasp with need as an elusive peak shimmered in the distance.

Ares's hand on her breast squeezed hard, fingers trapping a nipple. Cassie suddenly wanted more, wanted to feel his mouth on her there, surrounding that tight peak in heat and moisture.

Ares took his thigh from between hers and replaced it with his hand. He cupped her through the soft denim, right there over where she throbbed. He moved his hand against her, watching her. Cassie felt a little exposed because he oozed such confidence and experience but suddenly she stopped thinking because she was pressing against his hand and he was moving in a rhythmic motion and a force she'd never felt before held her body in an alien grip before it exploded into a rush of pleasure so intense that she would have called out loud if he hadn't taken her mouth again and swallowed her orgasmic cry.

The world and reality came back slowly. The sounds of the bar, music. People laughing. Cassie was grateful that Ares was shielding her from everyone else. No one would know that she'd just had her first orgasm with a total stranger in a bar in Crete. *Ares.* Not a total stranger. But as good as.

A million and one things were rushing through Cassie as this sank in. Ares seemed to be watching her warily as if she were a bomb about to go off. She had just gone off, against his hand. Heat climbed into her face. She was glad of the dark.

He put his hands on her arms and somehow, sensing a shift in the mood, Cassie managed to straighten up. Her legs were still working. Albeit wobbly. He must think she was so gauche.

'I...' Her tongue felt thick as she tried to formulate something.

Ares shook his head. 'You don't have to say anything. Not a word. This is on me. My fault.'

Cassie felt a trickle of unease trace down her spine. That was an odd thing to say. 'What do you mean, your fault?'

He let her arms go and took a step back. Ran a hand through his hair, making it messier. He looked at her. 'Because we should never have come here.'

Something occurred to Cassie and she reared back. 'You're married.'

A look of disgust crossed his face. '*Theos*, no. I'm not married.'

Cassie was confused. 'You have a girlfriend?'

The disgust again. '*No.* I don't *do* girlfriends.'

He took her arm in his hand and had started to guide her back out of the bar, through the couples mingling and dancing, before Cassie even knew what was happening.

When they were outside and fresh air hit her, she stopped, forcing him to stop too. 'What are you doing?'

He let her go and looked at her. 'We need to leave.'

Something about the return of that censorious tone and the fact that *he* had decided to leave stung Cassie somewhere vulnerable. Had she been such a bad kisser? Had her orgasm been such a faux pas? A turn-off? The expression on his face hadn't been disgusted or bored, it had been intense. But had she imagined that?

She felt even more exposed. 'You might have decided that you no longer want to stay here but that's your decision.'

He gritted his jaw. He really was such a taciturn man. Cassie wondered what on earth she found attractive about him. *Everything.* She wanted to scowl. She'd certainly found him pretty attractive just a few minutes ago. Her body still felt hot inside, as if something had melted.

'I brought you here, I'll take you back.'

Now she was offended. 'Charming, like a parcel you've suddenly decided you no longer want.'

She tossed her hair and drew herself up to her full height, which was still a good few inches short of his. In heels. 'You don't have to *take* me anywhere, Ares. I've decided I like this bar and I'm staying. Goodnight.'

She turned and went to walk back into the bar, her insides fizzing and jumping with a mixture of hurt, confusion and anger, when from behind her she heard, 'It's not that simple, princess.'

Cassie's feet stopped. She wondered if she'd heard that right. *Princess.* Surely she was just being paranoid, he'd meant it as some sort of figure of speech. Inappropriate though, because clearly he had no interest in her and was just trying to salve his conscience now by returning her to where he'd picked her up. But it was still weird.

She turned around. 'What did you call me?'
'Princess.'
Her insides tightened. This man was a total stranger, he couldn't possibly—
'Princess Cassandra Mansur de Roche. Crown Princess, to be precise. You'll have to forgive me for not remembering your middle names, there are quite a few, but I'm assuming Cloe is one of them.'
For a moment Cassie heard nothing but a dull roaring sound, and then she was suddenly light-headed. She was going to faint. *No.* He moved towards her as if sensing her shock. She put up a hand between them, as the full enormity of what this meant rushed through her brain and body with a million and one ramifications hitting her all at once.
He said, 'I'm not from the press or anything like that. I'm a friend of your brother's. He sent me to track you down because he was worried about you.'
Cassie felt a flash of anger at her brother for interfering when she didn't need him and for not being around when she did need him. She knew there was no point denying who she was. 'I've taken some time off. He doesn't need to be worried. I told him I was OK.'
'But not where you were. If he'd seen what I saw earlier he would have had reason to be worried.' Admonishing her when a moment ago she'd been all but climbing him like a tree and orgasming into his cupped hand.
Cassie felt her blood start to boil, eclipsing the shock. This man had known who she was and hadn't been fully honest with her.
'For your information, Mr Ares Whatever Your Sec-

ond Name Is, I'm skilled in self-defence, I've been taking classes since I was small so I would have been absolutely *fine*.'

'Not if you'd been unconscious due to a drug in the drink. And my second name is Drakos, Ares Drakos.'

It suited him, she thought a little churlishly, curt and abrupt like him. 'I wasn't going to take the drink. I didn't trust them.'

'You trusted me.'

Cassie folded her arms at the humiliating reminder and it struck her then that perhaps, somewhere deep down, she'd suspected that he wasn't just some gorgeous man who'd appeared as her guardian angel. Ha! Guardian devil.

The sense of exposure was compounded now by feeling acutely self-conscious. She'd allowed herself to believe him to be a total stranger who had been overcome with lust for her. She'd revealed herself to him in ways she'd never done with anyone else. He'd brought her to orgasm. In public.

Mortification and the heat of shame crawled upwards through her body. 'You should have told me you knew who I was.'

'Yes,' he said immediately, 'I should have. It was a lapse of judgement.'

Cassie was a little taken aback by his straightforward admission of guilt. She frowned, thinking of something belatedly. 'Why did my brother call you?'

'I own a private security company. I will stay with you until your bodyguards have you under their protection again.'

Cassie shook her head and started to back away. 'No, you won't. We're done here, Mr Drakos. You found me and you had your fun at my expense.'

She looked around, feeling panicky. She needed to get away from this man and those dark eyes and that unsmiling face. And that mouth and those hands that had played her like an instrument for his amusement.

She saw a line of taxis about a hundred feet away and she walked quickly towards them. From behind her she heard, 'Princess Cassandra, wait.'

But she didn't turn around, she jumped into the back of the first taxi and, with her heart hammering and her insides tight with humiliation and embarrassment, she gave the address of her hotel.

She looked out of the window as the taxi turned to go in the right direction. He was standing there, a tall, powerful figure. And everything they'd just shared was tainted. He knew who and where she was now, her peace was shattered. In more ways than one.

She never wanted to see that man again.

CHAPTER FOUR

Cassie had sent her brother a text when she'd returned to her hotel last night.

Caius, I'm fine, please let me have this time to myself. You had your years of freedom. In a matter of weeks, I'll no longer have this luxury. I love you. x Cass.

Cassie hadn't received a response from Caius. But she knew that didn't mean much. He knew where she was now. He'd sent his *friend* after her. His friend, who when she'd looked him up online last night had suddenly appeared in numerous photos with her brother, coming out of various bars and clubs going back a few years.

It didn't look as if he'd been any happier in those moments, a stern, or even scowling, counterpoint to Caius's playboy-prince mischievous grin. Cassie had generally avoided looking at her brother's exploits online, naturally enough.

But if she had, then Ares Drakos might have been familiar to her last night. Because clearly he'd enjoyed playing the playboy along with her brother and apart from pictures of him with Caius there had been plenty of him at glittering functions with a stunning woman on his arm. A different one every time. Blonde, brunette, redhead. He didn't seem to have a type. Maybe he was just the kind of guy who would hook up at any opportunity. With any willing woman.

Like last night. Cassie had to push down the resurgence of humiliation that had kept her awake with heartburn all night.

Ares Drakos was from one of Greece's biggest shipping dynasties and yet he'd broken relations with his family when he'd graduated high school, at the age of seventeen. He'd turned his back on his inheritance and the family business to go his own way.

He'd served with the Greek army before going into the special forces for a few years, but those details were hazy. There were several online rumours that he'd been involved in some of the most high-profile security engagements in the world, including several political prisoner swaps.

He'd emerged from his time with security forces and set up his own security company—Drakos Security. There was little information about it online except for the mention that Ares had invested in cutting-edge software that had made his security company one of the most in demand in the world. And worth billions.

Cassie huffed to herself now that he'd probably used this *software* to track her down.

She was dressed today in cut-off shorts, sneakers and a T-shirt that she'd tied in a knot at her waist. Her hair was now free of the temporary tie-dyed colours and up and stuffed under a baseball cap. She didn't have contacts in her eyes to disguise their colour.

She'd leased a sailing boat from a marina on the other side of the island. She was going to avoid any more troublesome interactions by taking to the seas and doing some island hopping.

That would give her space to think and enjoy her freedom. *Alone.* She ignored the pang of loneliness.

Well, she thought to herself as she jumped down from the boat to the wooden walkway to untie it, *better alone than being potentially drugged or mocked.*

She had the rope in her hand and she was about to step back onto the boat when the skin on the back of her neck prickled and she went still.

No.

Slowly she turned around to see an all too familiar tall, broad figure just a few feet away. He was wearing board shorts and a short-sleeved polo shirt. He had a baseball cap too and it shadowed his face but she could still make out the hard, bearded jaw and that provocative mouth.

In fractured moments of sleep last night she'd dreamt of that mouth. Touching more than her lips.

'What are you doing here?' As she asked that question she noticed that he was carrying a scuffed holdall. She pointed to it. 'What is that?'

He lifted it up and Cassie noticed the way his muscles bulged. She also remembered how hard his chest had felt against hers.

He said, 'It's my bag. I'm coming with you.'

Panic spiked. Cassie turned away and jumped lithely onto the boat. She turned to face him. 'No, you're not.'

He walked to where there was one more rope mooring the boat to the dock and he put his foot on top of the post. Cassie cursed inwardly.

'Yes, I am. Your brother has acquired my services until such time as you're done with this little trip and you're back at the palace.'

Cassie shook her head. 'No way, no how. He has no right to do this. I'll pay you double whatever he's paying you to leave me alone.'

'It's not about the money. He's my friend and it's a personal favour.'

Cassie smiled sweetly, belying the way her belly was cramping with tension. 'Well, we were pretty friendly last night, maybe you'll do me a personal favour and get lost?' She had never been so rude in her life. But something about standing up to this man was a little shamefully exhilarating, especially when she'd spent all her life trying to make everyone else happy.

Now he smiled and Cassie almost fell off the boat. His mouth was wide and his teeth were very white and the smile completely transformed his face. Even though she knew it wasn't a real smile. Lord help her if he ever did that. She scowled. She wasn't going to ever see him smile for real and didn't want to.

She secured the rope in her hand and went back down onto the walkway to untie the last rope mooring the boat to the jetty. She looked expressly at his foot and tried not to be so aware of his size. 'Can you move your foot, please?'

'Not until you tell me where you plan on going.'

She looked up from under the rim of her cap. 'Island hopping, not that it's any of your business. But after last night I'd prefer to take my chances with sharks at sea rather than the sharks on land.'

She bent down and pushed his foot off the bollard and lifted up the rope, moving back towards the boat. She hadn't even unbalanced him.

'I'm coming with you whether you like it or not, sweetheart.'

Cassie went rigid and turned back towards him. 'I am not your *sweetheart*. And I am leaving now on this boat. If you attempt to board I will call the marina police and have you arrested.'

'And how will that look in the papers, hm? Crown Princess Cassandra running from her duties to be queen?'

Cassie's mouth fell open and her eyes widened. 'You wouldn't dare.'

He shrugged one wide shoulder. 'I've been given a brief and I don't ever renege on an assignment and my assignment is you until you're back at the palace under the protection of your own guards again, who, admittedly, need a refresher course in how to protect you.'

My assignment is you. Those words sent more than a frisson of awareness into Cassie's blood.

'Now,' he said, 'we're not leaving here on a boat. I have a private plane standing by ready to take you wherever you'd like, preferably back to your palace but if you insist on wanting to island hop then that's what we'll do.'

A million things buzzed into Cassie's head—the sheer arrogance for one, that censorious tone again along with a trace of weariness, as if suffering a petulant child.

She very deliberately stepped back onto the boat that was now untethered from the jetty and, after securing the rope, she stood up with hands on her hips. 'Now,' she said, mimicking his tone, 'I am not leaving here, except on this boat that I have paid good money for. I have no desire to contribute to global warming by using a private jet when I don't have to. There's an app that you can download that'll allow you to follow the boat's progress—feel free to keep an eye on me that way. I'd really prefer it.'

Cassie turned her back on Ares and focused on turning the engine on to navigate out of the marina. She couldn't see someone like Ares Drakos dancing to her tune, so good riddance.

Ares looked at the boat and the back of Crown Princess Cassandra as she stood by one of the two big wheels. It had taken more strength than he cared to admit just to walk down the jetty to where she had been untying the boat. Not even her long, golden, slim legs and that high, curvy behind encased in demin could have stopped the clammy feeling of sweat on his brow and palms.

Or the bolt of electricity he'd felt when she'd looked up at him from under her cap and he'd seen those amazing blue eyes that she'd hidden under contacts last night.

He hated boats. Loathed them. *He still had nightmares about them.*

He'd been kidnapped when he was ten and the gang had held him on a boat, moving around to evade detection, as they'd negotiated with his parents for his return.

His parents had fought paying up, fearing it would set

a precedent, caring more for their vast wealth and reputation than the life of one son. They'd had another heir in his older brother, Axel, so they could afford to lose one.

Axel's academic prowess in contrast to Ares's struggles reading and writing had ensured that Ares was never going to inherit the family business, highlighted by the reaction to his kidnapping.

In the end, it had been a specialist team from the police department who had tracked down the boat and saved Ares, with no help from his family. It had shown Ares that the police force had cared more than his own flesh and blood about his welfare.

He'd returned home, traumatised and changed for ever. His brother had wanted to know what had happened but Ares hadn't been able to talk about it. And his parents had encouraged him not to talk about it. To just forget. Eventually Axel had stopped asking and had been drawn more and more into the realm of becoming successor to their father—cementing an even bigger gulf between the brothers.

His sisters had been too young and Ares had distanced himself from them too, finding their childish innocence terrifying—because he knew how quickly it could be taken away.

He'd vowed to make sure he was never that vulnerable again, by taking care of himself. It had been clear his family hadn't valued him as worth protecting, so as soon as he was of age, he'd left.

He'd also vowed to do his utmost to help those who needed it. Those who were left behind, forgotten by the ones who should be protecting them.

That was why he really, really resented his time being taken away from a more worthwhile cause than caretaking a wayward princess. And why he hated boats so much.

In spite of which, he knew how to sail, because his father hadn't allowed Ares's traumatic experience to be the reason he couldn't take control of a boat. It had simply been unconscionable that, as the son of a shipping magnate, a Drakos couldn't handle a boat and so he'd spent his teens white-knuckling and sweating his way through being forced to sail on many occasions.

But Ares had only been on water in recent years if it was absolutely necessary for a security mission. To save a life. Certainly not on the whim of a big brother who wanted his little sister protected at all costs. No matter how much he liked the guy.

She's not just anyone, a voice pointed out. *She's a crown princess, about to become a head of state.*

That held no sway with Ares. She wanted to have her cake and eat it. Privilege *and* freedom. She needed his protection about as much as a tiger did. Her biggest danger was making eyes at goons who would want to spike her drink. *Or going off with a stranger who then ravished her in a public place at the first opportunity.*

Ares's conscience stung. He couldn't put that on her. It had been all him and his wayward libido. The sun must have got to him yesterday.

Then he heard the engine revving and his tension spiked. He realised she had every intention of pulling out of this marina and leaving. In the midst of his churning guts he had to hand it to her. She wasn't afraid of him. *Because she expects you to jump to her bidding.*

Whatever. Ares wasn't here to pass judgement on her. He knew he had no choice. He would have to dance to her tune. For now. He swallowed down the rising panic and gritted his jaw before jumping lithely onto the boat, just as it started to move away from the jetty.

Ares swayed a little on the boat as it picked up speed out of the marina and gulped down more nausea. At least he wasn't deep below deck this time, locked into a tiny cabin.

At that moment Princess Cassandra looked around from the wheel and scowled at him from under her cap. Ares arranged his face into a smile that felt more like a grimace and said, 'I haven't had a holiday in years. This'll be fun.'

About thirty minutes later, Cassie's heart was still thudding. He was on the boat with her. In her peripheral vision on the seats that encased the deck where she was standing at the wheel. She was suddenly annoyed she hadn't hired a much bigger boat. This felt very intimate even though it was a family-sized sailing boat with a generous cabin area down below.

There was a compact kitchen, stocked with supplies, and a dining/seating area. A master cabin was in the bow with a small en suite, and two more small bedrooms and the head/toilet at the stern of the boat.

She was sure he'd get off at the first stop. He was just calling her bluff. But shamefully her dominant reactions weren't anger or frustration, they were something more like anticipation, *excitement*. She scowled into the warm Aegean breeze, trying to focus on navigating.

Ares Drakos was a busy man, no way was he going to settle for babysitting her, no matter how close to Caius he was.

That piqued her curiosity, in spite of herself. Caius gave off the impression of being charming and amenable and the life and soul of the party but Cassie knew well that he used that to deflect from the fact that, actually, he was a lot more serious and guarded than he wanted anyone to know.

So the fact that her brother obviously trusted Ares Drakos was intriguing to say the least.

She and Caius had both been affected by their parents' chaotic and destructive relationship and she knew that it had had a profound impact on Caius to find out that the king hadn't been his father. She could only imagine what that knowledge would do to your sense of yourself—suddenly finding out you weren't who you thought you were. The fact that he was still trying to protect her even though he'd had to step aside made her conscience prick. It hadn't been his fault that their world had shifted on its axis like this.

Then, just when she'd almost convinced herself that she was actually alone and not with a taciturn uninvited guest, Ares's voice came over the throb of the engine. 'So, I presume you know what you're doing if you're sailing this boat by yourself?'

Cassie glanced at him reluctantly and hated the way her heart skipped a beat. He was sitting, legs sprawled, bag on the seat beside him. Arms out across the back of the seat. For all the world as if he had chartered the boat and she were just an employee.

She wasn't used to people making her feel prickly and she didn't like it. 'We'll soon find out, won't we?'

She turned back to face the horizon as he said, 'Wouldn't it have been easier to hire a catamaran with a crew? Plenty of space to lounge about and work on your tan.'

Cassie made sure the chart plotter was set with the right coordinates and turned back to face Ares and folded her arms, glad she was wearing more clothes this time. Well, apart from her cut-off shorts.

'My aim was to take this boat trip *alone*.'

Ares took off his baseball cap and ran a hand through his hair, making it even messier. And was his jaw even more stubbled today? But did he look a little pale under his tan? Green, even? Eyes a bit pinched? He seemed supremely relaxed but Cassie could sense a very subtle tension in his form. Before she could wonder about it too much he said, 'Don't you have any friends to play with?'

Cassie's hackles reached nuclear levels because he was unwittingly highlighting the fact again that she was alone and hadn't anticipated feeling this... *lonely*. At all. She did have friends; they just had pretty normal lives and weren't available to go sailing on a whim.

She gritted out, 'Not that it's any business of yours, but I do have friends. Good ones. And maybe I want to be alone to gather my thoughts.'

'Ah yes, no doubt to contemplate the new job you alluded to last night, becoming Queen of Sadat Sur Mer.'

Casssie's jaw gritted even more. 'You mean last night when I was led to believe you had no idea who I was?'

He had the grace to look sheepish. 'I told you that was a mistake. You had a right to know who I was.'

'Yes, I did. But clearly it was far too tempting to mock me and make a fool of me.' Cassie was surprised at the depth of emotion that spiked. As if he'd somehow had the power to hurt her by deceiving her.

She turned back to the horizon that was wide and empty except for little smudges of other boats and islands in the far distance.

'I'm sorry.'

She tensed, wondering if she'd heard right. Then his voice came again. 'My intent was not to deceive you, princess. I mean that.'

Cassie hated the way his apology made her tension dissipate. She glanced at him, and now he was sitting forward with his hands linked between wide-apart legs.

'So why did you?' And then she added, 'And don't call me princess. My name is Cassie.'

Last night she'd told him, *I'm Cloe.* She pushed the memory aside.

He looked as if he was gritting his teeth and then he said, 'Cassie.'

He couldn't be further from the intense brooding stranger from last night who had enveloped her in his strength and heat, coaxing her to a climax before she'd even realised what was happening. And he also didn't seem inclined to answer her question.

'Look,' she said eventually, 'I'm heading for Santorini. I'll drop anchor and bring you to the island on the tender. You can make your own way from there. You obviously don't want to be here and I don't need babysitting.' *You are going to be a queen.* Cassie could almost hear Pierre's scandalised voice in her head.

But Ares was already shaking his head anyway. 'No can do. While you're insisting on taking this little pleasure trip, I'm by your side.' He sat back again and regarded her. It was patently obvious that he judged her as selfish and spoiled.

Little pleasure trip. He riled her up so easily, it was a little scary. She knew she shouldn't let him get to her but she was putting hands on her hips and facing him. 'Did you ever judge my brother like this when you and he met up on *your* little pleasure trips to exclusive nightclubs and bars?'

He had the grace to flush slightly. Cassie felt ridiculously pleased that she could get to him.

He said, 'You looked me up.'

Cassie faced back to the sea, hands on the wheel. 'Of course I did. It's only because I don't snoop on my brother's social activities that I didn't recognise you, but now that I know you share his playboy…proclivities, last night makes a lot of sense. But if I had known who you were I wouldn't have let you come within five feet of me.'

Ares surged up from the seat in her peripheral vision and Cassie tightened her hands around the wheel. She looked at him. His face was dark.

He bit out, 'I am not a playboy.'

Cassie shivered a little inside. He was *so* intense. It called to that part of her deep down underneath where she'd resented having to be the sunny antidote to the animosity around her growing up.

Feeling as if she were playing with a great white

shark, she said, 'If it walks like a duck and quacks like a duck...'

'Those pictures with your brother were only taken because it's impossible to go anywhere with him without being tailed by paparazzi. We met for drinks. Maybe once or twice went clubbing together.'

Cassie was intrigued. She'd hit a nerve. He didn't like being associated with her brother's more debauched behaviour. Which admittedly hadn't been that debauched. He'd just developed a reputation for being seen at every exclusive glittering event and blazing a trail through Europe's most beautiful women, each of whom had desperately wanted to be his queen. Until they'd invariably found themselves waking alone in a bed long gone cold.

'So you didn't leave a string of broken-hearted lovers behind you like my brother did? All that means is you're more discreet.' That reminded her of how he'd been careful to shield her from the people in the bar last night. As she'd orgasmed. She turned away again, face getting hot.

Cassie said, 'My point is that you're allowed to go out clubbing, Ares, and so am I, if I feel like it. Maybe I'll try a couple in Santorini.'

'What exactly is it you're hoping to get out of this trip?'

Cassie felt exposed. How could she articulate to this unsmiling man that being crowned queen both excited her and terrified her? It would make the world her gilded prison. She would never have this chance again to try and be incognito and to try to taste some of the freedom her brother had been afforded because he'd naturally had a less restricted life just because he'd been a man.

It had almost been expected of him to carouse and make mayhem before settling down. Double standards. She didn't hold it against her brother, and she knew that his hectic social whirl had largely been a smokescreen to deflect from his own inner demons.

But that hadn't been her scene and it was only now she was realising what she'd missed out on. A chance to feel free and unburdened. As much as someone like her could. A chance to live an alternate existence for a while. A chance to live for her twin. No, she couldn't articulate all that to this man.

Cassie ignored his question. 'I saw that you came from one of Greece's most prominent shipping dynasties.'

Silence and then, after a long moment he responded with, 'It's no secret.'

'Nor does it seem to be a secret that you walked away from your inheritance at a young age.'

'Yes.' Clipped. Not inviting more comment.

Cassie looked at Ares from under her baseball cap. 'Well, I don't have that luxury. It's not as if I want to walk away, in any case. I'm happy to do my duty as Queen of Sadat. It's an honour and a privilege. But is it so bad to want to experience a little window of freedom before it's gone for good?'

Ares had no answer for that. He hadn't really considered the full reality of what she was facing. A life of duty. Being beholden to a nation, even a small one. Having to watch every step you took and word you said for fear of bringing scandal or infamy on your people.

Caius had worn that responsibility lightly and Ares had to admit now, a little uncomfortably, that his decadent behaviour had been all but sanctioned—he'd just been living up to his playboy reputation and making the most of it before his life changed.

Ares had seen glimpses of a much more serious Caius, hiding behind the flashing paparazzi lights, but they hadn't ever strayed into deeper emotional territory. There wouldn't have been enough whiskey in the world for that level of bonding. They'd both tacitly acknowledged that they had their own *stuff* and had skirted around it.

He could imagine the rolling of Cassie's eyes if he were to admit that. Strange, he'd only known her for less than twenty-four hours yet he felt he knew her better than others he'd known for years. *You made her come against your hand.*

Ares's body reacted to that provocative thought. He had felt jealous of his hand, last night. He'd wanted to be embedded deep inside her and he'd wanted to feel the pulsing strength of her orgasm around him, milking him.

The fact that she'd looked him up online made him feel exposed. He knew she wouldn't have seen anything of the kidnapping as his family had managed to all but expunge the unsavoury episode from the records to protect their reputation. But it was still there, in corners of the Internet. She obviously hadn't dug that deep.

Ares was grateful. The thought of her knowing about that...made him feel even more exposed. And something he hadn't felt in a very long time. Vulnerable.

He took a step back. 'Fine, Santorini it is.' He had to acknowledge now that the fact that she was helming her own boat without any crew or entourage contradicted his assumptions about her.

She stepped away from the wheel and control panel and said, 'I'm going down to do some unpacking while the coast is clear.'

'I'll keep watch up here.' Ares had very little intention of going anywhere near the below-deck area unless it was absolutely necessary.

'The boat is set on its course. I won't be long.' She came out from behind the big wheel and ducked down into the lower-deck area. Ares let out a breath and ran his hand through his hair again. This was going to be a long week, unless he could convince her to return home sooner.

But strangely that no longer had a sense of urgency about it. He had to concede that her desire for a slice of freedom before taking on a mammoth role wasn't completely unreasonable. And her brother had certainly taken advantage of his.

You could have one of your most trusted employees take over from you in Santorini. Ares knew he could. Caius would be OK with that, if it was still one of Ares's team. But for some reason, Ares wasn't reaching for his phone to make the call. And he wasn't about to investigate why. The fact that he wasn't taking the first opportunity to get off this boat was disturbing enough.

CHAPTER FIVE

'Why Santorini?'

Cassie wondered if she could ignore the question. Ares had insisted on coming with her onto the island. He'd seemed almost eager to get off the boat. She was regretting saying they'd walk the famous almost six hundred steps up from the old port to Fira instead of taking the cable car.

They'd docked the tender at the port. Donkeys meandered up and down the steps carrying luggage and, sometimes, people. One passed her by now with a tourist on its back. Cassie felt sorry for the poor donkey.

She glanced at the man who was keeping pace beside her easily. She noted there wasn't a hint of perspiration or exertion on his face, when hers felt as if it were about to melt off under the seam of the baseball cap she was wearing for protection from the late afternoon sun as much to hide her identity.

She'd changed out of the cut-off shorts and T-shirt into loose linen trousers and a sleeveless V-necked silk top. A bag containing water and other essentials was slung across her body.

'Because I've never been and I've heard the sunset viewed from Oia is spectacular.'

'It's just a sunset.'

Cassie stopped near the top—mercifully—and looked at him. 'Are you always this grumpy or is it my unique effect on you?' she asked and smiled sweetly.

He just scowled behind his dark shades that made him look like a movie star. After Cassie had unpacked earlier and returned up top on the boat, Ares had gone down into the cabin with his bag. She'd called after him with only a modicum of sarcasm, 'Feel free to use one of the rooms at the stern of the boat.'

He hadn't answered. But he had changed into a white short-sleeved polo shirt that made him look even darker and only emphasised his outsize muscles.

It wasn't just the climb up from the port that made her breathless. She went back to climbing the last steps and said, 'If you don't want to be here so badly why don't you send someone else? Maybe they'll be a bit more excited about a sunset.'

Cassie had more or less resigned herself to the fact that she would be shadowed for this trip, whether she liked it or not. She didn't fancy her chances of evading Ares or one of his staff, after reading about him and his company.

'All my staff are busy on assignment.'

Cassie sent Ares a look. 'No doubt protecting far more worthy clients.'

He seemed to stiffen. 'I never said you weren't worthy.'

'You didn't have to,' Cassie said without any rancour. She was actually finding it quite refreshing being around someone who wasn't overly obsequious. Or who she felt she needed to keep happy.

They were at the top of the steps now and Cassie saw

a bus being loaded up with *Oia* in the window. She was heading for it when a hand—a large hand—wrapped around her bare upper arm. An electrical charge jolted through her body. She stopped and looked at Ares.

He said, 'Where are you going?'

'Taking the bus to Oia. It's the best place to see the sun set.'

He shook his head. 'No, we'll take a cab.' He was all but herding her to the taxi rank nearby and within a nanosecond she was installed in the back seat with him alongside her, one long muscled thigh far too close for comfort.

He was giving instructions to the driver in Greek and then the car was on the move.

A little stunned at the speed with which the man moved for someone so big and imposing, Cassie said churlishly, 'This is *my* trip.'

'And you're my responsibility. When we're off the boat, I'll dictate the modes of transport.'

'Yes, sir,' Cassie said under her breath.

But obviously not far enough under because he said, 'That's more like it.'

She looked at him but his face was turned away towards his window. She could have sworn she saw the faintest upturn of one side of his mouth and that sent a wave of heat undulating through her body.

Disgusted with herself for being so weak and susceptible to a pretty face and a few bulging muscles, she looked out of her own window.

'This place is like a theme park.'

The words were gritted out from above Cassie's

shoulder. She'd taken off her baseball cap and it hung from the strap of her bag. Her hair was pulled back and she was wearing shades. She knew that she more or less blended pretty well with the rest of the tourists. If anything, Ares was the one attracting all the attention, moving through the throngs of people clogging the narrow pretty streets of Oia lined with shops and boutiques and restaurants.

That suited her fine. She loved this sensation of being anonymous among crowds. Then she spotted something and exclaimed, 'Ooh, I was going to try and find this—it's here!'

She veered to the left and heard a stifled curse from behind her. She ducked into the famous bookshop that was situated in a cave that had been turned into a building. Like many of the buildings built into the caldera walls of Santorini.

'It's a…bookshop.'

She turned around to face Ares. He looked stunned as he took it in. No doubt he'd expected her to make for the first exclusive boutique or jewellery store. She was interested in those too but she liked confounding him.

'I've always wanted to see this place.' Cassie wandered further in and gazed at the shelves and poetry written on the walls. It was quirky and coming down with books. Heaven.

She picked up a big glossy hardback of photos of Greece. She could sense Ares's tension beside her and glanced up. 'Look, if you—' She stopped talking when she saw the expression on his face. It looked pained.

She put the book down. 'What is it?'

He shook his head, expression clearing. 'Nothing, I'll wait outside.' He slipped his shades back on and ducked back out through the small doorway. After a few more minutes' browsing, Cassie followed him outside to find him leaning against a wall, hands in his pockets.

He looked relaxed but she could see the tension in those impressive muscles. He saw her and stood up straight. They resumed walking along the street. When it became clear that he wasn't going to elaborate, Cassie asked, 'What was that about?'

'What?'

Cassie rolled her eyes. He was being obtuse. 'You know very well—you looked as if you'd just eaten a side of cold suet pudding.'

The faintest glimmer of a smile touched the corner of his mouth. 'Suet?'

Now Cassie's mouth twitched. 'A particularly revolting dessert we used to be served in boarding scool.'

She felt him glance at her and he said, 'Boarding school?'

She nodded. 'Since I was eight, in Switzerland. I came home for holidays and half-term. But my parents let me do the baccalaureate in Sadat.'

He seemed to digest this and Cassie had resigned herself to him dodging her initial question when he said, 'I'm dyslexic. So...being surrounded by books makes me a little uncomfortable.'

Cassie felt a little punch to her gut at that admission. 'There are so many more ways to read now.'

He shook his head. 'I know, but not so much when

I was growing up. My parents weren't very willing to accept that a child of theirs was in any way imperfect.'

Cassie stopped in the narrow street, forcing people to swerve and go around them. She put her hands on her hips, filled with indignation. 'That's outrageous. Some of the most successful people on the planet have dyslexia. If anything it means you're above average because you've had to mask or engineer your way through life in a way that takes serious ingenuity and intelligence.'

Ares looked at her, eyes glinting, a minuscule smile playing around his mouth. 'That's quite a defence.'

Cassie flushed, embarrassed. 'There was a girl in my school who was constantly sidelined and put at the bottom of the class, just because she had difficulty reading and writing. It made me so mad. Anyone could see she was more intelligent than the rest of us.'

'You pitied her.'

Cassie let out a short sharp laugh at the thought of the only friend she'd really made at boarding school allowing anyone to pity her. 'No way, she pities *me*. She's a force. She's already working at the UN.'

Cassie started walking again, following the flow of tourists to the best vantage point for watching the sunset. She gestured to Ares, who kept pace easily beside her. 'You're one of those success stories.'

His mouth compressed and he said, 'It's more that I was bred to be a success no matter what.'

Cassie thought to herself that she was sure it was more than just breeding, but Ares put his hand on her elbow to steer her through thickening crowds and that made any more words dissolve on her tongue.

They were approaching the promontory now, a vantage point that afforded a ringside view for the setting sun, which was slowly but steadily getting closer and closer to the horizon.

Ares guided Cassie to one of the few spots that hadn't been taken and they sat down, surrounded by chattering tourists, all facing the same way, oohing and ahing as the sky started to go through a veritable kaleidescope of colours.

'You know, you'd be getting just as specatacular a view from your boat and it wouldn't be half as crowded.'

But I'd be lonely. Cassie wondered if she would have had the nerve to come and do this if she'd been on her own. She liked to think so but she hadn't thought twice with Ares. Even if he was here at the behest of her brother and not because he wanted to be. That stung a little.

'Oh, be quiet and enjoy the view,' she said.

Be quiet. Ares had never been told to be quiet by a woman. Or anyone, for that matter. And yet he wasn't insulted. He knew he was grumbling like a petulant teenager. This woman seemed to bring out aspects of him that he'd never encountered before.

And he had never, *ever*, willingly revealed to anyone about his dyslexia. The army had known, and his staff knew but that was because he would never let his dyslexia compromise a security situation. By now he managed it pretty well, but Cassie was right, he'd had to mask it for a long time.

She'd sounded so indignant on his behalf…it had

roused something suspiciously expansive in his chest. For a moment he'd imagined what it might have been like to have someone in his corner as a child—helping him navigate a world where letters and numbers had danced in front of him and refused to make sense.

He had to acknowledge uncomfortably that she wasn't at all what he might have expected. She was here, on her own, not just helming her own boat. No staff. No lackeys. Self-sufficient in a way that made him think she must have been on her own a lot as a child.

She was capable. And not looking to see who was looking at her. Ares glanced around briefly, instinctively checking who might be watching them as much as to see if anyone had recognised her. No. She did blend in with the crowd of golden-skinned tourists, watching a sunset. Of course, if anyone chose to really look, they might recognise the pedigree that she carried with a self-assurance that came only with birth. A high-born birth. But even now Ares could imagine her pointing out that she hadn't asked to be born into a royal lineage. And yet she seemed resigned to her fate. To carry on the line. To do her job.

After a few minutes Cassie turned to face him. She'd slid her sunglasses on her head and the brightness of those blue eyes cut right through him.

'Ready to go?'

He just looked at her. She waved a hand in front of his face. 'The sun has set.'

Ares tore his gaze away from her face and looked out over the sea to where the sun had indeed set below the horizon, leaving a lingering haze of orange and pink and yellow flooding the sky. It must have been spectacular but he wouldn't know because he'd been too busy looking at that sunset reflected on Cassie's rapt face.

He was losing it. He stood up. 'Let's get back, then.' He knew he sounded curt. Abrupt. But she rubbed him up the wrong way. *She rubbed you up the right way last night.* Ares gritted his jaw and let Cassie precede him out of the viewing point.

The lingering memory of that spectacular sunset was fast fading and being eclipsed by the way Ares's hand felt on Cassie's elbow and the jolts of electricity running through her every time their bodies collided as Ares herded her through the thronged main street of Oia.

Feeling a need to resist at all costs—this hijacking of her precious freedom, and this assault on her senses—Cassie stopped and dug her heels in. 'I'm hungry. I'd like to eat before going back to the boat.'

Waves of displeasure emanated from Ares. It was almost worth it to rise him. It felt like a dream that they'd shared such an incendiary intimate moment only twenty-four hours ago.

But then he looked down at her as people flowed around them and it came hurtling back. The delicious heat of it. The heart-pounding excitement.

He said, 'Fine, I could eat too. There's a place near here.' He started leading them again, veering off and down a little side street.

Cassie said, 'I thought you hadn't been here before.'

'I never said I hadn't been before, just that I think it's become an over-hyped theme park.'

They were going down wide steps now and emerged into a restaurant that was cut into the side of the caldera, with amazing views out over the sea. A waiter came and greeted Ares effusively, and brought them to a table, set apart from the others on a little point. The best vantage point in the place. Ares pulled out the chair that faced the sea and Cassie found herself being touched by his consideration that she have the view before she realised that he was most likely doing this out of habit, so that there'd be less chance of anyone recognising her.

After all, he was hardly Mr Charm. And yet…there was something seriously compelling about him. Cassie hated herself for it but she wanted to see him unbend. Smile. Relax.

They sat down. The stunning view of the high walls of the caldera with the white-roofed houses and blue trim built along the sides like little toy buildings was exquisitely pretty. But Ares Drakos easily eclipsed even such an amazing view.

Cassie focused on the menu, choosing a salad and a fish main. Ares chose similar and a local wine and they handed the menus back. Cassie tried to take in the view but her gaze kept returning to Ares, who was regarding her steadily.

The setting sun made him seem even darker. More saturnine. It made Cassie itch to provoke. The waiter poured some white wine into their glasses and Cassie lifted her glass. She smiled sunnily. 'To new friends.'

Ares didn't lift his glass in cheers. He took a sip of the wine and said, 'We're not friends.'

A dart of hurt along with irritation at his dogged refusal to bend an inch made Cassie open her eyes wide. 'As I mentioned this morning, I think we've already established we were quite friendly...' she lifted her bare wrist and pretended to look at a watch '...right about this time yesterday evening.'

Ares looked at a point over her shoulder. 'That was a mistake. My fault. You didn't know who I was.'

Cassie said nothing for fear of revealing that even if she had known who he was she might still have climbed him like a tree.

'Can we move on from that?'

He looked at her. 'You brought it up again.'

Cassie rolled her eyes. 'Fine, if *I* promise not to bring it up again can we move on? As it appears that we're destined to spend the next week, at least, together.'

'You sure you don't want to go home sooner?'

Cassie smiled extra sweetly. 'I'm sure. As I said, this is my only chance to enjoy some freedom while I can. Something you take for granted.'

'Are any of us really free though?'

'Spare me the philosophical debate, and yes, some are freer than others. My brother certainly enjoyed his freedom as crown prince, before he became king, after our father died.'

'Or, in his case, *not* his father.'

Cassie's smile slipped as she recalled that brutal bombshell. They'd found out mere hours before it had made international headlines and Caius had had to leave Sadat Sur Mer to avoid the scrum of paparazzi who had descended on the island. Not to mention the shock and ire of the people who had idolised him.

The starters were served, traditional Greek salad with a twist.

'No,' Cassie echoed, 'not his father.'

'What happened to you after your brother left Sadat to escape the press?' Ares popped an olive into his mouth.

Cassie tried not to fixate on those sculpted lips. She shrugged lightly, belying the fear she'd felt in those moments, all alone. Abandoned by her brother. 'I holed up in the palace and had to wait it out, as our advisors and press corps came up with a response, naming me as queen. There was no other alternative.'

She had to acknowledge, 'Caius wanted to stay, to shield me as much as possible, but people were angry. They felt betrayed. He would have caused more headlines staying in Sadat.'

'Overnight you became ruler.'

'More or less...but not officially until the coronation.'

Ares waved a hand. 'That's just a ceremony and paperwork.'

Cassie let out a laugh. 'I think Pierre, my chief advisor, who runs on anxiety and adrenalin, wouldn't quite agree. You're not a royalist?'

Ares took a healthy sip of wine. 'Why would I be?'

'Greece still has a royal family, even if it no longer has any power. You come from a dynasty that probably has traditions and bloodlines dating back as far as theirs does.'

Ares went still on the other side of the table. Cassie sensed it.

He said, 'You're not far wrong. Maybe that's why I'm not a fan of entitled privilege.'

'What happened to you?'

His eyes flashed dark golden for a moment. She was transgressing but she didn't care. He'd hijacked her peace. But then he shrugged and said, 'I didn't care to inherit something I hadn't worked for.'

Cassie was sure there was more to it than that but she just said a little mockingly, 'My, my, you must be dizzy on such high moral ground. No wonder your opinion of me is so low. I don't even have a business to inherit, just a rock of land and and an ancient title.'

He had the grace to look slightly shamed. He said, 'It's not quite the same, I grant you. My lack of love for royalty stems more from an unfortunate incident with a princess from another European royal family.'

Cassie's eyes widened. The waiter put down their main courses. She hadn't even noticed their starters being removed. She came forward and rested an elbow on the table, her chin on her hand. 'Do tell.'

Ares couldn't have looked less inclined to tell, but after spearing a morsel of food from his plate and wiping his mouth with a napkin he said, 'Princess such and such… I was tasked with protecting her as she did one public event in Paris and then proceeded to shop and party like a one-woman hen party.'

'So? That can't have come as a massive surprise. After all, my brother did his best imitation of a one-man stag party. Sometimes with you in tow.'

Ares glared at her. 'Not the same at all.'

Cassie swallowed a piece of delicious fish and smiled. 'Double standards much?'

'Your brother is not spoiled.'

Cassie looked at Ares. 'No, he's not.' And neither was Ares, she was beginning to appreciate.

Ares continued, 'I think we both know he puts up that playboy front as a smokescreen to prevent people getting too close.'

Cassie tried not to show her surprise at Ares's understanding of her brother. It unnerved her. If he saw her brother so clearly, would he see all the way into her where she felt as though no one had ever really seen her? Where she'd had to smile bright enough just to be noticed? To mitigate the tension and toxicity around her?

Her smile certainly didn't work on him except to rile him and the way that left her feeling a little out of control and unsettled made her say, 'Don't change the subject. This princess…'

Ares sat back, wine glass in hand. 'You won't let this go.'

She shook her head. 'Nope.'

'Fine. I went back to my room after a long and particularly tedious day of shopping and socialising to find her naked in my bed.'

Cassie let out a bark of surprised laughter and put her hand over her mouth. When she took it away again she said, 'How did you deal with it…without it…?'

'Ending up all over the papers?'

Cassie nodded, mirth making her mouth twitch

again. She could just imagine Ares going volcanic at such a stunt. But she could empathise with the princess. Whoever she was. A dart of something hot and not nice went through her at the thought that it might have worked. But the look on Ares's face was so disgusted it told her all she needed to know. He hadn't accepted her invitation.

'I booked into another room for the night. And she woke up to a new security team the next day.'

Mischievously Cassie said, 'So you're telling me that if I were to—'

'No.' The crack of Ares's voice made Cassie jump a little. He seemed to notice and said a little less curtly, 'You're not getting rid of me that easily and if you try a stunt like that, I'll put you below deck. For your own protection, of course. I'm sure your brother would understand.'

Now he smiled and Cassie scowled. She speared some more food into her mouth to stop herself from goading him any more.

But now it seemed to be his turn when he asked, 'So what is it exactly that you want to get out of this trip?'

Cassie sat back and pushed her empty plate away and took a sip of wine, wondering if she could possibly divert Ares with the spectacular view of the sky turning lavender and purple behind him as night fell. Stars popping out. But she knew that wouldn't work. He'd barely noticed the sunset earlier.

Eventually she said reluctantly, 'To be honest, I didn't really put a lot of thought into it. It just...suddenly occurred to me, as my advisor was asking me to look at prospective suitors, that I hadn't ever really taken time out for myself…and that, in a couple of weeks, it would no longer be possible. My every moment is scheduled, practically down to toilet breaks. My brother got to have his freedom, I wanted to at least…taste it.'

Ares raised a brow. 'Prospective suitors?'

Cassie nodded wearily. 'A whole file of them.'

'Let me guess, they're all from distinguished royal lines.'

'Of course.'

'And are any of them appealing?'

'Not in the slightest. But…when it comes down to it, I'll have to choose someone. But I won't lie, I'm hoping for something or someone better than those files are offering.'

Ares cocked his head to one side. 'In what way?'

Cassie bit her lip and then said, 'I don't want a marriage in name only…for heirs, like my brother was prepared to settle for. I want real companionship. Respect. At the very least.'

She also wanted passion and something much deeper but she could imagine the horror on Ares's face. Or worse, mockery.

Before he could quiz her on that she asked, 'What about you? Don't you want to marry some day? Have a family?'

He smiled but it was grim. 'No way, not for me.'

'Why? Unhappy childhood?'

He looked a little startled, as if he wasn't used to someone being so direct. He said, 'Something like that.

To our parents, we were seen as pawns to fit into the family business at strategic points, either in the running of it—for instance, grooming my brother to inherit the business—or by marrying my sisters off strategically to consolidate power.'

Cassie asked, 'Where were you going to fit in?'

Ares waved a hand. 'Some outpost where they figured I could do no harm with my limited capabilities.'

Cassie snorted, making it clear what she thought about that, and then she observed, 'We really don't come from such different backgrounds. You said "sisters"—how many siblings do you have?'

Ares shifted as if uncomfortable. Tough. He knew practically everything about her. He said, 'Just my older brother and two younger sisters. Both are already married with children.'

'And your brother?'

Ares shook his head. 'Not yet but he's under pressure. He's already CEO and his children will inherit the legacy and carry the name. I was never really interested in the business.'

'How could you have been if you were made to feel it wasn't your destiny?' Cassie observed. Ares said nothing, just looked at her.

Then she divulged, 'If I have children they'll carry my name.'

'That makes sense.'

Cassie's mouth twisted. 'You'd be surprised how many men would have an issue with that.'

'I don't see the issue. Once I walked away from my inheritance my name lost its value.'

'But you started in the army. That's hardly a fortune-making venture.'

Ares looked at her with a clear warning.

Cassie smiled. 'No-go zone.'

He looked at her. 'No-go zone?'

'Caius and I have "no-go zones", when one of us strays too close to something we don't want to discuss.' She leant forward as the waiter gave Ares the bill. 'Are you close to your siblings?'

Something very fleeting crossed his face, and disappeared. 'At one time, maybe, but not now. We haven't been in touch for years.'

It was an enigmatic answer but Cassie didn't push it. She said, 'That's sad. I don't know what I'd do without Caius. I always wished we had more siblings, to take the pressure off just us.' She thought of her twin, and how that might have changed so much. Or perhaps not much at all. They'd never know.

Ares shook his head. 'More siblings doesn't mean less pressure, it's just more opportunities for manipulation.'

Cassie was fascinated by all that Ares was revealing. 'Your parents were manipulative, then?'

He let out a bark of laughter. 'You could say that. But let's get back to what you want to get out of this… moment of freedom.'

No-go zone.

Cassie sighed, looked up and then back and said, 'You won't understand.' He would laugh at her silly wish list. But then, he didn't laugh so maybe he wouldn't.

He said, 'Try me.'

Cassie sighed and divulged, 'OK, I'd like to go to the Uffizi in Florence, during the most packed part of the day; I'd like to go horse-riding on a beach at dawn; I'd like to ride a motorbike along Route 66 in America...but I'd settle for an empty stretch of motorway anywhere really...'

Ares's eyes opened wide. 'You can ride a motorbike?'

Cassie nodded. 'Caius taught me.'

Ares muttered something that sounded like, 'Of course he did.' And then, 'Why the Uffizi on a busy day? When you could get the place shut down just for you?'

Cassie grimaced. 'That's exactly why. I went on a school tour and there were so many daughters of important people in my class that the place was shut down just for us...but I always felt ashamed. It was eerie. I couldn't enjoy the art. I felt like we were stopping people from enjoying it. So I'd like to go back, pay to get in and queue with everyone else...soak up the experience with fellow art lovers.'

Ares had a slightly arrested expression on his face and then he said, 'Is that it? Not an especially extravagant list.'

'I'd like to get a tattoo and go clubbing, proper sweaty-all-night-until-the-sun-comes-up dancing clubbing...'

Now he grimaced, and ignored the bit about clubbing. 'A tattoo? Isn't that a bit of a cliché? Don't tell me, not one of those Mandarin symbols that no one really knows what they mean.'

Cassie vowed there and then to never reveal why she wanted a tattoo. It was way too personal and poignant.

He looked at his watch. 'Is that it? I'm afraid your brother would have my hide if I let you get a tattoo but we could find a club here and by tomorrow be on our way back to Sadat. I'm sure you'll fit the rest of your wish list in over the years.'

Cassie pushed down the pang that he was so eager to be rid of her. It had no place here. That rebellious spark moved through her. She gathered her nerve, sat back and said casually, 'There's something else. I'm a virgin and I really want to have sex before I become queen and have to get married.'

For a second Ares didn't react. His wine glass was at his mouth, he'd just drained it and then suddenly he was sitting up and coughing and spluttering as the wine hit his throat and went down the wrong way.

His reaction helped lessen Cassie's sense of exposure for revealing that. But…he was the one who'd crashed her party and he wasn't going to stop her.

Ares took a gulp of water and glared at her. 'Did you just say…?' He sounded a bit hoarse.

Cassie helpfully provided, 'That I want to lose my virginity? Yes, I did.' She had to laugh at the mix of horror and shock on his face. She winked at him. 'The tattoo probably doesn't look so bad now, does it?'

CHAPTER SIX

IF HE DIDN'T think about what she'd said back at the restaurant, maybe Ares could pretend he'd misheard her. But, from the way she'd been sliding him twinkly blue-eyed glances since they'd left the restaurant and returned to the tender and were now almost at the boat, anchored in the sea, he figured that unfortunately he hadn't misheard.

What he had done was get them out of that restaurant so fast his head had been spinning, as if afraid she was going to go and start propositioning strangers there and then.

As if afraid she'd want to sleep with someone other than you. The incendiary thought crept into his head and Ares mentally snarled at it. He didn't want her. She was too bright and sunny and *royal* and his friend's little sister and totally out of bounds. She was untouched, for crying out loud. He did not touch untouched people. He was too…dark. Cynical.

A man like him and a woman like her did not mix. He would take her brightness and dim it.

But even as he thought of that he almost shook with the enormity of the fact that she was innocent, and what it might be like to be the one to touch her, to rouse her, to make her gasp and moan and plead and clasp around him so tightly that—

'So, I guess no clubbing tonight, then?'

Ares was pulled out of his feverish circling thoughts. The tender was at the boat now, and Cassie was reaching out to grab the ladder that they'd used to climb down from a platform that could be lowered at the back of the boat, while anchored.

'No,' Ares issued through his teeth. He was seriously considering his threat of putting her below deck and keeping her there. But that would mean going down there and even that short visit earlier had been enough to make him sweat. The last thing he wanted was for those far too bright and inquisitive blue eyes to notice. She already saw far too much.

She'd had him spilling about his family, who he never spoke about. And her perceptiveness had surprised him. How she'd put a finger on the fact that he'd never been encouraged to think of the family business as something he could be part of in a meaningful way because his parents had deemed him somehow not useful.

But far more disturbingly he now ached to be the first man to make her moan and clench as she had last night in the bar. If he'd realised then that Caius had spoken the truth and that she really might be innocent... *Theos*. It was too much.

For the first time in a long time, Ares was out of his depth and it was in a way he wasn't prepared for.

Cassie secured the tender to the boat and climbed the ladder. The night was still and warm. From above him on the boat Cassie said, 'That's cool. I heard Mykonos is the place to go clubbing anyway. Maybe I'll try there...'

For clubbing *and* a lover? Ares wanted to untie the tender again and sail as far away from this boat and woman as he could. But he couldn't. So he climbed up onto the deck. Cassie was standing, with her shoes in her hands, bag slung across her body, hair down and wild around her shoulders. She seemed to glow in the moonlight. It made something inside Ares's chest feel tight and achy.

She said, 'Well, goodnight, then, help yourself to one of the spare cabins.'

'I'll sleep up here.'

Cassie had been turning away and then turned back. She must have seen something on Ares's face because she shrugged and said, 'Whatever.' She turned away again and disappeared down into the belly of the boat. Ares shuddered just thinking about it.

He looked out over the dark mass of the sea. Why did it feel as though what should be the easiest assignment on the planet—babysitting a princess—had just become the most challenging?

The next day, after a light breakfast that Cassie had brought up to the deck to eat, they set off again. Ares had retreated to his taciturn self. He'd disappeared below, presumably to shower and change because he had changed, into board shorts and a T-shirt, but he'd been so quick that Cassie had barely noticed his disappearance as she'd focused on plotting the next stage of the journey.

She turned around and he was back and changed.

Only the fact that his hair was damp gave any sign that he'd showered.

His eyes were hidden behind dark shades and his jaw was as hard as ever. Cassie sighed. He was like a formidable piece of rock. And really, she'd not learned much about him last night. She suspected there was a lot more to his break with his family than just a desire to make his own way. No one joined an army to make a fortune. They went into armies to escape something.

'Where are we headed?'

'Mykonos,' she threw over her shoulder. 'It's famous for its clubbing scene. They call it the Ibiza of Greece.'

'Fantastic.'

'Oh, lighten up, you might even enjoy it.'

Cassie smiled to herself. She could feel the way Ares was bristling behind her. Was it wrong that riling him felt so right?

He sat on one of the benches in her peripheral vision, legs spread. She didn't have to look to know his bare legs were as muscled and strong as the rest of him.

When he didn't make any attempt to converse she asked sweetly, 'How was your night on deck?'

'Fine.'

'Is that a security thing? To keep an eye out?'

He huffed and said, 'Something like that.'

Cassie rolled her eyes and shut her mouth. She needed her wits to navigate through the Cyclades. Mykonos was on the other side of Naxos and Paros, so she focused on that for now and tried to block out the brooding muscled man-mountain sitting far too close for comfort.

When they approached the island, Cassie dropped the anchor in a sheltered spot and busied herself getting the tender into position.

'You're going onto the island now?'

Cassie turned from the small lower deck and looked up. 'Yes, that's my plan.' She smiled sunnily. 'You're welcome to join,' knowing full well he'd have to come with her.

'What's your plan?'

'Well, some lunch to start with, I'm starving, and then shopping. And then, later, clubbing.'

Ares didn't smile. 'Sounds delightful.'

After Cassie had secured the boat, and they were in the tender heading towards the old port, she tried her best not to be so aware of Ares. It annoyed her that he appealed to her so much. He was like a dark cloud. *A dark sexy stormy cloud.* And she hated that she felt the urge to make him smile, look happier. Because that pushed way too many buttons. She'd spent her life trying to make her parents smile and be happier and it hadn't worked.

To know that nothing you'd done had had a positive effect on the people around you in spite of your best efforts was not nice. It was why she'd oftentimes felt invisible. And yet she couldn't join Ares where he was, her inner spirit was just too buoyant no matter how much she might try to deny it.

When they had secured the tender, Ares said, 'Where to now?'

'Mykonos town.'

He hailed a cab and they were being spirited away

from the port within minutes. Cassie realised that she hadn't paid for anything yesterday and Ares had just handed the driver some euros.

She said, 'I don't expect you to pay. I'll give you what I owe, and for dinner last night.' He'd all but run her out of the restaurant after she'd told him she planned to lose her virginity. She still couldn't believe she'd had the gall to say that. But it had been worth it for the look of shock on his face.

The fact that he'd populated her dreams last night made it slightly less worth it. Because he was welded to her side for the foreseeable future and so the chances of her actually getting to lose her virginity with anyone seemed to be challenging in the extreme.

Unless you lost it to him, whispered a little voice. As if Cassie didn't already have that incendiary moment from their first night branded onto her brain for ever. Moaning into his mouth as she pushed herself into his hand.

'Are you all right? You've gone very red.'

Cassie saw the town centre approaching and said to the driver in a panic, 'We'll get out here, *efharisto*,' and she all but jumped out of the car as it was still moving in a bid to get away from that dark incisive gaze.

She strode forward into the shopping district and pulled a baseball cap onto her head, praying Ares would leave it alone.

An hour later, as Ares sat on a bench outside a boutique, sipping a small and perfect espresso, he had to acknowledge that he hadn't had this kind of time off in…*ever*, and, while it was disconcerting, it wasn't unenjoyable.

No wonder so many of his peers preferred babysitting royals and celebrities. This was positively civilised. If a bit mind-numbingly boring. Shopping bags were scattered at his feet. And Cassie had just entered the umpteenth boutique.

She'd said a short while before, 'I know you must think this is so typical but, for what it's worth, I never get to just…shop. I'm supplied with clothes by a stylist.'

She'd sounded so defensive and had been looking up at him from under the lip of her baseball cap in a way that had made him want to bend down and capture those plump lips against his, and press against her. So he'd said curtly, 'I'm not thinking anything.'

For a second she'd looked almost stricken but then those bright blue eyes had flashed and she'd said something like, 'Yeah, right, silly of me to assume so.' And she'd disappeared into another shop.

Strange, but Ares had almost felt…guilty. Because the truth was that he *was* assuming and thinking about her. So hard his head hurt. As much as his body. Ever since he'd laid eyes on her. *And your hands*. He gritted his jaw to stop that flood of memories. And he was certainly not imagining her right now, peeling off the knee-length cut-off jeans that hugged her high firm ass like a second skin, or the plaid sleeveless shirt that she'd tied at her waist. Or the plain flat sneakers on her feet and the cute little silver or gold anklet around one impossibly slim ankle.

A bell rang and Ares looked up to find the object of

his thoughts standing in front of him holding another shiny bag, smiling. 'Lunch? There's a salad bar nearby.'

Ares stood up and picked up the other bags. 'Lead the way.' Ares knew he was being a grim asshole but the sunnier she was, the grimmer he got, because if he cracked and let one ounce of that sunshiney lightness in, he wasn't sure he wouldn't disintegrate completely.

Just before they reached the restaurant though, a couple emerged, shouting volubly at each other. They were having a fight, the woman gesticulating angrily. They walked away, down the street, still arguing, and Ares moved to let Cassie precede him into the restaurant but she wasn't moving. Or smiling.

He looked at her. Her gaze was fixed on the retreating couple and her eyes were wide. Her face was blanched of all colour. She looked stricken. Or winded, as if someone had just punched her.

An unfamiliar sensation gripped Ares's insides… concern? He reached for her arm and put a hand around it. Not even that shook her out of the trance. He squeezed gently, ignoring the way her arm felt under his hand. 'Cassie?'

Eventually she averted her gaze and looked at him. And blinked. Ares was frowning now. 'Cassie? Do you know those people?'

She blinked again and seemed to come back from a long distance. 'Who?'

Ares jerked his head in the direction of the couple who he could still hear. 'The people having a fight.'

Colour seeped back into Cassie's cheeks and she

avoided his eye now. 'No, of course not.' She moved into the restaurant, dislodging his hand from her arm.

They settled into a booth in the restaurant. Ares put Cassie facing the view again, less chance of her being recognised. *And watched by others who could recognise a rare beauty?* He scowled. But his mind was still on that weird little moment outside.

Before he could ask her about it though, she was saying, 'One day the wind will change and your face will stay stuck like that.' She smiled cheekily and then she put a hand to her mouth and took it down and said even more cheekily, 'Oh no, that's what already happened, it's too late!'

She collapsed in a fit of giggles at her own joke and Ares couldn't help it, he felt an alien warmth spreading into his chest and his mouth tugging up and wide. The strange moment was gone. Maybe he'd imagined it? She looked impossibly young and lovely and yet all grown up too. A woman. Who hadn't yet been touched. Not even that reminder could stop her infectious mirth from reaching out and winding around him like a benevolent breeze urging him to just…unbend a little.

She pointed. 'Oh my God! I've done it. I made you crack. And all it took was—' once again she inspected that bare wrist, and looked back at him '—forty-eight hours? Is that a record? Has anyone beaten me?'

'Ha ha,' Ares said, feeling testy but also zingy.

The waiter came and took their orders. When he'd left, Cassie said, 'Lunch is on me, I insist. For that rare smile alone. I mean, I get it, you're in security. It's on brand to look hard and tough and humourless…'

Ares wanted to glare at her but he couldn't quite manage it. Was he really so humourless? He suddenly felt weary. As if he'd been carrying a weight he hadn't even recognised until this moment. He had been humourless for a long time. Since the kidnapping. Since it had become so painfully apparent that his parents couldn't have cared less if he lived or died. Since the chasm had grown between him and his brother and sisters because he couldn't articulate what had happened to him.

Before he could let it go completely he said, 'What was that back there?'

'What was what?' Cassie looked at him, eyes wide and innocent. He didn't trust it for a second.

'You know…the couple arguing and your reaction like you were taking it personally.'

She shook her head. 'Nothing. I just…had a moment. Déjà vu, or something.'

Then, before he could ask any more about it, she grinned and leaned forward. 'Hey, guess what I found?'

Ares tried not to let his gaze drop to the vee in her shirt where he knew he'd see the swells of her perfect breasts encased in lace. Or maybe nothing. Maybe she wasn't wearing a bra. His body jumped at that and blood rushed to his groin. He shifted.

He indulged her even though he had the definite sense she was distracting him. 'What did you find?'

She sat back, triumphant. 'A tattoo parlour.'

Ares shook his head. 'No way, you're not getting a tattoo, not on my watch.'

Cassie shook out a napkin with a flourish as their salads were delivered. 'I'm afraid to burst your bubble but you can't stop me. I'm a grown woman and you're literally not the boss of me.'

'No, but I am your protector.'

'Well, you can protect the entrance of the parlour while I'm inside. It won't take long. It's not a big tattoo, I promise.'

Ares put his hands up. 'I'm not the one who'll be under the world's lens with everyone debating the meaning of ink on your unblemished skin.'

She cocked her head. 'You think my skin is unblemished?'

Yes, damn her, every toned and golden inch of it. Ares cleared his throat. 'It's not becoming of a queen.'

Cassie speared some cheese and popped it into her mouth, saying, 'Well, it's a good thing I'm not queen yet, isn't it?'

'And did your parents never teach you not to eat and talk at the same time?'

Ares was surprised at the way her face momentarily fell, before she brightened again and swallowed her food before saying, 'No, they were too busy engaging in domestic warfare. But our nannies did their best, if they lasted long. Caius did tend to wear them out.'

Ares picked up on what she'd said and saw the arguing couple in his mind's eye and her reaction to it. 'Domestic warfare?'

Cassie's brightness dropped a few volts again and it was as if the sun disappeared behind a cloud. He hated to admit it but he didn't like it.

She said breezily, 'Forget I said anything, a slip of the tongue.'

To avoid thinking about that tongue and how it had felt tangling with his, Ares said, 'They didn't get on?'

Cassie looked at Ares warily. 'Did Caius ever talk about it?'

He shook his head. No, they hadn't talked about family. Because Caius was in the realm of arranged marriages, or had been, and Ares had no intention of inflicting the Drakos name on children he would inevitably mess up. His own parents hadn't even tried to save him when he'd been in peril and the rest of the time they'd had a series of cold and aloof nannies—how the hell would he know what to do?

In their worlds—his, and Cassie's to a greater extent—children were born to continue legacies or bloodlines. He had no desire to inflict that on a child.

He'd carved out his freedom and on that note he could actually empathise with Cassie. He knew what it felt like to want to break away.

'Well, there's not much to tell, except that...' Cassie stopped and blew some hair out of her face, which only drew Ares's eye to her finely etched jaw and high cheekbone. Those pouty lips.

'Look,' he said, regretting drawing her into this, 'if you don't want to—'

She cut him off. 'They despised each other, that's the truth. They fought all the time. It was like a minefield living with them. They both had affairs. They crucified each other.'

Ares went still. He could see it all too easily. 'That's what happened back there, wasn't it? Your reaction to that couple fighting.'

She shrugged minutely. 'I hate seeing people shouting at each other.'

Ares guessed it was more than that. Her response had been stricken, as if they'd shouted at her.

His parents hadn't actively hated each other but they certainly hadn't *loved*. Not that that even existed.

Cassie went on, 'When my father died in the skiing accident, my mother went on holiday with her latest lover, after pretending to be griefstruck for the cameras of course. And when *she* died a few months later, everyone said wasn't it so romantic, that she obviously hadn't been able to live without him.'

Ares heard the cynicism in Cassie's voice. And something more hollow. Disappointment?

'What had you expected?'

She looked at him with narrowed eyes. 'Was it too much to expect parents who respected each other at least and who showed the minimum of care for me and my brother?'

'No,' Ares said quietly. 'Everyone deserves that.'

With a mocking tone that didn't suit her, Cassie said, 'And some even get more than that, parents who actually love each other and who love their children.'

Ares bizarrely felt like comforting her. He pointed at her. 'Now that is way too much to ask for. That's just an urban myth.'

Cassie smiled but it was small and made Ares miss her full wattage. But wasn't this just proof that being in close proximity to him was only going to dim her light? Something moved through him, a need to restore Cassie's ebullience.

He called for the bill and when Cassie looked at him quizzically, he said, 'Well, if you're going to fit in a tattoo *and* delivering all that shopping back to the boat before going out tonight, we'd better move.'

When her eyes opened wide and she grinned at him Ares fought the counter urge to scowl. The fact that it had unnerved him to hear about her reaction to her parents' marriage and to see her lose her sparkle was far too disturbing to countenance. And why he was encouraging her in her pursuit of this wish list…he really was losing it.

'You're not going to let me see it?'

Cassie shook her head and held her arm against herself. There was a big white plaster over the tattoo that she'd got along the inside of her wrist. 'Not yet anyway. I need to keep it covered for twenty-four hours.'

They'd returned to the boat a while ago and Cassie had taken her shopping down to the cabin. Ares was delaying the moment he would have to go down there and shower and change. He was a coward. He knew it and it sat within him like an acidic little demon.

Cassie had prepared a light dinner of pasta and salad and it was surprisingly delicious. Ares asked, 'Where did you learn to cook?'

'Go on, you can admit it, I'm not what you had me boxed away as on first sight.' She grinned at him and it made his chest feel full.

'You are definitely a novel experience.'

'I was obsessed with cooking shows when I was small. The palace kitchen staff set up a small area for me so I could pretend to cook alongside them. The main cook, a woman called Maria, was probably more of a mother to me than anyone else. She was kind and warm.'

'Sweet story.'

Cassie just grinned even harder at him. 'What about you? Don't they teach you to cook in the army?'

Ares nodded. 'Rudimentary stuff, yes. I can cobble together a meal with whatever is there.'

'Great, then you can do dinner tomorrow night.'

Ares grimaced at the thought of lingering down in that cabin with the boat around him, encroaching on him. Darkness. Cruel hands and fists raining down on him. *He's just some rich kid who no one cares about.*

He swallowed it all down and looked at Cassie. 'That's fair.'

Cassie stood up and gathered the plates. 'I'm going to get ready. See you back up here in an hour?'

Ares nodded. The sun was setting, turning the sky pink and orange and ochre. But already he was dreading seeing what concoction Cassie was going to appear in because he knew she could be wearing an oversized sack and he would burn for her.

He smiled mirthlessly to himself. This was torture pure and simple. All of his sins were being called in and there was nothing he could do about it.

Cassie looked at herself in the mirror and her heart thudded too loudly. She'd heard Ares coming down, doing something with dishes in the galley area, and then after a silence he'd gone back up. It was as if he didn't like coming down into the cabin. Sleeping on the deck. She shrugged to herself. Maybe it was an army thing. He certainly hadn't held over anything, like being precious, from his days as an heir to a vast fortune.

She still felt a little raw after that far too revealing episode earlier when she'd reacted to seeing the couple arguing. They'd caught her by surprise, the violence of their words and actions hurtling her back in time before she could steel herself against it. She still had such an immediate visceral response to witnessing confrontations. And Ares had noticed. And put two and two together once she'd let slip about her parents. It had surprised her how easy it had been to reveal that, even if she hadn't revealed the extent of how much it got to her.

She'd sensed an affinity with him, as if he understood something of how it affected her.

She'd plaited her hair and coiled it up onto her head. She'd put in dark-coloured contact lenses again—just in case. Heavy eye make-up. Glitter across her cheeks.

She was wearing a light blue silk jumpsuit. Sleeveless and with a deep vee, gathered at the waist and at the ankles. Sticky tape holding it in place was preserving her modesty but she knew deep down with an illicit thrill that she didn't much care about preserving her modesty around Ares.

She wanted him. It beat deep within her. Even with all of his grumpy surliness. Today, she'd seen something lighter and that smile. She could still remember it, and how it had transformed his face. It had made her feel pathetically triumphant. But also something else, something more emotional.

No. Not emotion. Desire. She wanted to kiss him again. Feel his hands on her. She wanted him to show her how it could be, so that, no matter what happened, she would have this to treaure inside herself for ever.

She knew she wouldn't even notice another man while he was in the vicinity. He was magnetic. And…a small rogue part of her wondered what it would take to really make him crack open. Lose his control. The thought of being able to have that effect on him was seriously heady.

But doubt crept in. Maybe after that first night her gauche responses had put him off. And now he was here as her reluctant keeper and the last thing he'd want to do was sleep with her. He resented her. She was less worthy than any other client he could have.

And then Cassie shook herself out of it. She *was* worthy. When Ares looked at her, he really looked at her. She wasn't invisible to him. Except, earlier, when he'd told her he hadn't been thinking or assuming anything about her, that had felt like a knife sliding into tender skin. It had shocked her how much his words could hurt her. He was still little more than a stranger. And yet one who had become central to her existence.

Cassie suddenly felt vulnerable—Ares's opinion meant something to her. She wanted him to like her. Care for her. Respect her. *Want her.* And that was too dangerous. He already had the power to hurt her.

Maybe sleeping with him was not a good idea.

She vowed to try her best to slip away from him tonight. Find another man who could make her want him as she wanted Ares. Surely that wouldn't be so hard? He couldn't have ruined her for other men after little more than a kiss?

Ares wasn't sure how he was managing to command his motor skills because every functioning brain cell had migrated to his pants ever since he'd watched Cassie emerge onto the deck of the boat in a silk jumpsuit that bared her practically from throat to navel.

He'd hardly taken in the coloured lenses in her eyes or the glitter along her cheekbones making them stand out even more. The dark kohl around her eyes. Hair up in a braid and pinned to her head, making her look like a beautiful bohemian art student, exposing her graceful neck and that spectacular bone structure.

They were walking into the beach club now, famous for its legendary full moon parties that spilled onto the beach. Ares sent silent thanks up that it wasn't a full moon tonight. He felt feral enough as it was.

He steered Cassie over to a roped-off VIP area and ordered drinks. They were looking over the dance floor—heaving with lithe bodies and arms in the air as a world-famous DJ worked his magic at the decks.

When champagne had been delivered, Ares handed her a glass and said, 'Well, is it everything you'd hoped for?'

Cassie was staring around her, taking it all in. Ares hated the lenses dimming those blue eyes but it did make her blend in more.

She nodded. 'Yeah, it's pretty cool.' She looked at

him, 'This is nothing new for you—I saw pictures of you coming out of places like this with my brother.'

Ares made a face. 'It was more your brother's scene than mine, to be honest. I'm not a dancer.' Or a charmer, like Caius.

Cassie laughed and it sounded so light and joyful that it had a physical effect, rippling along his nerve ends.

'Believe me, Caius cannot dance.'

Ares gestured with his head towards the dance floor. 'They're not exactly dancing, more like jumping around.'

Cassie rolled her eyes. 'OK, Granddad, I'm going down to dance, or jump around, coming?'

Granddad. Ares swallowed down the urge to put her over his knee for her cheekiness. He'd enjoy it way too much. He shook his head. 'You couldn't pay me to go down there.' And yet he'd pulled her close and danced with her in that bar the other night.

She stood up, long legs even longer in the spindly heeled sandals she'd brought with her in a little backpack from the boat. He watched her walk down onto the dance floor, golden and lithe and beautiful. Graceful. Regal. She was used to people parting to let her aside—he watched as it took her a moment to realise she'd have to push through the crowd and it made him feel something very protective towards her, because she wasn't standing there stamping her foot. She was adapting to being a normal person.

She took such delight in things that he knew most people would have a fit over. Making her own food—

sharing it with him, it had to be said—steering the boat. Living with no frills. If he'd thought she wouldn't hack it on her own on a boat, he'd been sorely mistaken. He had to face the uncomfortable fact that even if he weren't here, it wouldn't have dented her enthusiasm for experiencing all of these little *freedoms*.

Finding a man to have sex with for the first time. Hot, acrid rejection at that thought filled Ares. And yet what could he do? He couldn't forbid her to bring a man back to the boat if she so wished. Or to go off with a man and spend the night with him.

Was he prepared to stand outside some door while inside she was laying herself bare for some other faceless, nameless man to touch her and glory in all that stunning innocent sensuality?

No way.

Ares looked down at the dance floor and it took a second to realise that he'd lost sight of her in the crowd. He kept searching for that distinctive blonde hair. The golden limbs. Glitter. Nothing. He cursed. He was losing his touch. This was the woman who had managed to evade her own security team after all.

Ares stood up and went to find her.

CHAPTER SEVEN

CASSIE WAS HAVING a bad case of the 'déjà vu's. Two guys were standing in front of her and trying to ply her with drinks.

'Come on,' wheedled one. 'They're nice.'

'Look, I'm here with a friend and—' The déjà vu hit even harder when a large shape appeared behind the guys and an arm reached in, a hand wrapping around Cassie's arm. 'There you are.'

Cassie didn't even bother to feign that she was annoyed Ares had sought her out. She said to the guys as she walked away, 'By the way, it's not cool to go after a woman and isolate her in a corner. It's creepy, OK?' They just looked at her, mouths falling agape.

As soon as she'd hit the dance floor, she'd known that there wasn't one man there who could match Ares and then she'd been cornered before she'd realised what was happening.

Ares was dressed in faded jeans and a plain white T-shirt. Messy hair, bearded jaw. He made everyone else look as though they were trying too hard.

He brought her back up to their seats. In spite of being grateful he'd come to get her, she didn't want him to know that. 'Would you not do that, please?'

Cassie sat down. 'I told you before, I can look after myself.' So much for sneaking off for her very first tryst. She wouldn't get as far as the door.

Ares's expression was dark—surprise surprise. He said, 'Some time I'm going to get you to show me exactly how proficient you are at self-defence.'

Between Cassie's legs throbbed at that ultimatum. At the thought of having Ares on his knees before her. *Making him your king.* Cassie shook her head at that totally audacious image. Wrong on so many levels. She wanted Ares for sex, nothing more.

And if she didn't make it happen now she'd lose her nerve. She picked up her bag. 'I think I'm done here.'

Ares couldn't hide the flash of relief across his face but he looked at his watch. 'It's another five hours until sunrise, are you sure?'

What had she been thinking? The thought of staying until sunrise had been slightly over-optimistic. She said, 'I'm willing to rejig my wish list. I can watch the sunrise from the boat.'

'OK, but, for the record, you're the one who wants to leave.'

Cassie hid a smile. As if Ares with his brooding disapproval weren't cramping her style anyway. But it wasn't him. This wasn't her scene but she knew that now.

They left and Cassie sucked in fresh air. The *thump thump* of the music faded behind them. They picked up the tender at the small pier and headed back to the boat, Cassie swapping out her heels for sneakers. She slipped the lenses out of her eyes and blinked to restore moisture.

As they were heading back out into the sea, Ares tensed and said, 'There's a storm coming in.'

Cassie looked to where he was pointing. Her skin prickled at the gathering clouds. She was suddenly conscious of the breeze picking up. She could handle a storm but it was obviously better not to have to if you could help it. 'That wasn't due to hit until tomorrow. I was planning on heading to a marina to tie up in the morning.'

Ares shook his head, just as the first smattering of faint rain drops hit them. 'No time for that. We'll take the boat somewhere more sheltered now and drop anchor. We'll have to wait it out. Looks like a squall.'

'You mean, I'll take the boat somewhere more sheltered,' Cassie pointed out.

Ares looked at her. 'I never said I couldn't sail. I just don't like boats.'

Cassie had no response for that, but when they reached the boat it was raining in earnest and Ares took control as if he were the skipper. Within minutes they'd secured the tender and Ares was saying authoritatively, 'Get the engine started and I'll pull the anchor up.'

Cassie was professional enough on a boat not to argue. Not in this kind of situation. They worked silently and quickly together, as the wind whipped up and rain battered down. They were soaked but Cassie barely noticed. Too intent on guiding the boat into a small sheltered nearby cove.

She knew enough since she'd been sailing with Caius as a child to understand how quickly storms could come upon you. And how dangerous they could be.

'Here is good. Cut the engine and I'll drop anchor again.'

Cassie did as Ares instructed. It was too much of a revelation to get her head around that he could sail. When the boat was secure she opened the door to the below-deck area and shouted over the wind, 'Come on, we need to get inside.'

Ares hesitated, looking at the opening to the cabin with an indecipherable expression. Cassie said, 'Ares? What are you waiting for? You can't stay on deck, it's too dangerous.'

Finally he moved and she went down into the belly of the boat. He followed her, securing the door behind him. Cassie put on some lights. She realised she was soaked to the skin, her silk jumpsuit plastered to her body.

So was Ares. Soaked. T-shirt practically see-through. She could count the ridges of his six-pack. She could see the dark shadow of his chest hair that went in a line down towards his navel and the top of his jeans. That were also soaked...moulded to his powerful thighs.

Cassie dragged her gaze back up. Ares's hair was wet, stuck to his skull. Water dripping off the ends, that almost reached his shoulders now. He looked like a pirate.

He was looking at her, eyes very dark, hard to read. Jaw clenched. So far so normal. When had he not looked brooding? Earlier...when he'd smiled at lunch. Before taking her to get her tattoo. Absently she glanced down at her arm. The plaster had come off her tattoo but she barely noticed now.

She looked back up and little fires raced over her skin at Ares's look. It was so...primal. 'Ares...' Cassie said. 'You're looking at me as if—'

He abruptly turned around and said gruffly, 'Sorry.'

Cassie moved closer behind him, kicking off her sodden sneakers as she did. Her hair was coming down, and she loosened it out of the plaits so it could dry.

She stood close behind him. He was so much bigger than her. He dominated the space. 'No,' she said, 'I didn't mean it like that... I like you looking at me.'

He shook his head and little droplets of water fell. The boat was rocking from side to side but Cassie hardly noticed. He said, 'No, princess, it was a transgression.'

'Don't call me that.' She knew he was doing that now to put distance between them and it made something surge inside her. Hope. Confidence.

He huffed out something like a laugh. 'Even though it's accurate?'

'Here and now I'm just Cassie. Ares...please.'

With almost palpable reluctance he turned around and she looked up. His eyes were burning. He shook his head again. 'Cassie...this...is not going to happen.'

She moved closer. 'It already happened the other night, Ares.'

His jaw clenched. 'My fault.'

'I wanted it too. I kissed you.'

'You didn't know who I was.'

'I don't care who you are.' She flushed. 'I mean, I do, but it doesn't matter. Here we're just two people. Adults. Who want the same thing.'

'It's not that simple.'

She moved closer, close enough to touch. She put her hands on his chest, his soaked-through T-shirt. His skin was firm, warm. Pectorals bulging under her palms. 'I think it's the simplest thing in the world. I'm just a woman, Ares, and I've never wanted a man the way I want you.'

'You don't know what you're saying.' Ares brought his hands to her arms as if he was going to push her away. Cassie dug her heels in. She wasn't going anywhere. The air crackled and pulsed between them. Between her legs. Her breasts felt heavy, nipples tight.

'Don't you want me, Ares?' She knew he couldn't deny it. It would be like denying there was a storm lashing the boat and sea outside.

His face was taut now, and his hands tightened on her arms. 'I wanted you the moment I saw you that first night, that's why I didn't tell you who I was when I had a chance. I didn't want you to turn away from me. I've never wanted anyone more.'

Relief flooded her. And sharp desire. 'Take me, Ares, please.' Cassie wasn't above pleading. If she couldn't have this experience with this man, she knew she'd regret it for the rest of her life.

'Cass...'

'Ares.'

Instead of pushing her away from him, he pulled her inexorably closer until their bodies were touching. He looked down at her, fierce. 'Are you sure you want this?'

'I've never been more sure of anything in my life. Make love to me, Ares.'

'It's not love, Cass.'

Cassie loved the way he said that. *Cass.* She shook her head, body going up in flames, pulse tripping so fast she felt breathless. She lifted her arms and wound them around Ares's neck. 'I don't care what we call it, I just want you, now.'

Ares would have to have been made of iron and stone to resist the woman twining herself around him, pressing those perfect breasts against his chest, rocking her pelvis against his raging hard-on.

Breasts that might as well have been naked the way the soaked material of her jumpsuit clung to them, outlining their high full curves and hard nipples.

She's not just a woman, she's a queen in waiting. She's your friend's little sister. These thoughts that were feverishly running through Ares's head were also being fast drowned out by the clamour of his blood.

On a very deep level, his body was recognising this woman in a way he'd never felt before. *He had to have her. She was his.* He knew if he pushed her away she was stubborn enough to wait out the storm and go straight back to that club. And he wasn't having that. She was his. It beat through him, the most right thing he'd felt in ages.

He took his hands off her arms and settled them around her waist, almost able to span it. That evidence of her femininity made something very carnal move through him.

She lifted her mouth to his and the last of Ares's control snapped. He lowered his head and met her, mouth to mouth, breath to breath and...devoured her like a starving man.

Cassie was clinging onto Ares, any sense of trying to pretend to be nonchalant or cool or confident obliterated. He was kissing her and she was fire and earth and water and air all at once. An amalgam of nerve-endings and atoms and cells all mixing to turn her into one big sensation, throbbing with need as he stoked the flames. Tongue to tongue. He tasted so good. And he felt even better, every rock-hard inch of him, and the part of him that she could feel jerk between them, against the denim of his jeans. Against her belly.

Between her legs felt embarrassingly hot and damp. Was it normal to be so...*wet*? Who cared? One hand was on her waist, gripping her, and the other was in her hair, tangling, tugging her head back so he could take the kiss even deeper.

Cassie wasn't sure how she was standing. The earth was moving and vaguely she was aware of the storm outside.

When Ares pulled his head back, Cassie opened her eyes. Everything was blurry for a second and she was gasping for breath, heart hammering. Terrified Ares would let oxygen get to his brain and realise this was a bad idea, she said a little shakily, 'Take your top off.'

He looked at her—eyes blurring, cheeks flushed.

Hair drying and wild. He smiled and Cassie's heart turned over because this man didn't have a big repertoire of smiles, as she knew well, but she knew she hadn't seen this one, even on that first night.

It was wicked and very sexy. It told her he was committed to this and something inside her eased and melted even more.

He arched a brow. 'Please?'

'Please,' she said. What was wrong with her? It was as if she'd been stripped of everything civil and she'd become the most basic form of a woman wanting to mate with a man.

Ares reached behind him and pulled his damp T-shirt up and over his head and off, dropping it to the floor. Cassie's eyes widened on his broad and muscled chest, with its smattering of dark hair.

'Oh my,' she breathed, hands itching to touch him.

He said, 'Go ahead.'

She looked up for a moment. She must have spoken out loud. She moved closer again and put her palms on his chest, fingers spread out. She felt reverent, as if she were worshipping a god. A Greek god. She might have giggled if she hadn't felt so serious about what she was doing.

His skin was warm, heart thumping under her palms. She moved her hands down and her nails scraped over his nipples, causing him to suck a breath in. She looked up. He shook his head. 'I'm fine, keep going.'

She went back to her task of exploration. Her hands moved down to that tantalising line of dark hair dissecting his flat belly. And then disappearing under the top of his jeans. Her gaze travelled further down to where there was a very obvious bulge against the denim material.

Her mouth watered. Her fingers were on the button. She looked up. 'May I?'

He said, 'Yes, you may.' There was a rough quality to his voice that sent a shudder of longing through her. She popped open the button and then slowly drew the zip down, releasing Ares from his confinement.

Suddenly it was too overwhelming. She took her hands away and stood back saying, 'Can you…?'

He seemed to read her mind and put his hands to his jeans, tugging them down and off, taking his underwear with them. Cassie's avid gaze was glued to Ares's very hard and very big erection. It was beautiful. *He* was beautiful.

'Now you.'

Cassie looked up and gulped. He was six feet plus of raw male beauty. An experienced man. How on earth could she hope to engage his interest? *He's interested,* prompted a dry voice. Maybe for the moment, thought Cassie, but as soon as he realised just how little she knew…

He reached out and trailed a finger along her jaw. 'If you change your mind, Cassie, it's OK.'

Cassie hadn't expected any of this. And she hadn't expected him to be so…*reassuring*. She shook her head. 'No, I want to… I just…no one has ever seen me naked, except for the women at the palace who dress me sometimes and even they…' She trailed off. Even they hadn't seen her fully naked. Exposed.

Ares found one of her hands and picked it up. He interlaced his fingers with hers and led her back through the space to her cabin. Her bed was a tangle of sheets. *Oh God*, would he think she was a spoiled brat? She didn't want him to be reminded now that she was a princess.

As if hearing her thoughts he turned to face her and said, 'Stop thinking.'

'I... OK.'

He put his hands on the shoulders of her jumpsuit and said, 'Is this OK?'

She nodded. Her skin was tingling where his fingers rested and then slowly he pushed the shoulders of the jumpsuit down her arms. She wasn't wearing a bra and the material loosened on her chest, exposing her breasts. She freed her arms.

She could feel her damp skin springing into goosebumps. Her nipples were tingling. She couldn't look at Ares but she heard his indrawn breath and then something like, *Theé mou.*

She glanced up and his gaze was fixated on her breasts. He said reverently, 'You're beautiful.'

Cassie blushed. Then Ares said, 'Turn around.'

She did and he pulled the zip at the back all the way down to the bottom of her back. He tugged gently and the material came down over her hips and fell to the floor. She stepped out of the legs. Now she wore only her underwear. Knickers. Lacy.

Ares gathered her hair and brought it over one shoulder. The ends tickled the upper slopes of her breast. He put his hands on her shoulders and stepped close behind her. She felt his heat and smelled his unique musky scent. Musky and spicy and something more exotic.

He turned her around again and now their bodies were almost touching, nothing between them. His erection pressed against her belly. Cassie moved closer and Ares's eyes flashed.

'Lie down.'

Cassie really wanted him to kiss her again. But she did as he asked, pushing the sheets aside to lie down. He looked at her, that dark golden gaze travelling over every inch of her. She didn't feel embarrassed or exposed now, just hungry.

Ares came down on the bed beside her and Cassie was unaware of the fact that they were in a small cabin on a boat that was being rocked and rolled due to the storm outside.

There was a storm gathering inside her and it grew under Ares's appreciative gaze. He bent his head and answered her silent plea, capturing her mouth with his, fingers tracing her jaw and angling her head so that he could make the kiss deeper.

Cassie explored Ares, wrapping her hand around a bicep and glorying in the strength of him, then up and around his shoulder and neck, fingers funnelling through silky hair, holding his skull.

She touched his chest, and down, fingers trailing over rock-hard abs and that slim waist and then to the potent evidence of his arousal. Instinctively she wrapped a hand around him, revelling in the sensation of all that power and strength under hot silky skin, the way it slipped up and down his shaft with her movement. Suddenly Ares reared back.

Cassie stopped. 'Am I doing something wrong?' Now she felt exposed.

His eyes were glittering and his cheeks were flushed. As flushed as Cassie guessed hers were.

'No, you're not doing anything wrong, but this will be over very fast unless you stop doing that.'

Cassie unpeeled her fingers from Ares's erection. She bit her lip and put her hand on his ass. 'Is this better?'

He huffed a laugh, making his whole face transform. Cassie wanted to make him laugh all the time. It made him look years younger. Less severe. Less…haunted.

Before she could dwell on that little revelation, Ares was squeezing the firm flesh of her breast and rubbing a thumb back and forth across one nipple. Cassie's head fell back and she let a moan come out of her mouth. It felt…exquisite. As if a wire were directly connected from her breast to between her legs.

And then, as if reading her mind, Ares's hot mouth closed over her nipple as he smoothed a hand down over her belly to between her legs. She opened them, tacitly giving him permission, and her insides burst into flame when his fingers delved between the folds of her sex to find the throbbing core of her body.

Cassie opened her eyes as Ares's wicked fingers explored how desperately ready for him she was. He lifted his head from her breast and watched her as he struck up a rhythm, fingers moving inside, massaging her body and then out again. His thumb circled her clitoris and Cassie's hips jerked.

'That's it...' Ares breathed. 'Let yourself go, Cass.'

This man had already given her an orgasm without even penetrating her body and now his fingers were inside, where she'd wanted him that first night, and suddenly a wave of sensation exploded outwards, suffusing Cassie in a haze of pleasure, her muscles clamping against his fingers.

'You're so responsive,' he said with obvious satisfaction, a look of stark hunger on his face.

Cassie was too dazed to do much more than let the waves of pleasure lap through her as Ares disappeared momentarily and then came back, rolling a protective sheath onto his body.

He came back down onto the bed, and pushed Cassie's legs apart. She'd never been more splayed, more exposed...more vulnerable. And yet she felt strong and powerful. Ares knelt between her legs and ran his hands up over her legs, up to the juncture of her body where she was still sensitive.

'OK?'

She nodded, and looked at his erection again. Had it grown? She suddenly felt trepidation that it would—

'It'll fit,' came Ares's amused voice.

Cassie scowled at him and he came down between her legs, nudging them even further apart. 'Don't worry, Cass. You're ready to take me.'

His hair-roughened thighs rubbed against hers, creating delicious friction. Everything about him was so unashamedly *male*, and Cassie had never imagined a man like him would turn her on so much, but right now she felt as if she'd been made just for him. For this moment. Even if it was in a tiny cabin on a rocking boat.

'Please, Ares…'

He came closer and the head of his erection teased the folds around her sex, where she was now aching for more.

'Patience… I'll have to take it slow.'

Cassie felt frustration and she growled, 'I've been riding horses and motorbikes for years, I think I'll be OK.'

Ares's eyes widened and his amused look was back. 'Greedy little thing, aren't you?'

But before she could say another word, he was breaching her entrance and spreading her wide. Cassie watched him as he slowly entered her fully, her body protesting at the invasion but then softening in increments around him. It wasn't painful, so much as uncomfortable. She moved to try and ease it and wasn't prepared for the flutter of pure electricity that shot all the way up to her brain. 'Ooooh…'

'That's it, just breathe, Cass…'

Cass. She melted and Ares went even deeper. She felt impaled, full. She couldn't speak. She could only feel. And then Ares pulled back out and her body didn't want him to go. She gripped his arms. But just as he was almost out, he slid back in again, and so began a slow and leisurely priming of her body to accommodate his.

And then as her body grew more fluid around him, an urgency built, unlike anything Cassie had ever experienced before. Building from her core and tightening inexorably. Brokenly she begged for Ares to do something to relieve this building tension and he bent his head and kissed her, saying, 'Not long now, *agapi mou*...stay with me.'

Their skin was slick. Cassie put her legs around Ares, heels digging into his buttocks, to try and alleviate the tension. He palmed her breast, trapping a nipple between his fingers, pinching.

'Your mouth...' Cassie whispered hoarsely, half deranged with the fire inside her. 'Put your mouth on me.'

Ares obliged, surrounding that taut peak in heat, teeth nipping at her tender flesh and it was that that finally pushed Cassie over the edge and soaring free, higher than she'd ever flown before. Her body wasn't hers any more, it was in the grip of something primal and timeless as she contracted around Ares's body.

Her orgasm was the end of him. He pulled back, trying to hold on, every muscle and sinew taut, but he couldn't do it, he fell too, joining Cassie in her sea of oblivion, bodies welded together, breathing hard. Hearts pounding for long minutes until, finally, the last pulses of pleasure ebbed away and left them at peace.

Ares's return to consciousness was slow. He felt as though he were climbing through a million layers, and then he had the gut-emptying sensation that he'd never find his way out to daylight again. He was aware he was half asleep and starting to panic. An all too familiar sensation. Claustrophobia closing in around him, suffocating him.

He came to with a start, sitting up in a bed, breathing hard, sweating. In an enclosed space. Very dim light coming through the only window. It took him long agonising seconds to place himself. He was in the cabin. On a boat. *Not that boat.* A sliver of relief went through him but not enough.

He looked beside him to see Cassie in a sprawl. Lying on her front, arms out beside her head. Long back. Hair wild, spread out over the pillow. Sheet covering her bottom. Not even that provocative sight could jolt Ares out of the increasing sense of claustrophobia. It was testament to how much he'd wanted her that he'd been distracted enough to make love to her down here at all.

He needed air. Heart pounding, skin clammy, fighting the waves of panic threatening to pull him down into a nightmare, Ares left the cabin.

CHAPTER EIGHT

CASSIE WASN'T SURE what had woken her but she knew before she opened her eyes that she was alone in the bed that took up much of the cabin. She also noticed that the boat was still, only rocking gently. The storm had passed. In more ways than one.

She turned over and cracked open her eyes to see pale daylight. Sheets in a tangle. She smelled *them* in the air, sex. It made her insides clench as she tried to wrap her brain around what had happened.

She was no longer a virgin. She'd never expected sex to be so...all-encompassing. Transcendent. *Amazing*.

She ached all over but pleasurably. Between her legs felt tender and her face got hot as she remembered how frustrated she'd been with Ares's teasing. And then, the exquisite pleasure/pain of him entering her body.

Where was he? There was no sound from outside the cabin. Gingerly, Cassie got up and cracked open the door. The main cabin was empty. The door leading up to the deck was open though.

She caught a glimpse of herself in the mirror in the en suite and groaned. Smeared make-up, glitter on her cheeks. She washed her face quickly and saw Ares's T-shirt on the ground and reached for it, pulling it on.

It reached to mid-thigh. She went up the small set of steps and emerged into a cloudless dawn morning. The storm well and truly gone.

Ares was at the stern of the boat, his back to her. Jeans riding low on his hips. He didn't seem to hear her. She went out, feeling suddenly shy after last night. She stopped a couple of feet behind him, near the control panel and wheel. She cleared her throat and saw him flinch. *What?*

Confused now, Cassie went and stood alongside Ares and looked at him. His hair was wild but his face arrested her. It was pale, almost green. Her initial thought was that he was seasick. It wasn't unheard of even after a few days at sea. And it had been stormy. 'Ares…are you OK? Are you ill?'

He looked at her and his eyes were wild. She noticed that he wasn't really looking at her. More like through her. He wasn't seasick. It was something else. A sliver of fear went through Cassie.

She touched Ares's arm and then down until she could take his hand. She tugged him over to the seat on one side of the deck. 'Sit down, Ares.'

He did. As obedient as a little boy. She came down on her haunches in front of him. 'Ares? What's going on?'

His glazed expression didn't change. He shook his head. 'I can't…'

Cassie thought of something and said, 'Wait here.' Even though he didn't look capable of going anywhere. She went back down into the cabin and hunted around until she found what she was looking for.

She went back up on deck and handed Ares a tumbler glass with a measure of whiskey. 'Drink this.'

He took it but she noticed his hand wasn't steady so she put her hand around his and lifted it to his mouth. He swallowed a drop. Cassie said, 'More.'

He looked at her and for the first time she noticed he saw her and felt heartened. He took some more. Cassie noticed his hand wasn't trembling any more. She came up on the seat beside him.

The sun was coming up, bathing the wide sky in shades of pink. After a few moments, Cassie said as lightly as she could, 'Was it that traumatic?'

Ares looked at her, uncomprehending, and then he got it. She was talking about him taking her virginity. He shook his head and the ghost of a smile touched his mouth. 'No, it's nothing to do with you.'

But had it been as amazing for him as it had been for her? She doubted that.

'Then...what was that?'

He looked at her and threw back the last of the whiskey. She took the empty glass and put it down. She thought he wasn't going to say anything and then eventually he said, 'I was kidnapped, when I was ten. They held me on a boat. Locked in a cabin for two weeks.'

It took a second for this to sink in, and for Cassie to grasp the magnitude and when she did she went cold all over. 'Ares...' she breathed. 'I didn't see anything online...why...?'

It all made horrific sense now, the way he'd always seemed reluctant on the boat, happy to let her navigate. Going down into the cabin as little as possible. *Sleeping on deck.*

'It's not online because my parents had it all but scrubbed from the web. It's still there if you dig for it but they don't like to be reminded of any chink in their armour, any sign of weakness.'

'What happened?'

'The kidnappers, an organised crime gang, asked for a ransom, but my parents refused to pay. My older brother, he was the smart one, they didn't want to risk him being kidnapped if they paid.'

Cassie shook her head. 'Ares, that's so wrong. Did they hurt you?' She couldn't recall seeing any physical scars but then she hadn't been much focused on taking a survey of Ares's body last night. It had been an instrument of pleasure. Not something to scrutinise. She wanted to though, some day. Lay him out on a surface and inspect every inch of him. She pushed that aside.

He let out a short sharp laugh. 'Not physically no, apart from some bruises from rough handling. A bump on my head. Maybe concussion.'

He didn't have to tell her the scars were inside. To this day. She felt guilty. She remembered him trying to persuade her to take a plane.

'Is it just boats or…?'

His mouth compressed. 'Mainly boats… I'm not great in small spaces with locked doors, but it's not as bad.'

Something struck her. The memory of how he'd taken charge during the storm. 'How did you learn to sail if you hated it so much?'

A flash of pain crossed his face. 'My father. He

would not tolerate a son who couldn't sail a boat. He made no allowances for what had happened—he insisted I sail at every opportunity. After all, I belonged to one of the world's biggest shipping dynasties. He saw it as akin to getting back on a horse after being thrown.'

Cassie's mouth fell open in horror. After a moment she said, 'What a monster. Ares, I'm sorry, if I'd had any idea…'

'No one knows how it affected me. Not really.'

Her chest felt tight. 'Your own parents compounded the trauma.'

'They didn't care. It wasn't them that rescued me, it was the police.'

Cassie sucked in a breath. Her parents had been focused on hating each other more than loving her or Caius but she knew they wouldn't have just abandoned them to their fate in a situation like that.

'That's why you broke with them.'

Ares nodded. Cassie sat back and absorbed this. It had been so bad and the abandonment had been so traumatic that not even inheriting a vast dynastic business and fortune had swayed Ares from his vow to break with his parents.

'What about your older brother? Did you ever talk to him about it?'

Ares shook his head. 'He tried to talk to me, but I couldn't articulate what I'd been through. The terror of not knowing what would happen, of knowing there was no escape. My parents didn't encourage me to talk about it with anyone. My brother was being groomed to succeed, my parents pushed us apart, I can see that now.'

'So you had no kind of therapy?'

Now Ares laughed out loud and shook his head. 'No.'

'Maybe if you had you wouldn't still be having panic attacks.'

He looked at her, sharp. 'How do you know what that was?'

'You saw my reaction to that arguing couple yesterday... I've had to learn to manage my anxiety around witnessing any kind of confrontation. I know it's not as traumatic as what happened to you but—'

He put a finger to her mouth and shook his head. 'It's not a competition, Cass. We've both been affected by what happened to us.'

CHAPTER NINE

ARES WAS MOMENTARILY ALONE. Cassie had gone down into the cabin to get them coffee.

He felt hollowed out after his panic attack, but also something else, a sense of calm. He'd never had that reaction in front of anyone before. He could still feel her hand on his arm, cool, then taking his hand, leading him over to the seat. Her compassionate eyes. So blue. Hair wild and tangled around her shoulders. Bare thighs. His T-shirt.

The fact that she knew what he was going through, albeit for a very different reason. He could still recall the way she'd frozen yesterday. Gone pale. Retreated somewhere inside herself.

The sense of being seen and accepted and understood was…as disturbing as it was profound. Throwing him off-centre.

She re-emerged now with cups of coffee and he took one. 'Thanks.' He noticed she'd put on shorts. He'd never been in this situation with a lover before. Because he didn't hang around or encourage them to hang around. And yet, in spite of exposing himself so spectacularly just now, he didn't feel the need to get away from Cassie.

To his relief, he felt something start to eclipse the

cold clammy dread as it receded. Awareness. Heat. *Desire.*

Last night...had been amazing enough to distract him from his surroundings. Not even sex would have done that before. But with her... Something uneasy moved through him. *She's different.*

Yes, because she was so out of bounds she might as well be from another planet.

'Last night,' he said and stopped. Not sure what to say. But Cassie spoke. 'You don't have to say anything.'

'I don't?'

She shook her head, her hair slipping forward to hide her face. 'I'm sure it wasn't what you're...used to.'

Ares huffed a laugh. 'You can say that again.' He absently rubbed his bare chest. He had to acknowledge that it felt as if something had freed up in his chest. Some resident tightness.

Cassie stood up and rounded on him. 'Well, there's no need to be rude about it. I'll dock this boat as soon as I can and you can sign me up with another babysitter, OK?'

It took Ares a moment to compute the hurt on her face. She went to go back down into the cabin and Ares caught her arm. *'Woah!* Wait just a second, where are you going?'

He saw the turmoil on her face and it lanced him right in the gut because he could see that she knew if she went downstairs he would find it hard to follow her. She pulled her arm free. 'That's the problem, there's nowhere to go.'

A moment ago Ares had been thinking that last

night couldn't happen again, she was out of bounds and maybe it would be best to just let her dock the boat somewhere and put in a call to have someone else take over, but now that she was saying that, he found it unpalatable. More than unpalatable. Downright impossible.

'Cass, look at me.'

It took her a second but she did, eyes flashing, jaw tight. He took the coffee cup out of her hand and put it down and then took her hands and tugged her towards him until she fell into his lap.

Yes. She belongs here. With me.

'Ares?' She was rigid in his arms, on his lap, where his body was responding to her luscious ass pressed close to his body.

'Cass, last night wasn't what I'm used to…*in a good way.*'

She relaxed into him a little. 'Oh.'

'How do you think I was even able to do that if you hadn't taken all of my attention?'

'There was a storm, we couldn't have stayed on deck… Maybe you were just looking for something to distract you.'

'I tried to resist you, remember?'

Her face went a pretty shade of pink. He saved her. 'You tempted me from the moment I laid eyes on you and judged you to be a spoiled party-girl brat.'

'I'm not a brat.'

'No, you're not.' She wasn't. Ares knew that now. She was genuine and sweet and more self-sufficient than most people he knew. And she was going to be taking on a job that would demand everything of her. For the rest of her life.

'I should be asking you if it was everything you'd hoped.'

She looked at him, suddenly shy. Bit her lip. 'I...' she said. 'It was the most... I never expected it would be so... Is it always like that?'

He shook his head. 'No, but with you...? I think so.'

He moved under her and saw her blush again as she registered what she was sitting on. And then a gleam came into her eye. 'Could we? Now?'

Ares nodded. 'We need protection.'

She jumped up. 'I'll get it.' She disappeared down into the cabin. The thought that he had debauched the future queen he was supposed to be protecting was not something he wanted to dwell on right now. When she came back, he said, 'Take off your shorts.'

She did as Ares stood and pulled off his jeans and sat down again. He reached for her. 'Straddle my lap.'

She did, the T-shirt riding up to the tops of her legs. Ares bit back a groan when she came into contact with his cock. He wouldn't last long.

'Are you sore?'

She shook her head. 'Not too sore.' She looked hungry. Ares pushed her hair over her shoulders and then cupped her face with his hands and kissed her, getting drunk on her sweetness and the way she opened up to him so trustingly.

She wrapped her arms around him and he let her face go to reach under the hem of his T-shirt—it had never looked as good on him—and found soft silky skin. The weight of her perfect breasts, those sharp nipples.

She gasped into his mouth as he rolled them, pinching gently. Then he pushed the T-shirt up, bunching it, and bent his head, to lavish each peak with his tongue and mouth, until Cassie was writhing against him.

He put his hand between them, finding where she was slick and swollen with need. It was all he could do to find the protection, rip it open and roll it onto himself so that he could say, 'Rise up a little.'

She did, bracing her knees on the seat either side of his hips. Ares angled himself so he was nudging her entrance and then he said, 'OK, come back down...'

'Ahhhh.' He let out a hiss of ecstasy as she slowly came down onto his body, encasing him in heat and silk and that exquisite grip of her inner muscles. He held her waist, guiding her movement. She looked at him as if concentrating on a very hard task. It made something move in his chest, so he kissed her again to push it away and focus on the physical.

Up and down she glided on his body and it was more exquisite than Ares had ever known. They fitted together. He could feel Cassie's movements becoming more jerky, faster, as she chased her peak, and Ares held her hips as he thrust up and deep, once, twice... on the third time she splintered around him with a cry, her body convulsing around his, sending him flying.

The panic and the claustrophobia was gone, banished. Cassie collapsed into him, head buried in his neck. His arms went around her, holding her lightly trembling body in the aftermath.

Even when the tendrils of his dread did come back to him, as sanity and reality returned, it didn't feel as acute. The sharp edges were softened.

A little later they were still at anchor in the sheltered cove where they'd come last night to avoid the storm, eating breakfast/brunch. The sun was up. It was a beautiful cerulean blue-sky day, no hint of the rain and wind from just hours ago.

Cassie had assured Ares a short while before that they would dock the boat as soon as she found the nearest spot for it. She wasn't sure what would happen now, but she knew she couldn't ask Ares to stay on the boat. And she didn't want to continue this trip on a boat with anyone else. The thought was repugnant and she knew there was no way he'd agree to let her continue without security.

A little hesitantly she asked, 'You're not going to… leave me?' She winced inwardly at how that sounded. Needy.

He looked at her. 'Only if you've decided to return to Sadat?'

Cassie shook her head. For the first time since it had become apparent that she would be queen, she resented the constraints on her life. The fact that she had mere days before she'd have to return and start her life of duty. *Without Ares.*

And even though they'd just had the most…transformative night of her life, and delicious morning sex, she wasn't sure where they were now. Ares was used to this. She wasn't.

Hating herself for feeling so insecure, Cassie said, 'What is this now...? What are we...?'

Ares took a sip of coffee and put the cup back on the small table. He looked at her. Thankfully he'd put on a T-shirt that Cassie had brought him. So he wasn't too distracting.

He gestured between them with a finger. *'This?'*

Cassie nodded, squirming. Ares was probably used to sophisticated lovers who didn't need anything spelled out. Well, tough. She raised her chin. 'Yes, *this*.'

Slowly he said, 'We are two adults enjoying a moment of rare chemistry.'

She registered the word *moment*. 'So this isn't... usual?'

He shook his head. 'No, Cass, it's not.'

Something fizzed inside her. It wasn't just her. 'If I had found someone last night to sleep with...to be my first...'

A thunderous expression crossed Ares's face and he reached for her from the other side of the table, pulling her into his lap. 'I wasn't going to let anyone else be the first to touch you.'

Cassie relaxed into Ares's steely strength. She believed him. He wasn't just helping her to tick off her 'last days of freedom' wish list.

He said now, 'I might have tried to deny it but I knew as soon as you told me you were innocent that I wanted to be the one.'

Cassie smiled. 'I'm glad you were. I wanted you to be too.'

A smile tipped up one corner of Ares's mouth. *'Wanted?'*

Cassie bit back a grin. She loved seeing him smile so much. She waved a hand airily and said, 'Oh, yes, I've moved on now. Twice was enough for me.'

Ares's arm tightened around her and his free hand delved under the opening of the robe she'd changed into after her shower to cup her breast. She sucked in a breath.

His smile grew and turned wicked. 'Are you quite sure about that? Not even one more time?'

Breathless now, Cassie said, 'Well, just to be sure, maybe one more time.'

Ares shook his head. 'Not here. Next time, I want to take you on a proper bed, where I can lay you out and explore every inch of you.'

Cassie's insides clenched at the thought of that, and of being able to do that to Ares. To have him spread out for her delectation. 'That sounds nice.'

His expression turned serious. Seriously sexy. 'Oh, it'll be more than nice.'

'This big bed...where would we find it?'

'Spetses.' Ares named another Greek island, in the Saronic chain of islands.

'Spetses,' Cassie repeated.

Ares nodded. 'I have a villa there.'

'That sounds...perfect.' She felt a little giddy at the thought he didn't want to run away from her at the first opportunity. She stood up from Ares's lap, dislodging his hands from her body. 'There's one more thing I want to do here before we hand the boat back.'

He looked up at her and he was so beautiful and wild against this oceanic backdrop that he took her breath away. Cassie undid the robe and let it fall from her naked body. She went and stood at the stern of the boat and glanced back over her shoulder. 'I've never been skinny-dipping before.'

And then she turned and executed a perfect dive off the boat into the clear blue-green waters. When she surfaced it was just in time to see an equally naked Ares poised to join her. He said, 'You're going to kill me before we even see another bed, aren't you?'

Cassie grinned and flicked water up at him and then watched with very feminine appreciation as he also executed a perfect dive into the sea.

Cassie breathed in, taking in her idyllic surroundings. Dusk was bathing everything in a lavender hue, and lavender scented the air as Cassie walked down a path lined by bushes and shrubs and cypress and olive trees.

A sprawling villa lay behind her and the sea glistened at the end of the path. She walked all the way to find steps leading down to a private beach.

She looked at Ares, who had come to stand beside her. 'This is just stunning. How long have you had it?'

'A few years.'

They'd landed on a helipad not far away a short while before in the helicopter that Ares had organised from Mykonos, after docking the boat at a small private marina where it would be picked up by the boat company.

Ares's estate on the Spetses coast was completely secluded and protected by trees and a perimeter fence. He'd shown her a beautiful infinity pool on the other side of the villa set at the end of a series of rolling lawns.

It was utterly quiet and still and it soothed something inside Cassie. The palace on Sadat was beautiful too but it was always busy and full of people. There was no corner that was truly quiet. She hadn't even realised until now how much she appreciated this kind of space and peace.

'Let me show you around the villa.'

He led her back up towards the building with its white walls and terracota-hued slate roof. One end of the villa was two-storey and Cassie could see a room with a balcony that would give views out to the sea. The master bedroom, she presumed.

The rest of the villa seemed to be one-storey and there was a patio on one side.

Ares walked in through open French doors, muslin curtains fluttering gently in the warm breeze. Cassie thought back to the moment earlier that day when she'd been in the sea, the water silky against her naked skin, after Ares had joined her, and how he'd swum under the surface, catching her legs and pulling her down, kissing her under water.

It had been magical. And so had drying off on the deck of the boat, which had inevitably led to more.

Cassie followed Ares into a large airy reception room, with soft couches and low coffee tables laden with hardback photographic books on every subject.

'As you can probably notice, I have more picture books than word books.'

Cassie's heart squeezed as she thought of his dyslexia.' She waved a hand. 'Word books are highly overrated.'

Then he showed her a formal dining room, which led into a huge state-of-the-art kitchen where a man in black trousers and black T-shirt was chopping on a marble island.

'Cassie, I'd like you to meet Declan, my chef. He's been kind enough to come and prepare some food for us.'

Cassie shook the man's hand and smiled. 'Nice to meet you.'

'You too.'

They kept going. There was an informal sitting room with a massive-screen TV. Guest suites. A gym. An office.

Upstairs, the master suite was indeed the one with the balcony overlooking the gardens and sea. It was unashamedly masculine, decorated in dark tones with a massive bed. Cassie glimpsed an en suite with a shower open to the elements and a bath as big as a small swimming pool. Two sinks.

As Ares stood beside her on the balcony she asked as casually as she could, 'So do you have many guests here?'

'Only royalty.'

It took Cassie a second to understand his meaning and when she did she looked up at him. 'You mean…'

'Do I have to spell it out?' he asked with a smile.

That smile made Cassie's insides melt. She shook her head. 'I don't think so.'

'Let me show you your room.'

Cassie appreciated his consideration in giving her

her own space. She followed him out of his suite and to another, further down the corridor. Ares opened the door, showing her into a sumptuous suite decorated in lighter tones than his. There was a vast bathroom and dressing room, where Cassie was surprised to see a woman hanging up her clothes.

'This is Marta, my housekeeper.'

Cassie shook her hand. The woman said in accented English, 'If you need anything, let me know.'

She left them, closing the bedroom door behind her. Cassie said, 'Marta and Declan...do they stay here too?'

'Marta lives with her husband, my caretaker, on the grounds, in their own smaller villa. Declan lives down in the town with his partner.'

The bed looked very inviting, dressed in cool white cotton.

Ares took her hand and led her over to the French doors. He opened them and Cassie saw that there was a small terrace outside, with views over the other side of the grounds and sea.

She felt inexplicably emotional for a moment, not even sure where it was stemming from. Swallowing it down, terrified Ares would see something, she said, 'Thank you for bringing me here...and I'm sorry again about the boat. If I'd known—'

He stopped her words by squeezing her hand. She looked up at him. He said, 'I told you, no one knows. Not even my own family.'

'Caius?' Cassie asked.

Ares shook his head. 'We don't go into too much personal stuff.'

Cassie let out a laugh. 'I'm not surprised. I call my brother the clam, he's so secretive.'

Then she thought of something and went a little cold inside. She pulled her hand free. 'Ares, did you just bring me here because it would be easier to keep me protected?'

It was certainly conveniently cut off from everywhere else and Cassie was just realising how adroitly he'd managed to get her to deviate from her plan. But then her conscience struck her. He hadn't faked that panic attack. She believed him about the kidnapping.

A sense of exposure skated over Ares's skin. Cassie wasn't meeting his eye. It would be so easy to say *yes*, that had been his plan, exactly. And it was a good plan to keep her out of the public eye and harm's way. But that hadn't crossed his mind once.

'No,' he said simply, turning his back on the view and resting against the terrace wall to look at her. 'You're free to go, Cass.'

She glanced up at him. 'And what would happen then?'

'I'd get one of my team to shadow you.'

Her hands went to the wall. 'So, you are ready to let me just…go?'

The thought of her leaving sent a visceral response through him. *No way.* 'No, I'm not. But if you wanted to leave, I couldn't go with you. It wouldn't be a good idea for us to stay together because I could no longer be professional.' *Ha!* Ares hadn't been thinking professionally since about five seconds after he'd seen her for the first time.

'Oh,' she said.

'Yes. Oh. I want you, Cass. It's not about me letting you go, it's about whether or not you want to stay and to explore this…heat between us.'

She looked up at him, a smile playing around her mouth, her extremely distracting and provocative mouth. 'That's what it's called—*heat*?'

He reached for her, pulling her into him, relishing the feel of her lithe body and curves pressed against him. She made him feel lighter. *Thée mou*, he would pay for this transgression but not now. Not yet.

'Among other things like lust, chemistry, desire. Take your pick.'

'Yes, I'd like to stay, and I like lust,' she said with a devilish glint in her eye. Ares thought of watching her dive into the sea naked, how she'd looked like a faerie nymph, a mermaid, with her long golden hair and blue eyes and perfect skin.

She might have been innocent but she was a fast learner and she was moving against him now in a way that was fast short-circuiting his brain cells. Obeying some semblance of self-protection from deep down, he forced himself to say, 'You know that this…between us can't go beyond here, out into the world, into our real lives.'

She went still and pulled back, suddenly avoiding his eye. 'Of course, I know that. We both want very different things, and I…do want a marriage that will be as real as I can make it. Caius might have been happy to have a marriage in name only for heirs and appearances and keep someone on the side, but I want more than that.'

She was a romantic. She might deny it but Ares could read between the words. But then he thought of her with some chinless well-bred prince and a red mist coloured his vision. He told himself it was just because he felt possessive of her. He'd been her first lover.

But, no harm to put some space between them. He said, 'I should go to my office and make some calls, check in on things. Let your brother know you're safe.' *And thoroughly debauched.* Ares wouldn't be divulging that. Not if he wanted to keep his head attached to his body. And he wouldn't even blame Caius.

She was still avoiding his eye. She wasn't like the women he was used to. He caught her chin between his fingers and tipped her face up. 'Don't underestimate how much I want you, Cass. We'll have dinner later. Relax for now, make yourself at home.'

He pressed a swift kiss to her mouth and walked away before he changed his mind and his full weakness for her was made brutally apparent. *To her or to you?* asked a mocking voice. Ares ignored it.

Cassie looked at herself in the mirror. She felt different. Did she look different? She peered at her face. She was a little sunburned, there were freckles across her nose, visible even under light make-up. She could imagine Pierre's look of shock to see his pristine princess looking more human. She grinned. She didn't care. She felt reckless. *Free.* Which was ironic, or maybe tragic, considering that she was about to embark on a life of being followed and scrutinised almost every waking moment.

Her grin slipped when she thought of how Ares had made it painfully clear that there was no chance he would be a part of that future. Not that Cassie had imagined for a second that he could be. Even if he wanted to be, the pressure to marry someone *suitable* was immense. And Ares Drakos, even with his upper-class pedigree, didn't have blue blood running through his veins.

Cassie rolled her eyes at herself. Neither did she. It was red, like everyone else's. The only thing that marked her out was the fact that her upper-class family line could be traced back to pre-medieval times and at some point along the way they'd been decreed royal.

She knew what this was with Ares. A moment. A totally unexpected and amazing moment. She'd hoped for this, but hadn't really believed it might happen. And with someone so…compelling. And interesting. And intriguing. *Stop.*

She focused on checking her reflection again. She was wearing a dress she'd bought in Mykonos in one of the boutiques. White. Silk. Loose and flowy to just below her knee, the kind of thing she'd never be allowed to wear. It was too young, too sexy. Too revealing.

It was sleeveless and backless. A halter-neck design with a deep vee between her breasts. The top of the dress was held in place by a choker-style neck design, pearl buttons.

The waist was nipped with a band of the same material as the dress that met at the back, just above her buttocks, in a pearl clasp, matching the ones at the back of her neck.

She paired the dress with strappy high-heel sandals and a simple pair of pearl earrings and matching bracelet. Jewellery of her mother's that she'd brought with her. She pulled her hair back and up into a rough chignon.

Cassie stepped back and headed for the door. She was going to meet her lover for dinner. *Her lover.* The thought of seeing Ares made her feel bubbly. Effervescent. Light. Who knew that the taciturn man she'd first met would sneak under her skin and change her life so comprehensively? That a smile from him could make her breathless with a sense of victory?

She knew it was dangerous to indulge in this little game they were playing, but she couldn't seem to care enough to stop it. To walk away. This was just a massive tick off her wish list, that was all. *Sex. Losing her virginity.*

Once she landed back on Sadat Sur Mer, her life would not be her own again, and she would have a lifetime to regret the choices she was making right now.

Ares stepped into the living/dining area holding a bottle of champagne and two glasses. But he stopped in his tracks when he saw the figure of the woman standing on the terrace through the open French doors.

She had her back to him. Her bare back, beautifully shaped and making his hands itch to touch. Hair pulled up, drawing attention to that graceful sweep of neck.

A choker of material was at her throat, little buttons at the back of her neck. A white dress, falling from her hips in loose, elegant folds.

Legs bare under the dress, high heels.

Ares knew that for the rest of his life, this image would be seared onto his brain.

As if hearing his thoughts she turned around and the front view was even more spellbinding. The dress had a deep vee at the front and he could see the tantalising curves of her breasts. His hand tightened on the bottle of champagne as he forced his legs to move in her direction.

She gestured at the dress. 'I'm probably a little overdressed but I couldn't resist. I'll never get to dress like this at home.'

Ares felt like telling her she could dress like that for him but he bit it back. She would be dressing for duty and, some day, her husband. He was glad he'd changed into dark trousers and a white shirt, at least.

'You look beautiful.' The words felt horribly inadequate. She was stunning. And she oozed an elegance and sophistication that didn't just come from her breeding and background. They came from her. She'd be elegant in anything. She humbled Ares.

'Thank you.' She ducked her head, some hair falling forward.

Ares poured her a glass of sparkling champagne and one for himself and put the bottle in an ice bucket. He handed her the glass. *'Yamas.'*

She looked up and smiled. *'Santé.'*

They took sips, eyes locked, sparks flying. For someone who'd always taken feeling comfortable around women for granted, Ares felt unaccountably tongue-tied.

Showing her consummate diplomatic skill, she asked, 'Did you get much work done?'

Ares huffed a rough-sounding laugh. 'Really? We're going to talk about work?'

She rolled her eyes. 'I'm interested. How many clients do you have at the moment? Not counting me.'

'I don't consider you a client.'

Her cheeks flushed and she bit her lip. Ares knew he wouldn't make it to dinner if she kept doing that. He reached out and tugged her lip free. 'Stop that. Your mouth is mine to bite.'

She flushed even more. 'So I'm getting a lover and a bodyguard rolled into one? That's a good deal.'

Ares scowled at her and then he spotted something—he'd spotted it before but hadn't had this chance to ask her about it. He reached for her right arm and lifted it up, turning the underside upwards so that he could properly inspect the tattoo she'd had done on the inside of her wrist.

He looked at the letters, only five of them, and read out loud, 'B-e-l-l-e. Belle.' The E ended in the shape of a heart. It was light and delicate. Discreet. Classy, as tattoos went.

He felt Cassie's tension. He looked at her. 'Who's Belle?'

CHAPTER TEN

CASSIE'S HEART WAS thumping and her chest felt tight. Not even Ares's hand on her arm could distract her right now. She should have known this would incite interest but she'd wanted to mark her sister in some way. Brand herself with her presence. Bring her with her on this journey.

Her voice was husky. 'She was my sister. My twin sister. Christabel. Born five minutes after me. She died shortly after birth.'

Ares's hand tightened around her arm for a moment. 'I didn't know.' He let her go and Cassie brought her arm into her belly. 'Not many do, to be honest. They didn't publicise the fact that my mother was pregnant with twins. She was superstitious. She'd had a miscarriage before I—*we*—were born.'

'I'm sorry,' Ares said simply.

Cassie looked at him. 'Thank you. It turns out she was right to be superstitious. It might sound weird but even though we never really met…except for in the womb, I've always felt her presence. As if I'm living a life for both of us. This whole trip…has been in part because I always wonderd if she'd have been more outgoing than me. More brave.'

'You are brave.'

Cassie looked at Ares and swallowed down the lump in her throat.

He asked, 'Would she have been queen?'

'Probably not as I was born first.' Cassie had always felt ridiculously guilty on some level, as if her successful birth had cost her sister's life. 'I always felt as if something or someone was missing. It made sense when I found out that I'd had a twin.'

'When did you find out?'

'I heard staff gossiping when I was around ten, and then I asked Caius.'

'I can't imagine what it must be like to feel like a part of yourself is missing.'

Cassie was surprised that Ares understood even that much. 'It's like a little ache that never goes away. I'm always conscious of her and wondering what she might be doing. We weren't identical.'

At that moment Marta appeared behind Ares and said, 'Dinner is ready.'

Ares turned around. '*Efharisto*, Marta.'

Cassie was glad of the diversion. She always found it emotional to talk about her sister. They followed Marta around to another section of the patio where there was a table set with white linen and china and crystal glasses. Flowers in a vase in the centre. Candles flickering. Cassie knew she couldn't let this scene go to her head—the woman was probably reading more into why Cassie was here with Ares—but it was lovely.

She complimented the housekeeper and the woman beamed.

When they sat down Ares looked at Cassie. The skin of her inner wrist was still tingling from where he'd touched her. He said now, 'You'll make a great queen.'

She looked at him, surprised. 'Why do you say that?' She'd hoped to make a competent queen at least and not let her people down.

'You're a good person and you care about people.'

Cassie couldn't deny the little glow at his assessment of her. But then it dimmed a little. 'I feel very selfish right now.'

'I didn't have a full appreciation of how much your life will be given over to your duties as queen, before I met you. Or how much of your life it's already taken up, just being princess.'

Cassie shrugged. 'It just was, *is*, my life. School was the only time I really had to myself. University. When I was young I would accompany one or both of my parents to events and functions. They'd be doled out between me and Caius. We rarely got to go together because my parents were usually at each other's throats.

'I would have liked to spend more time with Caius,' she admitted wistfully. 'But the abdication forced us apart. I'm ashamed to admit that I blamed him a little, as if it were his fault. When of course it wasn't.'

Ares said, 'Completely understandable. Overnight you were thrust into a position you'd never anticipated. He had his whole life to prepare and then when you needed him most, he had to leave.'

'Thank you,' Cassie said simply, touched by Ares's insight.

She said, 'He'll be there for the coronation—he's

insisting on weathering whatever the public and press reaction will be.'

'I'm sure by then it'll have died down and your people will be ready to accept and welcome their new queen.'

Cassie grimaced a little. 'I hope so. I would like to bring the people of Sadat closer, take away some of the fussy protocols. Open up the palace to the public. Be more involved in every part of society on a much more tangible level. Be more of an ambassador for the country to encourage people to come and visit. We're not as glitzy as Monaco, we have to work harder.'

Marta brought starters, delicious morsels of squid cooked with tomato and basil, washed down with local white wine. For a few minutes they ate contentedly—Ares was easy company.

When Marta cleared the plates away, Cassie sat back. 'So where are your family?'

Ares gave her a look—no-go zone—and she just arched a brow. 'It's a simple question.'

Ares sighed. 'Mainly Athens, that's where the head office is, but there are offices all over the world. Drakos Solutions is one of the biggest shipping and logistics companies in the world.'

'It's the biggest, according to the Internet. You don't regret turning your back?'

Ares made a face. 'I guess I'd be lying if I said I don't look them up, keep tabs on them. The company… *and* my siblings. Not my parents.'

Cassie was silent while Marta returned with the mains, seafood ravioli. When she was gone Ares said with almost palpable reluctance, 'I have nieces and nephews.'

Cassie's mouth opened. And shut again under his look. He probably hadn't intended divulging that much. Risking his censure, Cassie said quickly, 'Well, for what it's worth, they're missing out on a pretty cool uncle.'

Ares made a non-committal noise. Cassie could see Ares with kids. He'd be good with them. Knowing that she shouldn't push but not able to stop herself, she said, 'You could just…reach out. It wasn't your siblings' fault what happened. It sounds like your brother cared to know what had happened?'

Ares sighed and ran a hand through his hair, messing it up sexily. Cassie fought to stay focused.

He said, 'It has eaten away at me, the guilt of pushing them away. Losing contact. My brother is busy, he's now CEO of the company. My sisters…they have their families. The gulf has grown and it's my fault.'

Cassie offered, 'It's on them too but it's easy to let distance grow. Especially if they think they might be rejected.'

Knowing she was straying way into the no-go zone, she couldn't help asking, 'You really don't ever intend to have a family?'

This time Ares gave her an explicit look and said, 'Your food is getting cold.'

Cassie smiled and obediently took a piece of ravioli. It was delicious. When she thought Ares was going to ignore her question, he sat back and said, 'Why would I have kids when I have no idea how to parent them?'

Cassie put her head on one side. 'I could have the same attitude but I know that I want to do things differently. I don't want my children growing up in a domestic war zone and I want them to know they're loved, and...*seen*.'

'You didn't feel seen?'

Cassie shook her head. 'Caius was the focus, the heir. I think my father saw me like an ornament. He didn't know how to relate to me. My mother was too busy hating him and having affairs. As I got older I think she looked at me and saw herself ageing.

'When they were really going for it, during one of their many arguments, I'd do everything to try and distract them. Be as bright and happy as possible...'

Ares shook his head. 'It didn't work because they were so selfish they couldn't appreciate what was in front of them.'

That caught Cassie right in the heart where she'd always had that sense of being on the other side of a glass wall, unable to make anyone hear her, or see her.

'*Theos*, Cassie. Come here.' Ares took her hand and tugged her out of her seat and pulled her into his lap. Her silky dress was a flimsy barrier between her and the steely heat and strength of his body.

She looked down at him, heart tripping. His hand was on her bare back. 'No wonder you blasted me with your sunshine when we met. It's your defence and offence mechanism.'

Cassie scowled but inside she was turning into mush at his far too accurate assessment. 'What can I say? Your snark gave me permission to display my true self.'

Ares looked serious. 'I was afraid I'd dim your brightness.'

Cassie's heart skipped about a million beats. She shook

her head. 'No, you couldn't do that.' He'd given her something far more precious. A sense of who she really was.

Ares said then, 'There's another reason I never intended to have a family. I don't want to pass my dyslexia on to a child.'

Cassie wanted to reach out and punish his parents for being so awful and cold. 'Even if you did, it's not an affliction, it's just a different way of learning. I think it's an asset.'

'Anyway, it's not something I'll have to consider. My brother will have kids.'

Cassie felt like pushing back at Ares's certainty he wouldn't be complicating his life with a family but then she thought of him with someone who might have the power to change his mind and make him want things he'd never considered before. A cold weight lodged in her gut, because she was realising that *she* wanted to be the one who could change his mind.

The curse of every woman everywhere who had been told in no uncertain terms by a man that they were not interested in commitment but who fooled themselves into thinking they could be different. Or, worse, *the one*.

Cassie assured herself desperately that Ares had been her first lover, that was all, it was normal to feel emotions attached with sex. It had been a pretty profound experience.

Ares was not someone who wanted to step into a lifelong role of duty by a woman's side. Where he would be required to sire children to further the Mansur royal line. He was a lone wolf. And this was just a brief moment. And the fact that she was even thinking of him in those terms made Cassie lever herself off Ares's lap and back to her seat, forking some ravioli into her mouth before she could say anything else.

Ares just looked at her, as if he had her measure, but she really really hoped he couldn't see into her head because if he did he'd be running so fast in the opposite direction she'd have whiplash.

Cassie woke the next morning to a warm breeze over her bare skin and the scent of sea and pine and lavender. Scents that reminded her of home, but she knew she wasn't in the palace.

For one thing, she didn't sleep naked. And for another, she wasn't used to waking feeling achy but satisfied on a bone-deep level. *A soul level.* She let her mind skitter away from that far too revealing revelation. There was a much earthier smell, the smell of sex. She focused on that and smiled.

'Do you ever *not* smile?'

Cassie's eyes flew open and she was looking at an expanse of toned ridged belly muscles above the line of sweatpants. She dragged her gaze up to where Ares was sitting on the side of the bed.

Cassie's face got hot. Last night she'd lived out her fantasy of having Ares spread out for her very thorough investigation.

'Kalimera,' Ares said, with a very wicked glint in his eye, as if he too was remembering how she'd let him do the same to her, exploring every dip and curve of her body until she'd been begging him for mercy.

'Bonne matin,' she said, using her own language. A hybrid of French, Spanish and Italian.

He swatted her bottom under the sheet and stood up. 'Come on, I've got plans for you this morning.'

'Plans? What are they again?' Cassie rolled over onto her back. She could see that it was still early outside, just after dawn.

When she looked at Ares his gaze was fixed south of her face on her bare breasts. She revelled in his hot look. 'Are these plans…urgent?'

He came down on the bed again and put two hands either side of her, coming down close to her chest. She could smell his freshly washed skin and smiled wider. She'd realised that it cost her nothing to smile and be happy with Ares. It came from an easy place. Not needing to force it. 'I've just added something to my wish list—I want to shower with my lover.'

Ares's eyes flared. He stood up again and caught her hands, pulling her up. 'What a good idea.'

She was in his arms and he was carrying her into his en suite before she could take another breath. She'd never get enough of this evidence of Ares's sheer strength.

He put her down but kept an arm around her as he turned on the spray. Then he pulled down his sweatpants and brought them both under the steaming hot water. He set about soaping up Cassie's body, hands running over her with the same thoroughness he'd used last night. Standing behind her, cupping her breasts and then reaching down with his hand to slide his fingers between her legs where she was already ready, and, by now, wide awake.

He moved his fingers in and out, bringing Cassie to the brink of orgasm, and then he disappeared, saying, 'One second…'

Cassie whimpered a little, and turned around, resting against the wall, to see Ares return, rolling a protective sheath onto his hard erection. He stepped back under the spray and lifted her up. 'Put your legs around me.'

She did, and then gasped when he took her with one deep thrust. It was fast and furious, Cassie climaxing around Ares's body, clinging to him as he found his own release, a guttural groan coming out of his mouth as his body jerked against her, and he dropped his head into her neck.

Cassie felt unaccountably tender, spearing his hair with her fingers and holding him as their breathing came back to normal and the spray fell around them.

A little later, Cassie stopped in her tracks when she saw what was waiting for them outside the front of the villa. Her mouth dropped open as she looked from where the two motorcycles were parked to Ares.

'Ares?'

He smiled a little ruefully. 'I know the coast road of Spetses isn't Route 66 but it'll have to do.'

She couldn't believe it. Emotion surged. She couldn't remember the last time someone had done something so thoughtful. She tried to hide how touched she was, gesturing to her clothes, jeans, a T-shirt and sneakers. 'Now I know why there was a strict dress code.'

Ares was similarly attired. He held out a lightweight leather jacket. 'The bike shop sent this over too.'

Cassie pulled it on. Even though it was warm, she knew the leather would be protective and regulate the heat. She zipped it up.

Ares put on his leather jacket and instantly looked like a rock star. He showed Cassie her bike but she was familiar with the model. She got onto the bike, settling into the seat. Ares came over with a helmet in his hands and looked at her, shaking his head a little. 'I must be crazy to let you do this.'

Cassie took the helmet out of his hands, putting it onto her head. She grinned at him and turned the bike on, feeling the powerful throttle. 'Too late now.'

Ares's jaw clenched but he put on his own helmet and got onto his bike, then he said over the sound of the two engines, 'This isn't a race, Cass, follow me.'

Cassie bit back her smile. 'Aye, aye, sir.'

They set off from the villa and Cassie dutifully followed Ares as he made his way to the main coastal road that encircled the island. Ares drove fast but he was safe. Cassie liked that he obviously didn't feel the need to show off. He was confident enough not to. It was very sexy. And she was happy to stay in his slipstream. She guessed he was giving her time to take in the scenery. After about thirty minutes, when she figured they must be halfway around the small island, Ares slowed down and indicated left.

He turned off the road and went down a dirt track. Cassie saw the sea sparkling in the distance, olive trees lining the track until they emerged onto the edge of a secluded sandy beach. Not just secluded. Totally empty.

Ares stopped his bike and got off. Cassie pulled up beside him and cut off her engine. It was blissfully quiet, just the sounds of the waves breaking on the shore and insects in the undergrowth.

Ares took off his helmet and then came over to her, lifting hers off. She shook her hair out and unzipped the jacket. She could get far too used to this attention and consideration as Ares helped her off the bike.

Her legs were a little wobbly from the adrenalin. The sea had never looked so inviting.

Ares said, 'I found this not long after I bought the villa. It's usually very private here.'

She noticed then that there were two saddlebags attached to his bike and he opened them now, taking out an array of items. Swimwear, towels, and she could see what looked like a packed lunch. A bottle of wine in a cooler.

Ares carried everything down to a shaded spot. He glanced at Cassie. 'I took the liberty of packing for you.'

Cassie raised a brow. 'Did you now?'

He grinned and handed her a white string bikini. His grin distracted her from pointing out that he could have chosen the white one-piece she'd also bought in Mykonos. She took a towel too, and used it to change into the bikini. When she was dressed she jogged towards the water, not able to resist the lure.

She turned back to face Ares, jogging backwards, and almost tripped over her feet when she saw him pulling up a black pair of swim shorts that hugged his muscular physique and left little to the imagination. Not that she needed any help picturing what he looked like naked.

He jogged towards her, easily catching up, and she saw the mischievous glint in his eye and put out her hands. 'Ares...don't you even dare to—' but it was too late. Before she knew what was happening, the world was upended when he threw her over his shoulder and brought her into the water, ignoring her squeals and protests, dunking them both beneath the foaming waves.

When Cassie surfaced, gasping and blinking seawater from her eyes, she felt so full of gratitude for Ares giving her this experience that she wrapped her arms around him and kissed him before he could see the emotions that were bubbling ever closer to the surface with every passing minute.

Later that day when the intense heat had gone out of the sun, belly full and skin sandblasted and sunblasted, Ares sat by Cassie, knees drawn up. She'd fallen asleep under the shade and his avid gaze tracked over her golden curves. Her hair was spread out, wild and tangled from the sea. Blonde streaks highlighted in the sun.

She'd been so delighted with the bike, and then the impromptu picnic. It had been rustic and basic, but she'd fallen on it like someone who'd just been handed a ten-course tasting menu in one of the world's top restaurants.

The fact that she would be at home in either scenario was not something Ares had ever expected when he'd seen her that first night on the dance floor in the tacky bar.

She'd admitted to him that she'd felt out of her depth and lonely that night. Then she'd asked, 'Are you really here with me because you want to be?' His insides had seized at the thought that she suspected he was only with her out of a sense of responsibility. She truly had no idea of the depth of his desire for her. A desire that wasn't waning. It was growing.

He'd pushed that disconcerting thought aside and said, 'If I didn't want to be with you, Cass, I'd have handed you over to one of my team days ago. I've never wanted a woman the way I want you.'

Ares would never usually be so honest with a lover but Cassie knew where they stood. They were both on very different trajectories. This was just a…moment.

He knew he was playing with fire indulging in this rare chemistry with her. She'd been innocent. She'd had a pretty sheltered upbringing. She might be displaying her sense of insecurity, but he had an uneasy suspicion that it wasn't her he should be worried about protecting, it was himself.

As if hearing his thoughts she stirred and cracked open one eye and smiled. He knew now which smiles were genuine, and which ones were the ones she pulled up out of habit, to project that sunny nature. To defend and protect herself.

In a bid to try and regain a sense of control, Ares came down over Cassie on his two hands and bent his head to hers, hovering over her mouth for a moment, prolonging the delicious feeling of anticipation, and then she wound her arms around his neck and pressed her mouth to his and Ares fell headlong into the kiss, pushing aside all niggles and reservations and a growing uneasy feeling that he'd lost control a long time ago.

The next day…

'Go on, hit me, show me your moves.'

Cassie smiled sweetly at Ares as she moved around him on nimble feet. 'You think I can't take you?'

Ares let out a huff of laughter. 'Oh, don't worry, I've learned that you are not to be underestimated.'

Cassie's smile got sweeter and then she aimed a few jabs at Ares's midriff area and when he looked down she pushed her palm up to connect with his chin. If any force had been behind it his head would have snapped back.

He looked at her. 'Not bad.'

Cassie—still moving—gave a modest shrug. They were in the gym of the villa, and Ares had put mats down on the ground. After a leisurely breakfast he'd said, 'Get your workout gear on—now's as good a time as any to prove to me you could have taken care of yourself with those guys.

'OK,' Ares said now, walking her back towards a corner of the room, 'say I've got you boxed in like those guys had in the bar. What do you do?'

He crowded her, putting his hands up over her head, caging her in. Cassie wanted to scowl. He had an unfair advantage of being far too distracting in a sleeveless T-shirt and shorts. All she could see were muscles.

'What if I told you I'm a lover, not a fighter?' she said, hoping to divert him. Not because she couldn't take him but because she'd prefer to lick his muscles than pummel them.

'Nope. Not going to work.'

Cassie rolled her eyes and as quick as lightning ducked out under Ares's arm and was standing behind him tapping him on the shoulder. He sighed and turned around, and Cassie lifted a knee as if to aim a kick at Ares's groin area but he caught her leg. Cassie twisted to dislodge his hold and feinted away.

She went back into the centre of the room and Ares came towards her, not smiling. It reminded her of how he'd been and how different he was now. It was enough to distract her so she wasn't ready when he quickly sidestepped her and caught her in a choke-hold against his chest, a strong arm across her neck.

She wriggled her behind against a strategic part of his anatomy and when he relaxed infinitesimally, she aimed a sharp elbow at his ribs and used his arm as leverage to get free, while hooking her foot behind one of his legs to send him sprawling to the ground.

Instantly she was down beside him, concerned. 'Ares? Are you OK? To be honest I didn't even think I'd be able to budge you.'

He looked up at her and then, capitalising on *her* distraction, executed a move that had her under him in seconds. He commented, 'You little minx, you knew exactly what you were doing distracting me.'

She grinned, relishing his weight on her. He came down even closer and she wrapped her arms around him.

He said, 'I don't need to worry about you, do I?'

Cassie was torn. After years of her feeling like an object to be moved around, Ares was the first person—after her brother—who really looked at her. Saw her. Was it so bad to want to be worried about? Because that meant someone cared.

But she swallowed that down and said, 'No, I guess you don't.'

He lowered his head and covered her mouth with his and it was only a discreet coughing that became forceful enough to notice that had reality intruding and Ares lifting his head.

He looked up and Cassie's face flamed when she followed his gaze and realised it was Declan and he was saying, 'Sorry to intrude, boss, but your phone kept ringing and apparently it's urgent.'

Ares levered himself up from Cassie and she put a hand over her face to try and hide. But Declan was gone and Ares was on the phone saying, 'Caius?'

Immediately Cassie got up in a fluid motion. Ares was looking at her and saying, 'Yes, she's here. Hang on.'

He handed her the phone and he was grim. Cassie's insides turned over. 'Caius? What's wrong? Are you OK?'

Her brother's voice on the other end of the line said, 'I'm fine, Cass, it's not me. But I think you need to get back to Sadat. Your absence has been noted and speculation is building as to where you are. Some are even saying you don't want to be queen.'

Cassie gasped. 'That's not true. I'd never let them down.'

'I know, Cass, but you should probably get back and calm things down.' After a beat he said, 'I'm sorry you didn't have longer.'

Cassie was looking at Ares, who was watching her. Suddenly it was overwhelming to think that life was rushing back at her. And that this was it. Emotion rose, swift and sharp. Tears pricked her eyes, she turned away and terminated the conversation with her brother and gathered herself before facing Ares again.

He spoke before she did. 'You have to get back to Sadat.'

She nodded and handed back his phone. 'I should have figured that my absence would cause some confusion.'

Ares came close and touched her jaw. 'It wasn't too much to ask to have some time to yourself, Cass. You'll be able to carve out time again—you're resourceful.'

She shrugged minutely and struggled to muster up a smile. She felt flat. Cold inside, because it would be time without Ares. 'I should start packing.'

'I'll arrange your transport.'

Cassie felt that like a physical blow. He probably couldn't wait to be free again. She also suddenly realised there was still so much she didn't know about him. Abruptly she asked, 'Where do you even live?'

Ares blinked. 'You want to know where I live?'

Cassie felt foolish now. 'I just…realised I didn't know that about you.' Maybe she didn't know because he didn't want her to know.

But he answered, 'New York, mainly. But I have this place here, an apartment in Athens and a place in London, too.'

'Oh.'

'Cass…?'

She shook her head. 'Sorry, I just…wasn't expecting this to end…like this.'

CHAPTER ELEVEN

Cassie's words hung in the air between them. She looked as if the wind had been knocked out of her. Deflated. Ares was numb. He recognised shock. He had to admit he too felt a little blindsided after Caius's wake-up call. It had been all too easy to pretend there wasn't a real world waiting for them to return. Ares to his security business and Cassie to become queen.

What Ares didn't tell Cassie was that when he'd heard Caius's voice on the phone he'd had an urge to cut the connection and say nothing. Because he'd known before his friend had even spoken that this…was over.

But it was for the best. This little…*moment* had been an indulgence Ares should never have allowed to happen. It had been weak. Selfish. He'd broken all of his own rules to not let anyone get close enough to hurt him the way his family had done with their callous disregard. He amended that now. Not his *family*. His parents. His siblings…he'd never given them a chance really and he was only fully recognising that fact after all this time.

Cassie with her questions had made him acknowledge that they'd been pawns as much as he had. It wasn't as if they'd had any power to help him when he'd been kidnapped. And yet he'd cut them off, excised them from his world. One of the tenets of his life, the thing he'd built so much around—not needing anyone, being a loner—no longer felt so solid. *Or attractive.*

His very justified sense of injury was no longer so justified and the woman in front of him, who he'd been moments away from taking here on the floor of the gym like a feral youth, was the cause of this introspection.

Ares didn't need introspection. His life had been perfectly fine. And the fact that her usual sunniness was dimmed…shouldn't matter a whit. He took a step back and tried not to let his eyes travel down over that perfectly honed body, encased in clinging Lycra. Her little midriff-baring vest top and the leggings that cupped her ass like a second skin.

And he definitely couldn't think about the surprising strength that had caught him off guard. But then, that just summed up his whole experience with her. Surprising at every turn.

His voice sounded gruff. 'You should get ready, Cass.'

'Yes. I should.'

Ares mentally pleaded with her to smile, light up again, but she just turned and walked out of the room looking dejected and he had to push down the surge of protectiveness he felt at the thought of her facing everything ahead of her alone.

She wasn't his. And she wouldn't be alone for long. She'd find a husband and carve out a better existence than she'd seen from her parents. He knew she would.

A short time later they were at the same private airfield in Athens where, just days ago, Cassie had evaded her security team and headed off on a solo adventure. Everything felt different though. She was different. She felt as if a layer of herself had been sloughed away and a new layer of skin had formed. She felt more sober. Less inclined to smile for the sake of it.

She also felt heartbroken and she wanted to hate Ares for making her fall for him. But she couldn't. The thought of going back to Sadat and becoming queen wasn't daunting. What was daunting was the fact that she had to do it without Ares, and that he wouldn't be by her side. Ever again.

She was standing in a small vestibule now, eyes hidden behind sunglasses, as Ares spoke to officials to arrange her flight home. This was it. This was where he was going to say goodbye and then it would be as if these last few magical days had never happened—

'OK, let's go.' Ares had taken her arm and was leading her out of the small room onto the tarmac and walking towards the sleek jet.

Cassie tried to get her brain to catch up with her mouth. 'Where are you going?'

He glanced down. 'With you.'

Cassie's heart skipped a beat. 'What do you mean? Aren't you staying here? Or heading back to America?'

'I will be, but not just yet. We're making one stop before I let you go back to Sadat.' They were climbing the steps to the plane now. An air steward was waiting for them, smiling. Cassie smiled back and it slipped off her face as soon as they were in the plush cabin.

'Ares...?'

He was walking through the cabin checking the

space and turned around. He was wearing jeans and a dark shirt, sleeves rolled up, buttons undone revealing the top of his powerful chest.

He looked over Cassie's head to the steward. 'OK, we're good to go.'

Cassie folded her arms and cocked one hip to the side, eyes narrowed on Ares. 'Want to tell *me* what's going on?'

He reached for her and tugged her to a seat. He took the one opposite and as the plane started to move he said, 'Buckle up.'

'Not until you tell me where we're going.'

He looked at her and then reached across the divide and slotted her safety belt together. Cassie tried swatting his hands away but the sensation of his hands near her belly and legs made her clumsy.

She was tempted to undo her belt to have him do it up again but resisted the childish urge. Eventually under her death glare, as the plane gathered speed and lifted into the air, Ares said, 'We're making a little stop en route to Sadat.'

'I've gathered that much,' Cassie said dryly. 'Where exactly?'

'Florence.'

'Florence,' she echoed, struggling to understand.

Ares looked at his watch. 'Yes, it's a little over two hours.'

And then it hit her. Florence. Her insides turned to jelly. 'Are we going to the Uffizi gallery?'

Ares nodded. He said a little gruffly, 'I wanted to give you one more experience from your list.'

Cassie shook her head, overcome. 'Ares...' She undid her belt and launched herself out of her seat and into Ares's lap. His arms went around her and he commented, 'I don't think we're technically cruising yet, so you're in breach of safety procedure.'

Cassie knew that if the plane went down in that moment, as long as she was in Ares's arms, she wouldn't care. She felt like crying but she pushed it down and grinned at Ares and wriggled a little on his lap. 'I've got a new addition to the list.'

His eyes turned molten. 'I'm sure we can accommodate late additions to the list.'

A short time later, when they were safely cruising, Ares made good on fulfilling Cassie's wish list. They were in the bedroom at the back of the plane and Cassie was biting down on her hand to avoid screaming out loud.

Ares's head was between her legs, his hands holding her thighs apart, and his tongue was engaged in sending her spiralling into a paroxysm of pleasure so intense it was almost painful. She had her other hand on his head, fingers tangled in his thick hair, simultaneously pulling him closer and pushing him away.

When Ares finally lifted his mouth from her clasping body, he was smiling. He moved up her body, stopping to press kisses to her belly and then enclosing a nipple in his hot mouth, teasing the sharp point with his teeth.

He lifted his head. 'You've now been inititated into the mile high club.'

Cassie was still reeling from the intensity of the orgasm. A short sharp dart of jealousy struck her to think that this wasn't Ares's initiation into the club. But then this was the last time they'd— She reached for him to stop her mind going down that path.

'Kiss me, Ares.'

He obliged, with a deep explicit kiss. Cassie spread her legs wider and reached down, wrapping her hand around him, stroking his erection, making him stop the kiss and hiss. His cheeks were flushed. 'Cass… you're killing me.'

'I want you inside me. Now.' She sounded so bossy. He'd turned her into someone greedy.

He found protection and rolled it onto his length. Cassie already felt the pain of regret and separation and as he entered her, it tinged this lovemaking with an unbearable sense of poignancy. This time was different. Eyes connected, Cassie couldn't have looked away even if she'd wanted to. When the climax broke over her she didn't even care that Ares would see the moisture in her eyes, she couldn't stop it.

He chased his own completion, his body jerking against hers, and she lamented the barrier stopping his seed from spilling into her. She felt it on a very primal level, that she was meant to be with this man. In every way. But she bit into his shoulder to stop herself from saying the words that wouldn't be welcome.

And yet, as she gripped him close to her, legs wrapped around his back, hearts slowing down in unison, she desperately tried to tell herself that it was just hormones and amazing sex, that she couldn't possibly have fallen for this haunted lone wolf.

But she knew she had and that this would be her cross to bear for ever. She wanted to hate him for that. But she couldn't even do that.

'Wear this.'

Cassie took the baseball cap Ares handed her, and put it on her head. She'd tied her hair back into a bun. They were in a chauffeur-driven SUV being taken from the airport to the museum. It felt strange to be back in a busy city again. Jarring.

She still felt a little over-sensitised after the plane. She'd noticed that, after making love, Ares had washed and dressed and left her to do the same, saying something about making calls.

Since they'd landed he'd been solicitous but was clearly drawing back. Putting boundaries back in place. Boundaries that had never really been there. And it felt so wrong. Cassie wanted to stamp her foot and demand he look at her. She smiled at herself mockingly—exactly how a petulant princess would behave.

They pulled to a stop on the banks of the Arno river, in front of the imposing building that housed the famous galleries. It rose up, dominating the landscape. Cassie still couldn't quite believe Ares had thought of this.

He was out of the SUV now and holding open the door, looking around. She saw him nod to someone in dark nondescript clothing getting out of another vehicle and asked, 'Who is that?'

'Your security. They've been replaced by a new team, vetted by me.'

Feeling desperate at this evidence of her real world

encroaching ever more steadily, she said, 'But you can protect me.'

He took her hand, and said, 'I'm not taking any chances.'

Cassie couldn't help her bruised heart from wishing he meant *not taking any chances* because he cared for her, but she knew he was just doing his job. Before they took a step towards the galleries he faced her and said, 'When we're finished here I'm going to hand you back over to your team and you are not to try to evade them again, understand me?'

He sounded so stern that Cassie looked at him and said meekly, 'Yes.'

Still holding her hand, he led her into the main gallery. Ares had organised the tickets ahead of time and so they were able to join the throngs of other tourists, all drinking in the spectacular art. But already Cassie knew she'd have to come again because this trip was ruined by the distraction of knowing that these were her last few moments with Ares.

So, greedily, she clung to his hand. Not that he was pulling away. And she revelled in standing close to him. Smelling him guiltily like someone with a scent kink, rather than taking in the spine-tingling beauty of Botticelli's *The Birth of Venus*.

As they moved from one gallery to the next Cassie asked him, 'Where will you go from here? Back to New York?'

A muscle ticced in his jaw. 'No, not straight away. I'll go to London. I have some meetings lined up there.'

She squeezed his hand. 'I think you should contact your brother and sisters, Ares, let them in.'

He glanced down at her, a different man from the one who'd forced his way onto her boat. 'Like the way I let you in?'

But had he? Really? She forced a smile. 'Exactly, what could possibly go wrong?'

He looked a little arrested when she said that but then people jostled them from behind and his expression cleared and they continued moving with the flow of tourists.

After a while he said, 'I'll see.'

Cassie bumped him with her shoulder. 'No man is an island, Ares. Not even you, or my brother.'

She realised with a pang that they'd come full circle. They were back at the main entrance again. She wondered desperately if she could pretend that she hadn't noticed and go around the galleries again but Ares was saying, 'Your security team are waiting.'

She saw the sleek silver SUV and the guards. They looked stony. No doubt under orders not to mess up. Cassie felt sick. Nauseous. Desperate. She couldn't walk away from Ares without telling him…

She tightened her grip on his hand and looked up at him. 'Ares.'

Ares steeled himself and looked down. Cassie's upturned face was visible from under the lip of the hat and he felt as though he knew every curve and dip and line as well as his own. Better.

'Cass, you need to go—'

She shook her head. 'No, I need to say something first.' She looked effortlessly regal in that moment, even in her trousers and silk T-shirt and flat shoes, designed to blend in with the crowd. Her cross-body bag. Who'd he been kidding? She would never blend in. She was a queen.

Not his queen.

'Ares, do you really believe it's not possible to have more? Something real? Love?'

Ares's gut clenched hard. For the first time in his life it wasn't so easy to dismiss. Because something had changed in him. Some chink had opened up and illuminated a space for wanting something he'd never wanted before. And it was her fault. He hardened his heart. When had it become so damned soft?

The moment you saw her dancing in that bar, and you know it.

He shook his head. 'I'm sure it exists for some, maybe even for you, some day. But not for me.' His stubbornness was like a hard piece of granite inside him. And there was something else he was too cowardly to admit to. *Fear.*

Cassie glanced over at where her people were waiting and back to Ares, eyes wide and beseeching. 'You do know you deserve to be happy, Ares? These last few days…it's possible to have that. All the time.'

The notion that they could really have that glorious togetherness without the world getting in the way was so…huge that Ares shut it down. She was talking nonsense. It had just been a moment.

If she left now then she'd have a chance of retaining that bright nature, but if Ares did what his dark soul really wanted to do, which was to spirit her away and keep her for himself, then he *would* dim that light for ever. He couldn't give her what she wanted. *Deserved*.

Something had been irreparably broken in him when he'd been so traumatised at a young age. He'd lost a sense of childish optimisim and innocence. He'd cut himself off to protect himself and it was too late to change that now.

'Ares, I love you.'

She spoke the words and it was too late to demand she take them back. They existed. The chink was cracking open and Ares's very foundations were crumbling to pieces. *No*. She didn't mean it. He was not lovable. He would ruin her. A self-preserving protective reflex snapped into action.

'No,' he said fiercely. 'You don't. You think you do. It's been intense, that's all. You'll meet someone far better than me, Cass. Someone worthy of being your king.'

'*You* are worthy, Ares Drakos. I don't want anyone else. I won't. Will you?'

Ares looked at her and pushed down the ache in his chest and forced ice into his veins as he said as coolly as he could, 'Of course I will. Nothing lasts for ever.'

It doesn't, he told himself even more fiercely even as he felt as if a part of himself was dying inside. He still wanted her, that was all. It would fade.

He saw the way she went pale and a light went out of her eyes. He told himself it was a good thing, because she would get over this and him. He needed her to hate him a little. So she would go and get on with her life and not look back. She was a queen. He had no claim to her.

'You need to go, princess. They're waiting.' He

needed her to go. Now. Because the longer she stood there looking stricken, the more conflicted he felt.

But then he saw the way her eyes flashed at his use of *princess* and some colour came back into her cheeks. She took a step back and he saw her security team looking around, making ready.

'No doubt you're right, nothing lasts for ever.' She smiled but it was brittle. 'I'm just not as experienced in these matters as you. Goodbye, Ares.'

Oof. Ares felt the words like a blow. He deserved that. He'd made her hate him. Good. She turned and was walking away, through the crowds to the discreet SUV parked at the kerb. And then she was getting inside and the door was closing and the security guy jumped into the front and the car was pulling away and disappearing into the traffic. And just like that…she was gone and at that moment the sun went behind a massive cloud.

London, two days later

Ares was watching the news, specifically a report from Sadat Sur Mer about Crown Princess Cassandra and how she'd appeared in public for the first time in days to allay the rumours and speculation that all was not well in the palace of Mansur de Roche.

She was greeting a crowd, wearing a simple but smart blue dress, colour-toned to match her shoes. Hair up and sleek. Oozing regal elegance. It made him think of her in that white silk dress she'd worn for dinner, in Spetses. How she'd said, *'I'll never get to wear a dress like this at home.'*

She was bending down now to greet a little girl who

was shy. Cassie's smile was so infectious that the little girl reached out to touch Cassie's cheek and Cassie took her hand and spoke to her, making the girl giggle.

Ares didn't even realise he'd put a hand to his chest to alleviate an ache. She would be an amazing mother. And queen. The people clearly adored her.

'Ares... *Ares...?*'

Scowling at the interruption, Ares turned to find his assistant in the doorway. She looked at her watch. 'Your flight to New York is ready and waiting at the airfield. The driver is downstairs.'

It was time to move on.

Sadat Sur Mer, The Palace

Cassie opened the button at the top of the blue dress she'd worn for the walkabout. She felt constricted. She wanted to strip naked and dive into cool blue waters. Already, it felt like a dream—her Greek odyssey—and she hated that it was fading.

At night she dreamt of it though, and him, and it was clear and vivid. She'd woken with tears on her cheeks this morning. Pathetic.

There was a knock on her office door and she scooped Zoe up into her arms. The dog licked Cassie's face just as Pierre walked in and he couldn't hide his delicate shudder of disapproval.

He had a file under his arm, and Cassie already knew what it was. The dreaded prospective husbands.

'If these are the same as when I left I'm not interested. None of them were suitable.'

Pierre stopped in his tracks. Cassie knew she was

different since she'd come back. Less meek and unsure. Less amenable. But in a fair and firm way. Less smiley. Pierre said, 'No, these are new candidates.' He sent her a glance, not sure how to deal with this version of the crown princess.

Cassie sat down and said, 'You can leave it there. I'll have a look later.'

'But—'

She looked at Pierre and he stopped talking. 'Thank you.'

He cleared his throat. 'There's just one more thing, Your Highness.'

'Yes?'

'The pre-coronation ball.'

'Yes?' The ball would be held the night before the coronation, and would be a chance to welcome all of the VIP guests who'd been invited from all over the world. It would be Cassie's first properly formal event as almost queen. Her last as a crown princess. The eyes of the world would be on her. She instinctively covered her inner wrist where she'd had the tattoo done. So far she'd manaaged to keep it hidden from view. But Ares had been right, someone would inevitably notice it and her twin sister would no longer belong just to her.

Pierre was saying now, 'We feel that the ball would be a good opportunity to also invite any possible future consorts...so if you should find someone suitable among the new suggestions, let me know and we'll invite them.'

Cassie's insides roiled nauseously at the thought of even looking at another man. She swallowed it down.

She was a queen. She didn't get to have much of a choice in this matter. 'Fine, thank you, Pierre.'

When Pierre had left, Cassie put Zoe down on the floor and opened up the folder. This was her life now, she had to suck it up.

Much to her dismay, when she looked at the candidates there were at least three who she couldn't find any reason not to consider. One of these men might one day soon become her husband. She battled the resurgence of the nausea and picked up the phone, saying to Pierre, 'I have the names of three of the candidates. Are you ready?'

Pierre tripped over his words, he was so obviously ecstatic. 'Yes, yes, please, Your Highness, I'm ready.'

She rattled off the names and put the phone down. There. Her fate was now all but sealed. Within two weeks she'd be Queen of Sadat and there would be a marriage announcement.

As much as Cassie was genuinely looking forward to taking her place among the kings and queens of Sadat on her coronation day, she felt acutely lonely at the thought of doing it alone.

Even though Caius would be there, at least. The public appeared to be ready to forgive his lack of royal bloodline. And he would know what she was going through.

But the one person who she would really want to see there wouldn't be anywhere near Sadat. Ares. She hated him all over again in that moment for making her fall for him. For making her wish for his solid presence. For his beautiful body. The way he made her feel. The way he saw her.

But of course she didn't hate him at all. She loved him. The bastard.

CHAPTER TWELVE

Ten days later...

THE STREETS OF New York were too busy. Loud. Jarring. Ares had done his best to re-acclimatise since his return but the place he'd called home for years now felt like an alien planet.

Had it always been so grimy? So grey? So...closed in with tall buildings? Everyone seemed so much in a rush. So desperate. No one smiled.

A few days before when Ares had been leaving his office building after his final meeting, he'd smiled at his security guy. Who hadn't smiled back. Ares had realised he was smiling like a loon, in some attempt to be polite, or *nice*, and the man had been frowning at him as if he had two heads. 'You OK, Mr Drakos?'

Ares had promptly broken out in a cold sweat. What the hell was wrong with him? Smiling at people and expecting the same in return? He was in a city where that could be considered slightly homicidal behaviour. He'd once been a fully signed up member of the make-no-eye-contact, unsmiling public.

Before he'd met *her*. So now he was scowling as he pushed open the doors to his offices. He'd just taken a meeting with a new client in a hotel downtown and had walked all the way back, feeling too restless to sit in a car or take the subway.

He barely noticed the same security guard behind the desk, too busy fighting off memories and images.

He kept seeing Cassie disappear into the back of the SUV, the door closing behind her. The reality that he would never see her again, except on a TV screen or perhaps somehow through Caius, was like a burr under his skin. He'd had a dream the night before, of watching her get married to some faceless chinless prince. Beaming at him. Confetti. Kissing him.

Ares had woken in a sweat, heart pounding. He did smile now as the elevator carried him up to the penthouse office but it was grim. It was small comfort that nightmares of boats had been replaced with nightmares of Cassie with another man.

He got to his office—empty because his staff had long finished for the day. It was late. But he was still too restless to go back to his empty apartment nearby. It was on evenings like this he would have sought out the company of someone like Caius, but Caius was in Sadat, because the coronation was happening any day now.

Everything seemed to circle back to Cassie.

He could call up a woman. Sex. Surely that would alleviate this building sense of panic?

But the thought of a woman who wasn't Cassie... made his insides churn. Irritated with himself and his inability to just...settle back into his life, Ares poured himself a slug of whiskey and turned on the TV.

A news channel came on and as if the universe was

intent on punishing him, or torturing him, it showed images of Sadat Sur Mer and the reporter was gushing about the excitement of the upcoming coronation as images of Cassie proliferated in the background.

Cassie as a baby, then as a small cherubic child, and a slightly gawky teenager with braces and now... His heart ached. As a beautiful young woman ready to step into her own power. And what power that was. She was magnificent.

Then an image of a man came on the screen. Some blond pretty man. With a toothy smile. Ares turned up the volume as the reporter said breathlessly, 'Prince Stefan has been invited to the pre-coronation ball tomorrow night. It's widely rumoured that after the coronation there will be an announcement of nuptials...'

Ares muted the sound, unable to listen to any more. He could see that man and Cassie together. They'd make a photogenic couple. They'd have even more photogenic kids. Royal kids.

Something hot roared to life inside Ares, deep down, rising up. Jealousy. No. More than jealousy. *She was his.* Not that insipid man's. She'd told him she loved him.

Desperation replaced the panic. He couldn't let this just...happen. He needed to see her. Look in her eyes. See the moment when she'd show regret for what she'd said because she couldn't have possibly meant it. And then maybe he could walk away and feel some peace. Well, not peace, he'd never feel that again, but some measure of being able to get on with his life. If he knew for sure that she didn't want him.

Ares's heart pounded at the thought that he might look into her eyes and see something else entirely.

He should leave her be. But it was too late. She'd melted something inside him. Rewired him. Made him want…connection. A chance to strive for another kind of existence. Happiness. *Love.* He knew he loved her. He'd known it as soon as her happiness had become paramount to him.

Before he could overthink it, Ares dug out his phone and dialled his assistant, issuing instructions. After a few minutes his assistant said, 'Sorry, boss, it looks like tomorrow is the earliest I can get you out of here.'

Ares cursed. It would have to do. 'Book it.' On his way back out of his office building Ares stopped in his tracks by the security guard's desk. The man looked up. Ares said, 'You know, it wouldn't kill you to smile once in a while.' And then he walked out. Smiling.

Cassie's face hurt from smiling so much. She'd never felt less like smiling in her life. And her hand ached from greeting all of the dignitaries. And her feet ached in the high heels.

She was in full crown princess uniform in her midnight-blue silk dress with voluminous silk skirts overlaid with tulle. The strapless bodice was boned, tucking her in and allowing only an acceptable amount of cleavage. Family heirloom jewels, sapphires and diamonds, glinted at her ears, neck and wrist.

She wore a white sash across her dress, adorned with ceremonial ribbons and brooches to signify her country's glorious military history and its independence.

Her hair was up and teased into a complicated chignon and she wore a diamond tiara that was weighing heavier and heavier on her head.

Unfortunately Caius hadn't been able to help her with this. He was somewhere in the background, easing himself back into acceptability. At least he was here, even if not by her side. It had been good to see him again.

She was firmly shutting out the face of the one person she *really* would like to see but the prospect of him appearing in the endless line-up bowing before her was about as likely as a unicorn materialising.

Her insides tensed as she recognised the next person. Crown Prince Stefan de Wilhelm of Danzerra, a small monarchy in central Europe. A prime candidate to be her husband. She sensed the hush that went up around them as everyone watched to see them meet for the first time.

He bowed before her and Cassie noticed a bald patch on the top of his head. She had the bizarre urge to giggle and she knew it was hysteria. He straightened and smiled. She felt sorry for her unkind observation. He was a perfectly handsome and potentially good candidate for marriage.

She let him take her hand. 'Thank you so much for coming, Prince—'

Suddenly there was a commotion near them and Cassie looked away from the prince to see a tall man bearing down on them, with a visibly distressed Pierre running to catch up and several of her security guards.

Ares. *No.* She had to be dreaming. Hallucinating, Brought on by the exhaustion of this interminable line-up. She blinked. But when she opened her eyes again Ares Drakos was now standing beside the prince.

Cassie was struck by the almost comical disparity in *everything*. Their size, looks, charisma. And then she realised...this wasn't a dream. Ares Drakos was really standing here, in... She looked him up and down. In worn jeans and a loose shirt. Hair wild. Was his beard bigger? He looked deliciously scruffy and achingly sexy and thoroughly out of place. And yet so *perfect*.

Pierre pushed forward, sweating. 'I'm so sorry, Your Highness, this man somehow managed to get through the security cordon—we'll have him removed—'

But then another voice joined in. 'Ares? What the hell are you doing here?'

It was Caius. But neither Cassie nor Ares looked away from each other. She just asked, 'What *are* you doing here?'

She was in shock. Numb. But she could feel sensation returning and it was like when the numbness of icy cold retreated and the heat returned painfully. She realised she'd been cold since she'd walked away from him. After baring her heart to him. After his rejection.

She strove to not let herself melt. This could mean nothing at all. She hated him. *She loved him.*

'Ares?' The silence was so profound around them but Cassie barely noticed.

'I needed to see you. To look you in the eye when I asked you...'

'Asked me what?'

'If you really meant it. What you said in Florence?'

Cassie felt something bloom inside her. Hope. She arched a brow. 'You mean when I said I loved you?'

A gasp went up around them.

Ares said, 'Yes, when you said you loved me. Did you mean it?'

How could he not see it shining out of her like a bright light? She nodded. 'Yes, I meant it. I love you, Ares.'

He stepped forward and put his hands around her face, tipping it up. Cassie felt the tiara slide a little precariously and grinned. He was unravelling her already and she couldn't care less.

'I love you, Cassie, but I felt selfish. How can I ask you to be mine when you need someone who'll be so much more suited?'

Cassie put her hands on Ares's, sliding her fingers between his. 'I don't need some prince.'

Neither of them noticed the splutter of indignation coming from the prince who was still standing there.

Cassie continued, 'I need *you*. But I know it's a lot to ask. You'd be giving up a lot...for me.'

Ares shook his head, fervent. 'I would give up my life for you.'

There was a distinct sigh from the crowd.

Ares went on, 'My life means nothing without you. I want it all, Cassie. I want to give you everything you've ever dreamed of and I want to be happy. You've shown me that it's possible. With you, I know I can do anything.'

'We'd have to have children...if we can. They'll bear my name.'

Ares's eyes gleamed. 'They'll have the bravest and most magnificent mother in the world, why wouldn't they bear your name?'

He said, 'I'm sorry that it took me a few days to figure this out. I fell for you the moment I saw you in that bar, determined to have an experience.'

Cassie blushed. 'I adore you, Ares. You see me. I've never really had that, except for Caius and he doesn't really count.'

There was another splutter of indignation from Caius's direction but Cassie went on, 'I can't take on this role without a real partner. I'd hoped for respect and companionship but after meeting you... I want so much more. The thought of becoming queen and settling for someone else...has nearly killed me.'

Ares's eyes looked suspiciously bright. 'I'm so sorry I let you go, Cass.'

He gathered her to him and kissed her, deep and thoroughly. When he pulled back she said breathlessly, 'Don't be sorry... I don't think either of us were expecting this...'

They looked at each other dreamily for a long moment, until Caius's voice broke the intense silence. 'Will someone please tell me what the hell is going on?'

Ares took Cassie's hand in his. She was beaming. Sore facial muscles forgotten. Tiara askew. She tore her gaze from Ares's and looked around. The great and good of the world staring at them. The prince's mouth was gaping open like a stunned fish. Pierre looked as if he was on the verge of a heart attack. And her brother was murderous. She'd never been happier.

Ares said, 'Can we go somewhere private?'

She looked back at him and her insides liquefied

with desire. She nodded. But then she winced when she took a step and her feet protested in the new shoes.

Ares was immediately concerned. 'What is it?'

'Sore feet.'

Within two seconds he'd swept her up into his arms. One of her shoes fell to the floor. Ares looked at Caius and said, 'I know you want to break every bone in my body but the fact is that I love your sister and I'm going to go somewhere now to ask her if she'll marry me. If that's OK with you?'

Caius looked as if he were about to explode but then he looked at Cassie and he must have seen her incandescent happiness because after a long moment his features softened. He said, 'Aw, hell. Go. Not with my blessing, it's too soon for that. But just go.'

As Ares swept Cassie out of the ornate ballroom and away from the hundreds of guests she could have sworn she heard Pierre ask Caius, 'Is there any chance he's related to the Greek royal family at all? Any royal family?'

In the end it didn't matter that Ares was not related to any royal family. Their moment had gone viral around the world and everyone had fallen in love with Ares and Cassie and their love story.

Pierre hadn't had a hope of standing in their way. Neither had Caius, who eventually did come to terms with his best friend becoming his brother-in-law.

Cassie had been crowned queen, with Ares close by her side at all times. Soon afterwards their engagement had been announced by the palace to no one's surprise.

EPILOGUE

Five years later—Sadat Sur Mer, The Palace

CASSIE HAD WORKED hard to dissolve a lot of the old structures standing between the royal family and the people of Sadat and now the palace was regularly humming with community activities, visiting tourists, and the family were involved in day-to-day life in a way that no other royal family had ever been.

But here in this wing, their private wing, there were no intrusions. Cassie walked from her office across the hall to where Ares's office was. He'd moved Drakos Security to Sadat over the past few years and it had now become a hub for the latest security technology and best defence systems in the world.

His new office building was in the centre of the town, an architecturally cutting-edge structure, but Ares liked to use his office at the palace because his main priority was as the king consort. And husband. And now, father.

Cassie stopped in the doorway and chuckled at the sight. Ares was lying back on a soft couch, with two smaller bodies sprawled on top of him, all of them snoring gently. A book was strewn to the side.

They'd had twins three years ago. Isabella and Calliope. Bella and Calli. Bella was the firstborn, and a reference to Belle, Cassie's beloved lost sister. They were identical twins, taking after both parents. They had blonde hair but Cassie could see it was already turning darker, and they had the dark eyes of their father.

She put a hand to her distended belly. Their little boy was due in a couple of months. The girls' suggestions for names so far had ranged from Calli's favourite thing in the world—Unicorn! To Bella's suggestion—Baby Brotha!

Since the arrival of the children, Ares had reached out to his own siblings and they'd finally connected. It had been a happy reunion. It had been easier with his sisters, but Ares had also met his brother, Axel, and was making plans to work with him, providing security for Drakos Shipping, and so he was returning to the fold on his terms.

As often as they could, Cassie and Ares went back to the villa on Spetses and revelled in a few days of isolation and freedom. Sometimes alone when they could manage it, sometimes with the girls.

They updated their wish lists all the time and Ares was extremely assiduous in making sure they ticked off all the items. On their honeymoon to the south of Spain, Ares had taken Cassie horse-riding on Adalucian horses on the beach at dawn.

Motorcycling along Route 66 still had to be done but Cassie was sure they'd get around to it, some day.

Caius had gone on his own journey to find happiness but that was not Cassie's story to tell.

Much later, when the girls had been put to bed and

their nanny was on the night shift, Cassie moved against Ares. His heat and strength and love surrounded her as they moved together in a dance as old as time.

His hand was splayed on her belly and another hand cupped her breast as he took her from behind, thrusting deep inside and taking them both on a languorous sensual dance.

He put his mouth close to her ear. 'Remind me when we have to stop having sex?'

Cassie huffed a laugh. 'Never…never stop.'

And then she cried out as her climax broke over her, and Ares gripped her tight as he followed her. They lay in sated bliss for long moments and then Ares pulled the sheet up and curled himself around Cassie's body, arms stretching around her, to her belly, a hand over their son.

'Thank you,' he said into her ear, sleepily.

Cassie smiled and lifted his hand, pressing a kiss to it. 'Thank *you*, for coming back to me.'

'Always and for ever,' promised Ares.

* * * * *

*Did you fall in love with
Bodyguard's Royal Temptation?
Then make sure to check out the next instalment in
the Royal House of Sadat duet, coming soon!
In the meantime, explore these other
stories by Abby Green!*

The Heir Dilemma
On His Bride's Terms
Rush to the Altar
Billion-Dollar Baby Shock
Bride of Betrayal

Available now!

KEEPING HIS ENEMY CLOSE

KATE HEWITT

MILLS & BOON

CHAPTER ONE

'I'M SO SORRY, ASHLEY.'

Ashley Woodward's stomach clenched with nerves as she took several deep breaths, trying to stem the tide of panic that was rushing through her in an icy river of dread.

'I don't shoot the messenger, Ruth,' she managed with a decidedly wobbly smile. Ruth Boxall had been with her from the beginning, when Ashley had been determined to take the wreckage of her father's business and turn it into something trustworthy and true. Ruth had believed in her even when Ashley hadn't been able to believe in herself, and together they'd built a company that had gone from admittedly small success to slightly *less* small success...until now.

'I don't understand why,' she said for what had to be at least the tenth time as she opened her laptop and started clicking on various emails, scanning the lines she'd already read too many times, the words branded onto her brain, her heart—scars that would never, ever heal, because she was about to lose everything she'd worked for, and she didn't even know *why*.

Buying shares for nearly twice the amount they're worth... Galletti Finance is offering... Too good to refuse... I'm sorry...

How was this happening?

Ashley tasted the acidic tang of bile on her tongue, and she forced herself to swallow, even though her stomach was churning so hard she was afraid she might lose the cup of black coffee and breakfast bar she'd forced down at five o'clock this morning—and then only because her stomach had felt so empty, she'd thought it might eat itself.

She'd barely slept or eaten in thirty-six hours, since Galletti Finance, a company she'd never even heard of before, had swooped in and started buying up shares in Infinite Innovations—the company she'd founded—just after it had gone public. What was meant to have been the pinnacle of her achievement and aspiration had ended up being a surreal nightmare, as the company she'd poured her life's blood and sweat into was swiftly devoured by a faceless magnate.

Had she really held her head up high through the years of scandal and shame, been knocked back time and again and finally found her courage and clung to it—only to surrender to a stranger who seemed to be targeting her for no reason that Ashley could possibly discern? It was utterly intolerable and yet, according to Ruth, there was nothing she could do but let it happen.

'It might not be as bad as you think,' her right-hand woman said now in a tone of quiet calm that had reassured Ashley so many times since she'd started Infinite Innovations.

Capable and no-nonsense, a former housewife turned chief financial officer, Ruth Boxall had been the steady pair of hands Ashley had desperately needed when she'd started out on this road. She'd tried to found her own company at only twenty-seven years old, with very little experience and too much baggage that came with the Woodward name, baggage that Ruth understood all too well. Without Ruth Boxall, Ashley would never have had the confidence to take that wretched name and make it known again, this time for championing something that mattered, something she believed in passionately—not that it made any difference now.

Because now, just when she should have been celebrating that victory, instead she faced the most stinging defeat. Galletti Finance was on the cusp of owning controlling shares in Infinite Innovations. The last three days had been a rollercoaster of learning about the takeover, talking to various lawyers and business consultants to try to stop it as it steamrolled ahead and then coming to this point: the absolute nadir. Galletti Finance was about to walk into the building and claim it as its own.

At least, Nico Galletti, the CEO, was. He had ordered her to a meeting at nine o'clock this morning. It was eight-thirty now, and Ashley was not at her best. She hadn't showered in nearly twenty-four hours, she definitely hadn't slept and she felt exhausted, emotional and hopeless. Not the best state of mind to be in when she was probably about to be fired.

'How might it not be as bad?' Ashley asked as she closed her laptop and stood up, pacing the confines of the small office she'd taken when she'd become CEO. It was a far cry from the offices Woodward Investments had enjoyed—sixteen whole floors of prime real estate, her father having had an enormous corner office with soaring skylights, a private fitness centre and countless other luxury amenities. All of it had been liquidated long ago, along with just about every other asset her father had owned, both personally and commercially. By the time her father had finished with the company, there had been practically nothing left but its name—and the daughter he'd left behind to pick up the pieces as best as she could.

'Well, hostile takeovers don't necessarily mean the acquiring company fires all and sundry,' Ruth explained as she lowered herself into the chair in front of Ashley's desk with a small, encouraging smile. 'Sometimes,' she continued, 'They just want to keep it running as smoothly and efficiently as it has been. Nothing necessarily needs to change.'

'Do you really believe that?' Ashley asked. It was a slender thread of hope that she was desperate to cling to, but somehow she couldn't make herself. Maybe because the worst had happened in her life so many times before, and she'd long ago learned it was better to be prepared for it. Or maybe because of the way Galletti Finance had targeted her little company so relentlessly the very second that it could. Something about that felt...deliberately malevolent. But why?

That was the question that kept hammering through her brain: why target Infinite? Yes, it had just gone public, but it was still comparatively modest, quietly doing good and making an admittedly negligible profit without attracting much notice. There had recently been a glowing article in a prominent business magazine, but it hadn't made the cover, and was that really all it took to attract the circling sharks?

Or at least one shark in particular: Nico Galletti.

Ashley had looked him up three days ago, when Ruth had first remarked upon the flurry of activity among Infinite's shareholders. There had been surprisingly few photos of the man online, considering how rich and successful he was, and most of them were blurry paparazzi snaps from a distance, when he was leaving a building or getting into a car.

Nico Galletti was notoriously private. He'd also seemingly emerged from nowhere a mere six years ago, playing the stock market and encountering wild success. Now, with his own extensive portfolio of financial and property interests, he was known for taking financial risks, for being completely calm and in control even when the stock market wobbled or plunged...and for being utterly ruthless.

Infinite Innovations wasn't the first company he'd taken over and, while Ashley had taken some comfort from the fact that he'd kept employees in place at other institutions, it still didn't give her a lot of hope. There had been zero communication from anyone at Galletti Finance until this morning: not a single assurance that jobs would be retained, that employees didn't need to worry or that things would continue to run smoothly. The silence had felt ominous, like a thundercloud moving ever closer, the storm about to break right over her head.

Still, she told herself, she could face her imminent demise head-on, with her shoulders back and her chin up. She wouldn't cower or cringe, bow or scrape—not again, not ever and not for anyone. Not even Nico Galletti.

'I think I need to brush my teeth,' she announced. 'And probably apply some deodorant. I have a feeling I might smell.'

'Well, that's one way to offend Nico Galletti,' Ruth replied wryly, and Ashley rolled her eyes.

'I think I'd rather offend him by telling him he's a ruthless bully,' she replied. 'But somehow I don't think that will be a good bargaining tactic.'

'At this point, I'm not sure what would be.' Ruth hesitated, a frown marring her forehead. 'It's a mystery to me why he'd target such a relatively small company. Do you think he might be interested in our inventions?'

'A secret science geek?' Ashley surmised hopefully as she rooted around in her desk drawer for deodorant and hairbrush. 'That could work. Maybe he wants it as his own little pet project. Do you think he'd keep on the employees, then, at least?'

'Ye-es...' Ruth's hesitant reply had Ashley wincing in immediate understanding.

'Let me guess—but not the CEO?'

'The CEO usually is a necessary casualty in these takeovers,' Ruth admitted. 'I'm sorry, Ashley.'

'It's okay.' Ashley straightened, squaring her shoulders. 'I can take it,' she stated, even though she wasn't sure she could. Infinite Innovations had been her entire life, her life's blood for the last four years. Could she really walk away from it all?

It seemed as if she'd have to.

'As long as everyone else gets to stay,' she finished, and Ruth smiled sorrowfully.

'Like I said, maybe it won't be as bad as we think.'

'And maybe Nico Galletti will ride in on a unicorn,' Ashley quipped. She'd learned the hard way not to hope for happy endings. The only thing she could do was take the hard knocks on the chin and then do her best to stay standing. And if she could convince Nico Galletti to keep on everyone else but her... Well, she'd count that as a victory.

Ruth glanced at her watch. 'Ten minutes until D-Day. Shall I leave you to your ablutions?' She gestured wryly to the stick of deodorant in Ashley's hand.

'Thank you,' Ashley replied. 'And Ruth, whatever happens...thank you for everything.'

Ruth shook her head as her eyes turned glassy. 'Don't set me off,' she warned.

Ashley laughed, the sound ending on a trembling note. 'You'll set *me* off,' she warned, and the two women hugged briefly before Ruth headed back to her own office.

Alone, Ashley stared unseeingly out of the window for a few minutes at the concrete haze of midtown Manhattan. She had no idea what Nico Galletti wanted and, more importantly, how she should approach him. Coldly polite and professional? Come out swinging, to keep from being at a disadvantage? What she *wouldn't* do, Ashley resolved as her lips pressed together in a hard line, was beg or bend over backwards, especially not for a man. She'd done that for far too much of her life already, and those years hadn't just been wasted but had been incredibly, intensely damaging.

Starting Infinite Innovations had helped her to get her

life, her very *self*, back on track, and that was something she would never let anyone take away from her...not even Nico Galletti. Not if she could help it.

Nico Galletti eyed the unprepossessing brick building on the edge of midtown from the confines of his blacked-out limo, his lip curling in disdain. Either Ashley Woodward had fallen on *very* hard times or he was in the wrong place. The last time he'd been in a Woodward building, it had been all soaring spaces, sleek marble and endless chrome, right in the beating heart of midtown. This place looked as if it needed a serious refurb—or to be condemned.

'Mr Galletti?' his driver asked when Nico hadn't moved. 'Is this the right place?'

'I believe so.' Nico eyed the building once more. 'I won't be too long,' he informed the driver. 'Fifteen minutes, at most.' He intended to deliver the news and then make a quick, satisfied exit. He wasn't a cruel man. He didn't need to witness Ashley Woodward's *total* downfall. Informing her of it would be satisfaction enough. Admittedly, it was a pity Woodward himself wouldn't be there to enjoy hearing how his daughter's company was about to be dismantled like an old rust-bucket of a car, but Nico would settle for telling the treacherous woman to her face.

For a second, he let himself picture Ashley Woodward as he last remembered her—eighteen years old and unbearably icy, jade-green eyes narrowed in disdain, blonde hair held back in an elegant chignon with a few platinum tendrils framing a heart-shaped faced exquisite in its beauty. And as cold and unfeeling as if made out of marble.

Oh, yes, he remembered Woodward's daughter. Remembered how she'd turned away from him when her father had staged the melodrama of his arrest, as if she'd been *bored* by the fact that the young man she'd flirted with moments ago, the man she'd tempted, teased and *kissed*, was about to be arrested. The utter injustice of it still burned, an acid corroding his stomach and crawling up his throat.

It was an injustice he'd spent the last sixteen years doing his damnedest to right, and here was the culmination. What was left of Woodward Investments—the company that had completely destroyed his life, his family—was about to be destroyed in turn. Thankfully, revenge was a dish best served cold, and this one was icy indeed, but just as sweet. Nico knew he would look forward to Ashley Woodward's dismayed surprise and dawning horror as much as he would have her feckless father's—maybe even more.

Chase Woodward had already had his comeuppance and was now serving twenty years in federal prison for tax fraud and embezzlement. Ashley might have escaped unscathed from *that* scandal, but she wouldn't from this one. By the end of the day, she'd have nothing but memories of dear old Daddy to keep her warm at night. Nico would make sure of it.

With that thought causing his mouth to curve in a cold smile, he exited his limousine and strode towards the building. Infinite Innovations was on the twelfth floor, although once upon a time Woodward Investments had had its own building of *thirty* floors, in one of the most desirable sections of Manhattan. Nico still recalled the cramped cubicle he'd been given when he'd been just twenty years old, desperate and determined to work his way up.

Woodward had promised him so much.

'Work hard and you *will* be promoted,' he'd told him with that glinting smile that had seemed so trustworthy. 'I reward hard work and honesty and with you, Nico, I like what I see.' He'd clapped him hard on the shoulder, a man-to-man gesture that, at his young age, Nico had especially appreciated. 'You're going to go far, my boy. Trust me.'

Trust me. The words echoed through Nico's mind now as he walked through the unprepossessing foyer and then stepped into the lift. Chase Woodward had destroyed his life deliberately, strategically, luring Nico in with all those false promises: pretending to take a paternal interest; always so friendly and encouraging; nodding along to his ideas so that, for the first time in his life, Nico had felt as if he could finally make a difference.

Every aspect of that evil charade tormented him now, mocking him with his own shameful and humiliating naivety for trusting a man who had only wanted to use him as a stooge. To flirt with his daughter, and not just flirt, but *beg*.

Well, he'd vowed never to be so naïve again. Never to be so trusting, and certainly not with a Woodward—a*ny* Woodward.

The lift doors opened and Nico stepped out into a modest and even shabby foyer, with none of the glamour or bling he remembered from Woodward Investments, where every element had been a deliberate and ostentatious display of wealth. Here, everything was of decent, if not precisely good, quality: a couple of ergonomic chairs in black leather; a single picture on the wall; a photograph of space with a scattering of stars across an endless night, and a framed vision statement beneath that Nico didn't bother to read. He didn't care how worthy Infinite Innovations purported to be. It was about to be reduced to nothing more than a closed file on someone's computer.

In any case, Nico didn't trust Infinite Innovations' supposedly worthy aims. Chase Woodward had sold his financial firm as 'cutting-edge investments for the innovative opportunist', but in the end he'd been the only opportunist, and a complete scammer at that. Many of the investments he'd touted as 'cutting edge' had only existed on paper. The fact that Ashley Woodward's company also purported to champion such *infinite innovations* had made Nico even more cynical.

Like father, like daughter…in so many ways.

As he stepped into the foyer, the receptionist at the front desk, who only looked about twenty, clambered to standing, seeming terrified by his presence.

'You—you must be Mr. Galletti…?'

'That's right.' He kept his voice clipped. He was going to fire every single person on this floor, and there was no need to get their hopes up with even a modicum of friendliness. 'If you could let Miss Woodward know I'm here…or, better yet, just show me the way to her office.'

There was enough steel in his voice to have the receptionist stammering that Ashley Woodward's office was the last one on the right. He gave a terse nod before striding down the hall. He looked forward to surprising Miss Woodward with his unannounced arrival; he already had her on the back foot, but what he really wanted was her sprawled on the floor. Tripped up completely with no recourse, begging for his mercy on her knees, which he would coldly refuse… just as she had once so coldly refused him.

Yes, that was a pleasant thought indeed.

He rapped once on the door before immediately opening it and standing on the threshold of the office. He'd had an image in his head of this moment, he realised—Ashley Woodward looking like the haughty princess he remembered, elegant and aloof as she stood behind her desk in a huge corner office, her icy hauteur melting into shocked fear when she realised just what was happening to her company, to her *life*.

Nothing about what greeted Nico lived up to that vision. Who was this dishevelled-looking woman with her hair in tumbled disarray, her blouse unbuttoned and a stick of *deodorant* in her hand? For a second, he couldn't make sense of it: the woman in her simple blouse and skirt, both of which looked decent but cheap; the scrap of lacy bra he glimpsed from beneath her unbuttoned blouse moulding to high, firm breasts with creamily ivory skin; the cramped and unremarkable office she stood in. It didn't even have a *window*. Had he gone into the wrong room? He looked around, as if for clues, while the woman let out an indignant squeak of protest.

'Don't you normally *wait* for someone to say it's okay to come in?' she demanded as she hurled the deodorant onto the desk and pulled the sides of her blouse together. 'Let me guess. You're Nico Galletti.'

That voice. It was so different, without the elongated syllables and cool, cut-glass accent of the Ashley Woodward he'd once known, but it still possessed that upper-class lilt that had once made him struggle to soften his own Brooklyn accent. This *was* Ashley Woodward—looking very different, but still essentially the same.

'Considering this is only going to be your office for about three more minutes, I decided to dispense with the niceties,' he replied in a cold drawl before nodding at her blouse. 'But I suggest you button that up.'

'And I suggest you turn your back,' Ashley snapped. 'If you're a gentleman.'

Nico let out a laugh of genuine amusement. 'Oh, but I'm not a gentleman.'

'Why is that not a surprise?' Ashley muttered as she thrust her chin up defiantly in a way he definitely *didn't* remember, keeping his gaze the whole while. She began to button up her blouse so that intriguing scrap of lace and glimpse of creamy skin was hidden from view.

Perversely and annoyingly, Nico felt the loss. For a few taut seconds, he let himself be entranced by that enticing, disappearing view of her long, slender fingers slipping in and out of the button holes of her cheap blouse, a faint flush pinkening her porcelain cheeks. The way Ashley Woodward unblinkingly held his gaze the whole time with those deep, emerald eyes was strangely erotic, considering he was pretty sure she was *not* trying to inflame him—although perhaps he shouldn't put such a pathetic ploy past her. Sixteen years ago, she'd flirted with him on her father's command. Was she so deluded as to think the same cheap ploy would work twice?

Never. Although, Nico had to acknowledge, Ashley Woodward looked more furious than flirtatious, the colour deepening in her pale cheeks, her narrowed eyes sparkling like slits of jade, her hair in tumbled gold waves about her shoulders. He felt something in him stir in response and he decided he'd had enough of the accidental—or not—strip tease. Ashley Woodward had beguiled him once. He would not allow her to do so again.

'I think you knew full well I wasn't a gentleman already,' he remarked coldly, and Ashley frowned, her golden eyebrows snapping together as she shook her head, so a few more curling tendrils framed her face and fell about her shoulders. As beautiful as she was, she looked a mess—her skirt crumpled, her hair falling from its pins, a ladder in her nylons from thigh to ankle. He realised she wasn't even wearing shoes. Was all that a ploy too? Did she think this made her more approachable? Was she hoping he'd have *pity* on her?

Again, never.

'Why would I know that?' she asked, sounding both curious and exasperated. She bent down to hunt for her shoes, giving Nico a pleasant view of her rear, her skirt stretching taut over the firm flesh. 'I don't know anything about you,' she continued, jamming one sensible pump on her foot and then the other. 'Except the fact that you swooped in and took over my company for no reason at all that I can figure out.

It's like…like you had a *vendetta*, when I've never seen you before in my life.'

She shook her head in disgust as she straightened and finished tucking in her blouse before meeting his gaze directly once more, her jade eyes flashing but also disconcertingly clear and seemingly empty of guile.

For a second, truly flummoxed, Nico could only stare. All right, *this* he hadn't expected. He'd envisioned Ashley Woodward as furious, scornful, dismissive…or hurt, woebegone, weeping. He would have taken any of those reactions in his stride and enjoyed milking them for what they were worth… But Ashley Woodward was acting as if *she didn't remember him*.

Could it be possible? Could that tumultuous scene in the Woodward ballroom, when he'd been dragged away in *chains*, have been so insignificant to her that she'd forgotten her part in sending an innocent man to jail? A man she'd flirted with and even *kissed*, all as a way to trap him further. Had she managed to forget that too? Or what about the sham of a trial, when she'd sat stony-faced in the second row, never looking him in the eye once? For two weeks she'd come every day. Had she forgotten *that*?

Nico hadn't forgotten any of it. At twenty years old, he'd been both beaten down and hardened by his childhood of near-constant struggle, and walking into the Woodward ballroom had felt like stepping into a fairy tale. It was the first time he'd worn a dinner suit—Chase Woodward had lent him one—or tasted champagne. The first time he'd felt as if his life had possibility and hope. And Ashley Woodward, with her tinkling laugh and shy smile, had been, ever so briefly, part of that.

Of course, it hadn't taken him long to realise she'd just been entertaining him on her father's orders. Later, during the trial, the prosecuting attorney had argued that Nico had not only been helping himself to Chase Woodward's money, but to his daughter as well. He'd painted a picture of a man beset by greed and shameless entitlement, which had so clearly been part of Woodward's plan.

And Ashley had been part of all that... Nico would never forget the completely cold look on her face when he'd been handcuffed right in front of her. Moments before, they'd shared a sweet yet lingering kiss. And then, when he'd begged her to help him, she'd turned away without a word.

She *had* to remember. This was some elaborate ploy, pathetic and absurd, to make him take pity on her. Or was it an even more pathetic power play—an attempt to make him feel wrongfooted and at a disadvantage, as if he was so unimportant she couldn't even remember his arrest and trial? The old Woodward arrogance showing itself yet again...

Whatever the reason, Nico wasn't buying it.

'For someone who is purportedly a CEO of their own company, your memory skills are sadly lacking,' he told her coldly, but all he got was a blank stare in return.

'My memory skills?' she repeated. 'Of what?'

Annoyance bit deeply. 'This little game might be amusing to you, Miss Woodward—or maybe it's a last roll of the dice—but it won't work.'

She shook her head slowly, her arms folded under her high, firm breasts. 'Mr Galletti, I have no idea what you're talking about.'

Nico gave her a long, hard stare which she returned, her gaze clear but also fearful, although he could tell she was trying to hide it. For the first time, Nico considered the veracity of her claim. Could she really have forgotten him? Admittedly, it had been sixteen years, and since then she'd sat through another, far longer and more damning trial, that of her own father. And, in reality, what had been life-and even soul-destroying for *him* had barely impinged on the tranquil perfection of her glamorous socialite life, in which she acted as her father's hostess and cheerleader, attending party after party by his side.

But he'd still thought she would *remember*. The fact that she might not was utterly shaming, and shame was an emotion he no longer let himself feel. So the ice princess might not remember him…fine. If that really was true, he'd use that knowledge to his advantage—and it would make him enjoy Ashley Woodward's complete fall from grace all the more, because she wouldn't even know why it was happening. Let her wonder. Let her *reel,* as he once had, and have no idea why her world was falling apart.

He'd be the one to make it happen, but he wouldn't tell her why. That, Nico decided, would be an even sweeter revenge.

CHAPTER TWO

Ashley held Nico Galletti's gaze with effort, although everything in her screamed to look away, and fast. She'd worked so hard on not hiding, not cringing or apologising for *anything* any more. But, dear heaven, this moment, this *man*, challenged the inner strength that had been so hard-won after the pain and shame of her childhood. *Why* was he looking at her as if he hated her?

It didn't help that he'd caught her unaware—with her blouse unbuttoned, for heaven's sake! The memory made her cheeks scorch all over again. Any normal person would have had the decency to apologise and retreat. Any decent man would have been embarrassed by his faux pas, or even alarmed that his accidental over-step might be construed as some kind of sexual harassment.

Not Nico Galletti. He'd simply stood there and glared at her while she'd inwardly burned and quaked, refusing to look away as she'd buttoned up her blouse and tried to ignore the heat blooming across her skin and stealing through her body as his narrowed gaze had kept hers. It had been a petty power play on both their parts, but she wasn't going to concede an inch if she could help it. But the episode *had* given her an unfortunate insight into the utter ruthlessness of her adversary. She already felt as if she had the measure of the man, and she feared it was ominous for both her and her company.

Now Ashley waited for him to speak while he simply cocked his head, his steely gaze sweeping slowly over her in a way that made Ashley's entire body heat all over again in unexpected—and unwanted—awareness. Her blouse might be buttoned up, but she felt as if he were slowly stripping her naked, although she didn't think there was anything sexual about his gaze; it was merely considering. The heat, Ashley was pretty sure, was humiliatingly one-sided, and she was determined not to reveal her response.

So, fine, the man was clearly incredibly good-looking. She couldn't deny such a basic and overwhelming fact, especially when she basically never came across men like him. Her employees were women or science nerds, and so were the investors and inventors she dealt with. No one like Nico Galletti had ever walked through her door before.

He stood several inches over six feet, with a lithe yet powerful body encased in a grey silk suit, his dark hair cut close and threaded with silver at his temples that somehow only added to his predatory, panther-like appeal. As for his face…it was all sharply bladed cheeks and a knife of a nose, the unrelenting hardness of those features alleviated by thick, dark lashes and a mobile mouth that, annoyingly and embarassingly, Ashley's gaze kept being drawn to. In some hidden, feminine part of herself, she imagined those lips parting, coming closer, *kissing*...

Oddly, she thought she knew exactly what they would feel like—warm and dry, soft yet hard at the same time, and surprisingly sweet…

Good grief. What was wrong with her, imagining that man's *mouth* at a time like this? She had no business thinking about him as anything but her enemy. He so clearly thought of her as his, which she really didn't understand. Why, Ashley wondered again, did this feel so *personal*? Galletti didn't seem all that interested in enlightening her, and

Ashley wasn't interested in begging for information. The man already had her on the back foot as it was.

Needing to hide her confusion—both about Galletti's hostility as well as her own extremely inconvenient response to him—she decided to go on the attack. After decades of being defeatist, being the one to deliver the thrust would feel good.

And so, steeling herself, she subjected him to the same lingering once-over he'd just given her, letting her mouth twist sardonically as her gaze deliberately wandered up and down his body, unable to keep from noting—again—the hint of the defined muscles of his chest and abdomen beneath the expensive white cotton of the shirt that clung to them. The broad shoulders, the long legs, that *face*...

She saw the surprise flare in his eyes, irritation mixed with amusement by her wandering gaze, and didn't know whether to be gratified or cowed. If she was trying to pull off a power play, she had a feeling she'd failed—big time.

She crossed her arms and tilted up her head so she was looking down her nose at him, which was a little challenging when he was at least eight inches taller than her. 'Whenever you feel ready,' she drawled, 'You *can* speak, you know.'

'You don't,' Galletti remarked dryly, seeming completely unimpressed by her examination of him, 'Seem at all interested in currying my favor.'

'Oh, and does that annoy you?' The words slipped out before Ashley could help them. All right, this was so clearly *not* the way to convince Galletti to keep her employees, but it felt as if being combative was her only defence. Nico Galletti might want her to beg for mercy, but she wasn't going to. She had promised herself she would never beg again.

Not even to save your company?

The words, whispered in the quiet of her mind, gave Ashley serious pause. She'd thought she'd do just about anything for Infinite Innovations. She *had* done just about anything:

living hand to mouth so she could pour just about every single dollar she earned back into the inventions that meant so much to her; working all the hours of the day and night that God had given her, having zero social life and few friends as a result; holding her head up high even when the world around her had condemned her for her father's sins, over and over again, until she'd finally started proving them all wrong.

Was a little politeness too much to ask, a little kowtowing, even to a man she already had good reason to despise?

She took an even breath and then let it out slowly. 'I apologise,' she said levelly. 'In my…surprise at this situation, I've behaved rudely, and there is never any excuse for that.'

In response to this careful little speech, Nico Galletti's eyebrows merely lifted a fraction. He looked amused, which was galling. Clearly, he would never consider theirs as a meeting of business equals.

'That's the best you can do?' he queried, folding his arms so the smooth silk of his suit tautened across his impressive biceps. His voice was as smooth as his suit…or a snake.

Ashley already felt the undercurrents of something dark and dangerous swirling around her, pulling her under. She might only have met Galletti five minutes ago, but she sensed there were aspects to this takeover that she didn't understand, reasons she couldn't even begin to guess at. And, until she knew those, she wouldn't beg for anything.

'What is it you want from me?' she asked evenly, doing her best not to flinch as she met his iron-grey gaze. His lashes were soft and lush, but the look in his eyes was pitiless, and meeting it made her feel as if she'd slammed into a wall. Why, oh why, did this stranger act like he absolutely loathed her?

'Ah, now, that's the interesting thing,' Galletti said in a soft, dark voice that held equal parts amusement and menace. He took a step towards her, challenging Ashley to hold her ground, which she did, if only just. She breathed in the smell of his cologne—something clean and spicy, that seemed as dangerous as everything else about him. She wasn't scared, not exactly, but the feeling coursing through her definitely felt like alarm...as well as a treacherous excitement she was honest enough to admit, if only to herself.

As much as she wanted to, she knew she could not deny there was something intensely magnetic about this man; there was some innate, compelling force to him that made her want to step closer and scamper away at the same time. Another inch or two forward and she'd feel as if she'd fallen into a vortex of fascination and desire she had absolutely no intention of feeling. And yet...she still looked at his lips. Still imagined how they might feel on hers—soft and hard, dry and firm, lush and...

Stop.

A shuddery breath escaped her before she could help herself and she drew herself up, dragging her gaze away from the man's mouth. As much as she wanted to step forward and sprint back at the same time, thankfully sanity prevailed, and she stayed still, trying not to sway under the unrelenting force of his hard gaze, forcing herself to act like his unaffected equal, even if he so clearly didn't see her as one.

'What do I want from you?' Galletti mused, taking yet another step closer so she could feel his warm breath fanning her face, the heat of his body rolling off in intoxicating waves that caused the heat in her own to flare hotter. 'The answer to that, Miss Woodward, is...absolutely nothing.'

For a second, Ashley could only stare at him. The rush of awareness she felt morphed into something even more powerful—*hope*. For what she already realised was an infuriatingly futile moment, she thought he meant he didn't want her company. That this whole hostile takeover was a bad dream, or a joke. *That everything was going to be okay...*

But when had anything in her life been okay? When had she ever been handed a happy ending, no matter how charmed her life looked from the outside? No, she'd had to forge everything good for herself, with hard work, blood, sweat and many, many tears.

This was going to be no different, she realised with a leaden certainty as Nico Galletti turned away from her, effectively dismissing her, that magnetic tug she'd felt towards him severed in an instant.

'You can gather your things,' he tossed over his shoulder before checking the Rolex that gleamed on one muscular wrist. 'I want you out of this building in five minutes.'

Nico kept his back to Ashley Woodward as he struggled to compose himself. He might once have been boyishly attracted to the ice princess he'd known, but he'd really thought he'd left those schoolboy feelings behind long ago. The thirty-four-year-old Ashley Woodward he'd encountered today had clearly fallen on some hard times, judging by the quality of her clothes and the smallness of her office; and she wasn't, in many regards, anything like the couture-swathed socialite he'd known long ago. But she still possessed the same arrogant attitude…even if her obvious once-over had both amused and inflamed him, an unsettling response he had no intention of entertaining for a second longer.

He wanted her gone.

She still hadn't moved.

'Your five minutes,' he informed her without turning around, 'Started…' He paused to ostentatiously check his watch. 'Thirty-seven seconds ago.'

'Wait.' Ashley's voice was a whisper, and an elemental part of him surged with satisfaction. Now he'd have her where he wanted her: *begging*. As he'd once begged. Swiftly he pushed that humiliating memory to the far reaches of his mind.

'I know you hold all the cards in this situation,' she continued, her voice getting stronger, 'But can't you at least tell me what your intentions are for my company?'

Slowly, now completely and coldly in control of his wayward response to this infuriating woman, Nico turned round. 'I just did.'

'Yes, but...' She licked her lips, her tongue darting out to moisten their lush fullness, and Nico impatiently flicked his gaze away. He definitely did not need that kind of distraction. 'You haven't told me what your intentions for the *company* are. The employees... There are twenty-two...'

'Twenty-two?' he scoffed derisively, although he knew the number as well as she did. He'd done his research. Infinite Innovations had started four years ago as a small, private company investing in ridiculous inventions—science-fiction-worthy concepts that bordered on the absurd. The only reason that it had been viable for it to go public was due to one invention in which it had invested that had become moderately successful—a robotic toothbrush, of all things.

The whole thing had elements of the absurd—in particular that Ashley Woodward was the CEO seeking out such bizarre concepts. After their brief interaction at that ball, he'd assumed she was shallow and vapid, as well as cruelly indifferent. She *had* to be, to have acted the way she had back then.

When he'd researched Infinite Innovations, he'd presumed that it was as a front for some other, more nefarious business dealings, although he'd yet to find any evidence. It simply didn't have the reputation, or the resources, to champion such innovative causes. Really, all he was doing was putting this company—and its CEO—out of its eventual misery.

'We're not a large company,' Ashley replied in a voice quivering with dignity. 'Which is why the takeover was such a surprise. Most people haven't heard of us—'

'Obviously,' Nico cut across her, 'I had.'

'Yes, but *why*? Why do this?' Her voice rose, wavered and broke. Nico watched her with cool disinterest as she sucked in a breath, pushing her hands through her hair. 'I just don't understand,' she muttered, half to herself. 'Why would you take over a tiny tech company just to fire *me*?'

She lifted her tortured gaze to his, her moss-green eyes widening in sudden, fearful realisation. 'Wait…is this about my *father*?' She sounded incredulous.

'Your father?' he repeated tonelessly. 'Why would it be about your father?'

'Who, then?' she demanded, her voice rising once again, spiking with anger and impatience. 'And why won't you just *tell* me? This whole cryptic thing is very YA, you know.'

Nico frowned, feeling irritatingly wrong-footed by not knowing the term. 'YA?'

'Young adult,' Ashley clarified impatiently. 'Enough with the brooding princeling act, okay? Just tell me what's going on so I can *deal* with it.'

He almost laughed at that, although he couldn't have said why. Nothing about the Woodward family was remotely amusing. 'What's going on,' he informed her, 'Is I am firing you. It's now been five minutes so, if you don't get going, I will be very tempted to call security.'

He slid his phone out of his pocket for good measure. 'What's also happening,' he continued in the same mock-pleasant voice, 'Is that I am about to fire your twenty-two employees, inform your investors *and* inventors that Infinite Innovations is ceasing to operate, and liquidate any assets—and I know there aren't that many—to be subsumed into Galletti Finance. By the end of the business day today, Infinite Innovations will effectively cease to exist.'

For a few taut seconds Ashley simply stared at him. Her face drained of colour, and her eyes went glassy as her lips parted soundlessly. Then, without saying a word, she turned slowly away from him and walked to the desk, her narrow back to him, one hand resting on her chair, as if for support, as she bowed her head.

Nico felt the tiniest flicker of pity and then quickly quashed it. She deserved this, every single bit of it. He was not going to feel sorry for crushing her company, or even her dreams. Ashley Woodward had surprised him several times in the course of their brief interview, but that didn't mean she'd changed. It also didn't mean she was undeserving of what was coming to her.

She was Chase Woodward's daughter. She'd watched him get arrested. She'd conspired in keeping him at that damned ball, and she'd turned away when he'd asked for her help. And, besides all that, in her complete shallow selfishness, she might have even *forgotten* him.

This was happening. 'Well?' he bit out, his phone still in hand. 'Do I need to call security?'

'Please…' She turned around slowly, stretching one hand out in front of her in supplication. Nico waited, curious as to what ploy she was going to try now, wondering if she really would beg, when Ashley's face went the colour of paper. Her eyes turned almost black as her pupils dilated and she swayed, stumbled and then collapsed to the ground in a dead faint.

CHAPTER THREE

FOR A SECOND, Nico thought she was faking. She'd accused him of being—what was it?—a brooding princeling? Well, right now she was playing the damsel in distress to complete and ridiculous effect. Then, when her face remained the colour of ash and she didn't move, he realised she wasn't faking after all. She was out cold.

Muttering a curse under his breath, Nico crossed the small room to crouch by her. As he leaned forward, he breathed in her scent—something almond, different than he remembered from before, when she'd smelled expensively of roses. Everything about her was different, he reflected, from the woman he'd recalled in his dreams—and in his nightmares. Had Ashley Woodward changed so much, or was he misremembering? After years of replaying that wretched night over and over in his head, torturing himself with every precious, privileged detail that had haunted him.

Or was Ashley pretending to be someone she wasn't? He'd figure out the answer to that one way or another, but right now he was pretty sure she wasn't play-acting being unconscious.

'Ashley...' He realised, it was the first time he'd said her name since he'd seen her again, and it sounded strange on his lips, familiar and forbidden. Because, after torturing himself for so long, he now tried never to relive the heart-stopping half-hour he'd spent in her presence.

'I don't recognise you,' she'd said, smiling, when she'd come upon him half-hiding behind a pillar, working up the courage to glad-hand the people whom he knew were subtly sneering at him, the Italian immigrant from Brooklyn whose dinner suit was a little too tight.

'I work for your father,' he'd said, awed by her cool, perfect beauty. She was so unbearably elegant, like something spun from glass, dressed in a white gown that was covered with Swarovski crystals so she shimmered every time she moved, an angel spangled in diamonds. Nico had both longed to touch her and been afraid to at the same time.

Ashley had cocked her head and leaned in so he breathed in her perfume—something delicate, of roses.

'Are you new?' she'd asked.

'I was hired six months ago.' He'd struggled to hide the accent he knew his colleagues secretly mocked. 'What about you? Do you always come to these things?'

'Oh yes,' she'd replied on something of a sigh. For a second, she'd looked sad, her green gaze turning distant, her lush mouth turning down at the corners. Nico had raised a hand as if to comfort her, but then she'd lifted her head, her suddenly bright smile seeming like a shield. 'Do you ever get bored at these things?' she'd whispered conspiratorially. 'Or intimidated?'

She'd nodded towards the mingling crowd, her expression turning thoughtful, assessing. 'All those people…'

She'd trailed off, shaking her head, and Nico had felt a surge of protectiveness for her which made no sense because *he* was the outsider, not her.

Ashley Woodward looked as if she belonged in that beautiful room, dressed in a ballgown that glittered every time she moved, her hair pulled up to show her long, graceful neck. She'd been born to that life, was privileged and pampered, and he was the poor boy who had been given an en-try-level job that was only a little more than minimum wage. Chase Woodward might be trying to help him, but everyone in that office looked down at him, with his rough ways and his Brooklyn accent. Even Woodward himself would be less than enthused to see him talking to his daughter, Nico suspected, but he felt so out of place at th event, and she'd been kind enough to seek him out...or so he'd thought.

'I've never been to something like this before,' he admitted. 'So I'm not bored yet. And certainly not when I'm not talking to you.'

She blushed at that, and Nico felt a thrill of victory.

'I'm usually bored at these things,' Ashley confessed with a faint, sad smile on her lips. '*And* intimidated.'

'I can't believe you're intimidated,' Nico protested, and she laughed softly.

'Oh, believe it. I'd rather be upstairs in my room, reading a book. What about you?'

He thought for a moment. 'I'd rather be getting a pizza and a beer back in Bensonhurst,' he admitted, and she laughed, a sound that drew him in, making Nico feel as if they shared something.

'Why do you go to these things, then?' he asked. 'If you don't like them?' He tugged on his bow-tie, feeling uncomfortable in the penguin suit he'd never worn before. He knew he was a fish out of water in this Fifth Avenue mansion and wished he wasn't...for this young woman's sake.

She shrugged then, casting her gaze downwards, her golden lashes fanning porcelain cheeks. 'I...have to,' she said in a tone of such resignation and even grief that Nico felt as if there was a world of unspoken burden in those three little words, a history of expectation he didn't entirely understand, yet he related to it.

'I have to' was the reason he'd dropped out of school at sixteen and worked two jobs. 'I have to' was why he'd taken every pathetic pay cheque home, knowing it wouldn't even cover the rent and groceries, never mind his little brother's medical expenses. And all the while his mother was his brother's full-time carer, and his sister made bad choice after bad choice.

It had been a hard life, a *very* hard life, which was why he'd been so pathetically grateful to Chase Woodward.

At least now, he reflected, he possessed the power to make it better, not that his mother would take anything from him. They hadn't so much as spoken since his trial. Chase Woodward's treachery hadn't just affected him, but that was a dark place he couldn't bear to go, so he pushed the unwelcome memory away.

Nico touched Ashley's cheek now, amazed and a little concerned at how cold it was. This wasn't what he'd meant by thinking of her as an ice princess. Why didn't she wake up?

'Ashley…' he said again. She didn't stir.

A sudden, hard knock at the door had Nico turning, and then a neatly dressed middle-aged woman opened it, looking shocked even before she saw Ashley crumpled on the floor.

'Mr Galletti…' The woman's eyes widened as she caught sight of Ashley. 'What did you do to her?' she demanded.

For a second, Nico was catapulted back to that ballroom. *What have you done?* Woodward had asked him, pretending to sound confused, and Nico had had no response, because at that point he hadn't even known what he was accused of.

But he wasn't that naïve, powerless boy any more, and this woman, whoever she was, was now under his authority, whether she recognised it or not.

'I haven't done anything to her,' Nico replied coolly as he straightened. 'She fainted and I'm waiting for her to come to.'

'She most likely fainted because she hasn't slept or eaten

in nearly two days, since this whole thing started,' the woman replied as she shook her head, her tone implying that it was his fault.

'Maybe you should call for a doctor,' Nico suggested in the same cool tone. 'And for some food.' He slid his phone out of his pocket. 'On second thoughts, I will.'

The woman watched him as he called one of his staff and bit out the necessary instructions, and he could feel her animosity as well as her curiosity, a pulsing, palpable thing.

'No one here understands why you took over Infinite Innovations in such an aggressive way,' she remarked as he slid his phone back into his pocket and then stooped to pick up Ashley. She was surprisingly light, curling into him with a faint moan that stirred his senses. He tamped down the instinctive, sympathetic response. She might have fainted, but she still deserved everything that was coming to her.

'We can't help but wonder,' the woman continued, 'if you have some secret agenda.'

'No secret,' he replied as he laid Ashley down on the love seat against one wall and left it at that. He wanted Ashley Woodward conscious for this conversation. 'An EMT will be here in a few minutes,' he stated, 'to check her over.'

The woman was still staring at him, her eyes narrowed in assessment, and then flaring with recognition. 'Wait a minute, I recognise you,' she said with dawning realisation. 'Rossi... You're Nico *Rossi*.' She shook her head slowly, looking incredulous. 'Right?'

Nico spared the woman a brief, cold glance. He'd changed his name to his mother's maiden name nine years ago and never looked back, but his past was not the shameful secret so many seemed to think it should be. 'Once upon a time,' he conceded coolly.

The woman drew a breath. 'I was at that ball,' she said quietly.

His whole body tensed as he absorbed that simply stated fact, before he raked her with a dismissive look. 'Enjoyed the show?' he drawled.

She squared her shoulders. 'I'm Ruth Boxall. My husband, Phillip Boxall, was the CFO of Woodward Investments.'

His immediate supervisor. A lightning streak of rage flashed through him, hard and fast, obliterating every other thought for a few blistering seconds. 'The man who stood aside and said nothing,' he finally remarked in arctic tones.

'Five years ago, he went to prison with Ashley's father.'

He arched an eyebrow. 'Do you expect me to feel sorry for him? Or you?'

'No,' she said quietly. 'Of course not.'

'Good, because I don't.'

'But…' Ruth Boxall glanced down at Ashley, still supine on the sofa, her golden lashes brushing pale cheeks. 'If this is some kind of revenge, you must realise that Ashley had nothing to do with any of that—'

'I'll be the judge of her involvement,' Nico cut her off.

Her eyes widened in alarm. 'I'm serious.'

'So am I.' His voice was as hard as iron. He neither needed nor wanted to hear this woman's pathetic excuses.

'We didn't know it back then, that you were innocent,' Ruth Boxall said quietly. 'I didn't, and Ashley didn't either. And in any case… This might come as a surprise, but she doesn't even—'

'Save it for someone who cares,' Nico snapped. The old injustice, and the accompanying fury, rose in him in a hot tide and he didn't have time for these feelings. He'd come here for one purpose—to destroy the last remaining Woodward holding—nothing else.

'As for believing I was guilty…' he couldn't resist adding bitingly, 'The twenty-year-old hireling managed to embezzle millions even though nothing was ever found in his bank account, his lifestyle hadn't changed at all and he'd only been working for the company for six months? That all makes such perfect sense.'

'Chase explained all that,' Ruth protested. 'In court.' She sounded regretful, which made Nico seethe with fury. Even if Phillip Boxall or Ashley hadn't known—and that was an absolutely enormous 'if'—the idea that anyone thought it mattered that they were sorry *now*, sixteen years later, just added insult to grievous injury. 'He said you'd sent the money to some relatives in Italy,' the woman explained. 'There were bank transactions; they showed them in court...'

'Transactions he'd made in my name, to people I didn't even know.' Nico shook his head, the old anger racing like fire through his veins once more, threatening to ignite with the injustice of it. Dismantling Infinite Innovations was hardly fair recompense for all he'd suffered, but it was a start.

On the sofa, Ashley stirred, and Nico stooped down once again. 'An EMT is coming,' he murmured, annoyed by the sense of protectiveness that surged up in him, just as it had all those years ago, but he told himself it was surely a normal response to any woman in distress. He was a decent man, despite what Ashley Woodward and her sidekick might think of him.

'Did she recognise you?' the woman asked in a hoarse voice. 'She wouldn't, though—'

'No,' Nico cut her off. He had no interest in hearing why Ashley wouldn't recognise him. He'd already realised himself how unimportant the boy he'd been was to her.

'And will you explain—?'

'I won't waste my time. In about fifteen minutes, all of you will be unemployed and this company will no longer exist. Explanations aren't necessary.'

Ruth shook her head slowly, almost in wonder. 'You're

so ruthless,' she observed, her tone sorrowful rather than condemning.

Nico straightened and met her gaze head on. 'Five years in prison will do that to you,' he replied evenly, and for a second they simply stared at each other, until Ruth looked away first.

Nico glanced back down at Ashley and saw that her eyes were fluttering open. She gazed up at him, dazed, as colour crept into her cheeks and light into her eyes. Nico stared down at her, determinedly unmoved. His conversation with Ruth Boxall had raked up all the old wounds and feelings again—the shock and horror of his arrest, his stammering explanation, his desperate plea…

The whole thing had been a stitch-up from start to finish—his hiring, the responsibility Chase Woodward had supposedly entrusted him with, his invitation to that ball and his arrest. Everything had been orchestrated by the father of the woman now sprawled at his feet.

And she'd been there, had seen it and done nothing—*less* than nothing. She'd played her own part, unwittingly or not, and for that she deserved everything she got.

And yet, as much as Nico wanted to turn away from her now, he found he couldn't. Reluctantly, his mouth set in a grim, hard line, he stooped down and reached out one hand to help her up.

Ashley blinked up at him, still dazed as she reached out to take his hand—and then yanked it back.

Why was she lying down? Ashley's head was whirling, her stomach seething, as she almost took Nico Galletti's hand before she remembered that he was about to fire not just *her*, but all her employees, and she yanked it back.

This man was a *monster*.

'Ashley…'

She turned to see Ruth gazing at her in concern. 'You were out for a while.'

Silently Ashley eased herself into a sitting position, her head in her hands, her whole body still reeling. She couldn't believe this was happening. In all her worst imaginings, she hadn't considered the utterly grim possibility that Nico Galletti would destroy her company simply for the sake of it.

He might absorb it, yes, take it as his own, but even in the worst-case scenario in which she and her board were all fired, she'd thought *some* employees would be able to keep their jobs. That some of the inventors she believed in so passionately would still have a place to live out their dreams.

But *this*…this was willful, wanton destruction, and she couldn't think why…until she remembered what she'd said about her father. Ashley knew her father had hurt a lot of people with his treachery: investors who had trusted him as well as employees who had believed in him, like Ruth's husband Phillip, who had gone to prison with her father even though Ruth had insisted he was innocent.

Had Nico Galletti been similarly hurt by her father? But surely he had to know she'd had nothing to do with her father's fraud and embezzlement? The modesty of her life now was proof enough she hadn't benefited from the millions her father had spirited away into offshore accounts before his arrest.

Slowly Ashley lifted her head from her hands. 'Did my father do something to you?' she asked, and Nico gave a short, harsh laugh.

'You could say that.'

'Ashley…' Ruth murmured, and Ashley swivelled to face her friend, even though it made her head swim.

'Do *you* know?' she asked, sensing something in Ruth's tone, and Ruth glanced at Nico before nodding tautly. Ashley shook her head, also not a good idea, she discovered, when she felt so faint and nauseous. 'Can someone please tell me what is going on?' she demanded.

Before Nico or Ruth could answer—not that either seemed inclined to—a knock sounded at the door. Nico called for the person to enter, a fact which rankled, because it was *her* office... Even if, Ashley realised with a plunging sensation, it wasn't any more.

'This is an EMT,' Nico informed her shortly, nodding at the man. 'He'll have you checked out.'

'What—?'

'You fainted,' he explained, sounding impatient now. 'I will not be accused of any kind of cruelty or neglect when it comes to the logistics of this takeover.'

Ashley had to laugh at that, a short, sharp sound. 'So, it's not cruelty when you're destroying my whole company *for no reason*?'

His eyes flashed then, streaks of silver that reminded her of lightning—and gave her the same kind of electric charge. Ashley jerked back as if she'd been struck, even though no one had moved.

'Hardly no reason,' Nico said in a quietly lethal voice, and then he turned and walked out of the room.

'Ruth...' Ashley began, and she shook her head.

'We'll talk after you've been checked out.' Her old friend sounded so defeated but, Ashley realised, also something else: something that made her feel even uneasier. She needed to figure out what was going on, why Nico Galletti had targeted her company...and then decide what she could do about it.

Fifteen minutes later, having had all her vitals taken by the efficient EMT and choked down an energy drink and a granola bar, Ashley slipped out of her office, determined to get the bottom of whatever mystery she'd stumbled on, figure out how her father had hurt Nico Galletti and then convince the man that destroying her company was not the right kind of revenge. Simple. Although, when she remembered that fierce look in Nico's eyes, maybe not…

As Ashley came out to the open-plan office, she felt as if she'd come upon a funeral. All her employees sat slumped at their desks, looking shell-shocked. A couple of them were crying quietly.

'Let me guess,' she said heavily. 'Nico Galletti…'

'Just fired us all,' Tom, one of her recent hires, said, sounding despondent. 'We have ten minutes to clear out our desks.'

'He only gave me five,' Ashley told him, trying for a wry note but, she feared, only sounding bitter. *How* could Galletti be so cruel? These people had done nothing wrong. Didn't he care about due process, severance packages, a sense of *decency*? Nico Galletti didn't seem to concern himself with any of those kinds of things, and certainly not the last.

Fury spiked through her. The man really was a monster.

'Where is he?' she asked her employees, and Tom shrugged.

'He left.'

'Left?' So he'd lobbed a grenade into her office, her whole *life*, and then just strolled away from the wreckage? Typical.

'Just a few minutes ago,' Denise add, an administrative assistant and single mum of two. 'He said his staff would make sure we were gone.'

Ashley shook her head in despair. These people needed their jobs, or at the very least some kind of severance. She could not let Galletti treat them this way.

Fired by both outrage and a desperate sense of purpose, she whirled around and strode back towards the hall.

'Where are you going?' Tom called.

'After him,' Ashley shouted over her shoulder with grim determination. She'd taken too many things in her life lying down to let this one pass. Nico Galletti was going to know the full force of her anger.

Knowing the lift would be too slow, Ashley made for the stairs, clattering down twelve fights in a way that left her breathless but even more determined. Down in the foyer, she sprinted for the front doors—just to glimpse Nico Galletti stepping into a limousine.

'Stop!' The word came out in a roar that had the security guard startling. Ashley raced for the doors, hurling them open and hurtling through, stumbling once in her pumps so that pain blazed through her ankle, and then half-sprinting, half-limping to the car door that was just about to close.

'You can't do this!' she burst out as she yanked open the door, and then, her ankle giving out in another blaze of pain, she pitched forward with a yelp of surprise…landing right on top of Nico Galletti.

CHAPTER FOUR

For several stunned seconds, Ashley couldn't think. Her ankle was a blaze of pain, her mind a haze of…awareness.

Awareness of the long, lean body, warm and taut, lying under hers, thighs moulded to hers. Her breasts squashed against a hard, muscled chest that made them both ache and tingle. She felt the heat of him, touching every pressure point in a way that was exquisite and incredibly unsettling, especially considering she'd raced after him for an angry confrontation, not for…*this*. Whatever this was.

After what felt far too long, Ashley lifted her startled gaze to meet Nico Galletti's.

Instinctively, she braced herself for whatever expression she expected to find in those silvery-grey depths—bemusement, derision, fury or some combination of all three. What she hadn't expected to see was desire, making his pupils dilate and his irises flare. From a distance they looked grey, or even silver, but from this close she saw they were rimmed in gold, like little sparks of fire. And those eyes, those magnificent eyes, were filled with heat and locked on hers.

The moment, which was already unsettling, suddenly turned fiercely electric. Ashley felt as if she could practically see the sparks in the air, hear the vibrating hum of energy; every breath was charged as they simply stared at each other.

Silently, without breaking her gaze, Nico half-rose from where he was sprawled on the seat and slowly, almost languorously, shifted Ashley higher up on his body. Her legs slid along his, her hips settling into his as a sizzling sense of awareness raced through her veins at every point of contact. Then, with one hand, Nico closed the limo door, rapped once on the tinted screen that separated them from the driver and they sped away from the kerb. And all the while Ashley couldn't break his gaze. She couldn't even move; as the car cut through traffic, she realised she was *still* lying on top of him, with far too many agonizing points of contact between their two bodies, each ragged breath a loud rasp in the quiet confines of the limo.

Then Nico put his hands on her hips and adjusted her, so she was cradled between his thighs in a way that felt even *more* intimate—and exposing. Her breasts were flat against his chest, her mouth inches from the lean, brown column of his throat. Everything in her felt sluggish, hazy and yet at the same agonizingly sensitised and aware. How she could feel both at the same time, Ashley had no idea, and yet she did.

She was achingly conscious of every part of him: the warm skin beneath her body, the smooth cotton of his shirt under her palms. She could feel his heartbeat thud against her hand—slow, steady beats that increased in speed as the moment stretched on and spun out—and still neither of them had spoken. He was as affected as she was, she realised with a thrill of wonder as she kept staring at his throat, too overwhelmed to lift her gaze to his face once more.

She realised Nico's hands were still on her hips, and Ashley wasn't so much of an innocent that she couldn't feel the evidence of his desire beneath her own aching thighs. It sent another pulse of longing through her, like liquid fire racing through her veins. How had this happened so fast? How had this happened at *all*?

And it should stop, it should definitely stop, because she had people depending on her, and a company to save, and...

Nico lifted one hand to the back of her neck, his long fingers tangled in her hair as he drew up her head, so she was forced to look at him once more. His eyes blazed into hers. For a second, Ashley thought he was going to say something. His lips parted, and his gaze, still locked with hers, turned fierce, almost desperate. Everything in her tensed—and yearned. She didn't know what she wanted him to do, and yet she did. Oh, how she did.

And then he did it… With one hand on her neck and another on her hip, he hauled her up so his lips met hers—not in a tentative brush, or a sweetly inquisitive question of a kiss, an opening gambit, but rather in a clash of mouths that felt like a brand and was instantly hungry, ruthlessly plundering from the second it started.

This kiss was a demand rather than a plea, raw, aggressive and utterly enthralling. Ashley had been kissed precious few times in her life, and never like this. She was being devoured, *consumed*, swallowed up whole by a kiss that went on and on, taking everything from her, and yet she knew she would have willfully given it away gladly, wantonly—because all she wanted was more of this kiss, more of him.

His hand moved from her neck to her breast, cupping its fullness as if he owned her, as if she was his, and in that moment she *was*. His thumb flicked across her nipple and Ashley couldn't keep from moaning aloud. She'd never been touched like this before. She'd never *felt* like this before. The last scrap of sanity she'd been clinging onto was willfully surrendered as the fingers of his other hand slid under her skirt, skimming her thigh.

Instinctively, she pressed against him, and now he was the one groaning against her lips as he pressed back, and for a few tantalising seconds they engaged in a primal dance that was more erotic than anything Ashley had ever experienced before and yet didn't feel remotely enough.

Then, in the midst of this whirlwind of heat and sensation, a voice came, like a bucket of ice water poured all over her.

'Mr Galletti? We have arrived.'

Ashley jerked up, feeling as if she'd slammed back into herself after several heady minutes of existing on an entirely different plane. She was aware of several things all at once: Nico Galletti's flushed face far too close to hers, his eyes glittering like sparks of lightning, his hand still cupping her breast, his other one up her skirt. Moments ago, it had felt thrilling, but now it only seemed sordid and humiliatingly shameful. Knowing what she did about him, how could she have responded to him in such a way?

She did her best to scramble off him, but then her ankle made its agony known again, and she let out a moan of pain rather than the pleasure she'd been consumed with seconds ago, reaching down to cup her foot.

'Are you hurt?' Nico asked, and he sounded frustratingly calm, even disinterestedly polite. He was already sitting up, running a hand through the hair she feared *she'd* mussed up. Had she had her hands in his hair? Yes, she was pretty sure she had. How on earth had she lost control so quickly, so completely? Nothing like this had ever happened to her before.

'I twisted my ankle,' Ashley admitted through gritted teeth. The pain wasn't as excruciating as the total humiliation she felt in that moment. She'd come here on a mission, and she'd failed beyond her wildest imaginings. Even as her body thudded with the after effects of desire, she only felt shame. She couldn't even blame Nico—he might have kissed her first, but she'd been lying on top of him, her heart, or at least her lust, in her eyes. She'd been *ridiculous*.

'So that's why you fell on top of me?' Nico remarked dryly. 'I thought maybe you were begging me to save your employees. Not the most novel way to do it, but I suppose it might work with some men.'

Tears of anger as well as mortification stung her eyes. 'You certainly acted like it could have worked with you,' she snapped. 'But, as it happens, I tripped. I certainly wasn't begging,' she stated with as much dignity as she could muster, which was precious little. 'And I never would like that.'

'Oh, no? You'll kiss a man to sign his death warrant, but not to save someone else?'

For a second, Ashley could only stare. There were spots of colour high on Nico's bladed cheekbones, and his eyes glittered not with desire but with anger, even rage. The mood in the limo had changed suddenly and completely, and she was aware of an entirely different kind of danger emanating from this man that she couldn't understand at all.

'I have no idea what you're talking about,' she stated flatly. 'At all. So, if you care to enlighten me…'

'I don't,' Nico replied shortly. 'You can get out of my limo and limp back to wherever you came from. But not to Infinite Innovations,' he informed her with lethal silkiness. 'The building has been taken over by my staff and is in the process of being cleared. Your things will be in the lobby, should you care to retrieve them.'

She did the hurt princess look very well, Nico thought sardonically, and she'd been the one to accuse him of being some kind of brooding princeling! Her big green eyes were glassy with tears, her face pale, her lip caught between her straight, white teeth.

'Please…can't we talk about this?' she whispered.

'So you can throw yourself at me again? As entertaining an idea as that is…' He made a mocking show of checking his watch. 'I'm a busy man, princess.'

'*Don't* call me that!' The words exploded out of her, low and savage, surprising them both.

Slowly Nico lowered his arm. 'Don't call you princess?'

'No.' She wrapped her arms around her middle, bending over so her hair fell down in gloriously tangled waves, so he couldn't see her face. 'Don't.'

Nico stared at her, curious as to why she'd reacted so strongly to a simple word, but also determined to remain unmoved. 'I won't call you anything, because you're about to get out of my car.' To make the point even clearer, he leaned over and opened the door, trying not to react to her vanilla and almond scent or the way her silken hair tickled his cheek as he loomed over her.

Ashley ignored the open door. 'What-whatever my father did to you…' she began haltingly, her head still bowed, 'This company has nothing to do with him. *I* have nothing to do with him. I haven't seen him since he went to prison.'

'Such a loyal daughter,' he mocked. 'I'm not surprised. Most people cut bait with a con, I find.' He couldn't keep the bitterness from spiking his voice. He'd lost all his family and a lot of friends once he'd gone to prison. His mother had blamed him for his arrest, even though she'd known he was innocent.

You should have known better, Nico. For the sake of your brother, you should never have aimed so high.

Other people had preferred to pretend they'd never known him, even after his innocence had been proved. He was still tainted, which was why he'd changed his last name. He wasn't ashamed, but neither would he have his prison sentence define who he was now by having it appear every time someone searched for his name.

Slowly Ashley lifted her head. Her face was mottled with distress, her lip pearling with a tiny droplet of blood from where she'd bitten it. 'If this is some kind of revenge, you really are targeting the wrong person,' she insisted, her voice trembling. 'If you want me to beg, fine, I'll do it. I'll beg.' She knotted her shaking fingers together, holding her clasped hands out in front of her. '*Please* don't do this. You're hurting innocent people. My staff—'

'Can get other jobs.' Nico forced himself to sound dismissive, although she'd prodded his one weakness without even realising it. He did not want innocent people to suffer… but Ashley Woodward was *not* innocent. As for her twenty-two employees, once they were vetted and cleared of any involvement in Woodward's affairs, perhaps he'd consider finding jobs for then.

'Did you invest in his company or something?' Ashley asked desperately. 'Did you lose money?'

Nico leaned forward. 'I lost my *life*,' he snarled. 'And everything and everyone that mattered to me. And you were part of that, *princess*, so enough with your "damsel in distress" act. I'm not buying it, and I never will.' With that, he gave her a purposeful push towards the door, his hand on her shoulder.

Ashley stared at him, her eyes wide with confusion and shock as she caught herself with one arm flung out to the door handle. '*I* was?'

Nico had had enough. *'Go.'* He raised his hand as if to push her again, although he knew he wouldn't. He'd already made his message clear. As he'd told her before, he wasn't cruel—not the way her father had been.

Finally, Ashley seemed to accept defeat. Her eyes still sparkled with tears and her lips trembled before she firmed them into a line. Lifting her chin a notch in a way that gave Nico an unexpected flicker of admiration, she eased herself out of the car. She closed the door politely, not slamming it, and left him alone with his revenge.

Nico exhaled slowly, willing himself to feel the sweet satisfaction of that delectable dish best eaten cold, but he felt nothing. He was empty inside, as if a cold wind was blowing right through him. He'd finally achieved what he'd set out to do—the last remaining connection to Woodward Investments, as it was, was about to be dismantled and destroyed. Chase Woodward was in prison and his daughter had nothing. Why did he not feel the way he'd thought he would, the way he *needed* to? Maybe if he gave it time…

Irritated with himself, he rolled down the window to check that Ashley Woodward was good and gone, only to see her standing a few metres away, limping pitifully. Her ankle really was injured, maybe even sprained. For the second time that day in relation to this woman and her ailments, Nico swore under his breath. And then, hating himself for his own weakness, he threw open the limo door and climbed out, striding toward Ashley.

'You're in no condition to go anywhere,' he snapped, his voice sharp with irritation. 'Why don't you hail a cab?'

'I don't have my wallet or phone,' Ashley replied with trembling dignity. 'But please don't trouble yourself on my account. You haven't so far,' she flung at him, 'So I'm not sure why you'd change now.'

Again, Nico felt that flicker of admiration for her courage…and promptly squashed it. He didn't need Ashley Woodward appealing to his sympathies.

'You obviously need that ankle tended to,' he told her gruffly. 'You can come into my office building and be seen to. Then I'll get you a car to take you wherever you need to go.'

She turned to stare at him in disbelief. 'Why would you help me now?' she asked, sounding genuinely curious as well as completely defeated. 'You've already taken *everything* from me. What does being decent do for you now?' Her lips twisted bitterly. 'Does it give you a little thrill? You don't need to kick me when I'm down. You can just pretend to help me up.'

'I *am* helping you,' Nico replied through gritted teeth. Her words pierced him in a way he hadn't expected and didn't entirely understand. Ashley Woodward had been complicit in his unjust arrest and imprisonment. Whether she remembered her part in it or not was irrelevant…even if the fact that she might have forgotten remained galling. He thought he'd almost prefer her to be deceitful. 'Now stop arguing,' he added, wanting to cut off any more uncomfortable accusations she might make, 'And come with me.'

He took her by the elbow, intending to help her into his building, but by the way she limped he realised she couldn't put any weight on her ankle at all so, swearing again, he lifted her into his arms in one sweeping movement and strode towards the office doors.

CHAPTER FIVE

ASHLEY KNEW BETTER than to protest as Nico carried her into the sleek skyscraper off Wall Street that housed Galletti Finance. Her ankle hurt too much, and Nico was clearly a man who didn't like to be challenged.

And, in any case, she was just too *tired*. She'd fought and lost too many times today, and after thirty-six hours with little food or sleep she simply didn't have a protest for pride's sake inside her. Maybe she really was weak, as her father had always said. Weak enough, even, to rest her head against Nico's strong, hard chest as he carried her because she was too tired to arch away from him—even though she knew she should, as a matter of principle, especially after that entirely unexpected and scorching kiss...

Not that she was going to think about that kiss, especially with what had come *after*... What on earth had he meant, that she'd been part of him losing his life? It didn't make any sense, but Nico Galletti hadn't struck her as someone prone to exaggeration. Surely there had to be some mistake? She'd never met him before. She'd had nothing to do with her father's business, besides playing his hostess at various events. Nico Galletti simply couldn't have any reason to blame her.

Without even realising she was doing it, Ashley closed her eyes. She was too tired to fight any more, even to *think* any more, and it felt weirdly comforting to be carried in someone's arms. Even Nico Galletti's.

Especially Nico Galletti's, she forced herself to acknowledge. Caught up in his strong arms, she felt small and safe in a way she secretly relished. For the last four years, she'd tried so hard to be independent and strong. She'd *had* to be, because with her father in prison and her mother in care there was little choice. But right now, just for a few moments, it was nice to feel someone else was in charge. Even if that person was wrecking her life.

Ashley heard the swish of the automated doors as Nico strode into the foyer, and then the startled gasp of a few people as he walked toward the back.

'Mr Galletti?'

'Can I help?'

'Should I call…?'

Ashley let her eyes flutter open for a few seconds—she glimpsed a vast and soaring foyer of black marble and a gleaming bank of lifts at the back—and then quickly closed them again, doing her best to ignore the whispers of speculation as Nico carried her towards the lifts. Really, there was something fun and fairytale-like about this whole scene that she perversely enjoyed. She'd have to open her eyes soon enough and face the music—or at least, this man.

Nico stepped into a lift, and it soared upwards at a dizzying speed, making her clutch him a little closer. She could tell he noticed from the way his arms tensed around her, and he drew in a sharp breath. As long as she kept her eyes closed, Ashley told herself, she didn't have to be embarrassed by the fact that she was practically *cuddling* Nico Galletti. She breathed in the scent of his cologne—clean and woodsy with a hint of leather. Even with her eyes closed, she could tell her lips were alarmingly near his throat, just as they'd been back in the limo.

But she wasn't going to think about that time-out-of-time back in the limo. Not without feeling extremely embarrassed and unsettlingly confused, anyway. The lift door opened, and Nico stepped out. Then he walked swiftly for a few seconds, nudged open a door with his foot and then deposited Ashley on what felt like a bed—a very soft, wide, comfortable one.

Her eyes flew open and she took in her surroundings: a sumptuous bedroom decorated in shades of grey, a floor-to-ceiling picture window overlooking Wall Street. 'Where are we?' she demanded, her voice coming out in something like a squeak.

Nico's mouth quirked, his eyes glinting silver as he shrugged off his jacket. 'We're in my bedroom so we can finish what we started in the limo.'

'*What—?*' This time her voice was a positive squawk.

Nico's lips quirked again. 'Relax, I'm not about to relieve you of your dubious virtue. You're in a spare bedroom at my office. I'm sending up someone to look at your ankle.'

'You don't have to.'

'You're obviously hurt. And, regardless what you think of me and my methods, I'm not a monster.'

That was exactly how she'd thought of him back at her own office. Now she didn't know what to think of him. He was being kind, and he clearly had reasons to act as he had, even if she had no idea what those were. And, when he'd kissed her, she'd forgotten who she was, never mind who *he* was. It was too much to process all at once.

Ashley leaned her head back against the pillows and closed her eyes once more. Life was so much easier, she reflected, if you kept your eyes closed. After a few seconds, she heard the door click shut behind Nico and she knew she was alone. Her breath came out in a rush, and she relaxed further against the pillows, their softness enveloping her. She was so very tired, and there was too much to think, wonder and worry about, with Nico Galletti at the top of that list.

At some point, she fell asleep, only to startle awake when a competent-looking woman opened the door.

'Hello, you must be Ashley. Did I wake you up? I'm sorry; I'm Pam, a nurse practitioner. Mr Galletti asked me to look in on you.'

'There was no need,' Ashley mumbled, pushing her hair out of her face. She felt discombobulated from having fallen asleep, and being in Nico's bedroom of all places, even if it was some kind of office guest suite, made her feel vulnerable. She needed to get out of here, and back to the shattered pieces of her own life.

'Always pays to be careful,' Pam replied cheerfully. 'Do you mind if I have a look?'

Ashley shook her head. The nurse examined her ankle, prodding it gently, making her wince. 'It does look swollen and is probably sprained,' she said, 'But I don't think an x-ray is needed, although Mr Galletti offered to have you taken to the hospital for one if I felt it was necessary.'

'No, thank you, I really don't think I need an x-ray.' She needed to get out of here, Ashley thought with something approaching panic. For a little while there, she'd been lulled into complacency because she'd been so tired and it had felt so nice to be taken care of.

But Nico Galletti certainly wasn't taking care of her employees, and she had to get back to them—and Ruth Boxall. Ruth had seemed to know something about Nico, and Ashley needed to find out what it was. Maybe her friend would have some information that would help her make Nico Galletti see sense.

'Well, I wouldn't walk on it for a few days at least,' the nurse told her. 'Mr Galletti is having some food and drink brought here for your refreshment. I advise you rest for a few hours and elevate your ankle.' Smiling, she reached for a pillow and put it under Ashley's injured foot.

'Actually... I kind of need to go,' Ashley told her with an apologetic smile. Belatedly, she realised she still didn't have her phone or bag. How was she going to get home? 'Could I borrow your phone?' she blurted. 'I just need to make a quick call...'

Pam frowned. 'I'm sorry, I don't have a phone on me. But I'm sure Mr Galletti will see to all your needs.' And with that, she rose from the bed and, with one last friendly smile, left Ashley alone in the bedroom, as good as a prisoner. She sank back against the pillows with a frustrated sigh.

A few minutes later, a woman brought a tray of food, leaving it on a table by the door. Ashley hobbled up from bed to examine it—fresh fruit, bread, cheese, a lentil and couscous salad and a vegetable quiche. It all looked delicious, and she *was* hungry, but it would feel like a betrayal of some kind of eat Nico's food. To accept his hospitality when he was firing all her employees. What about Tom, who was only twenty-one and on his own? Or Denise, who had two children to support, including one with complex needs? Or Laney, who was eighteen months from retirement? She'd never get another job at her age.

Ashley ran through the list of her employees—all of them wonderful people who needed the work she'd provided for them. She felt responsible for each and everyone. How, she wondered despondently, could she get Nico Galletti to change his mind?

'We have a problem.'

Nico snapped his gaze away from the view of lower Manhattan he'd been contemplating—except he hadn't been regarding the city at all. He'd been picturing Ashley sprawled on top of him, her pupils dilated and her lush lips parted, the little mewling sound she'd made in her throat when he'd touched her, the way her whole, delectable body had come apart under his hands...

Why couldn't he get that image out of his head? The memory alone was enough to have him shifting where he stood, restless with the desire that remained painfully unsated—for his *enemy*, the woman he'd sought to destroy. Nico had always been in control of his emotions, his urges—everything. He'd had to be, to survive five years in prison. It made no sense now to have this overwhelming want for a woman he despised. *That* was his problem, but it wasn't the one Tony, his head of PR, was talking about.

He turned round to face him, shoving his hands in his pockets as he rocked back on his heels. 'What kind of problem?' he asked. 'And how quickly can you make it go away?'

Tony shook his head, looking grim as he closed the door to Nico's huge corner office, with floor-to-ceiling views of the city on two sides. 'This isn't going away, boss. Not easily, anyway.' He frowned unhappily as he took out his phone and started scrolling. 'It's about the takeover of that tech company. It's not going well.'

'I thought it went very well,' Nico replied in a deliberately mild voice. At least it had on the surface, a textbook case of how to take over a company in three days with very little damage. The fact that he felt very unsettled in his own mind about it all was another matter entirely.

'Buying out the shareholders did,' Tony confirmed, 'But there's been pushback, and it's not pretty. One of the employees did something on social media, and two hours in it's already going seriously viral.'

Nico frowned as he held out his hand. 'Show me.'

Tony scrolled on his phone for a few more seconds before wordlessly handing Nico the device. Nico glanced down dispassionately at the video of a tearful woman sitting at an office cubicle, shredding a tissue as she detailed how she'd lost her job and had to clear her desk in ten minutes, a security guard menacingly standing over her. She was a single mother with a disabled son, she wept, and she had no idea how she was going to survive without her job.

He handed it back to Tony without watching the whole thing. 'So? One post.' He shrugged. 'People lose their jobs all the time and any business venture of this kind attracts this sort of notice. It's par for the course.'

'Yes,' Tony replied, 'But this post has racked up six hundred thousand views in just two hours, and there's more every minute.'

Nico's frown deepened. That, he had to acknowledge, was a lot of views. 'How?'

'Some celeb reposted it, apparently.' Tony shrugged in dismissal. 'Who knows how these things happen? The point is, it's now blowing up. I've already been contacted by *four* media outlets. And it's not just the media,' he continued darkly. 'Your front-facing interests are already suffering. The Galletti Hotel in Los Angeles has already had a raft of cancellations, with guests citing this as the reason.'

'What?' Nico could hardly believe it. He understood a little online faux-outrage, but people actually *cancelling* reservations because of one woman crying into her camera? 'All because of this?' he demanded. 'Why do people care so much about a simple takeover? They happen all the time. Usually, they barely make it past being buried in the business pages.'

Tony pressed his lips together. 'I suppose people want to know why a billionaire tycoon like Nico Galletti has been ruthlessly targeting such a relatively small company that helps at-risk people…and why he felt the need to fire everyone who worked there.' Judging from his head of PR's tone, it seemed as if Tony was wondering the same thing.

'These news stories last a second,' Nico dismissed impatiently, ignoring Tony's spin on reality. 'You just wait them out...' He stopped, frowning as Tony's words trickled through his mind. 'Wait, what do you mean, "at-risk people"?'

'The tech company,' he explained. 'Infinite Innovations. All their inventions are—or rather, *were*—to help differently abled and other at-risk people. Destroying it for no apparent reason is not a good look, especially in this day and age, when a company's ethical profile is so crucial.'

'Right.' Nico turned back to the window, raking his hand through his hair. Somehow, when researching the solvency of Infinite Innovations, he had missed the part about the inventions being *aimed* at anyone, especially people with special needs. All he'd cared about was that it was run by a Woodward, and what that meant for his bottom line.

He blew out a breath, his gaze on the view from the twenty-second floor, but his mind's eye picturing Ashley: that surprisingly stubborn tilt of her chin; the emerald flash of her eyes; the tremble of her lips as she'd tried desperately to hold it together when he'd told her he was destroying her company...

And then he thought about his brother, his mother's words ringing through his mind.

This is your fault, Nico. If you'd been here, Roberto wouldn't have...

He clamped down hard on that train of thought as he swivelled back to face Tony. 'So, considering the situation,' he asked, 'What do you advise I do?'

'Damage control, stat,' the other man replied immediately. 'Be seen in public with the tech company's CEO. Make a statement about being committed to preserving jobs. Promise to educate yourself about the issues that have been raised. Donate a *shedload* of money to significant causes. And then, maybe—and only maybe—you might limit the damage.'

Nico shook his head slowly, more amazed than alarmed. He could weather a few cancellations and some negative press, and he knew damage control wasn't as important to him as it was to Tony. But if he'd done something he would regret…for several reasons…

'You really think it's that bad?' he asked.

In reply, Tony held up his phone. 'Over a hundred thousand views in the last fifteen minutes. Yes, it's that bad.'

Half an hour later, Nico was back by the window, staring blindly out at the city. He'd spent most of that time scrolling on his phone to discover more information about Infinite Innovations. Just a few minutes had been enough to make his stomach seethe with guilt and regret. Of all the companies he could have chosen to destroy, Ashley Woodward's might have been the worst, both for public *and* personal reasons.

He'd read about the robotic toothbrush that those with paralysis or dementia could use to help brush their teeth and the communication device the company was helping to market to help people with speech difficulties. He'd learned about the bracelet that monitored brainwaves and could warn people they were having seizures as well as transmit messages to carers; and about an all-terrain wheelchair that was impossible to tip, and the prosthetic arm that could restore a sense of touch. All of the technology had been invented awhile ago, but Infinite Innovations was helping to bring it to a wider, more accessible market.

He'd read an interview with Ashley in which she'd explained how hard it was to get investors, because people with disabilities were so often at the bottom of the list, but that these were inventions that would truly change the world. He'd watched a snippet of a video in which she'd spoken passionately about needing to champion these causes, and how every single one of her employees had been hired based on their connection to someone who had complex needs.

Reading it all had made him realise what a huge mistake he'd made. And why Ashley Woodward must truly think he was a monster. Right then, he *felt* like a monster. He'd destroyed a company that was, at its heart, perhaps the noblest and most altruistic business endeavour he'd ever heard of. One, in any other scenario, he would have fought hard to champion. And, according to the articles he'd read, it had been Ashley Woodward's brainchild. Her *baby*.

What did that say about the woman he'd dismissed as not only shallow, but scheming and treacherous? What did it say about him that he had, especially considering his own history?

He felt as if he didn't know anything any more, and that was a deeply unsettling sensation. He dealt in certainties. What Chase Woodward had done to him, with the help of his daughter, had affected every choice he'd made in the sixteen years since it happened. But, no matter how noble she might seem, he still couldn't trust her. He *wouldn't*, and that was a choice too, because he'd learned the hardest way possible how much trusting could hurt. He would not let himself be fooled twice. He refused to be that naïve or hopeful with anyone ever again, the way he had once been, and especially not with a Woodward.

But Nico acknowledged with a grimace that he still needed to talk to Ashley…and find a way out of this mess.

CHAPTER SIX

Ashley had just finished eating—the quiche had been particularly delicious—when the door opened and a suited, blank-faced member of staff stood there.

'Mr Galletti will see you now.'

'Oh, will he?' Ashley fired back before she could think better of it. 'I wasn't aware *I* wanted to see *him*.'

The man's expression didn't change in the slightest as he simply held open the door. Deciding she'd have to face Nico Galletti at some point—and she had a few choice things to say to him, anyway—Ashley slowly limped through it. Her ankle was feeling marginally better, but she still walked haltingly and painfully as she followed the man down an opulent, thickly carpeted hall, past several closed office doors. The atmosphere was both awed and expectant—although maybe that was just how she felt. Nerves fluttered low in her belly as they approached a set of double doors in black walnut at the end of the hall. They had to lead to Nico Galletti's office.

The man knocked once on the door and then, at a terse command to enter, opened it before gesturing for Ashley to step through, which she did with equal parts trepidation and curiosity.

It was a massive office, with floor-to-ceiling windows that made her feel as if she were hovering over the city. A huge mahogany desk was at one end, a leather sofa and chairs at the other. And Nico Galletti stood right in the middle, looking as darkly forbidding as ever and, Ashley had to admit, as sexy as hell.

Ashley felt as though meeting his gaze was one of the hardest things she had ever done, because as soon as she did heat flooded her face and memories tumbled through her mind of her lips on his throat, her hands in his hair, his body...

She needed to scrub her mind of that brief episode, scrub her whole *body*, because even now, when he gave her nothing more than a level look, heat prickled everywhere and awareness trickled through her veins like molten lava, making her yearn.

'How,' he asked, all solicitude, 'Is your ankle?'

Ashley forced her chin up and was grateful when her voice came out sounding mostly normal. 'It's all right.'

'Why don't you sit down?' He gestured to the sofa and Ashley frowned at him.

'Why,' she couldn't help but ask, 'Are you being so polite?'

'I believe we need to clear up a few things,' Nico replied smoothly. 'Come. Sit.' He strolled over to her, cupping her elbow under his palm as he helped her over to the sofa. Ashley wanted to resist, but she knew she needed his help, and she also needed to sit down. She did her best not to react to the heat of his palm under her elbows, the spicy scent of his cologne hitting her nostrils and the sight of him without his suit jacket, so she could fully appreciate the breadth of his shoulders and the sculpted definition of his powerful biceps.

After she lowered herself into one of the deep leather sofas, Nico sat opposite her, crossing one leg over the other, his arms stretched out along the back of the sofa. He looked every inch the powerful magnate, totally at ease and in his element...whereas Ashley felt downtrodden and at a disadvantage. She still hadn't showered *or* brushed her teeth today, her hair was a mess and her ankle throbbed. And then there was her business to think about, or lack of… The memory of this morning's events made her stomach cramp, far from the first time, and, taking a deep breath, she launched into her plan of attack.

'Look, whatever my father did to you—and I'm assuming it had something to do with money, because he stole a *lot* of people's money—I had nothing to do with it. I never had anything to do with my father's business interests whatsoever. He'd wanted a son, you know, to pass it all onto, and overall I think I was a pretty big disappointment to him, in a lot of ways.'

His eyebrows drew together at that, and Ashley hurried on. 'I know Infinite Innovations might seem like some sort of reinvention of Woodward Investments, but it really isn't. I mean, there weren't even a couple of computers left after the police went through it all. Everything was either seized or sold, right down to the last pen.'

From somewhere, she found a desperation-tinged laugh. 'Destroying my company will have *zero* effect on him, I promise you. He's in some minimum-security prison in Florida, probably conning all the guards out of their life savings.' She rolled her eyes as if it was some joke, when in truth even thinking about her father was enough to have her feel the start of an anxiety attack. She took a careful breath, willing her heart to stop racing. 'He had absolutely nothing to do with it whatsoever,' she stated firmly.

Nico cocked his head, his gaze resting on her thoughtfully. His eyelashes were impossibly thick and lush, Asley thought numbly; his lips too. What man had eyelashes like that, especially such a potently masculine one as Nico Galletti? Or lips? And why was she thinking about them, remembering how his lips had felt on hers, so thrilling and yet also weirdly familiar, almost as if she'd remembered his touch…?

'Phillip Boxall was your father's right-hand man,' Nico remarked in a voice that sounded disconcertingly pleasant, considering how narrowed his eyes were; they were like slits of silver, his mouth pursed in what seemed like condemnation.

'Yes…he's my godfather,' Ashley explained uncertainly. 'He went to prison because he couldn't convince the court that he hadn't known about my father's dealings, but I believed him when he said he didn't, and so did Ruth. I've known her for a long time.'

Did Nico suspect Phillip or even Ruth of colluding with her father? She was sure nothing could be further from the truth. Ruth had been unfailingly kind since she'd helped Ashley start Infinite Innovations. 'She was…there for me,' she said haltingly, 'After things…fell apart.' And that was all she wanted to say about that.

'Just like her husband was there for your father,' Nico pointed out in that same pleasant voice.

'He worked for him,' Ashley corrected. 'And he thought he was his friend. Trust me, Phillip was not—'

'*Trust* you?' Nico cut her off, and now his voice was as hard as iron, making Ashley feel as if she'd run face-first into a brick wall. She blinked, reeling from his unrelenting tone. 'I will never,' he informed her curtly, 'Trust a Woodward ever again.'

She stared at him uncertainly, her lips parting soundlessly as she took in the colour that slashed his cheekbones, the blaze of fury in his eyes. 'What did my father do to you?' she whispered.

'You honestly don't remember?' The words were bitten off, spat out.

What? 'No, why would I?' Ashley cried. 'I told you, I had nothing to do with his—'

'You were there.' The words, spoken with such quiet finality, made Ashley fall silent, even more shocked than before.

'Where?' she finally asked helplessly.

'A charity ball at your house. You held it every year, apparently.'

'The fundraiser for breast cancer,' Ashley confirmed slowly. 'Yes, my mother arranged it. Her sister died of breast cancer when she was just in her thirties.' And from the age of sixteen Ashley had been forced to act as her father's hostess, no matter that she'd hated the role. 'But what does that ball have to do with…' she gestured helplessly between them '…this?'

Nico hesitated, and then in one abrupt movement he rose from the sofa and walked to the window, his hands thrust into the pockets of his trousers so his shirt stretched tautly across his powerful shoulders as he stood with his back to her. A full minute ticked by with neither of them saying anything.

Had she met Nico at one of those balls? Those years were a painful blur she'd done her best to forget, Ashley acknowleged. It was too painful to remember her father's cold anger which had been masked by an easy charm that, stupidly, had made her want to please him, even as he'd belittled her and her mother time and time again. It had been a pattern she had never had the courage to break, and, in its own way, his arrest had provided a freedom Ashley knew she'd never have had the strength to seize otherwise.

But she didn't have any recollection of Nico, and he was surely a man she wouldn't have been able to forget, no matter how much she might want to forget those pain-filled years.

'There's no need to rake over the past in this way,' Nico finally remarked, his back still to her. Now he sounded different, diffident, as if the issue was of no matter to him, all the fury and fire gone. He turned around slowly, his face as expressionless as a beautiful, blank canvas, and somehow the emptiness of his expression was even more unnerving. 'What matters is the future.'

'The future,' Ashley repeated uncertainly. She wanted to agree with him, but… '*What* future?' she made herself ask. 'As of this morning, Infinite Innovations *has* no future, at least according to you.' His expression didn't change, and yet something about his stance, his silence, made hope stumble through Ashley's chest like a drunken sailor. She lurched upright, even though it hurt her ankle. 'Wait…are you saying you might have changed your mind?'

Nico stared at her imperturbably for another endless few seconds. 'A good businessman is always willing to change his mind when new information becomes available,' he finally stated tonelessly.

'New information?' As tired and overwhelmed as she was, Ashley struggled to make sense of his words. 'What new information?'

'Why don't you tell me,' Nico suggested as she strolled back towards the sofa, his hands still in his pockets, 'What the impetus for starting Infinite Innovations was?'

Ashley stared at him, taken aback by his sudden curiosity. Was this some sort of trap? She didn't like talking about her background because it hurt too much, for all sorts of reasons, and she really didn't feel like talking about it with Nico Galletti, who seemed sure to use any such information against her…or her mother. She couldn't allow that to happen.

'I saw…a niche in the market,' she answered after a moment.

'No, you didn't.' Nico's rejection of her prevarication was swift and certain. 'Everything about Infinite Innovations screams passion project. I'm amazed you've made any money out of it at all. If not for that robotic toothbrush being picked up by hospitals and care homes, you probably wouldn't have.'

Ashley couldn't help but wince at that, because she knew he was right. 'Why do you want to know why I started it, since you only took it over to destroy it?' she asked, her voice wobbling more than she wished it would. She wanted to come out swinging, but right now, with everything that had happened, she felt so pitifully weak. And it didn't help that Nico was standing right in front of her, staring at her with eyes like lasers, as if he could see straight into her head, her heart, and was analyzing every thought she'd ever had.

'Why aren't you willing to go to bat for it now, if you care about it so much?' he challenged. 'I asked you a simple question, a question that most CEOs would be *begging* to answer, frankly, and you can't be bothered to tell me the truth.' His gaze was unrelenting, like a spotlight on her soul. 'Why?'

'Because it's *private*!' she cried. 'Because anything I tell you will probably be used against me. Because I met you this morning and yet somehow it seems like you've hated me for years.' She shook her head slowly, hating that tears were starting in her eyes. She never cried, not any more, yet here she was, having to blink hard to keep tears from falling. She drew a ragged breath as she willed back the tears. 'Why should I tell you anything?' she demanded in a broken whisper.

Why should she tell him, indeed? Nico rocked back on his heels as he gazed at the woman before him who was trying so hard not to cry. Either Ashley Woodward was not at all who he'd thought she was…or she was a hell of a good actress. But, if she was as sensitive and thoughtful as she now appeared, why had she not even remembered him?

That one little fact kept tripping him up. Yes, it was galling to know a woman he'd had at the forefront of his mind far too often hadn't even recalled he existed. But, beyond that, it was *odd*. Surely most people remembered seeing someone they'd talked to, had even *kissed*, had seen handcuffed in front of their very eyes and then seen standing in the dock for two *weeks*? That was surely too much personal history to have simply slipped one's mind?

Which led Nico to the only other conclusion: that she was lying. But for what purpose? He could understand keeping up such a pretence for a little while, whether to humiliate him or make a desperate bid for pity, but hours…longer? It was absurd.

And so, all he could deduce from the whole sorry debacle was that somewhere in this tangled web of truths was a deception. Ashley Woodward was lying to him…about something. Maybe something important.

'If you tell me why you started it,' he told her, 'I'll consider keeping on all your employees.'

Her eyes widened to mossy pools as her lips parted—lush, moist lips that Nico remembered the feel of all too well. 'You…will? Or are you just saying that?'

'I will,' Nico repeated seriously. He'd already decided he would, not that Ashley needed to know that just yet. 'So?'

She drew a deep breath as she raked her fingers through her tangled hair, clearly trying to compose herself. 'If you use this information against me…' she whispered, her eyes briefly fluttering closed at the thought.

Impatience bit at him. Surely she was being a little melodramatic? 'Why would I use such information against you? And how could I do so, even if I wanted to? All you're telling me is what inspired you to champion these inventions.'

She gave a huff of disbelief as she opened her eyes. 'Why *wouldn't* you do so?' she demanded rawly. 'Since you marched into my office this morning, you've done nothing but use *everything* against me. You've made no secret of wanting to destroy not just my company, but *me*, so why would I tell you anything personal that I cared about?' She shook her head in despair, brushing at her eyes with her fingertips as she angled her body away from him. Clearly just saying that had made her feel more vulnerable than she liked, and Nico felt uncharacteristically chastened. When she said it like that, well, it made him see things differently.

But if she really was lying…

'I promise,' he said quietly, 'I won't use anything you tell me against you. I'm just trying to…understand.' Although *why* he was, he still didn't know. Only that something about Ashley Woodward felt very…*off*, and he needed to figure out what it was.

She stared at him for a few moments, her eyes still wide, her whole body taut. 'Fine,' she said at last. 'When I was sixteen, my mother had a massive stroke. She was paralyzed on the right side of her body and had pretty severe motor and memory issues. She became bed-ridden—a shadow, a shell of who she'd once been…' Her voice choked, and her breath hitched. 'She struggled so much, and I couldn't do anything to help her. My father was ashamed of her, how she was, and he basically acted like she'd died. I hated that, even as my mum seemed to understand it and accept it, because my father was such a public figure. She was proud, too; she didn't like people seeing her the way she was after the stroke.'

She sniffed, dabbing at her eyes again. 'And so…this company was a way of helping my mother, and people like her, and also just…making sure they were seen and heard, because…' She pressed her lips together, her gaze becoming distant, veiled. 'My mother wasn't,' she finished flatly.

Nico felt there was even more she wasn't saying, yet she'd told him so much. So much he'd had absolutely no idea about it. He hadn't even thought about her mother once. He hadn't realised Ashley had that kind of painful history, history he understood all too well. 'I'm sorry,' he said, meaning it. 'That all sounds very difficult.'

'It was,' she replied shortly. 'And I...don't like to talk about it, because my mother is a very private person. She never wanted to be the poster child for my company by any means, and I would hate her to be...used, in some way, so I don't talk about her very much, at her own request. But... she's the reason, if you must know.' She looked away, still clearly struggling to regain her composure.

'Where is she now?' Nico asked.

Ashley hesitated before answering, 'She's in a care home outside the city. Her needs are too complex for me to take care of her at home, unfortunately, but I visit her as often as I can.' He heard the guilt in her voice, and he understood it. He had so much guilt for letting his mother down, his brother... He couldn't even *think* about his brother without the guilt pouring through him like acid, corroding everything it touched.

And yet... Ashley had been *sixteen* when her mother had had a stroke. He'd met her at that ball when she'd been eighteen. That didn't necessarily mean anything, Nico knew, and yet he couldn't reconcile the Ashley he'd known then with the woman before him now. If her mother's stroke had been the catalyst for some kind of personality change, why had it happened *before* he'd met her? Something still didn't make sense.

'So now I've told you,' Ashley said, straightening and flashing him a look of spiky challenge. 'Will you keep all my employees?'

'I said I'd *consider* it,' Nico replied. 'And I will.'

'They need their jobs,' she persisted, clearly not willing to let the matter go. 'Go ahead and fire me,' she continued defiantly. 'I'll figure something out. But those people depend on their jobs. They have families they take care of, with children or siblings with complex needs.'

'I'm aware,' Nico replied tersely. He didn't need to feel any guiltier than he already did. Once again, he thought of his own brother, and how he hadn't been able to take care of his needs. The knowledge was like a pulsing wound inside him, and not something he had any intention of sharing with Ashley Woodward. Some things were simply too private, and she thought little of him already.

'And the inventions,' Ashley continued, her voice rising. 'What we do, the projects we're pioneering and investing in...they're *important*. If you want to absorb Infinite Innovations into your own behemoth of a company...' she threw one arm out to encompass his financial empire in a way that felt stingingly dismissive '...go ahead. But still keep it going, so these inventions get made, because they *need* to be.'

'Your company was barely breaking even,' Nico felt compelled to point out. He sympathised with its aims, but he also had to be pragmatic. 'If I kept it going, it would be little more than a pity project.'

'You don't need to pity anyone,' Ashley replied hotly, her eyes flashing fire. 'That is *not* what Infinite Innovations is about at all.'

'I didn't say I did pity anyone,' Nico replied, keeping his voice mild. 'But, Ashley, you must have realised yourself, very few of these technologies are what I could call money spinners. Until they become cost effective, Infinite Innovations doesn't have a chance. The only reason you were as successful as you seemed was because of that robotic toothbrush.'

'But there are other inventions that could be just as successful,' Ashley insisted, her voice wobbling. 'Shutting the whole thing down because you're annoyed at my father—'

'I'm not *annoyed*,' Nico bit out. His patience extended only so far, and she made him sound—and feel—petty. 'This runs far deeper than some minor irritation.'

'Then tell me.'

He wasn't ready to reveal that information, not until he understood her more. Not until it made him feel less vulnerable. But, as Tony had said, Nico needed to do damage control. 'We have more to discuss,' he told her. 'There's a charitable gala I need to attend tomorrow night. I'd like you to go with me.'

Ashley's jaw dropped before she snapped it shut. 'As your *date*?' she asked incredulously.

Nico gave her a cool smile. 'No, as my potential business partner. If you want to save Infinite Innovations, then you'll attend with me and make a nice show of how we're so happy to be working together.'

Ashley's golden brows snapped together. '*Are* we working together?'

Nico bared his teeth in a smile. 'What do you call this?' he asked.

CHAPTER SEVEN

Ashley opened the door of her apartment with a groan, kicking it behind her before she shuffled over to the sofa and collapsed on it in a veritable heap. Today felt like the longest day she'd ever known, and it was only five o'clock. Yet her world had shattered, come back together and shattered again in the space of a few hours.

Ashley still don't know what to think about any of it. What did Nico Galletti even *want* from her? This morning, he'd seemed intent on cruel destruction, and then this afternoon he'd rowed back on it all…*maybe*. Ashley still couldn't tell if he was merely toying with her. *Why* have her attend this gala event, and why make it seem as if they were working together, if he had no intention of taking on her company, even as a "pity project"?

The questions seethed through her mind, filling her with uncertainty…and that was without thinking about that scorching kiss they'd shared, which she'd been doing her best to block out and act as if it had never happened.

Yet now, as she lay on her sofa in her studio apartment, Ashley let herself remember. She luxuriated in the memory of his strong arms around her, his hand sliding up her thigh, his fingers tantalizing her flesh and cupping her breast… His lips, so soft and full, yet hard and demanding at the same time…

Heat bloomed inside her at the mere thought, snaked

through her veins and filled her with wanting. Ashley had been kissed only a few times in her life, and it had all been unremarkable, confirming her suspicion that romance was nothing more than a distraction and worse, a weakness—one she had no intention of giving into the way her mother had. She'd been in thrall to a man who had as good as disposed of her when she'd outlasted her usefulness.

And, Ashley suspected, Nico would be a similar kind of man. Maybe he didn't possess the subtle yet devastating cruelty her father did—although there was no real reason for her to think he *didn't*—but in any case, she was under no illusions that that kiss had meant anything to Nico whatsoever. If anything, he'd been trying to demonstrate his power over her, something she had no intention of giving him. She would, she decided, never let him kiss her again.

Even if she'd agreed to attend this ball with him tomorrow night. With the fate of her business in his hands, what else could she do? But, as Nico himself had said, it was a business engagement only, and Ashley intended to be every inch the consummate professional.

The buzz of her intercom had Ashley heaving herself from the sofa with a groan. She didn't get many visitors, because she didn't have many friends, but this day had been one surprise after another...

'Delivery for Miss Ashley Woodward,' the voice on the intercom informed her after she'd pressed it.

'Can you leave it in the post room?' she asked. Usually deliverymen just chucked whatever packages or parcels arrived in the small room intended for such things.

'I'm afraid Mr Galletti's instructions were to have it delivered directly to your apartment.'

Briefly Ashley closed her eyes. She had no idea what Nico had sent to her apartment, but she was not surprised a deliveryman was determined to obey his fearsome instructions.

'All right, thank you, you can send it up,' she said wearily, and she pressed the button to unlock the front door. She supposed she should be grateful to Nico; he'd provided her with a car to take her home from his office after she'd—reluctantly—agreed to attend this event.

'If it's black tie, I don't have anything to wear,' she'd warned him after he'd told her, irritatingly, to 'dress appropriately'. 'I gave away all my formal clothes years ago.'

His brows had snapped together at that. 'Why did you do such a thing?'

'Because I had no need for them and I didn't want the reminders,' she'd replied shortly. She'd not been about to explain how she'd hated every dress her father had forced her to wear, intent on her being the consummate hostess, the perfect *princess*. How giving them all away had felt like freedom, a huge weight sliding from her bowed-down shoulders.

'But if this is a *business* event,' she'd told Nico with emphasis, 'Then I can attend in business wear, so we should be fine.' She'd bared her teeth in a steely smile and, to her annoyance, Nico had given her a little quirk of his lips in return, as if her petty little power plays merely amused him. She'd wondered if he'd still be amused when she showed up at the charity event in off-the-rack business separates.

As Ashley opened the door to her apartment, a groan escaped her. There was not just one deliveryman, but *three*, and they carried a portable clothes rack with at least a dozen plastic-swathed hangers that looked to hold designer dresses. Clearly Nico had not approved of her suggestion that she wear her usual business attire. She wasn't surprised by his high-handedness, but she was certainly aggravated by it, especially when she considered her history with her father and all the dresses he'd made her wear.

'I don't need these,' she informed the first deliveryman

as he held out a receipt for her to sign. 'You can take them back.'

The man shook his head resolutely. 'Mr Galletti said you might say something like that. He insisted they stay.'

Ashley nodded resignedly and signed the receipt. She wasn't going to take her ire out on a hapless and innocent deliveryman, but neither was she going to wear these designer gowns. 'Thank you,' she told him and, after closing the door on all three men, she turned to face the dozen dresses hanging from the rack.

She stared at them hard for a second as a visceral shudder went through her. The days of designer dresses and glittering balls were long behind her, but just the sight of a single plastic-swathed hanger had a reaction rising up that she could not suppress. She had to curl her hands into fists to keep herself from yanking those hangers off the rail and hurling them to the floor, which she'd never done when her father had made his demands.

You'll look beautiful tonight, princess, because that's all you're good for.

Doing her best to banish that hard voice, Ashley turned her back on the clothes and headed for the bathroom. She wanted a long, hot shower, then a mug of hot chocolate and an hour of brainless TV. Maybe then she'd figure out if she had the brass neck to ignore Nico Galletti's gowns and wear what she'd intended to all along—a perfectly serviceable business suit.

An hour later, swathed in a thick terry cloth bathrobe, her damp hair falling in ringlets about her face, Ashley was gratefully sipping from a very large mug of hot chocolate. She'd already fielded over a dozen emails from employees, asking about the rumours now swirling around that they might be able to keep their jobs. She'd tried to call Ruth, but her phone kept switching to voicemail. She'd get answers eventually, Ashley supposed, but it would have been nice to find out what Ruth knew—and to understand just what she was up against.

She'd also had six voicemails from various media outlets, asking her to comment on the video that had gone viral. It hadn't taken long for her to figure out what they were talking about: a couple of clicks, and Ashley was watching Denise tearfully explain how much she needed her job.

A sigh escaped her, along with a weary and cynical chuckle. So *that* was why Nico had changed his mind about dismantling Infinite Innovations. Nothing to do with a change of heart or an interest in the inventions, but merely a way to control the damage to himself and his company. She should have guessed.

Ashley put her phone on mute and tossed it aside. She was not going to talk to any media, she resolved, and she was going to do her best not to think about Nico Galletti until at least tomorrow morning. For a few hours, she would enjoy numbing her brain with back-to-back episodes of *Is It Cake?* and forget the wretched man even existed.

Surprise rippled through Nico as his limo pulled up in front of the decidedly dilapidated building on Fort Washington Avenue, up in the most northerly reaches of Manhattan. This was not where he'd expected Ashley Woodward to live. Yes, he'd suspected she'd fallen on harder times; but, considering the last time he'd seen her before today had been in the ballroom of her Park Avenue mansion, a box-like apartment in a less than salubrious neighbourhood on the very tip of Manhattan seemed like a fall too far. Was this really where she lived—and why? Her father might have lost the Woodward fortune, but there had to have been *something* left; something he'd squirrelled away in an offshore account for his family.

'Marco, there's no need to wait,' he told his driver. 'I'll take an Uber back.' If he could get one all the way up here.

Stepping out into the balmy spring evening, Nico raked his gaze up and down the street. Cherry trees with blossoms like puffballs framed a trash-strewn pavement. No, this was not the neighbourhood he'd expected Ashley Woodward to live in. Once again, she'd surprised and unsettled him, and he was determined to get to the bottom of the mystery—tonight.

Frowning in thought, he mounted the crumbling stoop to her building and pressed the button for apartment 6B.

'Yes?' Her voice on the crackling intercom sounded cautious, as well as exhausted.

'It's Nico,' he told her briefly, expecting her to buzz him up. Instead, there was only silence.

Then, finally, 'What are *you* doing here?'

That, Nico knew, was a very good question. There was no real reason for him to visit Ashley in her home. He'd sent the dresses; that had been message enough that he wanted her to wear something appropriate. And yet something about her reaction to the whole question of what to wear had bothered him. Surely, as a competent businesswoman, she saw the sense in wearing a dress to a black-tie event? Yet, that afternoon, Ashley had seemed determined to do things her way. Nico was here to show her they would be doing things his way…every time. He *might* be willing to salvage her company for expedient reasons, but he wasn't going to humour her little fits of pique. Far from it.

'Well?' Ashley demanded through the intercom.

'Let me up,' Nico commanded coolly. He was not about to explain himself while standing on a stoop. After another taut few seconds, he was buzzed through.

The floor of the foyer was littered with flyers and, although the place had six floors, there was no lift. Nico started climbing the grimy stairs, shaking his head in disbelief that Ashley lived in a place like this. Was she trying to make a point? Surely she had money for something better? She was CEO of her own company after all, no matter how modest.

As he arrived on the top floor, he found Ashley standing in the doorway of her apartment, swathed beguilingly in a white terry cloth bathrobe. Her face was flushed pink, her hair in damp waves the colour of rain-darkened wheat about her face and shoulders.

For a second, Nico was blindsided by the most inconvenient desire. He wanted to slip that soft robe from her shoulders and glimpse the pearly, still-damp flesh beneath. Cup her breasts in his hands, slide his palms along the silk of her skin, draw her towards him...

He stopped those thoughts with a screeching halt as he glared at her. 'What are you wearing?'

She glanced down at herself. 'A bathrobe. Because, after a very long day, I just had a shower, and I wasn't expecting visitors.' She shook her head slowly, annoyance sparking in her eyes. 'What are you doing here?'

Nico moved past her into the apartment. 'Making sure you do as you're told.'

'Oh, *charming*,' she snapped, closing the door behind him.

Nico surveyed the apartment curiously. It was tiny—just one room, with a kitchen tucked into the corner, a double bed in the other, and a bathroom leading off. It was cosy, though, with plenty of personal touches—house plants on every windowsill and shelf, battered cookbooks on the one shelf in the kitchen, a loveseat tucked against one wall with a laptop open on the coffee table, with a close-up picture of a lurid green iguana on the screen.

'What are you watching?' he asked, more curious than

anything else, and in response Ashley hobbled over to her laptop and slammed the lid down on it.

'It doesn't matter.'

Now he was really curious. 'No, seriously, what?'

She blew out a breath, looking exasperated, as well as adorably embarrassed, her cheeks going even pinker. '*Is It Cake?*' she finally muttered.

'*Is It Cake?*' he repeated. He'd never heard of it.

'It's a show where you have to decide if something is made of cake or real,' she explained impatiently, folding her arms so the robe pulled across her breasts, inevitably drawing Nico's gaze downward. 'In this case, an iguana. Does it matter?' She huffed. 'And also, *why* are you here?'

'To make sure you wear one of the dresses I bought you.'

Her eyes flashed as she tilted her chin. 'That's incredibly high-handed of you, but in any case, the charity thing is *tomorrow* night.'

'Yes, but I have a busy day tomorrow, and I don't like surprises.'

She shook her head. 'Why do you care what I wear?'

'Because you can't come to these things dressed in a suit you bought at Walmart,' he replied brutally. 'You, of all people, should know these things, Ashley.'

She stared at him for a moment, confusion clouding eyes that still sparked with irritation. 'Why should *I* know?'

'Because,' he explained impatiently, throwing one arm out to encompass her cozy apartment, 'No matter what your life is like now, you were once the daughter of one of the country's wealthiest men, as well as one of the foremost socialites in all of New York *and* in possession of a closet full of gowns just like those.'

He pointed to the rack she'd shoved into the corner of the room. 'And maybe you like coming across all humble and serious now, but I am not about to walk into a premier event with you on my arm looking like you've been kicked to the kerb—by me.'

Understanding and ire flashed in her eyes, and her breath hitched as her chin tilted a notch higher. 'Oh, I see. This is all about *appearances*,' she drawled. 'More damage control. I saw that video, by the way, of Denise. Must have got you pretty worried.'

'I don't care about the video,' Nico snapped. 'I can ride out any bad publicity *easily*. But I'm not about to have you putting about a false narrative by looking like something the cat dragged in.'

'Oh!' The single syllable came out in a hurt gasp, and she whirled away from him, no doubt to hide the expression on her face.

Nico released a slow, pent-up breath. All right, he hadn't meant to sound *quite* so callous, and in truth that wasn't entirely the reason he'd come here. But Ashley Woodward put him on edge, the memories he kept coming up against colliding with the present reality, and the clash did not make any sense. *Who was she?*

'This doesn't have to be a battle,' he told her levelly. 'I simply want you to wear something appropriate.' He gestured to the rack in the corner. 'Most women appreciate a chance to dress up, especially when it's not paid for by them,' he added for good measure, unable to keep an edge from entering his voice. Why couldn't she at least acknowledge that he was doing her a *favour*, high-handed though it must seem?

'Well, I'm not most women,' she replied in a strangled voice, her taut back still facing him, practically vibrating with tension.

'You can keep all the dresses free of charge,' he offered, but if he thought that would sweeten the deal, he realised at once he was mistaken.

Ashley whirled round, one fist raised above her head as

if she wanted to wallop him. 'I do not,' she informed him through gritted teeth, 'Want to keep *any* of these dresses. I don't even want to look at them. I certainly don't want to wear them, and I really don't want you to make me wear them.'

'Why,' Nico demanded in exasperation, 'Are you being so unreasonable about *dresses*?'

'Why are *you*?' she fired back, her voice turning shrill, her face paper-pale, save for two bright spots of colour high on her cheekbones. Her breath came in gasps that had her bathrobe gaping open with each tautly drawn one, not that Nico was trying to notice. 'What kind of control freak are you, anyway,' she asked, her voice now shaking, 'To come to my apartment and *demand* to know what I'm wearing? I'll *go* to the event. I'll look presentable. Can't that be enough for you?'

She shook her head, her features twisted in sneering despair. 'Or is this some kind of punishment—more revenge for simply being my father's daughter?'

Nico let out a huff of incredulous laughter. Her reasoning skills seriously left something to be desired. 'So buying you a dozen designer dresses is punishment?' he surmised with a twist of his lips. 'Maybe in your pampered world it is, princess—'

'I *told* you,' Ashley shrieked, both fists clenched at her sides, '*Not* to call me that!'

Nico stared at her in disbelief. Her face was flushed, her eyes glittering like emeralds. She looked beautiful, everything in her so vividly and vibrantly alive…and yet in the grip of a fury he did not understand in the least. He'd bought her dresses. Why was she acting as if he'd mortally insulted her? Nico decided he'd had enough of her absurd theatrics.

'You'll pick a damned dress,' he snapped out. 'And you'll wear it.'

In the space of a single second, the colour leached from her face, her shoulders slumped and her fists unclenched. It was as if he was watching the life blood drain out of her. Wordlessly Ashley turned on her heel, walked to the rack and unzipped the covering on the first dress, withdrawing a gorgeous, glittering sheath of emerald satin.

'This one will do,' she said tonelessly, giving it no more than the most cursory of glances, and then she zipped the covering back up. 'You can take the rest away. I don't want them.' She stood there, staring off into space, doing her best to ignore him completely, along with the damnable dress.

Nico stared at her in disbelief. 'Are you not even going to look at the other dresses?' he asked, but Ashley did not respond. He almost wondered if she'd even heard him.

Then, before he could say anything else, she slowly sank to the floor, her arms wrapped around her waist, her hair falling in front of her face in a golden tangle. Nico's brows snapped together as he watched her in concern. Had she fainted *again*? The woman was a walking disaster zone.

Impatiently, he started towards her, and it was only when he crouched in front of her that he realised she was sobbing silently, her shoulders shaking from the effort, tears streaking down her face. It was as if her heart might break, or really, Nico thought with a savage twist in his gut, as if he'd already broken it.

CHAPTER EIGHT

CRUMPLED ON THE FLOOR, Ashley was barely aware of anything. Her mind was a blank haze, seeming disconnected from her body, so she only distantly registered Nico's hands on her shoulders, warm and strong. She recognised that he was holding her, his arms around her, her cheek pressed against her chest; and then he scooped her up into his arms, so he cradled her like a baby, and then finally deposited her gently on her bed.

Ashley *felt* all these things, and yet it was as if she couldn't process them. Her mind was frozen, stuck and empty. She felt like a receptacle and nothing more, as if all the energy and emotion had been leached out of her. She couldn't find it in herself to care…about anything.

She turned her face away to the wall, limply lifting one hand to brush her hair away from her face, and only then realising that her cheeks were damp with tears. Even then she barely registered the fact that she'd been crying; not a single thought entered her mind as she lay there for what could have been minutes or hours, her eyes closed and her face turned away.

She heard Nico moving around the apartment, and at some point, he spoke in a low voice to someone on the phone, but she couldn't make out the words, not that she even tried. She heard the door open and close and, with an unsettling mixture of disappointment and relief, she thought that he must have left. Eventually, without even realising it was happening, she fell asleep.

When Ashley awoke, the apartment was completely dark and the time on her clock read one in the morning. Her breath came out in a sudden rush and she lurched upright, the remnants of a dream she couldn't remember trickling icily away, a fear clamping her insides that she couldn't shake...

Slowly she came back to her senses, and a soft sigh escaped her. She was safe. She wasn't even sure what from, but she was alone in her apartment, and no one could make her do anything any more, ever...

The sound of someone shifting on her sofa had a soft scream of pure terror slipping from lips.

'It's only me,' Nico said quietly and, as her eyes adjusted to the darkness, Ashley realised he was still there, seated just a few feet away from her, his body half-hidden in the darkness. He must have been there all the while she'd slept.

'I... I thought you'd left,' she whispered. Her voice sounded croaky.

He shook his head. 'I couldn't leave you like that.'

His tone was grim, certain, and it made unease pool in Ashley's stomach like acid. 'Like...what?' she asked uncertainly, although she wasn't sure she wanted to know.

Even in the darkness, she saw, or maybe just sensed, his frown. 'Do you not remember?' he asked quietly.

The unease that had pooled in her stomach now crawled coldly up her spine, like some living thing slithering around her body, taking up all the space. It was an intensely vulnerable feeling, to have someone ask her that. To realise she didn't know the answer. 'Remember...what?' she asked unsteadily.

'Just...' Nico paused. 'How upset you were,' he finally answered, and his tone was like nothing she'd ever heard from him before: gentle, even tender, and full of pity. It made

Ashley feel even uneasier, because why was Nico Galletti talking to her as if he felt sorry for her? His pity felt as uncomfortable as his condemnation, she thought, if not more so. She didn't like either. She didn't want anything from this man. She certainly didn't want to be beholden to him.

'Upset...' she repeated cautiously. Why couldn't she remember what had happened? Nico had brought the dresses, she'd been annoyed... The rest, whatever it was, was a complete blank. The realisation was incredibly unnerving. Unless, Ashley thought, he was making it up. Was this simply another way to disadvantage her? Another one of his petty power plays?

Except it didn't feel like that. Nico had sounded so...*concerned*. And if he'd stayed here while she'd slept... Nothing added up.

Abruptly Ashley leaned over and switched on her bedside light. Too late, she realised her bathrobe had fallen open and she yanked it closed as quickly as she could, but she was pretty sure Nico had got an eyeful. She couldn't even worry about that now, because there was too much else unsettling to deal with.

She glanced at him, seated on her sofa, looking so inscrutable, his narrowed gaze watching her, observing and assessing. She pulled her bathrobe right up to her throat.

'I think I need a cup of tea,' she announced, striving for a sense of normality.

'I'll make it,' Nico told her. Now completely flummoxed, Ashley watched as he went to her little kitchen and filled the kettle at the sink. She glanced around her apartment, and realised the rack of dresses was gone. More strangeness.

'What did you do with the dresses?' she asked uncertainly.

'I had them removed,' Nico replied, his tone giving nothing away.

'Removed?' Ashley repeated. 'Why?'

'They were…clearly upsetting you.' He switched on the kettle and turned to face her. Ashley couldn't make out the expression on his face in the half-shadow. His hair was rumpled, his shirt creased and stubble darkened his lean jaw. Somehow, all these elements made him seem even more appealing, more human. Without his forbidding expression and tailored jacket, his aura of cold-hearted and calculating power, he seemed much more approachable. Friendlier; someone she could like and maybe even trust.

Even if she knew he wasn't. And, she was reluctantly compelled to notice, he was also insanely good-looking. Even now, in the midst of her confusion and wariness, her mind noticed and her body responded. She pulled her bathrobe even closer together, as if the act could ward off her own impossible feelings.

'You can wear what you like to the gala tomorrow night,' Nico told her abruptly, his arms folded as he leaned back against the worktop. His face was hidden in shadow, his expression impossible to read.

'Okay…' Ashley answered slowly, her mind whirling. 'What happened to make you change your mind?' She tried to sound wry but she feared she only sounded scared. What had freaked Nico out so much, and why on earth couldn't she remember it? She knew there were parts of her past she'd forgotten, but it had been a deliberate choice…or so she'd thought. She hadn't wanted to dwell on those upsetting aspects of her personal history, because who would? But she'd never had this kind of *blankness* in her brain before. At least, she didn't think she had… But now she found herself second-guessing everything. It was seriously alarming to feel as if she didn't know herself.

'I was over-reaching,' Nico replied tonelessly. 'It's a bad habit of mine.'

'Nico…' It was the first time she'd said his name, and

she could tell he noticed, although his stance didn't change. Something in his eyes, his mouth... It was as if she'd ignited a spark between them simply by saying his name out loud.

Somehow it had just slipped out, an intimacy that wasn't warranted and yet bizarrely still felt right. He had seen her sleep, after all. 'You're scaring me, you know,' she confessed. 'By everything you're *not* saying. What did you mean, the dresses upset me? I mean, yes, I was *angry* at you,' she continued, her voice getting stronger. Maybe there was no big mystery here, after all. 'For over-reaching, as you said. I remember *that*. But... I wasn't upset.'

At least, not in the way his tone had implied—unreasonably and unsettlingly, as if she'd had some kind of breakdown. She hadn't...had she?

She leaned forward, trying to make out his expression from across the room, craving some clue to what had happened, needing to fill in the blank space she was frighteningly aware still loomed in her mind. Nico simply stared at her without saying anything. The kettle started to whistle, and he turned round to make her tea.

Ashley leaned back against the pillows and closed her eyes. This felt like some surreal dream: the room cast in shadows and pools of light, a man she'd only met that morning making her tea at her own kitchen sink. And the dresses... Where were the dresses? Why had Nico had them removed?

He walked silently across the room and handed her a mug of tea. 'Thank you,' Ashley murmured, and took a sip. It was sweet and strong, like something she'd take for shock. She watched out of the corner of her eye as he sat back on the loveseat.

'I feel like I should apologise,' she ventured as she lowered her mug. 'But I don't know what for.'

Nico shook his head. 'You don't need to apologise.'

She tried to smile. 'You know you're just freaking me out even more when you say stuff like that?'

He smiled faintly at that, his eyes glinting in the darkness. 'I don't mean to.'

Ashley shook her head. 'Why are you being so nice all of a sudden?'

He shrugged one powerful shoulder. 'Maybe we just got off to a bad start.'

She managed a laugh at that. 'As *if*. Nico, you came into my office this morning and told me you were destroying my company. You gave me five minutes to clear my desk. You told me I'd had a part in ruining your *life*.'

All of those were necessary reminders, because for a few minutes while she'd sipped the tea, and he sat there looking so approachable and relaxed, it almost felt as if they were getting along. But they weren't; they couldn't be. Not if he was still intent on destroying her company and strong-arming her into presenting some kind of united front to boot, just so he could save face. 'What's changed?' she asked.

Nico was silent for a long moment. 'I don't know,' he admitted. 'I don't know if anything *has* changed. Maybe…' He released a pent-up breath as he raked a hand through his hair. 'Maybe nothing has,' he said, like a concession. 'But… I'm telling you, you can wear whatever you like tomorrow night.'

She supposed she should count it as a victory, Ashley thought, even if right now it didn't feel like one, not remotely. 'And Infinite Innovations?' she pressed. 'My employees, the inventions… You'll keep them on if I go tomorrow night?'

'Don't press your luck,' Nico warned her, but Ashley thought she heard a smile in his voice. 'One step at a time.'

Ashley managed a smile back, and Nico felt a pulse of relief that things felt normal again. The whole surreal episode had been extremely disturbing, mostly because he didn't understand it, and also because he didn't like seeing anyone—bizarrely, Ashley Woodward in particular—that upset. She'd seemed so...*broken*...over dresses. There was too much here that he didn't understand, and he didn't think Ashley herself could be the one to explain it to him, because he was pretty sure she didn't know either.

How could she not remember how upset she'd been, crying as if her heart would break, and then seeming so unnervingly lifeless when he'd carried her to bed? It was almost as if she wasn't even *there*. Then sleeping like the dead for hours, only suddenly to twist and twitch in a nightmare as she'd moaned, *'Don't make me...don't make me...'*

How was he supposed to respond to *that*? What was he supposed to think of Ashley Woodward now? Either she was playing some elaborate and twisted game, or...there were a lot of things she didn't remember.

'Okay,' she said, putting down her mug on the bedside table. 'One thing at a time. I'll show up tomorrow night in sweatpants.' She smiled to show she was joking, but Nico wouldn't have been surprised if she would do such a thing simply out of pique. He also knew he wouldn't mind...not any more.

She lay down with her head on the pillow, tucking her hand under her cheek, her knees tucked up towards her chest as she eyed him speculatively. Her bathrobe gaped open again and Nico tried not to notice that if he let his gaze drop he'd be able to see the shadowy curves of her quite perfect breasts. It had been hard enough to avert his gaze the first two times.

'Tell me something about yourself,' she said, and he started, surprised.

'You want to know something about me?'

A smile played about her lush mouth. 'Well, you waltzed into my life this morning...'

'I'm pretty sure I didn't waltz,' he felt compelled to object, and she laughed softly.

'Okay. But I feel like it would be better for both of us if we knew something about each other.'

They *did* know something about each other, Nico thought darkly. They'd once spent half an hour sharing life stories, teasing, laughing, flirting. And now Ashley looked at him the way he would a kindly stranger. Which was, he supposed, better than she'd looked at him before, as though he was a monster.

'Where did you grow up?' she asked.

He paused, instinctively reluctant to impart any information, and yet wondering if some of his answers might stir her memory. Finally he said, 'Brooklyn.'

Her eyebrows arched. 'Right here in the city?'

'Born and bred.' This, Nico feared, could get tense very quickly, at least for him. He'd once told her where he was from, and how many siblings he had, and how one day he was going to make a million dollars. It all sounded so childish now, and yet he'd meant every word. Telling her again would feel wrong somehow, as well as weirdly shaming. As though something that had once been important to him had been nothing to her. After tonight, he knew he was going to think very carefully before he told Ashley anything more about their shared past.

Perhaps she'd sensed this too, because the next question came out of left field. 'What's your favourite food?'

He paused to think and then answered honestly, 'Pizza.'

She laughed again, the sound whispering through him. 'Pizza…but aren't you a billionaire?'

'I wasn't always. And I don't forget my roots.'

'I'd like to forget mine,' she replied baldly, her gaze meeting and holding his. 'Maybe I already have,' she added with a wry laugh that ended on a wobbly note. 'Since I can't even remember this evening. Maybe there's a lot of things I've forgotten.'

It clearly unnerved her, this forgetfulness, more than she wanted to admit. Without even thinking about what he was doing, Nico reached forward and cupped her cheek with his hand, her skin cool and smooth beneath his palm. Her eyes widened as his thumb caressed the fullness of her lower lip, his palm cradling her face in a gesture that felt both intimate and tender and sparked something inside him—desire along with something deeper. 'Don't let it worry you,' he murmured. 'Sometimes…maybe…it's better to forget things.'

She kept her vivid green gaze on his, his hand still cupping her cheek, his thumb resting on her lip. For a few taut seconds he was sorely tempted to close the remaining space between them, settle his lips on hers and taste their honeyed sweetness again. But this time it wouldn't be the ravaging of earlier that day, when he'd been daring her to remember their first kiss, but a tender reckoning, a healing, a promise…but of what?

Then she asked in a whisper, 'What do you need to forget?'

Softly as it had been asked, the question slammed into him, reminding him that this was utter, utter foolishness. Nico shook his head, dropping his hand as he leaned back. He *couldn't* forget Chase Woodward's treachery, the years of imprisonment and injustice or the way it had wrecked his brother's life and torn apart his family. Those were things that he would always remember. He *needed* to remember them, because they reminded him of who he was, what he'd endured and how he had triumphed.

And, whether she knew it or not, Ashley Woodward was part of that. Even if she wasn't aware of it—and Nico still wasn't entirely convinced that she wasn't—she was his enemy. Getting emotionally involved with her, no matter how briefly, would be a big, big mistake.

'I should go,' he said brusquely. 'And you should sleep.'

Her eyes widened as if he'd rebuked her, and in truth Nico felt as if he had. But he couldn't shake the feeling that coming here, comforting her, had been a mistake. A complication he couldn't afford.

She didn't speak as he rose from the sofa and reached for his suit jacket. She watched him silently, her hand still tucked beneath her cheek as he shrugged it on.

'I'll send a car to pick you up at seven,' he told her, and she gave a small, playful smile.

'For our *not*-a-date,' she quipped, and Nico's whole body went still.

They were the same words, and even the same tone, that she'd used on that fateful night, right before he'd been arrested. For a dream-like half-hour, they'd talked and flirted, half-hidden by a pillar, and even fumbled through a soft, sweet kiss that had felt like the purest thing he'd ever experienced. He'd been twenty years old and as green as a young boy.

In thrall to his own feelings, he'd asked to see her again, blurting the words, even though he'd known the daughter of the CEO did not step out with the lowest and most recent hire—no matter that Chase Woodward, in his magnanimity, had invited him to this ball. He still wouldn't have wanted him dating his daughter.

Ashley's expression had turned troubled, her eyes shadowed as she'd leaned back against the pillar. 'I don't know if my father...' she'd begun, biting her lip, looking unhappy and nervous. He'd bumbled through something about how it didn't have to be a *date*; they could just go for a walk, a coffee, anything... He'd been so pathetically desperate. The memory scalded him now, even all these years later.

She'd smiled then, shyly, like the unfurling of a flower, her lovely, heart-shaped face tilted up towards his. 'All right, then. I'll go out with you, on something that's *not*-a-date,' she'd said, and he'd smiled and even thought about kissing her again, before a hand had clapped hard on his shoulder.

And now she'd just said it again. *Not-a-date*. Coincidence…or a slip?

Ashley Woodward, he reminded himself yet again, was the daughter of his enemy, the former CEO of a business he'd intended to crush, and still most likely would dismantle. No matter how innocent or vulnerable she seemed now, she'd once set him up and then walked away. How could he forget that? How could he let this little amnesia act convince him?

The realisation slammed into him with a force that nearly left him breathless. Ashley *had* to remember what she'd done, and she must have gambled that acting as if she didn't was the only way of escaping his revenge. It was so blindingly obvious that Nico felt ashamed for being pulled in by her 'adorably confused' routine. All those tears…were they really fake? Was it all an elaborate ruse to make him soft?

Could she be that cunning?

'Nico…?' she asked softly and when he turned to look at her, her green eyes wide, her soft, pink lips trembling, all he saw was a very bad actress.

He walked out of her apartment without saying a word, and without looking back.

CHAPTER NINE

ASHLEY STOOD AT the entrance to the ballroom in one of New York's most exclusive hotels, feeling entirely unprepared for the evening. After Nico had walked out on her last night, she'd lain in bed, staring at the ceiling, trying to figure out what on earth had happened, and why this enigmatic man touched her so tenderly one moment and walked out without a word the next. More worryingly, she wondered why she *cared*. In the course of a few hours, Nico Galletti had engaged her emotions in a way she had absolutely no intention of letting him do ever again.

It had been easier, or at least simpler, Ashley had reflected, when Nico had been nothing more than an obstacle she had to navigate to protect her employees and her business. Now he'd become a man who'd touched her tenderly, answered her questions and made her tea…well, that became intensely problematic. Especially if she let herself think about the other element of Nico Galletti she found so worrying: the way he'd kissed and, more tellingly, the way she'd responded to him.

All of it made coming to this ball to present some kind of united front a far more dangerous proposition than Ashley wanted it to be. And so, before she'd finally fallen asleep some time towards dawn, she'd decided she would treat Nico Galletti exactly as what he was, or at least what he was meant to be: a business associate and potential colleague, no more. She could not figure him out at all, and the best thing to do, she decided, was to stop trying.

She'd go to this event, present the united front he wanted and do whatever she could to save Infinite Innovations. And after that…? She'd try never to see him again, for the sake of her own sanity, because the last thing she wanted was to be in thrall to someone, to anyone.

When her father had gone to prison, she'd vowed that she would never let herself be controlled the way he had controlled her, with alternating flattery and abuse, so she'd never known what to expect or even who she was to him. For far too many years, she'd been confused and deeply unhappy and, worse, she'd had no sense of herself until she'd escaped his charismatic orbit at last. When she'd finally been free, she'd promised herself she'd never again let another person force her to fear, fawn, cringe or beg. Yet, if she wasn't careful, Nico Galletti could have her do all the above.

She could not, Ashley reminded herself, let any man make her feel that way again…not even for a day or an hour. And Nico Galletti would not tonight.

Throwing back her shoulders, Ashley surveyed the ballroom and tried to ignore the anxiety gnawing at her insides. It had been a long time since she'd been at an event like this, trotted out like her father's show pony and forced to do his bidding. Was Nico doing any different, asking her to present this united front so he didn't have to suffer the bad press that had been headlining the business section of most newspapers that morning? She was doing it for the business, Ashley reminded herself, and for her employees. Not because she was afraid, but because she was determined. There was a difference. At least, she wanted there to be one.

'Ashley, it's so good to see you here. It's been too long.'

A woman bedecked in diamonds and black satin came forward to kiss both her cheeks.

'Valerie,' Ashley greeted her, the name coming to her lips at the last second. She was the wife of one of her father's golf buddies who Ashley had seen socially when she'd acted as her father's hostess. 'Likewise.'

'How are you, my dear?' Valerie stepped back to survey her in concern. 'I read about the takeover. And just when you were starting to do so well after all that business…'

All that business. It was, Ashley reflected wryly, quite the euphemism for the complete and total destruction of her life—her father in prison, her house and every other trapping of her luxurious life sold or seized and almost everyone she knew turning their back on her because of the scandal.

Now she managed a shrug and a smile. 'It happens. I'm very hopeful Galletti Finance will let Infinite Innovations continue to operate as normal. That's why I'm here tonight.' No reason not to fire the first shot across the bow, she decided. She wasn't about to let Nico call them *all* tonight; she'd make sure there was something in this united front for her—and the company.

'Oh?' Valerie's eyebrows rose. 'Is that so? Because the media was painting a much bleaker picture, my dear.'

'Yes, well, you know how they like to hype up the news. Anything to generate interest or outrage.' It had been the same during her father's trial. Her name and face had been splashed across the headlines more than once, with spurious speculation about her involvement in Woodward Investments, simply because she'd been so often by her father's side.

Was *that* why Nico blamed her? Ashley wondered. Because, even though she'd had nothing to do with her father's business dealings, she'd been seen with him? It seemed a flimsy reason, but she couldn't think of any others.

As she faced Valerie, Ashley let her smile widen. 'As it happens,' she told her, 'Galletti Finance is keen to be seen to promote Infinite Innovations, and in particular to show their ethical support of inventions that champion those who are differently abled, which I'm sure you'll agree is a very worthy cause.'

'Of course, of course. And especially considering your poor mother…' Valerie dropped her voice. 'How *is* she?'

Valerie and her mother had once played tennis together, Ashley recalled. But, like just about everyone else, she'd dropped her after her mother's stroke. Her father had been embarrassed by his wife and had kept her hidden away, even after she'd recovered, at least as much as she ever would. Ashley was convinced that her mother's recovery would have been aided by seeing people and getting out and about. Instead, she'd been imprisoned, like Rochester's wife in *Jane Eyre*, as if she were a shameful secret to be forgotten.

'She's doing well,' she told Valerie firmly.

'Well, I'm glad to hear it, of course,' Valerie said quickly. 'May I say, you do look lovely tonight.'

Ashley glanced down at the dress she'd pulled out of her wardrobe, the one evening dress she'd kept from her years as a socialite, and in truth she couldn't have said why she'd kept it. When she'd been consigning all her clothes to charity, not wanting the reminders of a life she'd come to hate, this one dress had somehow spoken to her and made her think of a happier time, although she couldn't remember ever wearing it. She'd forgotten she'd even kept it, but she hoped Nico would be happily surprised that she wasn't coming to a black-tie event in the business-wear equivalent of a bin bag.

But why, Ashley wondered with a spike of frustration, did she care what Nico thought? It was such an easy and wearying habit to slip into, to want to appease and impress him the way she had her father. She would not let herself fall into that trap again.

'Good to see you, Valerie,' she murmured, and moved away.

Ashley continued through the ballroom, smiling and nodding at those she knew, and talking up Infinite Innovations every moment she could. She didn't see Nico anywhere, but at this point she decided she didn't need him. She was doing fine, talking up Galletti Finance and Infinite Innovation's 'amicable merger' on her own.

He was going to have some trouble backing down from all the promises she'd made on his behalf, she thought with satisfaction. As she assured every guest and acquaintance she came across, not only was Galletti Finance going to keep all of the Infinite Innovations employees, but Nico himself was going to investigate championing some of the new inventions they'd been seeking to fund.

'He feels very passionate about it,' she told one potential investor as she sipped her flute of champagne. 'Really, we couldn't be more pleased to be working together.'

'I have to say I'm surprised,' the man replied. 'The reports in the news...'

'Oh, but you can't believe everything you read,' Ashley replied sweetly. 'Best to get it directly from the horse's mouth.'

'Yes,' the man replied with a rather knowing smirk, 'But the filly or the stallion?'

Before Ashley could react to that particularly offensive statement, the man nodded to the doors of the ballroom. 'Because your so-called business partner isn't looking as thrilled as you've been making out right now.'

Ashley stiffened, then slowly turned, steeling herself to catch sight of Nico. She didn't need to search the crowded room; he stood out like a dark beacon of power and authority, framed by the double doors, devastating in a dinner suit. Even from a distance, the sight of him was like a sucker punch to her gut, or really an entire body blow that she struggled not to reel back from... Because in an instant she remembered *exactly* how his mouth had felt on hers, his hands moving so deftly and surely over her skin, fingers brushing, palms cupping...

For a second, she nearly swayed simply from the memory of her own desire. *How* did the man have such an effect on her, and from over a hundred feet away? Seeing him in formal wear only added to his appeal as well as his sense of power. The black fabric of his dinner jacket stretched across the breadth of his shoulders, the trousers showcasing his long, powerful legs. He stood half a head taller than any other man in the room, indifferent to the sycophants gathering around him in a fawning crowd.

'Really not pleased...' the man next to Ashley murmured, sounding as though he was enjoying himself, and that was when Ashley clocked the thunderous look on Nico Galletti's face.

He was staring straight at her, and he looked *furious*—eyes narrowed to silver slits, jaw bunched, lips firmed into a hard and unforgiving line. But more than that was the energy rolling off him in waves that she felt hit her from all the way across the room, waves of pure, undiluted rage. She'd only met him yesterday, and already they'd had several tumultuous encounters, but Ashley had never seen him look the way he did right now.

No matter how many little pep talks she'd given herself to stay strong and not cringe or cower in front of this man, right then, as his furious gaze locked on her wide-eyed one, the only emotion she felt was alarm, even terror.

Why on earth was he so angry? Was it just because she'd been talking up Infinite Innovations to the various guests she'd spoken with? All right, maybe she'd gone a *little* overboard, claiming Galletti Finance was fully behind what had once been her company, but he'd wanted a so-called united front, and in any case, the look on Nico's face seemed to be for something else entirely. Something primal and overwhelming, deeper and darker than a mere financial transaction.

And yet, Ashley was forced to acknowledge, even in his rage he was stunningly handsome, every taut line of his body radiating power and authority. Next to him every other man in the ballroom looked limp and washed out, irrelevant. Ashley forced herself to stay still as Nico started stalking towards her, cutting a path through the crowd with a long, determined stride.

As he prowled closer, the alarm she felt morphed into a delicious anticipation, admittedly still tinged with terror, which, she realised, only made it all the more exciting. He looked so thrillingly purposeful, his eyes hooded and flashing silver, his jaw set, his stride long and sure. Ashley's stomach swirled and cramped as excitement clashed with fear, and her senses felt heightened to an exquisite painfulness. Her breath hitched audibly, and the ballroom and its glittering crowds fell away as she focused on only one thing—the man stalking towards her.

'Nico…' was all she managed to say in a whisper as he came to stand in front of her. She could feel the heat of his body along with the anger, waves undulating through the air between them, and the look in his eyes was enough to steal the breath from her body and every thought from her head.

Then he reached for her arm, strong, lean fingers clamping around her wrist as he drew her closer to him so her breasts brushed his chest and their hips bumped, causing a thrill of awareness to twang through her body as if she were a tuning fork and he was playing the one, pure note of her longing.

Nico leaned in so his breath tickled her ear and the scent of him, musky and clean, with the metallic edge of his anger, overwhelmed her senses.

'What,' he demanded in a low snarl that vibrated with the force of his fury, 'The *hell* do you think you're playing at?'

With effort, Nico loosened his grip on Ashley's wrist. He didn't want to hurt the woman—not physically, anyway—but, by heaven, he had never felt the fury he felt now. All this time she'd been playing him, toying with and taunting him, no doubt thinking he was still the green, naïve boy she'd once known, despite the fact that he owned her company. He basically owned *her*, not that she'd ever acknowledge it. And, right now, he wanted to shake her into admitting that her pretty little amnesia act was nothing more than a pathetic ruse—and for what? What purpose could such an absurd charade possibly serve?

'Nico…' she said again, and although her voice shook, and her face was as pale as porcelain, she still managed to give him a pointed look, nodding towards the man standing next to her. 'Have you met Edward Sackett? He's with Lumos Ideas, a tech investment firm…'

Nico barely spared the paunchy, middle-aged man a glance. 'I might have met him once or twice,' he said dismissively. 'Now, we need to talk in private.'

Without waiting for her to reply, he started marching her across the ballroom.

'You're making a scene,' Ashley hissed as she struggled to keep up with his long strides, catching the glittering folds of her dress in one hand. '*And* you're hurting me.'

Nico loosened his grip, but only a little. 'If I could trust you an inch, I'd let you go,' he replied tersely. 'But I can't, as you know very well. Now, *move*.'

They didn't speak again until they'd left the ballroom, the

doors clicking closed behind them. Nico strode down the thickly carpeted hallway until they came to a door of one of the hotel's salons. He pushed it open and then went inside, checking the room was empty save for a few sofas and chairs. Then, closing the door behind him, and leaning deliberately and ominously against it, he finally let Ashley go.

She took a few stumbling steps away, rubbing her wrist. 'Well, *that* certainly presented the united front you claimed to want!' she remarked with a disdainful lift of her golden eyebrows, although Nico thought she still looked shaken. 'Well done. I think we convinced just about everyone there how much we enjoy working together.'

'Save your sarcasm,' he snapped. He was too angry to spar with her, to score such petty little points. The sight of her in that dress had far too much old emotion throbbing through him, obliterating every rational thought he'd ever had. 'And level with me for *once*,' he ground out, 'Or, I swear, I'll fire every employee you've ever *thought* about hiring, and make sure they never work again, anywhere, ever.'

Her eyes widened as she stared at him, her lush, pink lips parting soundlessly. '*Level* with you?' she finally repeated faintly. 'Nico, you're acting like a...a *madman*. I have no idea why you're so angry.' She frowned, her elegant shoulders twisting in a shrug, as if this was all just some simple misunderstanding. 'All right, maybe I did push a little hard with how Galletti Finance was going to partner with Infinite Innovations, but what did you expect me to do—?'

'I am not talking about our companies,' he cut across her, every word like the lash of a whip.

She stared at him for several seconds, her lips still parted, a faint frown marring her smooth, pale brow, her body lovely and lithe, swathed in silk and crystal.

She looked so much the same. It was like a dagger thrust to his soul, his heart, to see her like this—her golden hair up in the elegant chignon, and that *dress*… That dress covered with crystals that glinted every time she moved, as if she was a walking rainbow, a beacon of light. All these years, she'd kept it, even when just last night she'd insisted that she had given all her dresses away. All these years…and she'd chosen to wear it tonight.

Why? To mock him? To make him feel like the boy he'd once been, holding onto so much stupid hope and then having absolutely everything taken from him? Was she trying to remind him of who he'd once been, as well as who *she'd* been and clearly thought she still was?

Well, it was working. Right now, Nico felt as deceived, as duped and dumb as he had at twenty years old, and he hated that fact. He despised it with every breath in his body, every atom of his being.

Never trust a Woodward.

Abruptly, he pushed off the door he'd been leaning against and turned away from her, driving his hands through his hair. All the memories crashed through him like the waves of a tsunami, so he'd barely absorbed the shock of the first because the next one rolled relentlessly on. He remembered the way Ashley had tilted her head up for a kiss, the sweet look of wonder in her eyes, the soft breath she'd released before he'd brushed his lips against hers, her mouth had opened beneath his own and he'd felt happiness and hope explode in his heart.

And then after, with his hands cuffed behind his back, a policeman's hand hard on his shoulder, the whole room watching, stunned and silent.

'Ashley, *please*…you must know I didn't do this… Please help me…' His voice had choked, and he'd fallen to his knees right in front of her. She'd stared down at him for one endless second, her face an icy mask, and then she'd turned away without saying a word.

And now here she was, recreating that very evening in every detail, right down to her hair, her earrings, her necklace. She looked *exactly* the same…and was acting as if she had no idea why he was so angry.

'Do you think I'm a fool?' he asked, his tone turning quietly, lethally polite as he turned around to face her. 'Is that what you think? Or maybe you actually believe you have all the power, all the cards, in this twisted little game of yours? I am well aware that a Woodward's arrogance knows no bounds. Maybe you're hoping you can navigate me into a corner with this little power play of yours, get me to give you something just for old times' sake. Is that it?'

He gestured contemptuously to her dress while she stared at him in what looked and felt like complete confusion. Her forehead was furrowed, her eyes crinkled as she shook her head slowly.

'Nico…' she began unsteadily. 'I really have no idea what you're talking about.' One hand fluttered at her throat, and she looked so pale that Nico wondered cynically if she might faint again. How many times had she pulled the damsel in distress routine in the last thirty-six hours? Fainting, spraining her ankle, the episode in her apartment… That trick was getting decidedly old. He would not fall for it a fourth time. Three had been bad enough.

She took a step towards him, her green eyes huge in her face and swimming with tears as her lips trembled. 'I just want to save my employees…' she whispered.

'Oh, come off it,' Nico sneered. How had he ever been convinced by her, even in the slightest? 'I've had enough of the Saint Ashley act, behaving as if all you care about is other people, when I know for a *fact* you only care about yourself.'

She shook her head slowly as he started towards her, closing the space between them. He felt like grabbing her, shaking her, forcing her to admit why she was lying to him. Why she thought looking so breathless and confused would actually convince him of anything.

'Why don't you just tell me why you're so angry?' she asked in a tremulous whisper. 'And then…then we can talk about it.'

'How very reasonable of you,' he drawled coldly. He stood before her, eyeing her up and down, unable to keep from noticing the way the dress shaped to her high, firm breasts, her chest rising and falling in unsteady gasps. Her skin was pearly and luminescent, her face tilted to his just as it had once been before, her lips parted as if inviting his kiss…

It was the night of the ball over again, the attraction between them like a force field neither of them could resist. He remembered it from before, how he'd felt powerless to keep from kissing her, no matter what the cost. How she'd invited him to, with her eyes, her breath, her parted lips… just as she did now.

But this time the moment, once so full of wonder, was tainted with all that had gone before. Tainted by the knowledge of who she really was and what he'd suffered…and she hadn't cared.

And yet even as that knowledge reverberated through him Nico felt a stirring, and then a surge, of desire. And he knew, from the way Ashley's pupils dilated and her breath hissed out, that she felt it too. This magnetic pull was too forceful for either of them to resist. No matter that he was angry and she was afraid; the connection between them was real, and even now threatened to overwhelm both of their warring emotions.

Nico put his hands on her bare shoulders, his palms smoothing over her silky skin as he drew her to him. Ashley looked up at him, her emerald eyes glassy and huge in her pale face, her lips parted in invitation.

'Nico…' she whispered, and it sounded like a plea. He bent his head. She swayed towards him.

And then he kissed her.

CHAPTER TEN

FIREWORKS BURST IN Ashley's heart and sparks raced through her veins as Nico captured her mouth with his own. It made absolutely no sense to welcome his kiss now, she thought dazedly, before she stopped thinking at all as Nico ravaged her mouth, his hands sliding from her shoulders to cup her breasts, squeezing and kneading as his thumbs ran over her peaked nipples, playing her body like an instrument, coaxing a sound from her lips she'd never made before—a mewling plea for more.

In the space of a single second, it felt as if the very air around them had ignited. Fear and fury were both obliterated in light of this—an attraction too strong to deny or resist. Together they stumbled back against the window, and then Nico hoisted her up onto the sill with her back pressed against the smooth glass as he raked her dress up high over her thighs so he could stand between them, his body hard and unyielding against her own softness.

Ashley drove her hands through his hair as she anchored him to her in a kiss that was both savage and sweet, demanding and giving, so one felt like the other. His hand slid along her bare thigh, and then his fingers brushed against her underwear and she moaned again, unable to keep from arching into his questing hand, his fingers knowing just where to go, how to move, how to make her utterly abandon every thought, every principle she'd ever had....

She was shameless, utterly shameless, Ashley thought, and she didn't care. She'd never felt like this before, never had someone have so much control over her body, her response...

Control... The word screeched through her dazed senses. She was letting Nico control her, both body and mind, maybe even *heart*, and in a far more devastating way than ever before. In a single, split second, the mood completely changed. Ashley put her hands flat on Nico's chest and shoved him away as hard as she could. Her feeble effort didn't even cause him to sway, but his hand stilled and he broke off the kiss, staring down at her, his face flushed, his breathing ragged.

'No,' Ashley said, trying to sound strong, but it came out like a whimper. 'No, please. I... I don't want this.'

He gazed at her for a taut moment, his expression inscrutable, before he jerked his head in a nod. 'Fine.' He stepped away, instantly in control, his expression turning cold. The colour was already fading from his face, while she felt like a puddle of contrary emotions, her legs rubbery, her whole body still trembling with shock and desire.

As Nico watched her dispassionately, Ashley forced herself to stand up straight, pulling her dress back down, which was all the way about her hips. They stared at each other for several long moments, the only sound the draw and tear of their still-ragged breathing. Or maybe that was just hers, Ashley thought miserably, because Nico looked frighteningly indifferent as he adjusted his dinner jacket, flicking an invisible speck of lint off one well-tailored sleeve.

'I don't understand you,' Ashley made herself say, trying to keep her voice from trembling. 'And at this point I don't think I want to. Frankly, you've messed with my emotions enough—'

Nico let out a sharp bark of laughter, the sound reminding

Ashley of the crack of a gunshot echoing through the empty room, as he raked her with a single, sceptical glance. '*I've* messed with *your* emotions?' he repeated disbelievingly.

He spoke as if she was the one who had been unreasonable, Ashley thought numbly, when he had half-dragged her in here, berated her and then kissed her senseless... It was the cycle of flattery and abuse all over again, she realised with a lightning-fast jolt, just like with her father, except this felt far worse.

A few moments ago, if he'd asked her, she would have given herself to this man, in a way she never had before. The thought was intensely humbling as well as painfully shaming and, with another lightning streak of realisation, Ashley knew she could not let herself surrender to Nico Galletti in any fashion—not physically and not emotionally. Not by cringing beneath his condemning stare—or responding to his passionate kisses.

'Yes, you,' she asserted as she straightened her spine. 'What do you call being incredibly thoughtful one moment and an absolute *ass* the next?' As strong as she was trying to seem, her voice still rose to a high, trembling note. 'Destroying my company and then telling me you might save it. Demanding I do exactly as you say and then being tender and making me tea...'

She passed one hand over her forehead as a wave of dizziness overwhelmed her. Nico Galletti had been turning her into a basket case since the second he'd stepped foot in her office. 'I can't take it any more. I *won't*—' she began, only to have him cut across her warningly,

'*Don't* try fainting again.'

Ashley dropped her hand as she stared at him incredulously. She wished she had the strength to laugh, but she was far closer to crying. '*Try* fainting? What do you think that was this morning, some sort of tactic?' she asked. This time she did manage a laugh, a sorry huff of despair. 'If so,' she told him, 'It obviously failed. Miserably.'

'You've been trying such *tactics* with me since I first walked in on you with your blouse unbuttoned,' he drawled coldly, folding his arms across his chest. 'Too bad you can't stick to one act. You have to be either the fainting lily or the hard-nosed businesswoman or the beguiling temptress, not all three in turns.' He bared his teeth in a steely smile. 'Otherwise they play against each other, and it doesn't work.'

He seemed to be speaking in riddles he thought she should understand. Ashley shook her head, weary now. In that moment, she didn't think she had the strength to fight for anything—not herself, not her employees, not Infinite Innovations.

'I really don't understand you,' she told him wearily. 'And I don't think I ever will. What I do know is that you mess with my head and my body way too much for me to keep going back for another round. I think… I think I need to walk away from this. From you. From…everything.'

She nodded slowly, her insides leaden, as the realisation spread heavily through her. She couldn't fight for Infinite Innovations any more, not against this man. Not for the sake of her own sanity, her own self. She'd have to find some other way to help the people she'd hired that did not involve Nico Galletti.

'You can have the company,' she told him, flinging her hands up. 'I mean, obviously, since you already do. Dismantle it, destroy it, do whatever you want.' She shrugged her shoulders dispiritedly, unable to meet his eyes, hating the thought of seeing triumph gleaming in their silvery depths. 'I can start over,' she stated, clinging to that one fact. 'I did it once already, and I'll do it again.' Even if she couldn't imagine having the strength to do so right now. One day she would; she'd make sure of it.

Nico Galletti might have taken everything she'd worked hard for, but he could not take her sense of self. He could not rob her of her future. 'This ends here,' she stated, and was glad that she finally sounded strong.

Lifting her chin to give him one last look, his own expression utterly inscrutable, she turned for the door. Walking out on Nico Galletti would be her last act of defiance. As her legs wobbled and her ankle gave a punishing twang, she just hoped she could make it to the door.

Each step felt endless, although it was only half a dozen yards. Nico didn't speak, and Ashley felt a prickling between her shoulder blades, sensing his iron-hard glare directed right at her as she forced herself to put one foot in front of another. One step, two steps, three...

Finally, she made it. A pent-up breath of relief escaped her in a soft rush. Then, as Ashley's fingers curled around the door handle, Nico finally spoke.

'Why,' he asked quietly, 'Did you wear that dress?'

The rage had left him, like a tidal wave that had surged up suddenly and obliterated everything before receding, leaving only devastation in its wake. For a few minutes, he had not been able to think or respond clearly to anything. To *Ashley*. And from within the embers of that rage had come the most inconvenient, overwhelming desire... It was unsettling, to feel so much in relation to this woman, and not to be able to control it, because he'd always prized himself on his steely sense of self-control. Yet Ashley Woodward had been able to obliterate it with one calculated move.

Except, judging from her response in these last few heightened minutes, it *hadn't* been calculated. Yet how could it not have been? To wear that dress and the jewels, even style her hair the same... Surely that had to have been intentional?

It was, Nico determined, time finally to get some answers. Answers that weren't clouded by Ashley's obfuscation or his own painful memories of just how treacherous the Woodwards could be.

For several seconds, she remained standing with her back to him, her hand on the door, her head slightly bowed so a single golden curl rested against the nape of her neck and trailed onto one smooth shoulder. Nico had the most inconvenient urge to lift that curl, kiss that sensitive skin... He forced himself to banish the thought.

Slowly Ashley turned round. She looked exhausted, defeated, her slender shoulders slumped and shadows like bruises beneath her jade-green eyes.

'The dress?' she repeated. 'Why are you asking about my *dress*?'

'I just want to know why you wore it.' He kept his tone even, determined not to give into the anger he still felt lapping at his senses. Was she really playing dumb even now? 'You must have had a reason.'

She twisted her shoulders in a shrug that felt stingingly dismissive. 'It was in my closet. I needed something to wear.'

'Don't,' he warned her in a low voice, 'Be flippant.'

'I am struggling to understand why you care what dress I'm wearing,' Ashley replied. She sounded exhausted rather than angry. 'You had a dozen brought to my apartment. Presumably any of those would have satisfied you.' She glanced down at the crystal-strewn dress he remembered so well. 'Why not this one?'

'The question remains, *why* this one?' Nico asked, his tone sharpening. She was making him appear foolish or even strange for fixating on the dress. Was that part of her plan? 'I just want to know what you're playing at,' he stated. 'Because it's obviously something.'

'What I'm *playing* at?' she repeated, taking a step towards him. Colour flared in her pale cheeks and her eyes glittered like the crystals on her dress as she drew in an agitated breath. 'I'm not playing at anything. But, while we're at it, why don't you tell me what *you're* playing at? Why did you get so angry tonight? Because I don't think I've seen anyone so furious, and I still have no idea what it was about. My *dress*?'

She sounded so incredulous. Once again, Nico had no idea what to think. *Could she actually be innocent?* Had she somehow forgotten the whole episode, *everything*, the way she'd forgotten her breakdown last night?

He stared at her, wishing he could see beneath those stormy eyes, that silken skin. 'You wore that dress,' he finally ground out, 'The night we met.'

Ashley's eyes widened and her whole body went still. 'The night we met?' she repeated in a whisper, sounding shocked.

'I said you had a part in ruining my life,' he reminded her. 'Didn't you realise we must have met before?'

She shook her head, a few tendrils of hair falling from her elegant chignon and framing her pale, heart-shaped face. 'To be honest, I thought that was just a bit of…hyperbole.'

'It wasn't. *Trust me.*' He deliberately echoed the words her father had used time and time again as he'd asked Nico to send emails, open accounts or add figures. All of it had been to incriminate him, and he'd been too trusting and dumb to believe it.

'When…?' Ashley licked her lips, her wide-eyed gaze locked on his. 'When did we meet?'

'At that fundraising ball for breast cancer. The one your mother set up. I told you before.' He couldn't keep from sounding impatient, because to him it was so obvious. The fact that she hadn't pressed him on any point before just made her look guiltier. She must have known. She so clearly remembered.

'Yes,' Ashley replied slowly, 'But… I didn't realise… You

didn't say we'd actually *met*...' She shook her head. 'I think I would have remembered that.'

'I suppose you met a lot of people,' Nico replied evenly, daring her to agree. To say their meeting hadn't been significant in any way, when he'd already told her it had changed his life.

'Yes, but...' She was silent, her teeth sinking into her lower lip as she frowned in thought. 'Obviously it must have been a fairly significant meeting,' she finally said, 'To have the effect you claim it had. To "ruin your life".'

The words would have gratified him, save for the needling note of doubt in her voice. *That* sent a fresh wave of fury through him, but he tamped it down. 'I don't *claim*,' he bit out. 'I know.'

'All right.' Ashley lifted her chin and, in the tilt of it, as well as the set of her lips and the flash of her eyes, Nico knew that, just as he'd doubted her, now she doubted him. 'Then tell me about it. How did we meet? What did we say? And how on earth did meeting me ruin your life?'

She sounded scornful now, and Nico had to wait several seconds before replying to make sure his voice was as cold and even as he needed it to be. 'I'm not about to go into all that here,' he told her.

Her eyes flashed with more scorn. 'Then where?'

'My apartment,' he decided. 'We need to talk in private.'

'I am not,' Ashley informed him, her eyes flashing all the more, 'Going to your apartment so you can...can...' She shook her head, unwilling to finish just what they both knew he could do, and what she would welcome.

'Trust me,' Nico told her with acid sweetness. 'You're not that irresistible.'

'Neither are you,' she fired back, but the flush rising to her heated cheeks told otherwise.

He took a step towards her. 'Do you want me to prove that

to you?' he demanded in a low voice, and for a heightened second it felt as if the very air between them twanged with electric, sexual energy.

They stared at each other as a thousand memories of what she'd felt like in his arms, beneath his hands, flashed through his mind, reminding him of just how truly irresistible she was, never mind him.

'No, I don't,' she said at last, her voice little more than a husk. 'Which is why I'm not going to your apartment.'

'And if I promise I won't touch you?' He didn't want the complication either, no matter that desire was already racing through him, tightening every muscle and heightening every sense.

She tilted her chin. 'Is that a promise I can trust you to keep?'

'I don't break my promises,' he assured her stonily. 'And I don't force myself on unwilling women.' He held her gaze, daring to deny it. They both knew just how willing she'd been.

'Fine,' she finally said shortly, the colour still surging in her cheeks. 'As long as we're both clear that neither of us is irresistible.' Her mouth quirked cynically, and her chin lifted once more. 'Lead the way.'

CHAPTER ELEVEN

ASHLEY FELT AS if she were walking into the lion's den or even the very mouth of hell as she stepped into the lift that soared straight to Nico Galletti's penthouse apartment in SoHo. They'd barely spoken as they'd gone from hotel to limo to building; Ashley had asked whether they should make one last appearance for their guests, but Nico had dismissed the idea.

'I think they've seen more than enough,' he'd replied tersely, taking her elbow to steer her out to his waiting car.

On the ride downtown, with the limo sliding through darkened streets, Ashley had wondered if she was making a serious mistake. She didn't trust Nico Galletti about anything, she knew that much, but she didn't know much else… which was why she'd agreed to come back with him.

She needed to figure out why Nico was so suspicious of her. Had she really met him back at that ball? Those tumultuous years had blurred together in her mind, a kaleidoscope of images and emotions she'd longed only to forget, and had been grateful when it seemed as if she had. But she hadn't thought she'd forgotten *that* much….

But what if she had? She'd managed to forget an entire episode from last night. Had she forgotten more than she realised? Or…was Nico messing with her mind, another one of his little power games? He had accused her of playing at something, and now Ashley was wondering if *he* was.

But if it really was some kind of simple misunderstanding…

Except nothing about this situation felt remotely simple, Ashley acknowledged, and she doubted a single conversation was going to clear anything up. Maybe it would make things even more complicated, because whatever had happened between them back then seemed to have struck at their very hearts and souls…and left scars. A few quick words of explanation—an apology, heartfelt or otherwise—wasn't going to undo the damage. It might even make things worse.

But for the sake of her own conscience as well as sanity, as well as that of her employees, Ashley knew she needed to get to the bottom of whatever had driven Nico Galletti to initiate a hostile takeover of a company that shouldn't mean anything to him.

'Some place,' she remarked dryly as she stepped into the soaring space of his penthouse apartment, everything sleek and modern, with floor-to-ceiling windows on three sides overlooking the southern tip of Manhattan. 'Especially for a boy from Brooklyn.'

'Isn't it just?' he replied in an even dryer tone as he shed his dinner jacket, the muscles of his shoulders and arm rippling under the smooth white fabric of his shirt. Ashley jerked her gaze away. She definitely did not need that distraction right now.

She moved through the open-plan living space. Leather sofas and coffee tables that looked like sculpted pieces of modern art were scattered around to make the most of the view of the city stretched out far below them in a carpet of light. A galley kitchen with a marble island stretched off to one side and a hallway led to bedrooms on the other.

'I feel like I'm upside down,' she remarked as she came to stand by the window. 'And I'm looking at a sky full of stars.'

'A lot of this evening has felt upside down,' Nico replied,

and she slowly turned to face him. He hadn't turned on any of the lamps, and the ambient light of the city below cast half his face into shadow, and half into light, which seemed fitting. She really did not understand this man and his shifting moods...but maybe tonight she finally would.

'So tell me about when we met,' she said, and a muscle ticked in his jaw. She had the feeling he was restraining some powerful emotion that both intrigued and frightened her. *What on earth had happened that night?* 'I wore this dress at the ball,' she continued. 'And we spoke, I presume?'

'We did.'

'About what?'

'A few things.'

She shook her head, already exasperated. 'You brought me here to talk about it, so why won't you explain now?'

'Because I still can't decide whether you're lying to me or not,' Nico told her flatly. 'And I have no intention of rehashing that night, which ranked as the worst of my life, simply for your amusement.'

Ashley blinked at that startling and scathing indictment 'Nico,' she said quietly, taking a step towards him, one hand instinctively outstretched. She sensed so much pain beneath his anger, and it filled her with an emotion she had not felt for him before—a deep and abiding sympathy, along with a desire to comfort him. Somehow to make it better. 'Do you honestly think I'm that kind of person?' she asked in a low voice. 'Who would...torment someone simply for her own amusement?'

'You were,' Nico replied, his steely gaze locked on hers, 'That kind of person on that night.'

'What...?' The single word escaped her in a shocked breath as Ashley dropped her hand. 'What are you saying? What did I *do*?'

He wheeled away from her, heading to a drinks table

on the side of the room, where he poured himself a large whisky. 'I just can't believe you can't remember,' he muttered, half to himself.

'To be fair,' Ashley told him, a tremor in her voice, 'Those years are kind of a blur to me. I suppose I shouldn't be surprised I've forgotten. I've tried to forget a lot of what happened back then, but I didn't realise I'd blanked things out quite so completely.'

'Oh?' He turned round, his tumbler raised to his lips. 'And why have you tried to forget?'

He wasn't the only one who didn't want to reveal the painful episodes of the past, Ashley reflected, but one of them was going to have to take that fearful, flying leap into vulnerability, and she supposed it might as well be her. Someone had to go first. 'Because back then I was very unhappy,' she explained carefully. 'And I suppose no one likes to dwell on times in their life when they were unhappy.' *To say the least.*

Nico didn't reply for a long moment. 'There's a difference between not *dwelling*,' he said at last, before raising his glass to his lips and taking a long swallow. He lowered the glass, his silver stare skewering her once more. 'And forgetting completely.'

'That's true,' Ashley was compelled to agree. 'Which is why this whole thing has taken me by surprise.'

'Why did you keep that dress and none of the others?'

The abrupt switch had her blinking for a few seconds. 'I... I don't really know,' she admitted slowly. 'I gave away all my fancy clothes after my father went to prison. I didn't need them any more, and so many of them had painful memories attached to them.'

'Painful?'

She swallowed hard. 'My father...chose my clothes and forced me to wear them. I know that doesn't sound like anything much, but...he could be cruel about it. It kept me on edge for a long time, because he'd be so charming one minute, telling me how I was his pretty...p-princess...' She stumbled slightly over the word, the memories making her throat tighten. 'And the next he'd be...unkind.' It was all she was willing to say about that, at least for now. 'After my mother's stroke, I was forced to act as his hostess, and I wasn't very good at it, which...he didn't like.'

She had to swallow again as she recalled the icy precision of her father's rage, always hidden behind an easy smile in public, to be released in private, so that every social occasion had become a source of dread for what invariably came after. 'I never liked parties,' she explained, 'Or socialising, or small talk, and back then I would have rather been—'

'Up in your room with a book.'

Ashley's gaze widened as she absorbed what Nico had said so knowledgeably. 'Ye-es,' she said slowly. 'How did you...?'

'You told me.'

For a second, Ashley felt as if the room were spinning. Memories suddenly whirled through her mind...snatches of ideas, emotions, words...and then were gone again, leaving a fathomless longing in their wake.

'I... I think I need a drink,' she said unsteadily. 'Do you mind...?'

He gestured to the drinks table behind him. 'Whisky?'

Ashley had never had whisky in her life, but she nodded. 'Yes, please.'

Neither of them spoke as Nico poured her drink and then handed her the glass, his fingers brushing hers. He gestured to one of the sofas by the window, its cushions warmed by a spill of light from a building across the way.

'Maybe we should sit,' he suggested quietly. 'You look a little shocked.'

'I feel...' She didn't even know how she felt. It was as

though she'd fallen down a flight of stairs, mentally speaking. She still didn't know where she was, or how badly she hurt. Ashley slowly walked over to one corner of the sofa and curled up in it, drawing her dress—the one that had started it all!—around her ankles. She still hadn't told him why she'd kept it, and she didn't even know if she could. She took a cautious sip of whisky, wincing at the taste, which drew a wry chuckle from Nico, who had sat on the opposite sofa.

'Not your usual drink?' he surmised.

'No.' She lowered her glass as she gazed at him, determined get to the truth of that evening. 'So, we spoke that night. Significantly, it seems.'

'Yes.' He stared back steadily, but his expression was still impossible to read. It looked even, but she felt as if he was still holding himself in check.

'What else did we talk about?'

'Lots of things.' He gave a little shrug. 'Our favourite books, what we thought of the city, how we both felt like outsiders at the ball.'

Fascinated, Ashley shook her head. 'I can't believe I don't remember all that.' She felt as if she would surely remember a man like Nico entering her life even for a moment, especially at the impressionable age of eighteen.

'That's not actually the part I'd have expected you to remember,' he replied, and she leaned forward, intrigued as well as apprehensive.

What had he still not told her? 'What, then?' she asked.

He hesitated, rotating his tumbler of whisky between his long, lean fingers. His head was slightly bent, his face cast in shadow, so Ashley could only see the blade of his cheekbone, the straight line of his nose and the fullness of his lips. He was as beautiful as a Greek statue, and in that moment, he felt just as remote.

'While we were still talking,' he finally said, his voice low and toneless, 'I was arrested. Right in front of you. Handcuffed and dragged away.'

A soft gasp escaped her as her mind formed the seemingly impossible image. 'In the middle of the *ball*?'

He glanced up at her, and the bleakness in his eyes made her gasp again. 'Yes.'

Ashley shook her head instinctively. Surely she would have remembered *that*? And yet...already jagged pieces of a puzzle flashed through her mind: a scream, a sob, her own choking fear... Her fingers tightened on her glass.

Nico leaned forward. 'Do you remember now?' he asked in a low voice that thrummed with intensity.

'Not...not really.' Her voice was thick. 'Just... I don't know. Just...flashes of feeling.'

'What kind of feeling?'

'Fear, mainly,' she admitted numbly, the sensations still swirling through her. 'My own overwhelming fear.' She had to swallow hard. 'But I don't know if it's from that night. Who can say...?'

'Why,' Nico asked, leaning back, 'Would *you* be afraid?' He almost sounded scornful, and Ashley couldn't blame him.

She needed to be more honest. 'Because I was terrified of my father,' she admitted. 'Back then.'

Nico frowned, his dark brows drawing together. 'Terrified...?' he repeated, still sounding sceptical.

Ashley looked down at her glass, and then took another sip of whisky, this time managing not to wince at the taste. She needed the fire that stole through her, giving her the courage to say more. 'Yes, terrified,' she stated baldly, meeting Nico's gaze once more. 'He wasn't just unkind, like I said before. He was...abusive, for many years.' Admitting as much made her feel as if she'd exposed her raw nerves to touch and light, everything in her twanging with the anticipation of pain. Nico said nothing but simply stared at her, waiting for more.

'Mainly emotionally,' she continued stiltedly, 'But also sometimes physically. And if I was talking to you and he didn't like it for some reason...' The knowledge trickled through her, coldly and surely. 'I would have been utterly terrified that night,' she finished flatly, 'Of what he might do to me after.'

Which might have something to do with why she'd forgotten it so completely...and disastrously.

Nico stared at Ashley, noting the strained pallor of her face. Her eyes were huge and dark, her lips pressed together. Her fingers clenched her glass, so her knuckles were sharp and white. Whatever else she was hiding, he realised he believed her about this. He just didn't know how much it changed things.

Maybe nothing. Maybe everything. He took a sip of his own drink as he tried to organise his swirling thoughts. 'I'm sorry about your father and how he treated you,' he said at last. 'I didn't know.'

'It was a well-kept secret. My father was known to be incredibly charming. No one doubted it, at least until he was arrested.' She smiled thinly, but Nico found he couldn't smile back.

'Yes, I can believe that,' he replied tightly as his stomach clenched with memories. He knew just how charming and convincing Chase Woodward could be. 'But...' He paused. 'You didn't seem terrified to me,' he told her honestly. 'I'm not saying you weren't,' he added, 'Just that...it felt different.' When they'd been talking, it had felt warm and sweet. As for afterwards...it had been all cold indifference, her face a blank mask.

'I was good at hiding my feelings,' Ashley told him with a small, sad smile and a little shrug. 'I had to be. My father punished me for a week when someone asked me if I was unhappy in front of him.'

Nico felt himself go cold at that carelessly given detail. 'What do you mean, he punished you for a *week*?' he demanded.

She shrugged again, this time even more dismissively. 'Oh, he had all sorts of tactics. On that occasion, I think he just locked me in my room. It could have been worse.'

'*Locked* you...?'

'The housekeeper snuck me food,' Ashley assured him. 'It wasn't that bad.' She pressed her trembling lips together. 'It was the more...humiliating punishments that I couldn't stand.'

Humiliating...? Nico did not like the sound of that, and he could tell from the way Ashley's throat worked, and her lips still trembled, that she didn't want to say anything more. 'I had no idea,' he admitted in a low voice. Even when she'd said her father had been abusive, he hadn't quite grasped just how much. 'I'm sorry.'

She shook her head as she blinked rapidly. 'You don't need to be sorry. My father is the only one to blame—and me, I suppose, for letting it go on for so long.'

'You were a child—' he protested.

'It didn't stop until he was arrested,' she cut across him, her quiet voice full of self-regret. 'I was twenty-nine years old at the time. Hardly a child.'

'Still,' Nico insisted, angry on her behalf. 'You can't blame yourself.'

'I don't,' Ashley told him, but he didn't think she sounded convincing. 'At least,' she amended with an attempt at a wry smile, 'I try not to. But it can be hard, when you look back on how you once were, and you wonder why on earth you just *took* it for so long.' She shook her head, her hair tumbling from its chignon to frame her face in unruly tendrils. 'Why wasn't I smarter? Stronger? I've asked myself that so many times.'

'Yes,' Nico agreed, his voice turning hoarse. It was a question he had asked himself many times, as well. *Why* had he trusted Chase Woodward so completely and naively? Why had he let himself be led, like a lamb to the slaughter, without even so much as a suspicion about where he was going?

Like Ashley, it was hard not to blame himself…which was why he'd fixated on getting his revenge. He'd thought it would finally satisfy him but so far, he had to acknowledge, it hadn't. Taking over the last remaining bastion of Woodward wealth had only left him with questions and confusion when he craved certainty and closure.

'I'm sorry I don't remember,' Ashley remarked quietly, her voice laced with sorrowful regret. 'It's the strangest feeling, not being able to.' She shook her head slowly. 'After my father went to prison, I had…something of a wobble.' She gave a shaky laugh. 'Ruth Boxall helped me through it. Without her…'

She trailed off as Nico with effort kept his expression neutral. Ruth Boxall's husband had simply stood aside while Chase had framed him for embezzlement. The Chief Financial Officer of Woodward Investments *had* to have known what was really going on, and yet he'd said nothing. Had Ruth known too? Had Ashley, and she'd forgotten *that*, too?

'Anyway,' Ashley resumed, 'I saw a therapist, which was helpful, and it came up then that I couldn't really remember some things from that time in my life, but I was okay with that. I framed it, at least in my own mind, as just blocking out painful memories, the way anyone might. I didn't think I'd forgotten anything specific, anything that *should* be remembered. And I suppose I always thought that, if I wanted to revisit that time, I would be able to. I didn't think I'd suffered from some kind of *amnesia*.'

She paused, her expression clouding as she pulled her lower lip between her teeth. 'But then last night...when you said I'd become upset and there was just this *blankness* in my brain...it scared me. It made me wonder what else I've forgotten. So maybe I really do believe that I've met you and I just didn't remember, as incredible as that still seems.'

Nico couldn't keep a cynical laugh from escaping him. 'You think *I'm* the one who shouldn't be believed in this situation?'

She held out one pale, slender hand to him in appeal. 'Nico, try to understand. Imagine if someone told you they'd met you and it was life-changing, but you had absolutely no memory of it. Wouldn't that give you pause, at least? Make you wonder if they were lying, especially when that person had taken over your company?'

He finished the last of his whisky in one long, burning swallow. 'I have no reason to lie.'

'Nor do I.'

Which left them...where, exactly? They were both silent as the night settled around them, full of shadows and stars. He believed her, Nico realised heavily. With all the trauma she had suffered, she must really have forgotten. But did it change anything, truly? She'd still ignored him when he'd pleaded with her, something he had no desire to remind her of now. And, yes, maybe that was because she'd been afraid of her father, but he'd gone to prison—for *five years*. A character reference from Woodward's daughter on the witness stand might have strengthened his case, might have changed so much, not just for him, but for his family, his brother...

'You believe me?' Ashley finally asked into the silence.

'Yes,' Nico admitted heavily.

She gave him an unhappy little smile. 'You make it sound like it doesn't change anything.'

Nico set his glass on the table with a final-sounding clink. 'I'm not sure it does.'

'But…' Her forehead furrowed as her clouded gaze scanned his face. 'Why not?'

'Because whether you forgot or not doesn't really matter,' he explained. 'What happened still happened.'

Ashley leaned forward, her eyes brightening with both curiosity and urgency. 'But Nico, you still haven't told me what happened. Why were you arrested?'

The silence between them felt electric; if either of them broke it, Nico thought he would be able to see the sparks, feel the shock.

Finally, he spoke. 'For embezzling ten million dollars from Woodward Investments.'

Ashley's breath hissed between her teeth as she shook her head in instinctive denial. 'What…?'

'I didn't do it.' He waited a beat before adding, 'Your father did.'

'Oh…' The single syllable was released on a long, wavering note as Ashley leaned back against the sofa cushions and closed her eyes. She looked less surprised, Nico thought, than regretful.

'The memories coming back to you now?' he asked coolly.

Ashley's eyes flew open. *'No.* I just… I'm sorry that happened to you. Were you…?' Her voice wavered. 'Were you prosecuted?'

He laughed then, an ugly sound he couldn't help, because her question sounded so disingenuous, so *dainty,* as if she imagined that he'd had no more than a spot of bother, a night at the police station, perhaps, before it had all got straightened out. 'You could say that,' he told her. 'I spent five years in prison for your father's crimes.'

For a second, Ashley simply stared, her lips parting, her eyes going wide. As far as a reaction went, Nico found it spectacularly unsatisfying. He felt as if the reason that had fuelled him for so long had evaporated in a puff of smoke, a single gasp of surprise. How could he let revenge guide his decision now? And yet…how could he not?

What kind of man would he be simply to shrug his shoulders and turn aside from another man's utterly ruthless and scheming vindictiveness? To roll over and act as if it hadn't changed his life, his family's life, his *brother's*…?

But, just as Ashley didn't like to remember painful parts of her life, Nico thought grimly, neither did he. He tried never to think about Roberto, and what those five years had cost his brother. The medical treatments he could have had, if Nico had been earning. The care he could have been given.

'Nico,' Ashley whispered, her voice a raw ache. 'I'm so sorry.'

'So you should be.' His voice came out harsh, harsher than he'd meant it to, because, damn it, he *felt* far too much.

Ashley jerked back. 'You still blame me?' she whispered unsteadily. 'Even though I've told you…?'

'Do you really think you're all that innocent,' Nico demanded, his voice a throb of emotion, 'Just because you don't remember?'

'But…my father…' she faltered. '*He* was the one. I might have forgotten our meeting, but I know I wouldn't have known *anything* about the embezzlement or your arrest. I never had anything to do with his business. He wouldn't have let me, even if I'd shown an interest.'

'You were there,' Nico told her flatly. 'You saw me arrested right in front of you. You saw me…' He found he couldn't go on. 'You did nothing,' he finished.

'What could I have done?' she cried, colour flaring into her cheeks.

Even now she strove to absolve herself, to insist on her innocence. Some things never changed. Nico shook his head in dismissal, too weary—and still too angry—to continue.

'Nico, I'm serious.' To his surprise, she uncurled herself from the sofa and walked over to him, dropping to her knees in front of him, like a supplicant to the throne. 'What could I have done?' she whispered as she looked up at him.

She blinked back tears, her lips trembling. 'You spent five years in prison,' she whispered wonderingly. A tear spilled and trickled down her cheek. 'What could I have done to keep that from happening?'

CHAPTER TWELVE

Ashley didn't think she could bear the look of torment on Nico's face—his cheekbones slashed with colour, a world of grief in his storm-coloured eyes. And *she'd* caused it. She still could only remember that evening in flashes of feeling—the wonder of meeting him, her terror of her father—but she knew, instinctively and utterly, that something more had happened that night, something he didn't want to tell her, but which had hurt him deeply, to his very core.

Something she had done—or not done. Whatever it was, Ashley knew she was at its wounded heart, and she hated the thought.

'Whatever it is…' she whispered, lifting one hand to touch his cheek. 'I'm sorry. So sorry.'

Nico captured her hand with his own and, after pressing it briefly to his cheek, he started to draw it down but then stopped, his fingers curling around hers instead. For a few seconds they remained still, Ashley kneeling in front of him, his silver gaze blazing into hers. Time unspooled and the moment, so tearful and tender, became charged with something else. Something sweet and yet so very dangerous.

Except…right now, it didn't feel dangerous. Nico didn't. She wasn't afraid of him, or her own overwhelming reaction to him, Ashley realised. She wanted this. And so, without thinking too much about what she was doing, simply knowing she wanted and even needed to do it, Ashley reached up and brushed her lips across Nico's in a soft touch so different from the demanding plunder of their previous kisses. His mouth stilled under hers and the feel of his lips against hers, so sweet, tender and *familiar*, had her suddenly drawing back in surprised realisation.

'We kissed before!' she exclaimed softly. 'At that ball.' She couldn't remember it beyond the feel of his lips, a thrill of giddy wonder...

Nico's fingers tightened on her own. 'We did.'

Was that what he'd been keeping from her, or was there yet more? 'How could I have forgotten *that*?' Ashley murmured, and was rewarded with a faint chuckle before she kissed him again, deeper this time, letting her lips play over his, her tongue dart between, causing a tingling pleasure to dart through her veins like flashing, silver minnows.

Nico growled low in his throat and this time he was the one to pull back. 'Ashley...' He threaded his fingers through her hair, anchoring her head as she stared at him levelly, feeling surer about this than she had about anything since she'd met him. The certainty resonated through her, spread out to the very tips of her fingers and toes. 'Don't tease me,' he warned her throatily. 'Not now. Not about this.'

She kept his gaze as she whispered, 'I'm not teasing.'

His hooded gaze dropped to her mouth. 'Then you're playing with fire.'

She lifted her chin. 'Maybe I want to get burned.'

He shook his head, lifting his eyes to hers once more, looking both resolute and resigned. 'After what you told me about your father, the abuse you suffered at his hands... you're vulnerable. I'm not going to take advantage of you, and especially not tonight.'

She pressed her hand to his cheek, letting her thumb graze his mouth. 'You're vulnerable too.'

He jerked back slightly at that, and then a sigh of reluctant acknowledgement escaped him. His eyes closed as he leaned forward to rest his forehead against hers, their hands still clasped. For a moment they both simply breathed, their foreheads touching, their hands together against his cheek.

'This doesn't make any sense,' Nico murmured. 'For either of us.'

'I know,' Ashley whispered back. 'But that doesn't mean we shouldn't do it.'

He laughed, the sound a soft rasp. 'Truth be told, I don't need much convincing.'

'Good.' She lifted her forehead from his and then she kissed him again, deeply this time, a demand. It felt surprisingly strong, to be the one kissing him, to feel in control... but only for a moment. For within a few seconds Nico was kissing her back, just as demandingly, a kiss that was fierce and primal as his lips slotted over hers and his tongue invaded her mouth, claiming her as his own, and Ashley could only surrender.

And what a glorious surrender it was, as his hands became lost in her hair and the kiss deepened and took over her every spinning sense. His hands moved from her hair to her back to her breasts, cupping them, his thumbs running over her nipples, causing her to shudder in response before he slid them down to anchor at her hips.

He broke the kiss, his hands still fastened on her hips, to ask her yet again in a low, raw voice, 'Are you sure?'

'Yes,' Ashley said simply. Maybe she shouldn't be sure; maybe she would regret this in the morning. Maybe it was an even bigger mistake, piled on top of several already substantial ones, and this time one that could have potentially even more heart-wrenching repercussions, at least for her. She didn't give her body to this man lightly.

And yet...the brokenness in her called to the brokenness she'd discovered in him. Together, perhaps, they could find a wholeness that neither of them had found anywhere else. She didn't delude herself that this was love, especially not after such a short time, but it was something more than lust. It felt deeper, more profound, a kind of healing...or at least it could be.

Or was she being completely ridiculous?

Ashley didn't care. She wanted this. She wanted *him*— Nico. No matter what regrets she faced later.

'I'm sure,' she told him again, and Nico needed no further reminders as he captured her mouth with his once more and then hoisted her up by her hips, sliding her gown up to her thighs as he stood up and she wrapped her legs around his waist to anchor herself as he carried her into the bedroom.

As Nico let her down, Ashley glimpsed an endless bed with a duvet of navy satin, the view of the city twinkling from the floor-to-ceiling windows on two sides, her legs sliding down his body, her breasts brushing his chest. Even now he seemed to wait for her to hesitate or even refuse. She smiled up at him instead.

Nico slowly ran his hand from her shoulder to her hip. 'This dress...' he murmured. 'The first time I saw you, I thought you looked like a...rainbow, or a shooting star. I couldn't believe my eyes.'

She reached up and touched his cheek, letting her hand slide from his cheek to his jaw to his shoulder, amazed at how empowering it felt to touch him in this way, to see his response in the flaring of his eyes, the shudder of his breath.

'Did I talk to you first?' she asked as she let her fingertips brush across his chest, and then daringly, even lower, sliding under his cummerbund before skimming up again. 'Or did you talk to me?'

'You sought me out.' For a second, his hand trapped hers, stilling it. 'I thought it was because your father ordered you to.'

She tilted her head to look up at him, seeing the way he searched her gaze, needing whatever truth she could give him. 'Why would he have done that?' she whispered.

'It came out in the trial that I was a little too big for my britches. Making a play for the boss's daughter as well as stealing his money. The jury didn't like that.'

Ashley felt the tension thrumming through him, and carefully she twined her fingers with his, lacing them over his taut torso. 'I don't think my father would trust me with that kind of thing,' she whispered. 'He only ever asked me to stand there and smile…and I hated that already.'

His fingers tightened on hers and he drew their hands up towards his heart. 'I thought it was a set-up. Afterwards.' It came out like a confession.

A soft sigh escaped her as the depth of his suffering and hurt reverberated through her again. 'Nico, I don't know what it was. I still can't remember anything but—but how I felt when I was with you. And how scared I was after. And how…how much I want you now.' She whispered the admission in a trembling voice before she stood on her tiptoes to brush a kiss across his mouth as he closed his eyes.

This really didn't make sense, Ashley thought as a shudder went through him, and then his hand stole around the back of her head as he angled his mouth over hers to kiss her more deeply. They were enemies, or at least they had been. Their shared past was painful and littered with secrets she couldn't even remember. As for their future…she had no idea what it held for Infinite Innovations, never mind for them as a couple. If there even *was* a them, which there almost certainly wasn't. Maybe she really was deluding herself now…

And yet, as he kissed her, all those tumbling thoughts blew away and left only the purity of their shared desire. A desire that felt healing and possessed the power to make them both whole.

Nico lifted his head as he gazed down at her with eyes that blazed his need. 'I've had so many fantasies of taking this dress off you,' he murmured. 'I never thought I'd get the chance.'

A frisson of nervous anticipation shivered through her. Maybe now was the time to tell him…

'There is a zip,' Ashley quipped, trying to hide the tremble in her voice as she turned to show him her back. 'If that helps.'

Slowly, sinuously, he tugged the zip down the length of her spine, all the way to her tailbone. The crystal-encrusted folds of the gown fell away, revealing her bare back; the dress's built-in bra had precluded her needing one of her own.

A soft gasp escaped her as Nico trailed one fingertip down the length of her spine before he slid the dress off her shoulders so it pooled about her waist. Ashley's breath hitched audibly as she felt the cool air hit the bared skin of her back.

Nico slid his hand around to her front, cupping her breasts with his warm palms as he drew her back against him. She felt the hard ridge of his arousal against her back as he moved his hands from her breasts to her stomach and then lower still, so the dress pooled about her ankles and his fingers slipped beneath the scrap of her underwear.

A moan escaped her, and she arched her hips as his fingers slid even lower, probing the soft folds of her most feminine flesh. Arrows of pure, sizzling pleasure shot through her with each expert touch of his hand, and she pushed against him instinctively, seeking to give him even greater access, her eyes closed, and her head thrown back. No one had ever touched her body the way this man had. No one had ever made her feel the way he could, trembling on the brink of an even more overwhelming desire…

With a sound almost like a sob, she wrenched round to

face him. 'I… I want to see you,' she admitted as she pulled his mouth to hers. 'I want to see you when I touch you, and you touch me.' She didn't want this to be just about the pleasure, although there was so much of that spiralling through her to dizzying heights. She needed it to be something more, although what it could be, and how much, was something she didn't dare let herself think about now.

And so she didn't, drawing him closer for another open-mouthed kiss, pushing away any troubling thoughts as she surrendered to him once again.

Nico's whole body throbbed with the force of his desire as Ashley moulded her soft, pliant body to his. Still kissing him, she scrabbled at his clothes, and he was in just as much a hurry as she was to rid himself of the cumbersome garments.

Unfortunately, removing a dress shirt took some time. He stepped away, managing a wry laugh, although he felt as if his whole body were on fire as he removed the shirt studs. 'Not to ruin the mood,' he managed, and she gave a shaky laugh as she brushed wisps of golden hair away from her eyes.

He hoped to high heaven that she wasn't having second thoughts, because it would just about kill him to stop now, but of course he would do it. Yesterday morning he'd desired nothing but revenge on this woman. Now the last thing he wanted was to hurt her.

Finally, he was free of the shirt and cummerbund, and he shrugged out of them both, enjoying the way her eyes widened at the sight of his bare chest. She tentatively reached out one hand and placed her palm flat on his chest, fingers stretching as her hand registered the heavy thud of his heart. Even that simple touch was enough to inflame him. His breath hissed between his teeth and then he drew his hand down to clasp it with his own as he brought her to the bed.

They stretched out on the smooth satin, Ashley's body pale and perfect, a scrap of silk the only thing covering her. She reached shyly for the button of his trousers. The feel of her fingers brushing against him nearly had him bucking in response. It had been a long time, a very long time, since he'd had this kind of reaction to a woman—and one that wasn't just a matter of the physical, but something deeper. This felt like a pure form of communication that their words, so halting, scattered and pain-filled, had not been able to express.

With trembling fingers, she undid the button of his trousers and then slowly, exquisitely, drew down the zip. She pushed his trousers down and he kicked them off, grateful for the liberation.

For a second, they simply lay there, staring at each other, nearly naked, feeling totally bare. At least, Nico knew he did, and he suspected Ashley felt the same kind of vulnerability, his body open to her. Nico knew this wasn't a simple matter of slaking his lust or even, as he'd shamefully considered yesterday, some sort of sweet revenge.

What it was, he wasn't ready to think about. In that moment, he told himself it didn't matter. He slowly reached out one hand and rested it on Ashley's hip. She trailed her hand from his shoulder to his chest and then dipped lower, her fingers tentatively encircling him as he let out a groan of pure pleasure.

She laughed softly in response, and he captured her mouth in another deep kiss until neither of them was laughing, and it was all sweet, sated need, hands, lips and tangled limbs.

'I have protection,' he told her as he reached over to the bedside table. 'If you...'

'I'm not... I'm not on anything,' she admitted, her face, flushed with pleasure, going even redder.

It was only a matter of seconds to slip on a condom, but it felt too long. Too long to be away from her arms, her soft surrender. Nico rolled on top of her, bracing himself on his forearms as she gazed up at him, her eyes wide with wonder, her lips swollen from his kisses, her face rosy. As he began to move inside her, she tensed, her body bucking a little, and shock reverberated through him.

'You're—'

'It doesn't matter,' she said quickly. 'To me.' She wrapped her arms around his shoulders as she pulled him deeper into her soft warmth, and Nico clenched his teeth against the onslaught of pleasure, determined to move slowly for her sake, even though everything in him was crying out to bury himself inside her.

She was a virgin. Why hadn't she told him? Did it change anything? The questions swirled in his mind before they were obliterated by the deep ripples of pleasure obliterating them both. Ashley arched up as they found their rhythm, their bodies moving as one, fused from mouth to hip, every part of them locked, joined, *united…*

A shudder went through Ashley, and she cried out, finding her release before Nico surrendered to his own, burying his face in her neck as the aftershocks reverberated through them both.

He'd never felt so close, so connected, to another human being before. And he had no idea what it meant, what it could mean, for the future of the companies…or for themselves.

CHAPTER THIRTEEN

ASHLEY AWOKE TO bright morning sunlight and an empty bed. She rolled over, surveying the expanse of smooth, empty sheet as a soft sigh escaped her.

What now?

Her body ached pleasantly in all sorts of places, and she was conscious of her own nakedness beneath the satin duvet. Last night, after they'd made love—although she knew she couldn't really call it that—Nico had asked her why she hadn't told him of her inexperience.

'I don't know,' she'd admitted, ducking her head and hiding behind her hair. 'I didn't want it to complicate things. Or…be a disappointment.'

He'd chuckled at that, a soft sound of affection. 'It was certainly not a disappointment.'

And soon after he'd shown her all over again just how much of a *disappointment* she wasn't. It had been very pleasurable indeed, and it had made Ashley start to yearn in a way she knew she shouldn't. As mind-blowing and life-changing as their time together had felt to her, she was savvy enough—she hoped—to remember that it didn't mean anything. And, no matter that last night Nico had wrapped his arms around her, tucked her close to him and insisted she stay over, in the bright light of morning everything felt different. Felt uncertain and also embarrassing. She'd told him they'd both been vulnerable last night, but she felt it far more this morning.

Still, Ashley knew there was nothing to do but face the elephant in the room—or, really, Nico in the next one. She had nothing to wear but her evening dress but, as she slipped out of bed, she saw that he'd thoughtfully laid a thick terrycloth robe at the foot of the bed for her. She shoved her arms into the sleeves, belting it tightly and combing her fingers through the tangles of her hair. Then, throwing back her shoulders, she headed into the living area.

Nico was already showered and freshly shaven, his dark hair damp, and dressed in a crisp shirt and trousers, his suit jacket slung over the chair by the window he sat in, reading the news on his tablet. He glanced up as Ashley emerged from the bedroom, his expression worryingly inscrutable.

'Good morning.'

His tone was as inscrutable as his face. Ashley wished he'd give her some clue as to what he was thinking, but then she realised that the lack of feeling was probably evidence enough that last night had been exactly what she thought it had been—one night, out of time and now over.

'Good morning.' She had to clear her throat.

'There's coffee if you'd like some.' He gestured to the gleaming, galley kitchen that ran along one side of the soaring space.

'Thank you.' Ashley gingerly went to pour herself a mug as Nico went back to scanning the news on his tablet. It felt as if all the beautiful things they'd shared last night—their heartfelt confessions as well as the most intimate parts of their bodies—belonged to someone else. This morning, Nico seemed like a polite stranger, solicitous but distant. It was hard to know how to handle the situation, and then Ashley decided she might as well just be honest.

'As you know, this is new to me,' she remarked, strolling over to the window as she took a sip of the hot, strong coffee. Nico glanced up from his tablet, eyebrows raised, his expression turning wary. 'The morning after,' she explained. 'The protocols for how to act. How cool I should play it.' She gave a little shrug, her bathrobe sliding off one shoulder before she quickly pulled it back up. 'So, how am I supposed to be?'

'How do you *want* to be?' Nico countered. 'From what you told me last night, you've spent far too long performing to someone else's demands and being deeply unhappy as a result.' His tone was matter of fact without being warm, and Ashley wasn't sure how to take his words. Were they a criticism, an encouragement or merely an observation?

'I suppose that's true,' she replied uncertainly. She'd been trying to be pragmatic, but she felt as if she'd fallen into the old trap of seeking only to please, and Nico had realised it before she had. 'But I don't know what I want,' she added, although that wasn't quite true. She wanted last night to have meant something. What or how much, she couldn't say, but, she suspected, more than Nico viewed it.

'Well, I know something you want,' he replied, rising from his chair to take his mug to the kitchen for a refill. 'You want your employees to remain in work,' he continued, his back to her as he poured more coffee. 'And I want to limit the damage to my reputation and my own business interests.' He turned round, bracing one hip against the worktop. 'So maybe we start there.'

Ashley clocked the coolness in his eyes and realised they weren't even going to talk about last night, which told her everything she needed to know—but wished she didn't.

'I imagine our exit from the event last night didn't help matters,' she remarked.

Nico gave a small grimace of acknowledgement. 'Indeed, it did not.'

'So what do you suggest we do now?'

'My head of PR wants us to be seen together today,' he told her, his mug raised to his lips, his gaze above it seeming deliberately bland. 'He thought you could introduce me to some of your inventors, maybe even see the robotic toothbrush in action.' His mouth curved in a small smile that felt slightly mocking. 'Have a few photo ops along the way.'

'You don't sound all that enthused,' she remarked slowly. Did he dread spending the day with her?

Nico lifted one powerful shoulder in a careless shrug. 'Needs must.'

Ouch. Ashley couldn't keep from flinching at his words—and his tone. 'As appealing a proposition as that sounds,' she said, forcing her tone to remain light, 'I'll have to pass.'

Nico frowned as he lowered his mug. Clearly, he had not been expecting rejection. 'What?' he demanded. 'Why?'

Now Ashley was the one to shrug. 'I'm not interested in photo ops,' she told him matter-of-factly. 'And spending an entire day with you when you clearly don't want to is a pleasure I'll happily forgo.'

His frown deepened, his forehead furrowing as his eyebrows rose. 'Even for the sake of Infinite Innovations?'

Ashley briefly closed her eyes. She'd always believed she'd do anything for Infinite Innovations…but this? Torturing herself by spending the day with a man who clearly had put her back in the box she'd been in before last night? 'Are you even interested in saving my company?' she asked as she opened her eyes. 'Or is this just about saving yours?'

'They're one and the same,' Nico replied evenly, and Ashley couldn't keep from flinching. Of course they were. She didn't have a company any more.

'Thanks for the reminder,' she said through set teeth. She put her coffee mug down, drawing in a steadying breath. She really did not want to lose it when Nico was acting so aggravatingly calm, but she definitely felt too many difficult emotions bubbling under the surface, ready to boil over. 'I think...' She sucked in another breath. 'I think I'll get going.'

'We haven't made arrangements for today,' Nico protested, sounding impatient.

'I already told you I wasn't interested.'

'Ashley.' He took a step towards her. 'If this is about last night...'

'Oh, so we're going to talk about last night?' she asked in a trembling voice. She pushed her hair away from her face. 'I'm not expecting unicorns and rainbows, Nico, or declarations of love and wedding rings, for heaven's sake. But... I thought we'd *talk* about it.'

'Fine.' He put down his coffee mug and folded his arms. 'Let's talk about it.'

'Such an invitation.' She shook her head, despairing now. She wanted to be a grown-up about this, but Nico's forbidding manner made it hard to feel anything but hurt. Had last night not meant anything to him at all? Why was she even surprised?

'Ashley...' He released his breath in a long, slow hiss as he ran one long-fingered hand through his hair. 'I don't want to hurt you, but last night was...last night. I'm not...' He paused, his beautiful face, all harsh angles and planes, hardening into resolve. 'I'm not interested in anything serious,' he told her flatly. 'And frankly I think any kind of physical relationship would complicate this merger at this point—'

'So it's a merge, now?' she interjected, grateful that her voice didn't shake, 'Not a takeover?'

'As it happens,' he informed her coolly, 'I'm willing to keep Infinite Innovations in some form. Your employees can have their jobs. But, whatever form the company takes, it will have to be a modified version—some of your proposed inventions were little more than vanity projects.'

'They were important to the people they could have helped,' she fired back, even though she knew he was right. 'And my job?' she asked after a moment.

Nico hesitated, his eyes flashing with...what...regret? Whatever it was, Ashley felt the need to brace herself for yet another body blow of a remark.

'I can't have a Woodward as part of my team,' he told her, his tone final. 'And I think it would be better overall if we didn't work together.'

So he still blamed her on some level, she realised numbly, absorbing the shock and pain of his flatly given statement. It was a delusion to have hoped for all the supposed healing and wholeness from last night, just as she'd feared.

'And yet you want a photo op today,' she managed shakily.

'For the sake of your team, I think you can manage it,' Nico suggested coolly. His arms were still folded, his gaze steely with resolve. He seemed a million miles from the man who had been so tender last night, who had touched her with such skill, sensitivity and pleasure. Who had held her in his arms and told her he didn't want her to go.

Had so much really changed?

Ashley shook her head slowly. 'Why...why are you being so cold?' she asked in a low voice. Surely at this point her honesty couldn't make things worse? 'I get that last night was last night,' she continued. 'Fine. I won't be asking for a repeat, don't worry. But I thought... I thought we were...' What—friends? No, not that, but *something*. 'I thought we'd got over all this animosity,' she finished. 'When we'd spoken...' She found she couldn't say anything more.

'I don't mean to be cold,' he said in the same matter-of-fact voice he'd used along. It *felt* cold. 'Just practical.'

'Practical...' She nodded slowly. Well, maybe she would have to be practical too. If she could convince Nico of the importance of Infinite Innovations and the inventions it championed…if these so-called photo ops would help the company and the employees she cared about, along with the people she was trying to help…well, she would do it. And then, after today, she'd never see him again.

Why did that thought hurt so much?

Nico had told himself he was being cruel to be kind, but it didn't feel that way. After last night, he'd wanted to get this morning on the right footing. Create a necessary distance and professionalism, because just remembering how intimate and honest he'd been last night had him mentally cringing in shame and anger.

Never trust a Woodward. Never be that naïve again. Never let anyone close enough to hurt you.

Had he learned *nothing* from his five years in prison?

It had to be this way, for both their sakes, but he still didn't like how wounded Ashley looked. Maybe he'd been too harsh.

'Look, I'd like to have an enjoyable day together,' he told her. 'Show me the things you care about. Give me a tour of the city.'

'A tour of the city?' she scoffed, her voice wobbling. 'You're from Brooklyn.'

'Pretend I'm a tourist,' he cajoled with a smile.

'Because this is all fake.' She spat the words out like bitter seeds. 'You can stop trying to convince me, not that you were doing a good job of it, because I'll do it…for the employees' sakes. And I think you're right. It's better if I don't work for you.' She bared her teeth in a smile. 'I can already tell that would be a *very* bad idea.'

She turned on her heel, stalking back to her bedroom. 'Now, if you don't mind,' she called over her shoulder, 'I'm going to go home and take a shower and scrub the memory of last night from my mind. Then I'll meet you wherever you choose so we can have our oh-so-important photo op.'

'Ashley.' He was caught between annoyance and guilt, even shame, that he'd so obviously hurt her. It had been the last thing he'd wanted last night. 'A day of sparring remarks and hurt looks,' he told her, 'Is not going to help either of our causes.'

'I'm not *hurt*,' she snapped, her eyes flashing jade sparks as she pressed her lips together to keep them from trembling further. 'I'm annoyed. There's a difference.' And then, her breath hitching audibly, she stalked into his bedroom, closing the door behind her with a sound somewhere between a firm click and a slam.

Nico sighed. This was not what he wanted at all. Another weary sigh escaped him as he turned to gaze out of the window. *Last night...*

He couldn't stop thinking about last night, thinking how good and even right Ashley had felt in his arms. The way she'd touched him, how he'd felt moving inside her...the sense of completion and wholeness that had suffused his whole being as he'd held her in his arms, as if he'd found a home when he hadn't even been looking for one.

It was the stuff of fairy tales rather than real life, and God knew he had enough knowledge of what real life was like. Enough hard-won experience of how trusting people was terrible, and believing people cared had only opened him to pain. Not just with Chase Woodward, but with his own mother. Sixteen years on, and she still wasn't talking to him. Still blamed him for Roberto, just as he blamed himself.

Another reason not to forgive. He might let go of his idea of revenge, but that didn't mean he was going to let a Woodward into his life. Ashley might not remember the way she'd turned away from him, but that one moment, if it had played out differently, could have changed his life… and saved his brother's.

Ashley came out of his bedroom dressed in her evening dress, carrying her heels in one hand. To Nico's dismay, he saw she was still limping a little. 'Is your ankle still bothering you…?' he began, and she shook her head.

'I'm fine. I've called an Uber.'

'I can have you taken in my car.'

'Let's keep this professional, all right? No favours.' She gave him a steely smile. 'And, after today, we don't need to see each other ever again, which I imagine will suit you admirably, since you can't want to involve yourself with a Woodward any more than necessary.'

She was saying the right things, Nico acknowledged, and falling in with the plan he'd come up with early that morning, when he'd slipped away from their bed and stared out at the chilly grey dawn, trying to figure out a way forward that kept his own sanity intact. So why didn't he like her saying them?

'Very well,' he replied after a moment. 'Since you'll be showing me around, why don't you set the itinerary? You can text it to my driver.' He held up his phone. 'I'll give you his contact.'

'Perfect.' She stared at him for a moment longer, her green eyes going glassy, her hair tumbled about her shoulders, and for a heart-stopping moment Nico wanted to close the space between them, take her in his arms, and tell them *both* to stop being so ridiculous. Yes, Ashley was a Woodward, but she wasn't her father. And, yes, she'd turned away from him in his greatest moment of need, but she'd been young and afraid.

He could forget all that, he could forgive it… But for what purpose? What future did they have? What future did he *want*? He wasn't remotely ready or willing to let anyone into his life, his heart, never mind a Woodward. And, no matter how practical Ashley was trying to be about the so-called protocols, he could tell from the way her lips had trembled, and her voice had shaken that she wanted more than he would ever have it in him to give.

It was better this way. It had to be.

CHAPTER FOURTEEN

On the way back to her apartment, Ashley gave herself a very stern talking-to. She was *not* going to come over all hurt and needy today the way, cringingly, she had this morning. She'd fallen right back into her old patterns—seeking to please, wilting at criticism, being desperate for praise. She'd promised herself never again, and she'd meant it. No more.

Today Nico would be nothing more than a business acquaintance. She'd be friendly, professional, pragmatic, optimistic and just that little bit distant. And she'd try to forget last night had ever happened. She'd obviously forgotten a lot of things in her life. She could forget this, too.

Ashley was just stepping into her apartment when Ruth Boxall called.

'Ashley.' Her friend's tone was full of relief. 'I'm glad to catch you. I was worried, after hearing about last night.'

'What did you hear about last night?' Ashley asked as she nudged the door closed with one foot before kicking off her heels with a sigh of relief.

'Just that Galletti created some sort of scene at a charity event, practically manhandling you from the room.' Ruth sounded both disdainful and concerned, and Ashley sighed.

'Oh. That,' she said. Was everyone talking about that little scene? 'Well, we've worked it out,' she told Ruth briskly. 'In fact, I'm spending the day with him today so the world can be reassured Infinite Innovations is experiencing a glorious new age of innovation and development.' She couldn't keep a slightly mocking tone from her voice, though she'd meant it. At least, she'd meant to mean it. 'Get Jim writing a press release,' she added.

'Really?' Ruth sounded seriously sceptical. 'I thought Galletti wanted to destroy the company.' Her tone turned cautious. 'Because of what happened before, although I don't know if…'

'I thought you must have known about that.' Yesterday, Ashley had suspected Ruth had more intel about Galletti than she'd shared with her. It looked as though she'd been right. 'The arrest at the ball, I mean,' she clarified, in case there was anything else, 'And the fact that my father framed him for embezzling millions?' She still felt as if Nico had held something back from her…but what could it possibly be?

'Yes,' Ruth admitted. 'Once I saw him, I realised. I didn't know it was him, though, until he came to the office. Back then, he went by the last name Rossi.'

Rossi. The name rang like a bell in the back of Ashley's mind, a faint echo of memory reverberating through her.

I've never been to something like this before. So I'm not bored yet. And certainly not when I'm not talking to you…

For a second she felt as if she were tumbling through time: she was leaning against a pillar, her head tilted upward, wearing this very dress, her stomach full of butterflies and her heart full of hope…

'Ashley?' Ruth asked, and she blinked, the memory vanishing like morning mist.

'Yes, I'm here,' she said, her voice only slightly unsteady, the memories still teasing her like the whisper of a ghost. 'I think Nico realised that revenge wasn't a good look for his company,' she explained, 'So he's decided to keep some form of Infinite Innovations on. Not me, which is probably just as well, but the rest of you.'

Ruth was silent for a moment. 'Did something happen between you two?' she finally asked, and in her shock Ashley nearly dropped the phone.

'Something happen?' she dismissed, her voice rising to a revealing squeak. 'No, of course not. We just came to… an understanding. Now, I'm afraid I need to go, to get ready for a big day of photo ops.' She said goodbye and ended the call without waiting for Ruth's response. The last thing she needed was her friend guessing what had happened between Nico and her last night.

That needed to stay a secret from everyone…even herself.

An hour later, Ashley was taking an Uber to a trendy café in midtown, where she'd hastily arranged for Nico to meet Andrew, a scientist developing hearing aids that used AI to adapt to different environments. After that, she planned to take him to a nursing home that used the robotic toothbrush, before finishing at a lab uptown where they were working on improving a belt that monitored abnormal electrical activity in the brain to warn people with epilepsy and their carers about potential seizures.

After that…she'd probably come home and collapse in a heap of exhaustion.

Still, Ashley was determined to remain upbeat as she stepped out of the car and started walking smartly towards the café. She'd chosen a professional look for the day—tailored trousers in navy-blue and a pale-pink blouse with mother-of-pearl buttons. Her hair was back in a sensible ponytail, and the only jewellery she wore was a pair of pearl studs her mother had given her when she'd been twelve. This morning, Nico had set the tone with his cool, practical manner. Now she would too.

Even so, Ashley's heart gave a little lurch at the sight of him standing in front of the café, wearing a dark-grey suit that clung to his broad shoulders and a crisp blue shirt and a darker blue tie, a pair of designer sunglasses perched on his nose and hiding his eyes. Next to the harried-looking businessmen and women hurrying by, he stood out like a beacon of authority, power and charisma. She saw several women sneak second glances at him, clearly affected by his magnetic appeal.

Well, she wouldn't be.

'Good morning,' she said briskly, as if she hadn't been in his bed just a few hours ago. 'Andrew Browning, a research scientist who is working on hearing aids, will be meeting us here shortly.' She glanced at her watch before giving Nico a perfunctory smile. 'Shall we go inside? Or would you prefer a photograph out here?' She saw he had engaged a photographer to document their co-working. It made sense, but it still annoyed her. This really was nothing more than a publicity exercise. Did Nico even care about the inventions that meant so much to her?

'We can go inside,' he replied shortly. 'The photographer would like to get some more candid-looking shots, so the best thing is to pretend she's not there.'

'Of course.' Easier said than done, when a woman dressed all in black was snapping away, but Ashley would do her best.

Nico held open the door for her, and as she went through she breathed in the scent of his aftershave and then wished she hadn't, because it brought back too many fresh memories: the warmth of his skin; her lips on his throat; his hands...

Nope, she wasn't going there. 'What can I get you to drink?' she asked.

'One of my staff will buy the coffees,' Nico replied in a

tone that Ashley tried not to take exception to. Clearly, he was the host, not her. 'What would you like?'

'An Americano is fine.' They went to an empty table by the window overlooking a bustling Rockefeller Center, every sense Ashley had thrumming with awareness. It was going to be much harder than she'd hoped to act normal today, she realised. To act as if she didn't know every intimate detail, or almost, of Nico Galletti's body. To forget that, for a little while, he'd been so tender with her, that she'd ached with emotion for him and, despite every intention otherwise, her heart had ached to get involved.

'Ashley?'

Nico's voice broke into her thoughts, sounding more concerned than impatient, and she realised she'd simply been staring into space.

'Sorry, a little tired today,' she murmured, and then blushed while Nico gave a small, knowing smile of acknowledgement.

'As am I,' he replied, a hint of laughter in his voice, and Ashley quickly looked away.

He wasn't playing the part he was supposed to, she thought resentfully. She'd expected him to be as cold and distant as he had been this morning, but he seemed far too relaxed, the look in his eyes too knowing. Was he enjoying teasing her this way, knowing what he did of her inexperience? Was he playing with her just because he could? But, surely, he wasn't that cruel?

'What were you saying?' she asked him, determined to remain practical and professional.

'I was asking how you found these scientists and inventors,' Nico remarked. He crossed one leg over the other, resting one long-fingered hand on his knee. 'Did you search them out or did they come out of the woodwork?'

'A bit of both, I suppose,' Ashley admitted. 'When we

were first starting up, we offered grants to scientists to pursue the commercial development inventions that would help those who are differently applied. A lot of these devices were invented a long time ago, but they never had any practical market reach. At Infinite Innovations, we're trying to take the abstract and turn it into reality. Take an invention that was too expensive or cumbersome and make it for the regular person. With that I mind, we invited scientists to make applications, and we chose the ones we thought had the most possibility.'

'Grants?' He arched one dark eyebrow. 'That must have cost a lot of money.'

'We had investors,' Ashley replied. 'We were pretty fortunate with an early injection of financial support. Ah, here's Andrew.' She smiled and waved at the young man who had dedicated his research to improving the lives of those with hearing difficulties. She realised she was looking forward to Nico meeting him.

'Hi, Andrew,' she said as the young man stood in front of them, smiling. 'This is Nico Galletti, the CEO of Galletti Finance, that has acquired Infinite Innovations. He wants to meet all of our key inventors and investors.' She signed the words as she spoke, noting Nico's faint eyebrow lift, the only sign of surprise he showed that Andrew was deaf.

'Nice to meet you,' Andrew replied, shaking his hand. His voice was carefully clear, slow and deliberate, and he kept his gaze on Nico's face as he spoke.

'Andrew is partially deaf,' Ashley explained, 'Which has motivated and informed his research. He also reads lips, so don't worry about needing to sign.'

'But you sign,' Nico replied after a moment, sliding her an inquisitive glance.

Ashley nodded. 'I taught myself a few years ago. Made

things easier all around.' She turned back to her colleague, giving him a bright smile. 'Now, Andrew, what would you like to drink?'

Ashley Woodward was surprising him at every turn. Nico sat back in his seat, sipping his coffee, as Ashley asked Andrew probing questions and the young scientist explained his worthy research, and how he was using AI to help hearing aids adapt to different environments, needs and hearing levels.

He'd first thought Ashley was shallow and grasping, and then, Nico acknowledged, he'd assumed she was broken by her experiences, weak in a way that had made him protective. Now he realised just how strong and truly amazing she was. She was intelligent, driven, resourceful and kind. He stayed silent as Ashely laughed with Andrew, giving him encouraging smiles, clearly as protective of him as she was proud.

This morning he'd made the decision to keep his distance. Now, just a few hours later, he realised he didn't want to.

'You didn't talk very much,' Ashley observed once they'd said goodbye to Andrew and were walking outside. It was a beautiful spring day, the trees lining the city street full of blossom, the sky bright and blue above.

'I was listening,' Nico replied. As they navigated the busy street swarming with pedestrians, he took her arm, startling her, and raised his eyebrows.

'I *am* a gentleman,' he told her dryly.

'That may be so, but you're not acting as I thought you were going to,' Ashley replied, and then looked away, her cheeks touched with pink.

'And how did you think I was going to act?' Nico asked.

'Like you did this morning—distant. Cold.' She paused,

pressing her lips together. 'I'd just like to be clear about where we are.' Before he could reply to that, she shook her head, rolling her eyes. 'Oh, of *course*. This is for those oh-so-candid photos. Silly me.' She nodded towards the photographer who walked a few feet behind them. 'Sorry. I won't forget again.'

For a second, Nico couldn't reply. The truth was, he'd forgotten about the damned photographer. He'd taken her arm because he'd wanted to, but did he really want to admit that to her now? He'd made things clear this morning. It was his own fault they were muddled up now. And he didn't know how much more muddled they were likely to get.

In Nico's car, Ashely edged all the way to the side, staring out of the window, while Nico couldn't help but remember just how close they'd been the last time they'd ridden in a car together. Ashley clearly didn't want to repeat the experience, even if he was sorely tempted.

'How's your ankle?' he asked.

She kept her face to the window as she replied, 'Fine.'

'Ashley.' He touched her shoulder, and she tensed. 'Look, I appreciate that you want things to be clear,' he said carefully. 'And I know I seemed very clear this morning. But… I'd like today to be pleasant. Can't we enjoy each other's company?'

She turned to face him, her expression. 'Can we? I am, after all, a *Woodward*.'

He sighed, wishing he hadn't said that earlier, and yet knowing he'd meant it. Even now, he couldn't forget…but he was starting to want to.

'And I'm a Galletti,' he told her. 'You have just as much reason to dislike me as I do you, considering how I took over your company. Can't we put that all aside, if just for today?'

She looked as if she wanted to argue but then, with a sigh,

she nodded. 'I meant to,' she admitted. 'I was going to be professional and friendly and nothing else. But my feelings keep getting in the way.'

His breath caught in his chest as he took in her flushed face, the softness of her lips and eyes. 'What feelings?' he asked quietly.

'I know it was just a one-night stand, Nico,' she said unsteadily. 'I can accept that, but… I'm a romantic at heart, I guess. Some part of me keeps wanting it to be more.' She held up one slender hand. 'I'm being honest because…well… because I'm tired of pretending, I suppose. But I don't want you to worry about it, or freak out that I'm going to ask things of you, because I'm not.'

'I'm not freaking out,' he replied mildly.

'This morning felt like a little bit of a freak out,' she shot back with a wry smile.

Compelled by her own honesty, he admitted, 'That wasn't because of you. It was because of me.'

'What is that supposed to mean?'

He already regretted admitting so much. 'I could care about you,' he said slowly, feeling his way through the words. 'And I don't have space for that in my life.'

Ashley was silent for a long moment. 'Why not?' she finally asked.

'Because…' He couldn't go into why—the people he'd lost, and how much it had hurt. Already pressure was building in his chest, and even behind his eyes, which appalled him. 'I just don't,' he said brusquely, turning to look out of the window.

If he'd thought his tone might put her off, he was mistaken. Instead, he felt the soft touch of her fingers on his hand.

'Okay,' she said quietly, an acceptance, and somehow that made him yearn for her all the more.

* * *

The car took them to a nursing home just outside the city, a gracious-looking building set in its own manicured lawns.

'So what are we doing here, exactly?' Nico asked as he stepped out of the car. They hadn't spoken for the rest of the journey, but it had been a surprisingly companionable silence.

'We're seeing the robotic toothbrush in action,' Ashley told him with a little smile. 'And we're visiting my mother.'

He turned to her in surprise. 'Your mother?'

'Her nursing home was the first place we trialled the toothbrush. Did you know,' she added as she fell into step with him, 'There's a direct link between dementia and tooth decay and gum disease? So it's actually a lot more important than just having clean teeth, although that, obviously, is very important too.'

Nico hadn't really considered what visiting a nursing home would entail, but what he hadn't expected was the memories that slammed into him as soon as he set foot in the door and breathed in that antiseptic smell.

For a second he faltered, and Ashley glanced at him in concern. 'Nico...?'

He blinked, an acidic taste on his tongue. The colourful walls, the cheerful care workers, the smell... they all brought it back.

Roberto... How he'd failed him.

'I know some people find nursing homes...challenging,' Ashley said quietly, and he shook his head.

'It isn't that.' He hated her to think he was just feeling nervous or queasy. It was so much more than that, and he could not bear to explain it. He forced himself to straighten, swallowing the taste of bile. 'I'm fine.'

And he was fine, pushing all the memories back as he followed Ashley into the day room and listened to a nurse explain how the robotic toothbrush worked and helped residents who struggled to brush their own teeth...just as Roberto had.

But, Nico reminded himself, he wasn't going to think about Roberto.

'Do you mind if I say hello to my mother?' she asked once they'd seen the toothbrush in action.

'No, of course not.' He was curious about this woman who was so much a part of Ashley's life, and yet at the same time had been so absent.

'Hey, Mom.' Ashley came into the private room where a pale slip of woman lay in bed, the expression in her eyes distressingly vacant...until she caught sight of her daughter, then her whole face brightened as her mouth curved into a lopsided smile. 'It's so good to see you,' Ashley continued as she gave her mother a hug and kissed her cheek.

Watching the two of them interact, seeing the joy on both their faces, Nico felt that pressure build in his chest again, and behind his eyes, which was seriously alarming. He wasn't about to *cry*.

Except, he almost felt as if he was. Seeing Ashley acting so tenderly with her mother brought back the memories, but it also made him appreciate her all the more—her strength and her grace, her kindness and her spirit.

She'd said she had feelings, but Nico realised he did as well. And what was even more amazing and alarming than that was he found he didn't mind.

'Mom, this is Nico Galletti,' Ashley said, gesturing for him to come forward. 'He's helping with Infinite Innovations.' She gave him a quick look of warning and he smiled back in reassurance. He wasn't about to tell this kindly woman, with all her struggles, that he'd just acquired her daughter's company in an exceedingly hostile takeover. He didn't want the reminder himself just then.

They talked for a few more minutes, and then it was time to head for their third appointment of the day, at a lab uptown.

'But maybe we could use some lunch first?' Ashley suggested uncertainly, and Nico nodded.

'Let me make a call.'

Half an hour later, they were seated at a secluded table in the alcove of a French bistro near Columbia. Ashley shook her head, seemingly rueful at how quickly he'd had it all arranged.

'Do you know everyone?' she asked as she picked up the menu.

'No, but I know a lot of someones,' Nico replied. 'And someones who know someones.'

She laughed, the sound clear and even joyful. 'I've enjoyed today,' she admitted as she lowered her menu. 'More than I meant to.'

'So have I,' he replied, and her eyes clouded with uncertainty. 'This isn't for the camera,' he told her. The photographer was on a lunch break, anyway, just as they were. 'This is just me being honest.'

Ashley nodded slowly. 'So...what are you saying, exactly?' she asked. 'If anything?'

What *was* he saying? What did he *want*?

Nico put down his own menu as he reached for Ashley's hand. 'I'm saying I like what we've started,' he told her. 'And I don't know where it could go, but I do know I don't want it to end.'

'Okay...' Ashley's voice wobbled as she nibbled her lip, clearly waiting for more.

'I have to go to Italy in two days, for some business meetings,' Nico told her. He laced his fingers through hers as he squeezed gently, feeling reckless and yet also so very sure about what he was going to say next. 'It's only for a week or so, and there would be plenty of time to do other things—explore the cities, the countryside…'

He paused, and in that brief silence he let Ashley imagine what other kinds of things they could explore.

Then, with his fingers still laced through hers, he asked simply, more of a command than a question, 'Why don't you come with me?'

CHAPTER FIFTEEN

Ashley stared out at the view of San Marco Piazza, still hardly able to believe she was here in Italy...with Nico.

The last ten days had been an utter whirlwind, something between a fever dream and a fairy tale. When Nico had asked her to accompany him on his trip, Ashley had been incredulous. Her instinct to say no, to stay safe and hold onto her sanity, had been short-circuited by the overwhelming longing she had simply to go. She wanted to have fun, yes, but more importantly she wanted to *be* with this man—wherever he was. Even if it didn't make sense. Even if it would have to end.

And even if it was dangerous...because, just ten days later, she knew she was falling in love with him. It was hard not to, when Nico was so attentive and generous, both in bed and out of it. They'd flown business class to Milan and then, after a few work meetings in the city that Nico had attended while she'd entertained herself, they'd spent three days in a private villa on Lake Maggiore, exploring the area...and each other.

Ashley blushed just to think of the things they'd done to each other in the privacy of their bedroom, and in a lot of other places as well. But it hadn't just been sex, as nice as that had been. It had been morning coffee on the sunlit terrace, them talking about their lives. She'd even dared to ask

Nico about his time in prison, to which he'd responded with a startling honesty.

'I won't say it was easy. But prison life wasn't the hardest part. It was not being free, and in being so not being able to help my family.' His face had tightened then, as if he was recalling certain things and not wanting to.

'Your family…?' Ashley had repeated, like an invitation.

'A mother, a sister and a brother. They all needed my help. Some more than others.'

'It wasn't your fault, Nico,' Ashely had said gently then, sensing he needed to be told, but he'd just shaken his head.

'I know, but it doesn't matter.' The tension had been dispelled when he'd reached for her hand. 'But thank you for saying so.'

After their time in the lakes, they'd gone to Venice, where they'd hired a private gondola to take them around the city's glorious canals, and had spent a beautiful day out on Murano Island, exploring the glass-making shops. Nico had bought her a beautiful necklace of deep-blue Murano glass.

He'd fastened it onto her neck, dropping a kiss onto her nape. 'Next time it will be diamonds.'

But Ashley didn't want diamonds; she'd had enough of them in her lifetime. 'Glass is enough for me,' she'd assured him, running her fingers over the smooth pearl-like glass baubles. What she hadn't said, even as the words had formed on her lips, in her heart, was that all she wanted was *him*. This.

As the days slipped by like pearls off a string, the reality of her life back in New York inevitably started to encroach. It had been such a relief to escape the pressures of her life in New York, if just for a short time. Ashley knew she'd need to get back soon enough—to see her mother as well as search for a new job. Without needing to discuss it, she and Nico hadn't talked about any of that while they'd been in Italy. Her former employees' jobs were safe, and for that Ashley was thankful, even if she longed for so much more for herself—for Nico and her.

'Ready to go?' Nico asked as he strolled into the room, looking as devastatingly handsome as ever in khaki trousers and a white button-down shirt open at the throat. He'd seemed more relaxed on this trip, lighter in both spirit and tone.

Today they were off to Rome, for Nico to attend to some business before they both flew back to New York. Ashley knew she would be sad at the trip ending, because she suspected that *they* would end too. Nico certainly hadn't made any noises about things continuing once they were back in their real lives, and at the start he'd made it very clear that he didn't see where this would go, or for how long. And, after all, she was a Woodward. That fact could not be changed or erased.

And yet Ashley still hoped. After all the things they'd done and said to each other, she knew she would struggle simply to walk away. But would Nico?

'Yes, I'm ready,' she said, turning away from the window as Nico took her in his arms and gave her a thorough kiss. It was the kind of thing Ashley knew she could get very used to. She pretty much already had.

'I'm afraid there's some sort of charity event I'm meant to go tonight,' he told her as one of the hotel's staff collected their bags. 'I know they're not your favourite thing, but I'd like to have you there.'

'But I don't have anything to wear,' Ashley quipped, and Nico smiled at her with a tender wryness that made her heart skip a beat—and yearn all the more. This last week and a half had been so wonderful. Why did it have to end?

'I don't care what you wear,' he told her. 'But if you *would* like a new gown, there are certainly plenty of couture boutiques in Rome that would happily send a dozen dresses or more for your perusal.'

'I think I'd like that,' Ashley said with an honesty that surprised her. The days of being browbeaten by her father were over. 'A new start,' she told Nico. 'I get to choose my own dress...and enjoy wearing it.'

He kissed her again. 'Indeed you do.'

They took a commercial flight from Venice to Rome, landing in the Eternal City in the early afternoon. A limo met them at the airport, to take them to yet another Galletti hotel, this one overlooking the Spanish Steps. All of Nico's hotels were small, discreet and catered to an elite clientele. As they had in Milan and Venice, they would stay in the penthouse, with its own private terrace and hot tub.

When they arrived, a dozen dresses were already waiting for her. For a moment, Ashley simply let herself stand in front of them, recalling, as much as she could remember, that the last time Nico had bought clothes for her she'd basically had a breakdown...all because of the memories, or lack of memories, of her father and the way he'd emotionally abused her.

Nico came to stand behind her. 'You don't have to, you know,' he said gently, his hands resting on her shoulders.

'No, I want to. I don't want the past to define me.' She twisted to turn to face him. 'This is part of reclaiming that and making it mine.'

'Then can I have a fashion show?' Nico asked, a smile lurking about his mouth and glinting in his eyes.

'Don't you mean a striptease?' Ashley murmured daringly, and he laughed as he caught her round the waist.

'Maybe I do...'

The dresses were beautiful. Each one Ashley tried on

slipped over her like liquid, silky-soft and clinging to her curves. And, instead of feeling trapped and burdened by the clothes and the expectations, she felt powerful...free. Seeing Nico's eyes darken with desire only added to the heady feeling of finally reclaiming her past and feeling in control of her life.

She settled on a halter-neck dress of emerald satin with a deep vee and a slit up the side to the thigh. Despite this, the dress was surprisingly modest, at least until she started walking, with every step showing a long, golden glimpse of thigh.

'You'd better take that dress off,' Nico growled as he reached for her. 'I don't want to rip it.'

'Take it off?' Ashley replied innocently. She reached behind to undo the tie at the back of her neck, and with a single shrug of her shoulders the dress slithered down to her waist. A twist of her hips had it slipping silently to her ankles, so all she wore was a tiny pair of pants and four-inch stiletto heels.

Nico growled again, low in his throat.

Ashley stepped out of the dress and strolled towards him, revelling in both the power she had in this moment and the power *he* had—because already she felt as if she were both melting and burning inside, absolutely desperate for his touch.

She came to stand in front of him and he fastened his hands on her hips, his mouth mere inches from the juncture of her thighs. 'These have to go,' he murmured huskily, and hooked one finger in the elastic band of her pants before tugging them firmly downward. Ashley stepped out of them, a moan escaping her as Nico brought her hips even closer, settling his mouth on the most intimate part of herself.

She anchored herself with her hands in his hair, her head thrown back as she swayed with pleasure. He explored every moist fold and kept coming back for more. It was the most exposing, intimate and vulnerable thing she'd ever done, being so open to him like this, having him know her even more fully than he had before, and she relished every minute.

When her climax came, rushing over her in an onslaught of sensation, her knees buckled and Nico swept her into his arms, striding with confidence to the bedroom, leaving all the dresses behind, including the one she would wear tonight, which was rumpled on the floor.

Ashley lay on the bed, dazed and flushed, the aftershocks of her climax still pleasurably zinging through her as Nico quickly shed his clothes.

'Do we have time...?' she murmured as he stretched out next to her.

He laughed throatily as he pulled her to him. 'Oh yes,' he assured her. 'We have plenty of time...'

Four hours later, Nico stood at the edge of the ballroom, a flute of champagne clasped in his hand as he watched Ashley make the rounds, talking up Infinite Innovations at every opportunity. She was radiant with purpose and joy. Her hair was held back the same way it had been at that ball so long ago, diamond drops on her ears that he had given her himself just an hour ago. The dress she wore was different, but just as beautiful, and, Nico reflected, more suitable for a woman of her maturity and elegance than the naïve eighteen-year-old girl she'd once been.

Everything felt like a redemption. These last ten days together had felt like a miracle, one he was so very thankful for. After his years in prison and the relentless grind of proving himself afterwards, he'd thought he'd lost the ability to trust anyone ever again. To love anyone ever again—and certainly not a Woodward.

Yet here he was, considering those two emotions in relation to Ashley Woodward, a woman he'd come to respect, admire, enjoy and, yes, maybe even love.

Love. The word reverberated through him. No matter how wonderful the last ten days had been, it made him uneasy, as did the feeling. Ten days was nothing when it came to actually knowing someone. Even if he was falling in love with Ashley, he didn't yet know her well enough to be able truly to trust her.

Did he? There were certainly things, important things, he still hadn't told her—such as how she'd turned away from him on that fateful night. He hadn't told her about Roberto, even though she'd asked about his family. He still kept the most private and exposing parts of his life to himself, but there had been moments when he'd considered telling her, when he'd wanted to unburden himself.

What was love without trust? And he did *want* to trust and love her? Over the last week and a half, he'd felt that he was starting to; it had been less of a choice than a compulsion, and it had been freeing and frightening in equal measure. It was so much safer, Nico reflected, as well as so much easier, simply to keep his guard up. To make sure not to let anyone in, especially a Woodward. But, he'd come to realise, it was no way to live: without love, without trust, without joy.

Now, in a moment of quiet, he knew he needed to take stock and ask himself honestly whether, considering all he'd already endured—some of it at the hands of Ashley herself—he could let go and truly let himself love her. Did he have it in him? Was he willing to let the last of his prized control slip from his hands?

'Nico!' Nico turned to see Adam Tyler, a business colleague from New York, strolling up to him. 'I didn't know you were in Italy,' the man remarked.

'Just checking in on my real estate,' Nico replied dryly.

'And you?' Adam was CEO of a luxury tourism business that often recommended Galletti hotels.

'Visiting all the locations for a new tour we're offering,' Tyler replied with a grin. 'It's a tough job, but somebody's got to do it.'

'I'm sure.'

Tyler's eyes narrowed as he gazed out over the ballroom that held a fair few of Europe's and North America's most influential financiers and entrepreneurs, all gathered together to support an international charity for cancer research. It was, Nico thought, the perfect opportunity for Ashley to talk about Infinite Innovations.

'So what's the deal with you and the Woodward woman?' Tyler asked, jangling some keys in his pocket as his narrowed gaze lasered in on Ashley, who stood across the ballroom, gesturing enthusiastically with her hands as she chatted to another guest. 'You took over her company and now you're travelling the world with her?'

There was a slightly suggestive note in the other man's voice that made Nico tense. The last thing he wanted to do was talk about his relationship with Ashley with a veritable stranger.

'Something like that,' he replied.

'I always thought that company was a vanity project,' Tyler remarked. 'Most people see it as a money-laundering operation, although Chase Woodward won't get to use his hard-stolen cash for some time.' He let out a dry chuckle. 'Word is, though, he might get parole in a year.' Tyler shrugged while Nico went completely rigid, the casually spoken words reverberating through him like the aftershocks of an earthquake.

'Chase Woodward,' he stated carefully, coldly, 'Has nothing to do with Infinite Innovations.'

Tyler let out a guffaw of genuine amusement. 'And if you

believe that, I have some beachfront property I want to sell you in—'

'What are you talking about?' Nico demanded through gritted teeth, swivelling to face the man, his fingers clenched around the fragile stem of his champagne flute so tightly, he thought it might snap. It felt as if he were tumbling back through time to that night when he'd been so naïve, stunned into submission by sheer shock. Phillip Boxall had explained the reason for his arrest while they'd been handcuffing him, but Nico had only been able to shake his head in mute, shocked denial.

He'd been so stupid, so *foolish*, and now he felt so again—but this time it was even worse. Had Ashley been lying to him all along? Was he going to learn the truth from a virtual stranger, and not from her?

'You mean you really don't know?' Tyler asked. He looked pleased to be the bearer of such information. 'I thought it was common knowledge. Ashley Woodward set up the company right after her father went to prison and, even though she didn't know anything about business, somehow this dubious start-up got a sudden influx of however many millions. Everyone knew her father had squirrelled some money away in offshore accounts. Laundering it through his daughter's company seems a *little* obvious, but then butter wouldn't melt in her mouth, and it's such a worthy enterprise, no one wanted to question it openly. And as far as I know, no one has.' He shrugged, dismissive now. 'They say Woodward might be released soon, so I guess he wants his money.'

Nico turned and walked away from the man without another word. He was reeling, both emotionally and physically, memories pounding through him of the last time he'd been so blindsided, along with a fresh and terrible realisation that it had happened *again*.

Ashley Woodward had lied to him again. He'd asked her

where the funding had first come from, and with hindsight he realised how obviously and blunderingly she'd prevaricated, simply talking about an anonymous, generous investor. Had she been lying to him this whole time? Trying to keep him sweet, to see if there was any way she could get some of her father's money out of the company before he noticed? Or maybe she was trying to get him to change his mind so she could keep it for herself. He'd paused making any decisions about the future of Infinite Innovations until he was more certain in his mind about what he wanted to do. Was that what she'd been hoping for, with her endless dramatics—fainting, spraining her ankle, having that ridiculous little breakdown? Good Lord, but the woman was a failed actress and he'd fallen for it all!

Just like before, Nico's fury masked a far deeper shame. How could he have fallen for it? Was *everything* she did a lie?

For a second, he forced himself to stop and think calmly. One stranger's gossip should not make him doubt everything about Ashley…and yet it did. Because, he realised, he'd never known her that well at all. And the investment into her company *was* dubious—something she'd never explained.

And the last thing Nico ever wanted to do was be made to feel like a stupid dupe again by the same woman—and this time it was much worse because he'd thought he was in love with her! He'd been going to tell her about Roberto. He'd been thinking of baring his whole heart, offering it to her on a platter.

No longer. His heart, which had become so shamefully soft and pliable, hardened right back up, and it felt like a relief. He'd been right all along: keeping up his guard was the only sensible and sane thing to do. After all, he'd always known never to trust a Woodward.

His iron-hard gaze tracked the woman he'd almost fallen in love with across the ballroom. She looked like an emerald flame in her deep-green dress, a column of silk that clung to her lithe figure, hugging every slender and sinuous curve.

He was tempted to march over there, drag her out of the ballroom and let her know they were finished. But he'd played that card before and, he decided, he was not going to add to the drama. No, he'd tell her tonight, after the ball. He'd exult in letting her know the jig was finally, for ever, up, and then sending her packing. His heart would be intact, and Ashley Woodward would be gone.

It would be revenge, he thought bitterly…but it was anything but sweet.

CHAPTER SIXTEEN

NICO SEEMED VERY quiet in the car, Ashley thought as they drove back to the hotel. It was after midnight, her feet ached and her mind was spinning from a little too much champagne. She thought the evening had gone well, and she'd certainly chatted up Infinite Innovations but, looking at Nico's closed expression now, she wondered if he felt the same.

'I thought tonight went well,' she ventured, and Nico's jaw tightened.

'Oh yes,' he said tonelessly, his gaze trained straight ahead, his expression completely veiled. 'Very well.'

'Nico...' Ashley wasn't sure what to say. He looked and sounded as he had the first day she'd met him, all leashed fury and deep bitterness, hidden by a deliberately bland expression. Was she being paranoid, or had something happened that she didn't know about? And, if so, why wasn't he telling her? 'Is everything okay?' she asked, and he bared his teeth in a smile that made unease shiver along her spine and settle in her gut.

'Oh yes,' he said again, his voice now silkily lethal. 'Everything is absolutely fine.'

Ashley stared at him for a moment, trying to work out his mood. She realised he was acting the way he had the morning after they'd spent the night together—deliberately putting a distance between them, doing his damnedest to be cold and aloof—and it both frustrated and frightened her.

Was she always going to have to dance to his tune, play to his moods? That wouldn't be a relationship; that would just be another version of the dysfunction she'd had with her father, trying to please a man who refused to be pleased.

She didn't want the same with Nico. She wouldn't play his games, she decided with a surge of certainty. Not this time. Not ever again.

Ashley turned back to the window, staying determinedly silent. Neither of them spoke until after they'd reached the hotel. The blow came as soon as she'd walked into their suite, slipping off her heels with an audible groan.

'You can change,' Nico told her matter-of-factly as he shrugged out of his jacket. 'And then you can go. Let no one say I'm not generous—you can keep the gown and the earrings.'

The tone was cold, even cruel, as if he wanted to hurt her. After all they'd shared together, it felt particularly callous, and Ashley steeled her spine, determined not to beg the way she once might have.

'You want me to leave?' she asked slowly. 'Tonight?'

'The concierge will call you a cab.'

'And that's that?' she asked, lifting her chin as she stared him down. 'No explanation?'

'I don't think one is necessary.'

'And you don't think, after the last few days, you could have the courtesy of at least speaking to me politely instead of kicking me to the kerb?' Ashley was glad her voice didn't shake. She was hurt, yes, but she was also angry. Did he really think she deserved to be treated like this?

'How is giving you a gown and a pair of very expensive diamond earrings kicking you to the kerb?' Nico challenged in a dangerously quiet voice.

He was, Ashley realised with a sudden lurch, very, *very* angry. This wasn't just about him deciding to end things.

Something else was going on, something he didn't want to tell her, and already Ashley knew she wasn't going to guess. She wasn't going to play the supplicant just so he could kick her when she was down. She'd done that too many times before, with her father. She'd be damned if she'd do it with a man she'd thought she loved.

'All right,' she said coolly, and saw surprise flare in his eyes. So he *had* been expecting her to beg... 'I'll go. But let me say first that I think, considering everything we've shared over the last few days, I deserve more than this kind of callous dismissal. But, if that's the kind of jackass you truly are, then I suppose I've made a lucky escape.' Her voice trembled but she managed to steady it. 'I'm not going to beg for answers,' she warned him. 'I've done that too many times before.'

Nico turned round to face her. The moonlight streaming in from the window washed half his face in silver and made it look as if he were wearing a mask. Maybe he'd always been wearing a mask, Ashley thought numbly. Maybe she'd never truly known the man she'd thought she'd been falling in love with.

'That's rich, considering you already know the answers,' Nico snapped. He took a menacing step toward her. 'I must say, you can be a very good actress when you choose. I actually believed the fainting routine, and the sprained ankle, and the little mental breakdown. Good Lord, but you played every trick in the book! What was next—a stroke, like your mother?'

Ashley gasped and reeled back from the shocked pain of such a deliberately cruel remark. 'That was low, even for you,' she whispered. 'No matter what stupid conclusions you've come to.'

'You *lied* to me,' Nico growled. 'You lied to me time and time again. You never forgot anything, did you? Have you been laughing behind my back this whole time? Snickering with the Boxall woman that I've bought your pathetic little act hook, line, and sinker?'

'With *Ruth*?' Ashley demanded, shaking her head. She took a step back as he loomed over her, colour slashing his cheeks, his eyes like burning coals. 'Do you really believe that?' she demanded. 'After everything...?'

Nico took another menacing step towards her. 'Tell me,' he invited in a dangerously pleasant voice, 'Who gave you that initial seed money to offer to inventors? Those millions—where did they come from?'

For a second, Ashley could only stare. This self-righteous fury, this cold dismissal of everything they'd been to each other...was it all about *money*?

She folded her arms and met his cold stare. 'Where do you think it came from, Nico?'

'I know it came from your father. Something you chose not to divulge. Have you been in touch with him this whole time?'

'And if I was?' She shook her head slowly. 'You could have asked me, you know,' she told him. 'We could have had a normal, rational, adult conversation, instead of firing all these accusations at me.' Realisation trickled coldly through her. 'But I guess that was beyond you, wasn't it? You *wanted* it to be beyond you.'

'Don't make this about me,' he warned, and she let out a high, broken laugh.

'But it is about you. Because if you are seriously breaking things off with me because of how my company was funded...'

She shook her head helplessly. 'Look me in the eye and tell me that's not just an excuse,' she demanded. 'Tell me you're not afraid of what you're feeling for me and...what I'm feeling for you...and you didn't grasp at the first thing that gave you a way out of all that. What a relief it must have been,' she exclaimed brokenly, 'To retreat to your ivory tower of self-righteous fury! What a comfortable place that is for you to be, all by yourself.'

'That is not,' Nico told her through gritted teeth, 'What is happening here.'

'It's exactly what's happening here,' Ashley snapped. 'And what is *not* happening is me begging you to understand and believe me again.' She slashed her hand through the air. 'I'm done with all that. And,' she added, yanking the earrings out of her ears, 'I'm done with you. I'd say when you can have a mature conversation that isn't motivated by your paranoia, come talk to me, but on second thoughts, don't.'

Tears stung her eyes, and she forced herself to blink them back. 'I thought I was falling in love with you,' she choked as she flung the earrings at him. 'I guess I was wrong, because a man I loved wouldn't treat me like this, and I sure as hell wouldn't let him.'

And with that, not trusting herself to keep her composure, Ashley strode from the room. Nico didn't follow her as she yanked out a bag and started packing clothes—*her* clothes, not the outfits he'd bought for her. She wouldn't take a penny from him, she vowed. Not a single one.

A man I loved wouldn't treat me like this, and I sure as hell wouldn't let him.

The words echoed through Nico, making him start to soften with doubt and regret. Then he reminded himself that, no matter what she said now, Ashley had lied to him, or had at least been sparing with the truth. Even if she hadn't been, it was better this way. He was better off on his own. Love was for fools and saps, and he was neither. No longer.

He heard her moving round in the bedroom, and as she came out he turned to face the window, his back to her. He wasn't interested in saying goodbye. And he didn't trust himself not to break.

She drew a breath and he tensed, waiting for her to fire a parting shot. Or was he hoping she'd ask to stay, beg to explain? Was that even what he wanted?

But, in the end, she didn't say anything. Her breath hitched and then the next sound he heard was the closing of the door.

Nico closed his eyes and bowed his head. He was alone, which was what he wanted, but already he felt an emptiness sweeping through him. If this was victory, it sure as hell didn't feel like it.

Two weeks later, Nico was back in New York, working harder than he ever had in his life, all in an attempt to shut out the memories of Ashley—and, worse, the regrets. He'd second-guessed his actions too many times, wondering if he'd been too harsh, her own words coming back at him like a taunt.

A man I loved wouldn't treat me like this, and I sure as hell wouldn't let him.

And how, Nico had wondered more than once, would a man treat a woman he loved? Because he'd convinced himself he'd been falling in love with Ashley, and it was proving harder than he'd hoped to convince himself that he hadn't. Two weeks on, he wished he could forget, even as he steadfastly refused to.

A knock sounded on his office door, and Nico looked up from his laptop screen at which he'd been blankly staring for at least ten minutes.

'Yes?'

'Ashley Woodward is here to see you.'

'What?' Nico stared at his assistant in blank incomprehension even as a wild hope lurched inside him. Ashley was *here*? He'd thought she would never darken his door again.

The woman shrugged. 'She said she had to talk to you. Should I send her away?'

'No,' Nico said quickly—too quickly. In that moment, he realised just how much he wanted to see her, to explain…if he could finally have the courage. Because she'd been right: he *had* been afraid. He took a steadying breath as he rose from his desk. 'Send her in.'

Less than a minute later, but after what felt like an eternity, Ashley stepped into the room. She looked pale, resolute and incredibly lovely, her blonde hair pulled back into a sleek ponytail. She also looked thin, Nico noticed, the silk blouse and pencil skirt highlighting a body he remembered so well, but which now looked a little gaunt. Was that because of him?

'I'm sorry to disturb you,' Ashley told him stiffly, her gaze focused somewhere to the left of him, so she didn't have to look him in the eye. 'I just wanted to tell you that I spoke to Ruth Boxall, and you were right—my father's money did provide the seed investment for Infinite Innovations. He had money squirreled away in offshore accounts, and Ruth accepted it for my company. She did it without telling me, because she thought I might object, but she felt it would be a good use of the money he'd hidden. I've made arrangements for it to be paid back, through the company's profits. It will take some time, but I won't have my father's money sullying the reputation of a company I truly believed in.'

She paused. 'I've also tendered my resignation as CEO. I know you'd once said I could keep the role in the restructuring, but I thought, all things considered, it was better if I didn't.'

'Ashley…' Nico's voice caught on her name. Seeing her like this was killing him, as was knowing he had to be the cause. Every hard word he'd hurled at her was coming back to haunt him now, yet he didn't know how he could have done things differently.

Just as she'd said, he'd been too afraid. And he was *still* afraid to reveal his heart to himself, as well as to her. Yet she'd told him she'd been falling in love with him... Could he believe that she still might be?

'I don't think there's anything more to say,' she said quietly, and turned to leave the room. Nico watched her go, one step and then another. She was walking out of his life, just as he'd demanded she do two weeks ago, and could he blame her?

More to the point, could he finally dare to be different?

Her hand was on the doorknob.

'Wait.' He snapped the word out, and she stiffened, her head bent.

'I really don't think there's anything more to say,' she said again in a low voice.

'I... I wanted to explain,' Nico began stiltedly. 'About before.'

Ashley slowly turned around. 'I think you explained your position perfectly,' she remarked, her tone decidedly cool. *'Trust me.'* She echoed the words her father had once said to him, her eyes glittering with unshed tears, and Nico realised afresh how much he'd hurt her.

'You were right,' he blurted, and her eyes widened. 'I was afraid. Afraid of what I was feeling for you. Afraid of being rejected...again.' It cost him far too much to admit that, but he could tell Ashley still didn't understand, and he would have to explain it to her. Lay himself bare in a way that felt like pure torture.

'When did I ever reject you?' she asked in a voice soft with remembered pain. Nico knew he'd been the one who had done the rejecting, at least in her mind.

'After they'd arrested me,' he explained quietly. 'You were

there, watching the whole thing. I *begged* you to do something: speak to your father, *say* something. Anything.' His voice choked as he remembered just how much he'd pleaded with her. He'd wept like a child, on his knees, like a supplicant. 'And you didn't say a word. You wouldn't even look at me. You just turned away.'

'I...did?' Ashley's face was deathly pale, one slender hand pressed to her cheek. She shook her head slowly. 'I... I don't...'

'Remember?' he filled in. 'I know you don't. And I didn't want to tell you, because...it felt humiliating.' He glanced down, unable to look her in the eye as he confessed, 'I wasn't able to let go of that. And so, when I found an excuse to keep from feeling anything more for you, I took it. It felt like the safer option...just as you said it was. I'm... I'm sorry.'

She nodded slowly, her face still pale. 'So am I.'

Was this how they would end it? Nico wondered, even as he acknowledged there was more for him to explain. 'I know you saying something might not have made any difference,' he admitted. 'We barely knew each other at the time, and expecting you to speak up for someone who was practically a stranger, against your own father...it was too much. I understood that, Ashley, and accepted it. Even though...' He drew a shaky breath and released it. 'That prison sentence cost me my brother's life.'

Her face went even paler as her hand fluttered by her throat. 'What...'

'Roberto had cerebral palsy,' Nico explained heavily. 'Some of the inventions your company has championed would have benefitted him greatly. When I went to prison, my mother, who had been his full-time carer, had to go out to work. She couldn't afford more than a few hours a week of someone to look after him. There were neighbours too, and friends, but sometimes he was left alone.'

Nico fell silent as the memory of his mother visiting him in prison two years after his trial came back to him—the bleakness on her face, along with the hatred, as she'd told him what had happened. 'When he was alone one afternoon, he choked and died.' Ashley let out a soft gasp of shock. 'Alone,' Nico emphasised. 'With no one to help him or comfort him. And my mother has always blamed me for it.'

'But it wasn't your fault.'

'Does it matter?' Nico asked bleakly. 'Yes, she knew I was innocent, but she blamed me for accepting the job at Woodward Investments in the first place. Aiming too high, she said. Even now she won't speak to me or accept so much as a penny from me, even though she could sorely use some help.'

'And so you blamed me for all that?' Ashley whispered.

'No,' Nico told her. 'I didn't. But all those memories kept me from wanting to feel for you what I did. Made me afraid to take a risk on—on loving someone, when love just feels like handing someone the power to hurt you. So, yes, discovering you'd used your father's money for the investment felt like a lifeline to me, a way to escape what I was feeling, except of course it wasn't.'

She stared at him, looking at a loss, and he finished quietly, 'So you were right. I really was just afraid, and I let my fear guide me.'

She opened her mouth and closed it again as she gave a little shake of her head. 'Thank you for explaining,' she finally said, her tone so formal that Nico had a sinking sensation it was all too late. What he said no longer had the power to make a difference, and he couldn't blame her for that.

And yet neither could he let her walk away, not without saying what was in his heart. Not without finally being truly brave, as she'd been brave…even if it didn't make a difference to her now.

'I don't know if it matters now,' he told her with a crooked smile, each word coming with painful care, costing him something, 'But I am in love with you. I behaved like a stupid ass, and I don't have any right to ask for another chance... But I want you to know, at least, how I feel. That I fought it and lashed out and pretended I blamed you, but... you were right all along. I was falling in love with you. I *am*,' he corrected. 'I am falling in love with you.'

Saying so much felt horribly revealing and yet, in an oddly good and liberating way, like a bandage being ripped off, the wound finally feeling the healing freedom of fresh air. 'Before I heard about the money laundering,' Nico explained, 'I was going to tell you about that night. About Roberto. And... that I was falling in love with you. And then the money became the excuse not to risk saying any of it.' It was so obvious to him now, but it hadn't been back then. He hadn't let it be.

'Oh, Nico.' Ashley shook her head, and Nico's heart sank. It *was* too late. 'I'm to blame, as well,' she whispered. 'I was so determined not to repeat the old patterns of trying to please, like I did with my father. But maybe it made me stubborn, too stubborn—'

'No,' Nico said quickly. 'You were right to act as you did, Ashley. I was the one who was to blame.'

'Well, we both have a lot to learn, maybe,' she said with a small smile.

Nico could hardly dare hope. 'You mean...'

'You already know I'm falling in love with you,' she told him with a shaky laugh.

'I thought you might have stopped, considering the way I behaved,' Nico admitted, his voice filled with tenderness and choked with emotion. 'But I'm very glad to learn you might not have.'

'I couldn't have stopped, even if I wanted to,' she replied, brushing at her eyes. 'But, the truth is, I didn't. I came here today in part just to see you again.' She managed a wry smile. 'Telling you about the money was really just an excuse.'

'We're very good at finding excuses,' he murmured, his heart overflowing with love—and thankfulness.

'So what now?' Ashley asked, looking far more uncertain than Nico wanted.

'Now,' he told her, 'I think I take you in my arms and tell how sorry I am. And also, how I'll probably still be scared and do stupid things… but I want to try. With you. For you.'

And then he did just that, took her into his arms and, as she tilted her face up to his, he kissed her, the seal of the promise they'd made to each other so many years ago.

Everything really was a redemption.

EPILOGUE

One year later

IT WAS A family barbecue, Brooklyn style, in the yard of the Brownstone in Park Slope that they'd bought after they'd been married two months ago. Ashley stood at the window of the kitchen as she watched Nico's two nieces run around the yard. Her gaze moved from that happy sight to the even happier one of his mother sitting in a folding chair, looking nervous and uncertain, but there.

Over the last year, she and Nico had worked hard at reconciling with his mother. It had involved a lot of painful conversations, and many tears on both sides, but finally Nico's mother was speaking to him. She'd admitted that she'd blamed him because she couldn't bear to blame herself, which was what she really had done. Healing, Ashley reflected, was such a gift.

An even greater joy than that was her own mother's presence in their home. Nico had insisted he hire a full-time carer so her mother could live with them, and Ashely had been so very glad and grateful. It wasn't all easy, but it was wonderful, and maybe that was how all of life was.

'I think we need more burgers,' Nico announced as he came into the kitchen. He was master of the barbecue and clearly enjoying the role. Ashley loved seeing him like this—

so much lighter and happier, as if a heavy weight had rolled from his shoulders. And one had rolled from hers as well. Together, they'd both been able to escape the regrets of the past and face a future.

A future that now involved more than just the two of them...

'How are you feeling?' Nico murmured as he came up behind her to wrap his arms around her waist, his fingers splaying protectively across her abdomen. 'Still nauseous?'

'It's getting better.' Ashley leaned her head back against his chest as she revelled in the simple moment. In seven months' time, they'd welcome a son or daughter into their lives. Nico was already fiercely proud, Ashley incredibly grateful.

She had so much to be thankful for, not least that she was still working for Infinite Innovations and would be until she took maternity leave. With new investors, the company was going from strength to strength...and had escaped the long shadow of her father's reputation.

After having been denied parole, her father was still in prison, which was both a sorrow and a relief.

'You'd better get those burgers,' Ashley murmured. 'People look hungry.'

'*I'm* hungry,' Nico replied, and nuzzled her neck.

She laughed, tilting her head to give him greater access. Even nine weeks into her pregnancy, and feeling tired and hormonal, she always welcomed his touch. She could always be sure of his love...as could he of hers.

Ashley twisted in her husband's arms and wrapped her own around his neck to give him a proper kiss. 'Later,' she murmured against his mouth, and reluctantly he detached from her.

'That's a promise I'm going to take you up on,' he warned as he got the burgers out of the fridge.

'It's a promise I'm going to keep,' Ashley replied with a smile and, laughing, she strolled out with her husband into the sunshine of a new and wonderful day.

*****

Were you captivated by
Keeping His Enemy Close?
Then why not try these other passionate stories
by Kate Hewitt?

Pride and the Italian's Proposal
A Scandal Made at Midnight
Back to Claim His Italian Heir
Pregnancy Clause in Their Paper Marriage
Spaniard's Waitress Wife

Available now!

MILLS & BOON®

Coming next month

HIS FORCED SICILIAN BRIDE
Jackie Ashenden

'That's why you took me, isn't it?'

Caterina's pointed chin lifts, her expression half defiant, half imperious. 'So you could finish the job you started twenty years ago?'

So, the little *gattina* remembers me. I wasn't sure if she did.

'If I wanted to do that, you'd be dead already,' I observe. 'But you were right back there in the cathedral.'

Her long, thick black lashes flutter as she blinks rapidly. 'You kidnapping me, you mean? Oh...' Understanding dawns. 'I'm a hostage.'

I give her a slow smile, because I do like an intelligent woman. 'Excellent answer. Ten points to you.'

'My father will—'

'Your father,' I interrupt, 'is irrelevant, no matter what he will or won't do. I'm afraid, *gattina*, no one is going to save you this time.'

The delicate bow of her mouth, highlighted by some kind of shimmery, pink lipstick, compresses into a line, and fear flickers briefly in her eyes.

I expect her to cower in her seat, but she doesn't.

Instead, she stares back at me, undaunted despite her fear. 'So? I'm going to be your prisoner?'

'No, *gattina*,' I correct her gently. 'You're going to be my wife.'

Continue reading

HIS FORCED SICILIAN BRIDE
Jackie Ashenden

Available next month
millsandboon.co.uk

Copyright ©2026 Jackie Ashenden

COMING SOON!

We really hope you enjoyed reading this book. If you're looking for more romance be sure to head to the shops when new books are available on

Thursday 23rd April

To see which titles are coming soon, please visit
millsandboon.co.uk/nextmonth

MILLS & BOON

FOUR BRAND NEW BOOKS FROM
MILLS & BOON MODERN

Indulge in desire, drama, and breathtaking romance – where passion knows no bounds!

OUT NOW

Eight Modern stories published every month, find them all at:

millsandboon.co.uk

TWO BRAND NEW BOOKS FROM
Love Always

Be prepared to be swept away to incredible worldwide destinations along with our strong, relatable heroines and intensely desirable heroes.

OUT NOW

Four Love Always stories published every month, find them all at:

millsandboon.co.uk

OUT NOW!

Available at
millsandboon.co.uk

MILLS & BOON

LET'S TALK
Romance

For exclusive extracts, competitions and special offers, find us online:

- **f** MillsandBoon
- **X** @MillsandBoon
- **◉** @MillsandBoonUK
- **♪** @MillsandBoonUK

Get in touch on 01413 063 232

For all the latest titles coming soon, visit
millsandboon.co.uk/nextmonth